THE SECRET EX-BOYFRIEND

CIRCUS IS FAMILY

KRISTA & BECCA RITCHIE

also by

KRISTA & BECCA RITCHIE

ADDICTED SERIES

Addicted to You

Ricochet

Addicted for Now

Thrive

Addicted After All

CALLOWAY SISTERS SERIES

Kiss the Sky

Hothouse Flower

Fuel the Fire

Long Way Down

Some Kind of Perfect

BAD REPUTATION DUET

Whatever It Takes

Wherever You Are

LIKE US SERIES

Damaged Like Us

Lovers Like Us

Alphas Like Us

Tangled Like Us

Sinful Like Us

Headstrong Like Us

Charming Like Us

Wild Like Us

This book contains adult language and graphic scenes, including situations that may cause trigger reactions. Such situations include: grief & loss, bulimia, depression, kleptomania, and various forms of abuse. This story is meant for readers eighteen years or older.

PROLOGUE
LUKA KOTOVA

Date: January 1st
Subject: Happy New Year AE Artists
From: Marc Duval, Creative Director of Aerial Ethereal
Bcc: Luka Kotova, *and other undisclosed recipients*

Aerial Ethereal Artists,

A new year means big changes. Please keep this in mind as we begin the process of hiring new & veteran artists. As a reminder, the current Aerial Ethereal show roster is as follows.

Touring Shows: Somnio, Noctis, Seraphine
Resident Show in Montreal (The Palace Blitz): Nova Vega
Resident Show in New York (The Opal Hotel): Celeste

Resident Shows in Las Vegas (The Masquerade Hotel & Casino):
Viva, Amour, Infini

I'd also like to remind every artist (i.e., acrobatic performers, clowns, instrumentalists, dancers, singers, etc.) of the Wellness Policy that you're **<u>required to follow</u>** while under contract with Aerial Ethereal.

On behalf of the company, I wish the cast of Viva all the best with their performance tonight.

Marc Duval
Creative Director of Aerial Ethereal
marcduval@aerialethereal.com

I cup my phone and read the email. Everyone in the Masquerade's backstage dressing room pauses to check their cells. I hate mass company emails—almost as much as I hate *personal* company emails.

One of my cousins grumbles, "Damn Wellness Policy," and simultaneously reads the email while jumping into a spandex costume: forest-green, silver splashes of glitter on the neckline and sleeves.

I set my phone aside and return to the mirror.

Bulbous lights outline the frame and illuminate my features: tousled brown hair, captivating gray eyes (just not as much as my brothers'), and sculpted but lean arms and torso.

(I have to lift one of my cousins on my shoulders, for fuck's sake. And he's a two-hundred pound *dude*.)

I touch my carved jaw, my face a contradiction of hard and soft angles—and depending on the day, I suppose my personality is just like that too.

My cheeks are half-painted. Vibrant green swirls form leaves, but I have to add more yellow detail. I work on my eyes, blending green shadow into gold.

If someone out there wants to grant me some luck, tonight will be the *last* time I do the Viva makeup.

"Twenty minutes until opening!" someone shouts into the room.

Swiftly, I swipe out of my email and into my music. Earbuds in and makeup brush in hand, I nod my head to the rhythm and prepare for my job.

Date: January 16th
Subject: Welcome to Infini
From: Antoine Perrot, Director of Infini
To: Luka Kotova

Luka Kotova:

I'd like to formally welcome you back to Infini. This season, we're hiring a brand new choreographer who'll oversee every act in the show.

Including your discipline: Wheel of Death.

We want you to take these new changes with stride, and as a veteran artist, I need you to set an example at work. I hope we can count on you.

Antoine Perrot
Director of Infini
antoineperrot@aerialethereal.com

I dance. Half-intoxicated by the liquor in my veins. Half-intoxicated by the bass thumping the Vegas club called *Verona*. Raising my phone up, I squint at the bright screen and try to read the work email. I retain about a quarter.

It goes something like: *welcome back blah blah blah new choreographer blah changes blah blah.* Then I shove my phone in my jeans.

I just *dance.*

Date: January 17th
Subject: Congratulations
From: Marc Duval, Creative Director of Aerial Ethereal
Bcc: Luka Kotova, *and other undisclosed recipients*

Aerial Ethereal Artists,

On behalf of the company, congratulations to all the new artists who have signed on for the upcoming year(s). We'd also like to give the warmest welcome to the new female aerialist Thora James, who'll be a lead in Amour's aerial silk act.

As most of you may already know, AE has had to make serious changes with our veteran shows. Infini alone has recast 90% of its roles. We appreciate all the support **and compliance** moving forward. We expect to make more changes in the coming months.

We're a company striving to improve in all avenues: creative and financial.

Marc Duval
Creative Director of Aerial Ethereal
marcduval@aerialethereal.com

Shoving a piece of pizza in my mouth, I jog towards the performance gym inside the Masquerade Hotel & Casino. I'll probably puke. (Nothing new.)

In my other hand, I grasp my phone, trying to read and walk.

Multitasking like a motherfucker.

———————◆———————

Date: January 19th
Subject: Infini News
From: Geoffrey Lesage, Choreographer
Bcc: Luka Kotova, *and other undisclosed recipients*

Infini Artists:

Firstly, I am not here to be your friend. I'm here to make Infini the best damn show on Aerial Ethereal's roster. Most of you choreographed your own routines in the past.

Not happening this year. All acts will be created and approved by **me**.

Here's the sad truth: **Infini is stale.** It's why more than half of your co-workers were fired (or shifted to other shows). If the audience is bored to tears, do you think they'll return for a second and third viewing? No. They'll just go gamble at the casino instead.

No whining. No complaining. If I see any empty chairs in the audience this season, I'll push you all harder. Don't kid yourself, **<u>Marc Duval will axe Infini if it underperforms this year.</u>** You. Must. Sell. Tickets.

No excuses.

No exceptions.

While we wait for new artists to fly in and get accommodated at the Masquerade, remember to condition. **Do not waste my time.** First meeting/practice is February 15th.

For those asking for cast sheets, Antoine Perrot and the rest of the creative team are keeping Infini's shakeups quiet from the press. You'll meet all the artists in person on the 15th.

Geoffrey Lesage
Infini Choreographer
geoffreylesage@mailme.com

My older cousin's brash and crude voice blares through my phone, complaining about the email from Geoffrey.

While he curses, I toss the cell on my mattress and empty my pockets. Three packs of Junior Mints. Five bottles of tiny hotel shampoos. A Masquerade souvenir keychain. A half-opened bag of Skittles. My gym card.

———————— ✦ ————————

Date: January 20th
Subject: you there?
From: sergeikotova@aerialethereal.com
To: Luka Kotova

Nik says you blocked my number and that's why you haven't responded to my texts. Unblock me. We need to talk.

- Sergei

I slam the washing machine closed with more force than I intend. It's old anyway.

The hotel hasn't updated the 42nd and 43rd floor communal washers and dryers since I moved to Vegas three years ago. And they were already archaic back then. I glance back at my phone.

I hesitate.

And then I swipe right to delete.

———————— ✦ ————————

Date: January 21st
Subject: Reminder
From: Marc Duval, Creative Director of Aerial Ethereal
Bcc: Luka Kotova, *and other undisclosed recipients*

Aerial Ethereal Artists,

<u>The Wellness Policy is not optional.</u> All artists need to maintain in good standing in order to perform. We will not hesitate to suspend you from a show.

Marc Duval
Creative Director of Aerial Ethereal
marcduval@aerialethereal.com

Cigarette hanging loosely between my fingers, I blow smoke in the frigid air. The gray plume is visible in the night. Flashy, multicolored lights stretch along the never-ending Vegas strip, radiating.

So fucking bright.

——————◆——————

Date: January 21st
Subject: you there????
From: sergeikotova@aerialethereal.com
To: Luka Kotova

I'm your brother. Unblock me so I can at least text you. That is if you're even getting these fucking emails.

- Sergei

I hesitate again, for longer than a split-second. I pass my phone from one hand to the other.

And then I delete the email.

ACT ONE
LUKA KOTOVA

Date: January 22nd
Subject: Masquerade Room Changes
From: Marc Duval, Creative Director of Aerial Ethereal
Bcc: Luka Kotova, *and other undisclosed recipients*

Aerial Ethereal Artists,

In the past week, each of you should've received a letter from Human Resources detailing your new room assignment. I should not even have to send out this email. Nor should any of you be contacting me or AE's creative with trivial complaints. No one in the company, and I mean no one, will accommodate any room changes. They are set for a reason.

New seasons mean new changes. You know this.

In an effort to reduce costs, we had to reduce artist housing from two floors in the Masquerade to one floor. As a result, there are 4 occupants per room instead of 2.

Need I remind you that each artist still has free room & board at the Masquerade's luxury suites. This huge bonus should not be overlooked. If you're unhappy with your room assignment, you have the option to pay for apartments or housing in the Las Vegas area.

Any further complaints about room assignments will not be tolerated.

Marc Duval
Creative Director of Aerial Ethereal
marcduval@aerialethereal.com

I recheck the email—surprised it wasn't directly addressed to me. A few days ago, I learned my new room assignment and sent Marc a short but pointed email.

Something like: *I've roomed with my little brother for 19 years. His whole life. Nearly all of mine. Can you please change my assignment? It's kind of bullshit. (Sent from phone)*

It was an emotional response. One that I regretted the moment I pressed *send*. I didn't even sign my name at the bottom. Just figured he'd recognize me by my work email.

I've been Corporate's Least Favorite Kotova since I was fifteen. And with an extended family that fills one-third of all Aerial Ethereal shows, being the *worst* or *best* Kotova takes actual effort.

Circus is family.

For most of us, we mean it literally.

My email to Marc probably sealed my *least favorite* title. And I'm twenty-years-old now.

Look, I understand the whole corporate hierarchy better than anyone. Marc is the founder of the entire Aerial Ethereal troupe and rarely has contact with the artists unless it's through company emails. The only time he does one-on-ones is for terrific news (a long-term contract) or fucking horrific (you're harming the company's standards).

I've met him twice.

Obviously for *horrific* reasons.

An artist's fate lies in many corporate hands, but Marc Duval's hand encases all of the higher-ups. Emailing him directly is like whining to God. He could've easily fired me on the spot.

Shit, if Nik even knew I sent it…

I rake my fingers through my dark brown hair, panicked that I've now started the season on the *worst* footing. I don't actively shoot for "good"—just somewhere between "okay" and "mediocre" but not *worst*.

(What can I say? My name is Luka Kotova. I'm an irresponsible fuck-up. Thanks for your time. Now let me be.)

I ride the Masquerade's elevator to the suites. Alone. Numbers tick higher and higher, and then the elevator glides to a stop.

42nd floor. The doors open to mayhem.

Overflowing boxes, clear plastic tubs, lamps, rugs, and other household belongings fill the hotel hallway. Voices emanate from ajar doors. People rush in and out. Carrying as much shit in their arms as they can since no luggage cart can fit through this disaster.

I step over a drum set and what looks like an empty aquarium. Ducking beneath a coat rack, I spot my suite towards the end of the hallway.

Cardboard boxes are stacked outside the door, the name *Timo* scribbled on the flaps.

Reality hits me all of a sudden.

We have to move.

If the email hadn't already cemented our future, the apocalyptic hallway and my little brother's boxes just did.

Aerial Ethereal has always given artists the 42ⁿᵈ and 43ʳᵈ floors of the Masquerade. Taking away an entire floor is another swift kick in the gut and the ass. AE has so much control over our lives.

At last notice, they can change *anything*.

All we have are our contracts, but even those usually only last one year. Then they're rewritten all over again. Our lives are in constant flux, and as much as I love the circus—this one aspect never stops eating at me.

With a heavy breath, I slip through the cracked door.

"Shit," I mutter at the barren state.

It's a typical two-bedroom, modern hotel suite: sleek black and white furniture, floor-length windows that, from this side, overlook the ginormous Vegas pool. After being here for three years, the living room had real character.

An old New York Knicks blanket and throw-rug are gone, and walls that once housed *West Side Story* and *Les Misérables* posters are stark white.

Timo removed the cactus-shaped thumbtacks that said *don't be a prick*, my glass bowl of jelly beans, and his own ceramic Warhol coasters.

I turn left and right. Mixed emotions bearing on me. My jaw and lip twitches, and my throat bobs as I swallow hard.

I'm grateful that Timo packed up so I don't have to, but mostly, the disappearance of all my shit makes me uneasy. It's not like I haven't moved before.

I have.

Plenty of times growing up.

But for a while there, I felt rooted to something.

It's one fucking floor, I remind myself and comb my hands through my hair again. *One floor.* It's not a big deal. My family sees me as the "go with the flow" Kotova, and in a lot of ways, I am.

I'll go with the flow with this. With everything.

It doesn't mean it won't knot my stomach. Doesn't mean that I'm unfeeling, like some of my cousins believe. It just means I'm not going to whine or throw a tantrum.

Faster, I pass the kitchenette, sponged-clean, and head to my bedroom. When I push inside, I immediately spot my sixteen-year-old sister.

Katya peers beneath the wooden frame of my stripped bed. I shut the door, and her head pops up. Long, straight brown hair sticks to her overdone pink-glossed lips.

I frown at my little sister. When did she start wearing makeup on regular weekdays?

Her saucer eyes widen even bigger on me. "Oh crap," she says, clutching a...*really?*

I sigh. She grips a black heavy-duty trash bag, partially filled.

"It was Timo's idea." Katya picks herself off the floor, skinny and long-limbed like a ballerina but with prominent, ethereal features: orb-like eyes, pronounced ears, and big lips. "He said that you wouldn't mind if we packed up for you."

I don't mind.

What bothers me is that he enlisted Katya's help to *throw away* my things. Here's the deal: I'm really close to Timo and Kat—as close as most siblings come—but they still have no clue what I can't get rid of.

(The cactus paraphernalia better not be trashed.)

"Can you say something?" she asks. "You just look...sad."

"I'm not sad," I say coolly. "Just please don't trash my shit unless you ask, Kat."

She drops the garbage bag like it's suddenly toxic waste. "I won't again. I promise." Guilt sweeps her youthful face.

My features soften almost instantly, and I nod. Kat, more than anyone, respects my privacy. Whenever our older brother Nikolai tries to pry through my things, she's the most vocal: *just trust Luka, Nik. Why are you searching through his gym bag?*

I ask, "Where's Timo?"

She points to the walk-in closet.

I shuffle around an open box, stuffed with my wardrobe: a lot of gym clothes, plain T-shirts, some jeans, and baseball caps. Nothing flashy or brazen.

At the closet, I stretch the door further open. I distinguish the back of my brother's head that bounces to the beat of music. He's wearing earbuds, the song inaudible.

Timo is also lost in a mound of shoeboxes and towering stacks of snow globes, and to be completely honest, a lot of shitty Vegas paraphernalia that has no place or name.

It's junk.

I can admit that any day, any time.

Timo rifles through a shoebox, not noticing me, and after careful examination, he chucks the box into his trash bag.

"Timo," I call out, loud enough that he spins around.

Items clatter beside his lean, athletic frame, but he manages to crawl out. Sweating, he shoves the longer strands of his dark, disheveled hair out of his charismatic face. He's only a year and a half younger than me, but I'm an inch taller.

His gray eyes glimmer like a thousand-watt bulb, and he smiles an incredibly contagious smile. To the point where I *almost* forget that I'm supposed to be irritated.

Timo pops an earbud out, an upbeat song blaring through the tiny speaker. "Hey, Luk." Then he unplugs the cord, music booming through his phone. Timo swings his head heavier to the rhythm and shifts his body with the harmony, goading me to join his dance.

My body craves soulful rhythms like an animal craves an endless field to sprint. To run.

For me, it's unnatural not to dance. I don't know how, and it takes effort to force my body still and not move to the beat.

Timo must see that something's off with me, so he lowers the volume of his music. His black cross earring sways, and he pockets his phone in his cut-off shorts. Wearing a leather jacket, no shirt beneath—Timo is the kind of guy you wish you knew. Intriguing. *Captivating.*

I'm the shadow to his ceaseless light.

(Don't pity me.) I'm grateful to be anything next to Timo. Even a shadow. That's how much I love him.

I nod to the garbage. "Dude, what the hell is that?"

Timo eyes me weirdly. "Trash…?" His mouth falls. "Are you glaring at me?" He rocks backwards, surprised.

"You can't just throw away my shit without asking." My knuckles whiten as I grip the door frame harder.

Timo touches his chest. "I'm doing both of us a favor. Didn't you read AE's email—no, scratch that, you probably skimmed it. Which is why you're not panicked." He tosses the garbage bag past me. Glass clinks, the trash thudding by my bed.

"What do you mean?" I don't scroll through my emails for proof. I trust Timo to tell me the news.

He raises his brows. "We have to move by *five p.m.* or else they'll fine us a grand."

"Fuck," I groan.

"We're way past *fuck*, brother. Aerial Ethereal isn't playing games with this one." He strolls past me and effortlessly hoists himself on my dresser.

I spin around, unable to detach from the closet door. On the floor, Katya refolds my clothes and places them more gently in the boxes.

Our salaries aren't that great, but none of us perform for the money. We do it for the art and to be close to our family.

And because I literally don't know how to do anything else. I was *raised* for this. Only this.

Timo catches my gaze. "You could give me a hundred bucks and I'll turn it into a grand downstairs. Buy us extra time."

"No," I decline fast. He could easily spend all day at the casino tables and slots, and while he does win a lot, he loses too. I haven't given him cash to gamble in about a year.

"Kat?" Timo asks, pouting his bottom lip.

"I can't afford to share my money anymore," she says, her words sounding rehearsed.

Timo and I exchange a confused look.

I prod first. "Why not?"

"I'm saving up." She avoids our intrusive gazes by refolding my shirt. "It's private, so don't ask *what for*."

"Ouch." Timo wears mock hurt, but more than a fraction of that is actually real.

I thought we were closer than that, I want to say, but I'm harboring a secret bigger than either of them have ever imagined or considered.

It involves a girl.

I nearly shut my eyes and yell at myself, *don't think about her. Don't fucking think about her.*

So I stay quiet in terms of Katya's declaration. She fills the tense silence. "I'm sixteen," she tells us like we've forgotten. "I'm a woman."

"No shit," Timo says.

I'm not catching on either.

Katya sighs. "You wouldn't understand."

"Okay," I say, really baffled.

In our profession and our family, the ratio of men to women is severely off balance. I'm not great at math, but it's pretty much all male around here. Sometimes I really don't understand my little sister's female needs.

I unfasten myself from the closet and snatch my Knicks hat from a box, fitting it on backwards. My younger siblings watch me take a seat on my bare mattress.

"What's left to pack?" I ask Timo.

"Your closet, mostly." He holds my gaze, a thousand uncomfortable words passing silently between us. I hate each one because they're all about the shit stuffed in my closet. "You know—"

"Don't say it," I cut him off.

He tilts his head. "I was just going to tell you that I rolled all of your Broadway posters into tubes."

(So I love watching sports, preferably pro-basketball, and Broadway. If anyone wants to laugh or call me a pussy, the exit is stage left.)

Timo adds, "I even took better care of them than my film posters."

"Yeah right," I say casually. Where I thumbtacked my posters, Timo framed his favorite foreign language and classic films. *La Belle et la Bête* and *The Red Shoes* were preserved behind glass.

Timo gapes. "I glued the torn corner of *Chicago* for you—and you know how much I dislike that one."

Katya starts singing "All That Jazz" off-key. She takes my side over his, and Timo clutches his heart firmer and drops off the dresser. Gasping for air.

"You've killed me, sister," he chokes, pretending to die better than most people ever could or would.

My lips quirk.

It's difficult being upset at them. For anything. He settles down when I push the trash bag with my sneaker. I feel the heat of their gazes.

Timo rolls onto his side. Propping his head up with his hand, he grabs a Santa Claus snow globe from the bag, the price sticker stuck to the bottom.

"Technically," he begins—*don't say it.* "These aren't really your things." He shakes the globe hard, and fake flurries swarm the glass.

My muscles cramp, and I just stare off. Most stores leave on price stickers, even if you buy the item. But I didn't buy that.

I didn't buy *any* of it.

Timo sits up and leans against the dresser, the globe limp in his hand. My brother and sister know that my room is full of useless, stolen shit.

I seize my brother's knowing gaze again, and I speak through my own eyes: *like you don't have your own issues.*

His reply: *this isn't about me.*

Katya swings her head back and forth, realizing one of us is about to explode.

Look, over anyone else, we'll usually vent to each other about a bad day's work, grievances, personal bullshit. Because we're certain that we won't fucking blab.

We're in a workplace where everyone knows everyone. Each Aerial Ethereal show employs around 50 to 100 performers tops, and rumors and gossip reach every single ear.

Katya couldn't even keep her first period a secret. Our cousins (all male) sent her boxes of tampons and pads by the *hour.*

On top of that, I never attended a typical high school. Aerial Ethereal hires tutors for all minors in between practices and performances, but I bet the gossip here is about as bad as a locker-lined hallway or college campus.

Kat examines us one last time before standing. "I'll go pack the last of your fridge."

Our biggest fights start when two of us gang up on the other one, so Kat willingly pulls herself out of the confrontation.

I don't like when she's in the crossfires of anything.

Remember how I said there's a shit ton of Kotovas? Well in our generation, Kat is the *only* Kotova girl by blood—which means she's been protected and bubble-wrapped a thousand times over by all of us.

"What about your suite?" I ask as she reaches the door. Kat lives with our older brother, Nikolai, and since she's still a minor, he's her legal guardian.

He used to be all of ours, too.

"Already boxed and moved hours ago," she says.

(Of course.)

Nik wouldn't wait until the last minute for any Aerial Ethereal deadline, and Timo has probably been working just as long to clean up our place.

My little brother is one of the most professional artists here. Always on-time for rehearsals, stagings, and meetings. Goes above and beyond at practice, and would *never* send Marc Duval an email that called his decision bullshit.

As soon as Katya shuts the door on her way out, Timo says, "You said you wouldn't start hoarding."

"Dude." I sigh heavily. "I'm *not* hoarding. I have no attachment to most of this stuff. You can throw out a ton of it."

(Just not anything that reminds me of her—it's all I have left.)

I ache to say it, to plead, to tell him all that's weighed on me for years. But I do what I have to do.

I push her aside. I try to forget.

Yet, I'm still clinging.

Timo balances the snow globe on his bent knee. In smooth Russian, he tells me, "*I'm just worried.*"

In the same language, I say, "*You shouldn't be.*"

He rolls the Christmas globe into the trash bag. "Luka…"

"It's just my shit to deal with, okay?" I'm upset because I don't want them to see how much I've been stealing recently. I wish I threw out all that stuff ages ago, but I just put things off. Shove them aside and try not to look back.

That's my life.

I cram my figurative drawers full of shit and more shit and pretend it's all nonexistent. That it's not bearing on my chest like a fifty-ton elephant.

Timo rests the back of his head against my dresser. "I like focusing on your Robin Hood tactics. It helps take my mind off our new room situation *and* the fact that my life is completely fucked."

I kick the trash bag out of our way. "Your life isn't completely fucked."

Timo laughs once. "*You*, Luk, are the best roommate in the world. You don't hound me when I stumble in late or blare music. You don't care when I bring my boyfriend over and fuck loudly. Really, it takes extreme work to piss you off." He pauses, as though saying, *seeing you pissed today scares me.*

I rotate my baseball cap, brim in front.

Lately, I just feel like I'm losing all of my control with Corporate. Not that I had much to begin with, but I was artfully fooling myself for a while there.

"Henceforth," Timo continues, "my new roommate will never be as great as you." (Likewise, Timo.)

I give him a look. "*Henceforth?*"

"It annoys John when I say it." He smiles wide, a magnetic grin that could make grown men and women bow in adoration.

I shake my head. *Henceforth.* "I don't think you're using that word right." Maybe he is. I don't really know.

"That's the beauty of it," Timo says easily. "Henceforth, I will say it however I want."

I smile, my chest lighter just talking to him. He has that effect on most people.

As the quiet falls, we skim the emptied room and the trash bags. Half of my life is filled with garbage. The other half with necessities. The problem is trying to sort out which is which.

Nineteen years of living with Timo. *Gone.*

In one fucking email.

"Who are you rooming with anyway?" I ask him.

He scratches his temple, his face a little pained. "I'll tell you later."

Timo has no enemies. Where I'm the Least Favorite Kotova, he's without a doubt the Most Beloved. Last year, Marc Duval said he was "life and youth personified"—and he's never slept with anyone in Aerial Ethereal, so he's pretty drama-free too.

"Okay," I say, not pressuring my brother. I know he'll open up in his own time.

Timo nods to me. "What about you?"

I dig in my pants pocket and pull out the crumpled letter from HR with my room assignment. I hand the paper to Timo. I've read it a hundred times already.

Artists Assigned to Room 4303
L. Kotova
D. Kotova
Z. Li
B. Wright

That last name—B. Wright—skids my heart to a complete stop every single time. It's not a good feeling. No matter how much I wish it could be.

Her name so close to my name is just bad.

ACT TWO
LUKA KOTOVA

The exact layout of my suite is the same as the last one, but two things are noticeably different.

One: the window-view is of the Vegas strip, not the hotel pool.

Two: three other people live with me now.

That's four people total in the same sized space.

I didn't focus on this detail until I entered my new bedroom, and I was met with a bunk bed like I'm at summer camp. No box springs. Not even a real mattress, just some blue vinyl-wrapped foam insert that pretends to be one.

I prop my arm on the doorway, my gray eyes plastered onto the atrocity that Corporate calls a bed. My older cousin paces the length of our tiny, shared room and rubs his unshaven jaw and chin. Completely distraught.

"What…I…*what*…" He lets out a gnarled sound. This might be the first time I've seen Dimitri Kotova lost for words.

"Hey," I say with a nod and shake my box of Junior Mints, dumping candy in my palm. "You can take top or bottom, whichever you want."

Dimitri is *tall*, not just for an acrobat's standards. Everyone calls him "the tank" for his muscle mass and towering height.

He's 6-foot-5-inches like my older brother Nik, but the difference: Nik is more agile, more *natural*—a gifted, talented artist. He out-flips, outmaneuvers, and outperforms everyone.

Except for Timo.

Dimitri tries ten-thousand times harder to do what Nik can do in one breath. I know what it's like to be second-best to people you love. Hell, not even second-best.

Third best. Fifth best.

In some scenarios, *the worst*.

So yeah, I like Dimitri, even if he has a lot of undesirable qualities.

Dimitri stops by our plain dresser, the only other furniture in here. He blinks a few times, and I pop a Junior Mint in my mouth. Waiting for him to wake the fuck up.

When the shock escapes him, he finally acknowledges my presence. "Are you looking at me?"

I nod again, brows raised. Wondering where this is going.

Dimitri points to his chest. "Do I look like a third-grader? Huh? What in the *fuck* is Aerial Ethereal smoking?" His face nearly shatters at another thought. "How am I supposed to have sex on this thing? As soon as a woman sees this, she's going to laugh right in my face."

Dimitri sinks down on the "mattress" and the whole structure creaks. He looks simultaneously murderous and wounded. Covering his face in his hands, he's one step away from proclaiming *my life is over.*

My cousin loves sex, women, and the teeterboard. Not always in that order.

In his family, Dimitri is the oldest of ten children, and at twenty-six, he's six years older than me. But we were all born into the circus life together. Four generations. No other options.

Only one love.

By the age of five, I was a kid actor, collecting props. Clearing the area for the next act. Performing simple floor acrobatics in group routines.

Our job is to produce magic for an audience. No bunnies in hats or card tricks. With our bodies we do the *unthinkable*. Scale walls without handholds, lift people twice our size in perilous positions, slice through air with the strength of one arm—flips and twists that'd make most gymnasts go, "What the fuck?"

All while creating an aura of pure, raw beauty. Visceral, full-bodied magic thrums through our veins, and we hope it'll reach an audience. I love the adrenaline, but even more than the rush—when I perform, I feel the closest to my family.

Hearts and souls are left on that stage, and by ten, I fought to leave mine too. I began specializing in a variety of high-risk acrobatics, a required milestone for all Kotovas. Russian swing, Russian bar, trapeze, teeterboard, and aerial apparatuses (hoops, silks, straps, metal cubes, *chandeliers*).

All the while, I spent two to three months in cramped hotel rooms before traveling to the next city, the next country, the next continent.

At thirteen, Corporate said that I'd settle down in New York City and join the cast of a new show called *Infini*.

I was happy. Like wish-upon-a-star, blow-out-all-your-birthday-candles kind of happy. For the first time, I'd live in one place. I could unpack my suitcases for real. I could memorize city streets knowing I wouldn't have to forget them in a couple months. I didn't even care that Corporate housed us in dingy apartments. For one brief second, I was *happy*.

Then the second passed. Stupidly, I never looked at the fine print.

The cast list didn't include handfuls of my aunts, uncles, some of my cousins, and all the older generations. And most glaringly, my mom. My dad.

None of them were joining Infini.

Our huge overwhelming family was being split apart in several directions. My parents were recruited for Somnio, which would tour Asia, Europe, and South America for five years. Where Corporate says you go, you go.

"It's our living," my dad would tell all of us. Fight back and Aerial Ethereal could easily replace us. What kind of life would we be living outside of the circus? No one toyed with the idea.

I figured I'd lose some contact with my mom and dad. Halfway across the globe, too busy, all the time differences—so much separated the touring side of our family from us. Now I barely speak to any of them, and not long after my parents left, Nikolai became my legal guardian.

He was just twenty.

He was the age that I am right now. I think about that a lot. Could I've done what he did? Could I've taken care of Timo, Katya, me, and all of our emotional baggage in a big, brand new city?

(Not at all.)

I barely have my own head on straight. Sadly, too, my brotherly relationship with Nik disintegrated the day our parents left. Sometimes I wish he could be more like Dimitri.

More of a big brother than a dad.

Then I hate that I think it—because I'm sure he wishes he could've filled that role over the parental one.

I swallow my Junior Mint almost whole and focus my attention back to Dimitri. Who still mourns the dismal future of his sex life.

"We have a couch," I remind him. "Just screw there." He knows I don't care.

Dimitri drops his hands from his face, strong-jawed and broad-shouldered like all of us, but his ocean-blue eyes contrast the usual Kotova gray. "Let me do that, and then watch our two other roommates cock-block me and take a steaming dump on my work life. I don't shit where I eat."

When I was eleven, he told me that fucking anyone who works for AE is like swimming in a "polluted pussy ocean"—his ineloquent way of saying: *extremely dangerous*. And in some cases for our careers, *fatal*.

I didn't listen to his advice.

I usually don't.

I straighten off the door frame. "Speaking of that other roommate…" I can't even say her name. I think of *B. Wright* and all of my muscles tense. I shake the rest of my candy into my mouth.

Dimitri scrutinizes me. "Huh." He stands up. "*That* roommate? Are you talking about Baylee Wright?"

I shrug. *Don't think about her.* My stomach overturns, and I have to clutch the doorway. I crumple the Junior Mints box in my other hand.

"Little Kotova," Dimitri jeers when he thinks I'm being an idiot. "You're out of your mind if you believe HR put Baylee in our suite. For one, she has a cunt."

His crudeness is a second-by-second occurrence. With that kind of consistency, I've become overly desensitized. And maybe I shouldn't be.

"Second…" He seizes my gaze like he's trying to pry this fact into my skull. "She's *Baylee Wright*."

I feel sick.

My past—with her—tries to burrow deep into my body. (I can't let it.) I lower my baseball cap so he's unable to read my features.

Dimitri still appraises me, and he wedges his towering build into the doorway.

So I have to confront him head-on.

"But you do realize she's in Infini?" He cocks his head and waves his hand at my face. "You there, hello?"

I roll my eyes as I lift my gaze. "Leave it alone, dude. I don't—no, I literally *can't* talk about her." When I say that I can't speak about Baylee, it has nothing to do with our feelings. They could be good feelings. They could be miserable, and it still wouldn't change this one fact.

I literally can't talk about Baylee Wright.

And she literally can't talk about me.

"I just want to know," he says roughly.

"Know what?"

"If you auditioned for Infini forgetting that you'd have to work with her again."

"I didn't forget." *I'd never forget.* When Infini moved to Vegas and I jumped to Aerial Ethereal's Viva, Baylee stayed in Infini. She's one of the few original cast members from its inception.

I never really believed Corporate would shift me back to Infini. Even if I auditioned, I always knew it was a long shot. Now that it's actually happening, it's still hard to process the reality. We have two entirely separate acts, so I've prepared for our paths to parallel—not intersect.

Now we have new choreography where I may actually work *with* her.

Now she's living in my suite.

I shake my head to myself but I say aloud, "I didn't mentally prepare for her to live with me."

"Good because she's not," Dimitri says with certainty. Off my confusion, his brows knit and he makes a face like he's about to disown me. "Don't tell me you forgot she has an older brother."

"Fuck," I say.

Fuck.

My whole face drops. I never put the pieces together. When I see those initials, my mind cements on Bay.

Not the obvious answer…

Brenden Wright.

ACT THREE

4 1/2 YEARS AGO - NEW YORK CITY

LUKA KOTOVA

My knees bounce.

Restless, I rub my sweaty palms on my gym shorts. I've never ventured this far into Aerial Ethereal's Manhattan corporate offices. Large, black-framed show posters hang on the waiting room's periwinkle walls, and fresh lilies sit in a ceramic vase.

On any other occasion, this place would seem inviting, but today, I'll meet Marc Duval for the first time. Any kindness will vanish as soon as I step into his office.

"Apologize and then stay quiet," my older brother coaches in his stern voice, darker and more severe than ever. "Let me do the talking."

He towers above me, not able to sit, and his broad arms won't uncross. Nikolai Kotova is intimidating in almost every circumstance, but now I can barely even meet his gaze, which carries forty-tons of parental disappointment.

As my legal guardian, my failings reflect poorly on him, and this wasn't a tiny hiccup. In his words: "this is a *colossal* fuck-up, Luka."

I know.

I slump forward, hands cupped together, my stomach coiling in vicious knots. I'm not sure what I should say to anyone. There's no denying that I broke a rule.

A rule that's been cemented into the foundation of this company.

A rule that's been upheld by every Kotova that ever existed.

I broke this rule every day, but I was caught only once. And that's all it takes.

Just *one* moment for everything to change.

Next to me, Dimitri Kotova pinches the bridge of his nose, and in all the years I've known him, he's never looked this distraught. Briefly, he glances at me, and a flash of remorse ignites his ocean-blue eyes.

"This is serious," Nik tells me, his voice low—even if we're the only three in the waiting room. Long pieces of his damp hair hang over a rolled bandana, tied around his forehead. Sweat stains the neckline of his gray shirt.

Corporate pulled all three of us out of practice today.

It's not like my older brother and cousin are cheering for "free time" off work. Most of us stress if we lose gym time, if we're not stretching enough or not rehearsing our acts. I screwed that up for them too.

Nik waits for me to acknowledge my mistake.

"I know it's serious," I say beneath my breath, blinking through my rampant thoughts and feelings. What more can I say? While I sit, my body bows forward. My emotions are teetering on a precipice, and I'm a second from falling off and puking.

"Do you?" Nikolai says, his muscles flexed. As tense as I feel. "Every single artist who has ever broken this rule has been fired from Aerial Ethereal. Not transferred to another show. *Gone.* Do you understand that? I can't help you." His face is full of brutal gravity.

And I think, *fired.*

The word still distorts in my head. A word with no meaning. With no context. I struggle to flip it over and make sense of it. I know the history of this rule.

I knew the inferno I was running through. Now that I'm burned, I try to sit numb instead of screaming in pain. "There are other troupes," I say with no emotion. "High Flyers Company and Emblem & Fitz—"

"Aren't your family," Nik interjects. "Aerial Ethereal is the *only* troupe with your family, Luk—and it's the best."

He says it like I still deserve the best, but I don't. An immeasurable amount of guilt fists my bare bones. Trying to shatter me. Trying to crush every limb. I'm not sure I can ever be absolved, and at the heart of it: I only regret being caught.

I don't regret one day of breaking that rule. Because it'd mean regretting every moment that I spent with Baylee.

And I don't. I just don't. I *can't.*

It feels like betrayal. Like a knife in the heart—and I'd rather gather her in my arms and shield her from this incoming misery than never *feel* what we felt together. Than never live as happily as we lived.

I stare at my cupped hands.

Fired.

I can barely picture losing my family. If AE sacks me, that's what'll happen. None of us have much time for people outside of the circus. And without this job, I won't be able to afford room & board at the Masquerade. I won't spend hours of every day working beside Timo and Katya. I won't be tutored with them. I'll need to go to public school—I've never even been inside a normal high school.

I'll be on the outside looking in.

I'll miss their lives, and they won't really be a part of mine. To go from being in each other's company daily, hourly, to being ripped out of their world—it kills me.

Everything that defines me resides in this place.

Everything and everyone I love is here.

Dimitri makes a wounded noise, seconds from screaming. He's bent over, his hand splayed over his eyes. It takes me a second, but I realize that my unbreakable cousin—the one that everyone calls "the tank"—is breaking down before me.

I'm immobile.

Physically here, but drifting. Leaving. Somewhere else. Somewhere that feels more *real* than this unbelievable moment.

"It's not your fault," Nik tells our cousin. "Luka was the one who made the mistake. He has to take responsibility for his own actions."

I'm unsurprised by Nikolai's lack of sympathy. He's always told me that same thing. He's always been a stiff, follow-the-rules kind of guy, and he constantly tries to drill the same sentiments into me.

Even now.

When it's too late.

Dimitri drops his hand, his face full of hard lines, and he nods rigidly in cold agreement. Of course he sides with Nik. Both the same age, Dimitri prides himself on loyalty, and as Nik's best friend, he'd stand by his side to the death.

There's no *tender* consoling happening. It's not like there really ever has been. Before my family split apart, I never felt like my mom was mine. I saw her like a friend or a distant relative. My mom and dad wanted this corporation to raise us. To feed us. Clothe us, teach us.

I can see how they'd rarely call now. I can see how they'd feel like their jobs as parents were done once we landed a career. Once we learned skills that furthered us in the world. Only this happened when I was five-years-old.

Right now, I don't have to look hard to know that there aren't any gentle hands. No one is here to wrap their arm around my shoulder and whisper, "it'll be okay," in my ear.

I face hard jaws. Muscular bodies. Overpowering masculinity, and look, I'm only human. Sometimes I'd like a mom to hug me.

Just once.

Nikolai doesn't blink, and his harsh gaze meets mine.

"Just say it," I tell Nik, my eyes burning. Reddening.

"You valued sex over your career, and there's no coming back from this."

I shake my head repeatedly, my features contorting. I didn't risk everything for sex. It was *more* than sex. It was always *more*. But how can I defend myself? The rule I broke was about sex—and that's all they see. A fling. A hookup.

Not *love*.

I fucking love her—and that means nothing to everyone but me.

I ache for compassion. Sympathy.

Everything that Nik can't give me.

"Would you even care…?" I say so softly he can't hear.

"What was that?" His gray eyes narrow on me.

I hoist my head, high enough to meet his intensity. "Would you even care if I got fired?" He'd be free of me.

His nose flares, suppressing a multitude of emotion. He believes that I am going to be fired. That there's no other alternative.

(There never has been.)

He's right to think this. I'm the one dreaming.

"No matter what happens," Nik says, "I'm still your guardian." He didn't exactly answer my question, but he pats my shoulder, trying to be comforting. Gentle.

It's a harsh pat, but I understand.

I see that he loves me, even if he has trouble expressing the sentiment outright.

No one says another word after that, and all my thoughts circum-navigate back to one moment. One night. Yesterday.

I wonder how long it'll haunt me. How many times I'll replay the past in my head.

After Infini's show last night, Aerial Ethereal threw a huge cast party for their patrons. Attendance was required so investors could shake hands and chat with all the artists. In hopes that they'd make a donation by the party's end.

I'd been to plenty before, and in my mind, the word "required" was a loose suggestion rather than an actual rule.

Wearing makeup and garments from the show, I snuck away with Baylee to the costume department. We had sex behind one of the dressing racks. A colorful array of sequined outfits shrouded us from sight.

My older brother will say that having sex was my mistake, but I believe my real and only mistake was not accounting on anyone else leaving the party.

Swept up in the moment, we didn't hear Dimitri or the Marketing Director of Aerial Ethereal enter the room, but they heard us.

Apparently Vince laughed about the incident and said something like, "Looks like this room is taken." Dimitri told me that Vince even motioned to leave, but my cousin was the one who stepped forward.

"Anton," Dimitri called out, humored, "if that's you, I'm going to tell everyone where you like to fuck."

I had just enough time to grab a dress from the floor and throw the garment to Baylee. Then Dimitri pushed the hung clothes aside and caught us.

As soon as he saw me, his smile fell, and before he could yank the costumes back to conceal us, Vince careened his neck.

One glance from a member of Corporate and our whole world came crashing down. Vince reported us to his supervisors, and his supervisors reported us to Marc Duval, who'd been in Montreal. Apparently he took the red eye to New York, just to have this meeting.

Baylee and I had been secretly dating for about a year and a half, and in that time, we never really believed we'd be caught.

We felt invincible.

I'm fifteen.

She's fourteen.

We're young enough to make mistakes, but we're old enough to be employed by a billion dollar company with strict, unbending rules.

Aerial Ethereal **minors** *(i.e. employees younger than 18) are not allowed to date or have sexual relations with other Aerial Ethereal employees.*

The line in my contract wreaks havoc on me.

On us.

Exactly 48 minors were caught breaking that rule in the past forty years. Exactly 48 minors were sacked from Aerial Ethereal.

There should be no hope for me or her, but I haven't accepted my reality yet. I just can't.

I glare at the door to Marc Duval's Manhattan office. Baylee is on the other side, and it's not like I had much of a choice in who went first. I would've taken her place.

Truth: I'd do *anything* to lift the consequence off Baylee. She doesn't deserve to be fired. This circus—it means *so* fucking much to her. Infini, especially. It's more than a job for Bay.

It tears at my insides knowing that I'm responsible for hurting her…in an insurmountable, unthinkable way.

And if I start focusing on what she means to me—I'll really puke.

(They won't split us apart. They can't.)

I feel how naïve I am. I feel young.

I feel fifteen for, maybe, the first time in a really long while. I've been independent most of my life. Able to take care of myself and make my own money. It's what my mom and dad wanted. I've never felt like I *needed* a parent. Not until this moment. Not until right now.

Isn't that what parents do? Make things right. Help carry the burden. Lift the weight.

I sniff and rub my nose, suppressing more emotion.

The door opens, and I immediately stand. My body thrums, nerves and dread compounding, and I feel like I'm on the edge of a cliff, grabbing for her hand, but she slips through my fingers.

And I watch her fall.

Really, I can't see Bay. Not yet. A young black woman purposefully shields the fourteen-year-old girl from my sight. Hourglass frame and fashion-forward clothes—I instantly recognize her as Baylee's Aunt Lucy.

But I just want to see Bay—to make sure she's alright.

Nikolai and Dimitri are on their feet in front of me, purposefully blocking my view. (Come on.) I try to sidestep, but Nik clamps a hand on my shoulder.

"Stop," he warns.

Stop. I freeze, but my eyes dance past him. I try to peer through the gap between his arm and Dimitri's.

Lucy hugs Bay tightly to her side, and all I can see is Baylee's loose brown curls. Through the small gap, Lucy finds a way to glare at me.

I'm stunned cold.

Since I met Lucy she's *always* liked me. Always.

The changes crash against my chest, my world shifting up and down and sideways. All off-kilter.

(I'm not okay.)

"Nikolai," Lucy greets, her voice unusually stone.

"Lucy." Nik nods back.

Baylee's legal guardian.

My legal guardian.

It doesn't faze me that our parents aren't here. Hers would be if they could.

Mine are traveling in some foreign country for a touring show. I can't even remember what continent they're on right now.

Baylee and her aunt walk hurriedly past, and I want to call Bay back. To shout her name, but my throat swells closed. I hear the door shut.

They're gone.

I didn't even see her.

I barely hear Marc call for us. Dazed, my brother or my cousin puts their hand on my shoulder and physically pushes me towards the office. Each step is involuntary. I'm on *automatic*.

Programmed to move.

Once inside, Marc shuts the door, and I sit on a chair between Nik and Dimitri, all of us facing Marc's oak desk. My gaze glues to his Aerial Ethereal mug, blue lettering with purple swirls.

As soon as Marc's ass hits the seat, he gestures to me.

My face scorches and aches like someone's taken a frying pan and whacked me several times. I open my mouth, struggling for a second, but then I find words.

"I take full responsibility for what happened," I say. "Baylee had *nothing* to do with it." I'm about to say that I forced her to have sex. A lie, but I'd do that. I'd literally do anything to protect her right now. "She—"

Marc raises his hand, silencing me.

(I'm going to puke.)

Nikolai glares at me like, *don't retch on his fucking carpet.*

I swallow acid.

Marc looks older than his early fifties. Shaggy blond hair, sideburns graying, and his dark blue eyes wield only criticisms. I've now met the face of all the dull corporate emails.

"The sentiment is chivalrous," he tells me, "but it takes two people to have intercourse."

Intercourse? I frown and try not to shake my head. It bugs me. That clinical term.

"And Baylee already explained that it was consensual." Marc holds onto a manila folder. "Before I pass over a termination contract, we need to talk."

Termination.

I can't look at Nik, but he's stone-cold beside me. Rigid and unbendable. Maybe he's trying to be a rock for me. Something I can hang onto as I fall.

I remember what Nik said to do. So I start to say, "I'm sorry—"

"Apologies won't fix this."

I sit straighter, back aching.

Marc sets down the folder. "Do you know why Aerial Ethereal has a rule about minors *not* dating or having sexual relations with other company members?" He phrases this like a quiz I'm supposed to fail.

I open my mouth to answer.

He interrupts, "You don't know or else you would have followed it. At least, that's the hope. Because if you knew the importance of this rule and you still *knowingly* broke it, then I don't just have an ignorant kid on my hands. I have a reckless teenager with zero respect for this company."

I've never felt this incapable of speech. Of *being*. Existing. I feel weak. And powerless. I hang my head, unable to look him in the eyes. Slowly but surely cowering to Corporate.

"Which one is it, Luka?" Marc asks. Testing me.

My gaze sears the longer I stare fixatedly at his mug. What am I supposed to say? What's right? What's wrong? (Someone tell me. *Please*. Tell me.)

What do I need to do? I'll do it.

I'll do anything.

(Just don't take my family away from me. Don't take my sister. My brothers. Don't take *her*. I need them all.)

I turn my head to look for help. For a parent. *Nik*.

Reading my expression, he immediately speaks up. "Luka respects the company—"

Marc holds up another hand. "I didn't ask you, Nikolai. I'd like to hear from your brother." The heat of his gaze boils my skin. "Luka?"

"I…" I lick my dry lips. "I didn't…I didn't know." My Adidas shirt suctions to my abs, sweating through the black fabric.

Nik clears his throat and leans forward. "I should've explained its importance. I'll take some responsibility for this."

He will?

Marc taps his pen to the desk. "So you didn't know about his relationship with Baylee Wright?"

"No. I thought they were just best friends. Had I known it went beyond that, I would've put an end to it from the start."

My brother isn't railroading me, but I wish there could be a scenario where he would've been on my side. Hearing him now just cements all the reasons why we kept our relationship secret in the first place.

No one could know. It'd leak to Corporate, and we'd become the forty-ninth and fiftieth minors to be fired for going "beyond" a friendship.

I guess we are 49 and 50 now.

Marc looks to Dimitri. "And you? Did you know?"

My cousin shakes his head.

Once more, Marc's attention bears down on me, and I thread my fingers, cupping my hands together. Trying to remain as calm as I usually am.

"I'll tell you what I told Baylee," Marc says. "Aerial Ethereal has many rules, but for minors this is the most *important* one. It's why we've never failed to terminate a minor after the violation." He rolls his chair forward, arms splayed on the desk. "We employ children, and these children, like yourself—"

I try not to flinch, but he makes me feel five years old. Not fifteen. I don't like feeling this small. Or this *drastic* loss of control.

I have to take a breath. I listen. I try to breathe.

"—well, these children will work for us throughout their precious adolescence. Our job is to maintain the safest work environment for minors. Safe does not include sexual intercourse. Safe does not include workplace relationships that can lead to sexual intercourse."

I wish he would stop saying "sexual intercourse" like it's a disease—
please God.

"We also do *not* advocate underage sex. This isn't high school. This is a professional company that has high standards of care and compliance." Marc places his palm on the manila folder. "As I said, this is a termination contract."

And then I watch him procure a second manila folder from his drawer.

He sets it beside the termination papers. When his authoritative eyes meet mine, I see something else in them. Caution.

Trepidation.

Like this next part—the second folder—is completely out of the ordinary.

"For how many times I've sat here and fired teenager after teenager, we've never offered a choice to any of them," he says. "But I gave Baylee a choice to remain in Aerial Ethereal. And now I'm giving you the same one."

Why? I don't even have to ask. He's already there, telling me.

"Her discipline is unique. It's harder to find a juggler of her skill-level than to find an aerialist of yours."

I nod, agreeing. (Don't fire her. Keep her. *Please.*) She deserves to be happy and safe. I just wish I could've given her that.

"We're also respecting the memory of Joyce Wright. Baylee's mother was an incredibly talented asset to Aerial Ethereal, and her contributions to Infini…" He pauses and collects himself before saying, "Her music is still heard."

I nod again. Trying not to get choked up. Bay's parents passed away around the beginning of Infini, and Joyce composed the score of the show.

"Why offer you a choice?" he asks what's on my mind. "You're a Kotova."

(Of course.)

"The chemistry and trust your family have on stage is irreplaceable."

I begin to relax, but then the dark look in his eye—it says *don't be happy*. I'm still being punished. Someway. Somehow.

He's going to skewer me.

"Here's your choice," he says and pushes forward the left manila folder. "You sign the termination contract, and you will be fired from Aerial Ethereal like every minor before you."

I watch him push the right folder towards me.

"Or you can sign this contract. In order for you to remain employed by Aerial Ethereal, we need to *bury* this incident so far down that no one will ever unearth it. Because if anyone finds out we gave preferential treatment, it will ruin this company. We'll have forty-eight lawsuits thrown in our faces, accusing us of wrongful termination from years past because we didn't fire *you* for the same offense. Are you following me?"

It makes sense. "Yeah." I sit up more, thinking that this is going my way.

Marc taps the manila folder. "By signing this contract, you're stating that you will have no further verbal or physical contact with Baylee Wright." *What?*

Blood drains out of my head.

"Also, with your greatest effort, you will not look in her direction or utter her name."

I can't move. Can't breathe. I'm not even allowed to *look* at Baylee?

"Make no mistake, *this*"—he pats the manila folder—"is a gift to you. We're giving you a chance to remain with Aerial Ethereal, but if you violate this new contract by reigniting anything with Baylee—a relationship, a friendship, a hand-shake, a *glance*—I will not only fire you but the company will be forced to go one step further."

What's further than being fired?

"To protect ourselves from liability and damages, we will have to enact a company-wide policy for hiring. AE will only employ artists over the age of eighteen. It's a *no minors policy*. This action will be swift and immediate and will cause the termination of every artist seventeen and under."

I rock backwards, his words sucker-punching me.

Dimitri's jaw tightens, and he shares an increasingly dark look with Nikolai. We're all attached to minors in this company. Our cousins. Our siblings. Our family. It's not just about me anymore. My little brother, Timofei.

My little sister, Katya.

Not to mention the hundreds of other minors in touring shows. They could all be fired. All out of work. If I sign and then violate this contract, I'll ruin them.

"If you're even *considering* running into her arms, hugging her," Marc says, "do not sign this contract." He keeps his hand on the folder.

What about when we're legal adults? Can I hug her then? I want to ask, but my throat is swollen shut.

Nik asks, "But he'll remain in the company if he complies with the conditions of the contract?"

"He'll still be employed by Aerial Ethereal, but as far as Infini goes, he'll be cut from the opening sequence."

Because Baylee is in it.

"However, he'll still participate in high-risk wall/trampoline and Russian swing." He looks up. "This does not leave the room, but AE is currently in negotiations for a deal at a Vegas hotel and casino. Maybe you've heard of the place?"

We glance at one another, guarded and wary.

"The Masquerade," Marc clarifies. "The hotel has been building a performance gym and two globe auditoriums. In a couple years or so, Infini will be transferred to Vegas, and Viva and Amour will fill the second auditorium. In that time, we'll ask Luka to switch to either one. You'll stay with your family, but the show-separation between you and Baylee will make it easier to abide by the contract."

Marc says he'll "ask me" to switch to Viva or Amour—but he means he'll tell me. He fabricates an illusion of control, but I feel the strings he attaches to my arms and legs. And I feel him *pulling*.

It's why I have trouble smiling and beaming at the "gift" he's offering me. I want to be grateful because I fucked up and here's a handout no one's been given before. But it's hard when I feel like he can cradle *my* fist and slam my knuckles at my own face. Breaking my bones.

"Since your on stage time is shortened, you'll have a pay cut," Marc says.

I don't care about the money.

"And these"—Marc slides over two new folders to Dimitri and Nikolai—"are non-disclosure agreements. You both will *not* speak a word about Baylee and Luka's relationship. Not to your friends. Not to your family. Not whispered beneath your breath. The only people who know about this incident are the four of us here, plus Baylee Wright, her aunt, and lastly, two trusted colleagues of mine that'll keep an eye on Luka and Baylee in the gyms." *Vince has to be one of them.* "As far as we're concerned, this never happened."

He's erasing my entire relationship. As though my feelings for Bay never existed.

I stare haunted at the two folders still in Marc's possession. He pushes them even closer to me. Until they sit right in front of my face.

Marc never peels his eyes off me. "You can call a lawyer to meet you here, but neither contract will change. Not a single line."

Everyone waits for me to speak or move.

For the first time, I edge forward. "The rule I broke…" I pause, the air tensing. "It's exclusive for minors. Adults in Aerial Ethereal can have relationships with other members of the company."

Marc nods. "We encourage adult relationships. Chemistry *off* stage can translate to chemistry *on* stage, but minors are different. They're not leads in shows, and we're nurturing professional careers and a safe environment. We have to protect children while they're employed by us."

The same question bangs against my brain. *What about when we're legal adults? Can I talk to her then?*

Marc sees. He knows where I'm headed, and he interjects before I ask outright. "The contract states that when you're both over eighteen, the established agreement will still hold."

I freeze. "I don't understand…why?" My stomach overturns on itself.

Marc stares at me like I'm a fragile kid.

Has he broken me already?

Am I in pieces right now?

"Because you're not taking advantage of this opportunity. We're offering you a chance to stay in the world's most renowned acrobatic circus, and you're not going to backhand us in three years because you're suddenly of age."

I'm numb.

"We're asking for a full commitment. Not indecisive, in-a-few-years-I'll-be-with-her impermanence. You sign this contract, and you're promising AE that you'll keep this a *life-long* secret. Our favoritism could potentially cost us millions of dollars. Are you following? Have I lost you?"

(You've gutted me.)

By signing that contract, I'll never be able to see Baylee smile or even frown. I'll never hear her talk or laugh. I'll never wrap my arms around her shoulders. I'll never hug her tight or kiss her—*fuck* I can't even say her name.

Forever.

"I want to be clear," Marc says, "if you sign this contract and you both decide to quit four years or even ten years down the line to be with each other, we'll still have to enforce a *no minors policy* in case anyone finds out about today's offer. You take this offer, and there is *no* turning back."

My insides are on fire.

Marc throws more facts at me. "When you're eighteen, you can date any adult you'd like in the company. Just not Baylee Wright. I'm not keeping you from her, Luka. You have a choice. If you're adamant about being with Baylee, sign the termination contract."

"He's not," Nikolai says firmly, his glare hot on me. Wondering how I can even *hesitate* to choose a girl over my future. The love I carry for Baylee is stronger than he understands, but it's a fucking cruel choice.

Because I wholeheartedly, undeniably *love* Katya and Timofei. And Nik. And my cousins, but really, it's Kat. It's Timo.

If I leave Aerial Ethereal, I lose them—and I can't.

I can't lose them.

I've spent nearly my entire life with my sister and brother. We're closer than friends. Closer than most family. We're bonded by experiences and time, and I'm scared to sever all of that.

"Just give me…" *a second.*

"You're fifteen, Luka," Nikolai says, speaking huskily and forcefully beneath his breath. "*Fifteen.* Whatever you have with Baylee now, it'll most likely end. You can't quit for her. It's naïve. This is your career. Your life."

I hear: *your family.*

Marc passes over pens to all of us. "Luka, you're young; you don't get it," he patronizes me, "but simply put, you aren't *entitled* to everything you want. You will lose something today. And you must choose."

I stare faraway. Marc pretends like I have a choice, but Baylee was just in here. She already made her decision—and I know that she didn't pick me.

Baylee didn't just choose this career. She chose her older brother. She chose the memory of her mother. She chose the pieces of her heart that preexisted me.

I understand, and I know I'm about to do the exact same. For nearly identical reasons. Our siblings—they lift us when we fall down, and we're scared to lose them now.

Maybe it'd be different if we were older.

Stable. With less voices telling us we're naïve and wrong.

I don't know. I can't know.

An unbearable loss compounds on my chest as I pick up my pen. And I put my hand on the contract with a thousand stipulations. It seems impossible to maintain, but with the threat of the no minors policy, I know I have to.

I know she will too.

We're both not the kind of people who'd destroy other kids for our own gain. We'd choose to be miserable alone first.

While I flip through the papers to find the signature spaces, something wet glides down my cheek. I rub my face roughly and sign my name.

I terminate a friendship. A thousand peaceful moments. And the possibility of a happy ending.

A few minutes later, we shuffle back into the waiting room—and right when Dimitri shuts the office door, I crouch and puke in a potted plant.

Breathing heavy, I hang onto the wicker vase.

Nik looks slightly relieved by the outcome, but he's still in damage-control mode. "We need to talk about what to tell other people. They'll ask questions about why we were called here and why you're no longer talking to Baylee."

Just completely depleted, I sit on the floor. "Tell them I fucked up."

Nik shakes his head once. "It's too vague. We need an explanation as to why you're demoted."

Nausea roils again.

"You and Baylee were doing cocaine," Dimitri suddenly says, as though he's been concocting this during the entire meeting.

I narrow my eyes. "What?"

"Yeah, you did coke." Dimitri nods, *really* believing this is a good idea. "I caught you in the costume department snorting drugs together.

You've been enabling one another—it's why the company wants you to lose contact. You've been demoted because you broke the Wellness Policy." He laughs. "Fucking brilliant." Nodding to Nik, he says, "I can spread this like wildfire."

I don't have to ask why he chose cocaine.

A few of my cousins have been suspended for it. Our profession relies on our bodies, and at times, our jobs are physically painful. Even when we're in supreme physical condition.

Stimulants, especially cocaine, can offer a high that not only alleviates pain but makes performing...*electric.*

I don't know from experience. I've never tried cocaine. Mostly because I fear Nikolai's disappointment, and I risk a lot—but I couldn't risk using drugs.

"Hey..." I sluggishly pick myself up. "Can you at least make it seem like it was my fault, not hers?" If anyone blasts her for this lie...

"I'll try."

Nik starts walking away, but he glances over his shoulder, ensuring that I follow. "Let's go home."

He never asks if I'm okay. Maybe because it's obvious that I'm not. I'm reaping the consequences and taking responsibility for my mistake.

But the price I paid feels gut-wrenchingly high. And as I leave the offices, a realization hammers inside of me like steel to bone. I will always wonder if we chose wrong. If we chose right.

I will always return to today and contemplate my *one* choice. I already feel it tormenting me.

And suddenly, I think...

I wish we weren't given a choice at all.

ACT FOUR
1 YEAR AGO - LAS VEGAS

LUKA KOTOVA

Second meeting with Marc Duval.

I'm nineteen. I've lost the ability to fear him. I'm not terrified of being fired. Not even nervous. In over three years, Aerial Ethereal buried me so far down the roster that I'm surprised they even remember to print my name on the program.

I have one source of disdain in my life. Just one.

It's at him. At Corporate.

Marc sips from his Aerial Ethereal mug while I sit across his desk. "If this is about what I think it is," he says, "you can leave. You're lucky I'm even entertaining this." He has no name for our spontaneous meeting. I didn't schedule one.

He didn't call me in to chat.

I heard he was in the Vegas office, and I stormed assuredly through the door with four words. *We need to talk.*

"It's been three and a half years." I sit on the edge of the chair. "We've obeyed every demand you made. We never texted each other. I haven't even *looked* at her face." It's been hard. Almost impossible.

But the last memory I have of Baylee is us…being caught behind a costume rack. And then her aunt blocking her from my view.

Marc just stares at me like he can't believe what he's hearing.

I add, "No one thinks we hooked up in the past. They all think we were caught doing drugs." And Dimitri doesn't lie to family. Never has, and never will again. "They're not going to draw the conclusion that we broke a rule and you offered us our jobs back…" I trail off at the heat in his eyes. "Come on."

"Let go of her."

I blink slowly, weight mounting on me. I can't accept it yet. "I'm not asking to date Baylee. I'd like to speak to her." I sit forward again. "Her eighteenth birthday was yesterday. I just want to wish her a *happy birthday* and know that you won't enforce the no minors policy."

(Please.)

Marc shakes his head. "It's not happening. You're not being rewarded for honoring a contract that you *have* to follow."

"Can I send her a card?" I try.

"And what does that do? Other than open the floodgates to a friendship that you can't have?" Marc actually rolls his eyes in exasperation. "This is *exactly* why I told you make certain you were sure of your choice…"

I tune him out.

Every day I question what I chose.

Every day of my *life* I wonder what my world would look like with her in it, but without the circus. Without my family.

I wonder. I question. And there is no answer.

Either way, we'd lose something insurmountable. Either way, I'd be grappling with the same grief I do now.

I catch the tail-end of his lecture as he asks, "Do you even know what you're fighting for?"

(Love.)

Marc says, "I'm going to do you a favor and help you understand so you can let go."

(Don't.)

"You're fighting for an adolescent fling from nearly four years ago."

I instantly shake my head.

"No? You're saying that you still love each other? You're saying that after years of silence, you truly think you're the same people you once were? That the juvenile feelings you experienced still exist in some capacity? Luka," he says, contempt coating my name, "*grow up*."

I look away, my muscles flexed.

"You're holding onto an idea. She's not in love with you anymore. Maybe she never even did—maybe you concocted it all in your head."

(Fuck you.)

"She never hesitated. I gave her the choice, and she grabbed the pen ten times faster than you."

I don't want to believe him. Not even if it'll hurt less. I don't want to believe that.

"Look at me."

I force my gaze to his.

"I'll say this plainly, Luka. You're in Viva. She's in Infini. You have no reason to communicate. If you'd like to speak to her, then I'll take this as your formal termination. In which case, the *no minors policy* will be instated—"

"No," I say immediately, resigning from this fight. I didn't come here to tear up the contract and ruin everyone.

I came here for one open window.

And he slammed them all shut again.

"I'm not quitting," I tell him as I stand.

"You'll respect the contract you previously signed?" Marc asks.

I nod, frozen inside.

"I need more than a head-nod."

"I won't talk to her." My voice is hollow. "I won't look at her." And maybe, one day, I'll forget what our love felt like. And I'll finally stop hanging on.

"We understand each other then," Marc says.

I nod as stiffly as before, and then I exit, my disdain replaced with cold numbness. I realize now that I did have something to lose.

I lost all hope.

ACT FIVE

BAYLEE WRIGHT

My Aunt Lucy once said that I'm unnaturally predisposed to shitty situations. That, and I'm far too obsessed with grilled cheese, a boy who is trouble, soca music, and dancing barefoot in living rooms. Sometimes all four were tangled together—in a whacky, *just right* kind of way.

Three days ago, right after the hellish moving day for all Aerial Ethereal artists, I found myself in another shitty situation.

I thought I'd be able to pull myself out of the quicksand. I groveled to Aerial Ethereal and complained to Human Resources, all to be met with *your thousand-dollar fine still stands*.

So I've succumbed to my shitty fate.

Technically it wasn't my fault. Someone stole my *last* cardboard box, after I already made eight trips upstairs to my new suite. Then after I ran around searching for the box, it somehow turned up in another person's suite on the 42nd floor at midnight.

The floor that AE were *desperate* to have cleaned by 5:00 p.m.

"The box has your name on it," they said. "Therefore, you were late on moving and incurred a fine. It doesn't matter if your suite had been empty. You cluttered another room."

Cluttered. It was *one* neatly packed box.

Still, the thousand-dollar fine stands.

I cringe thinking about the depletion in my already low bank account. It's not like artists make loads of money. Aerial Ethereal tries to justify pay cuts with "oh but you live in a Vegas hotel and casino for free. It's worth more than your salary"—yeah, but I'd like money to *eat* too.

I stand on the carpeted casino floor and wait for my brother.

Inside the heart of the Masquerade, slots ping all around me. And even though people gamble at velvet card tables and at flashing machines, I'm alone with my sad thoughts.

"Where are you, Brenden?" I mutter and crane my neck beyond the casino floor. I try to spy my older brother through the hoards of people. Some wheel their suitcases towards the elevators. Others meander along the Masquerade's indoor cobblestone walkway, which leads to bars, dance clubs, gift shops, and the ginormous pool.

Everything you could ever desire is at the Masquerade, or so the brochure says.

I check my phone for any missed texts. My Facebook app is currently up, clicked into a closed group.

INFINITE LOOPHOLE – TOP SECRET (cast only)

Description: if you're a part of this group, then you know what's up. Narks will suffer severe consequences. Don't be a nark.

pinned post Meet up at 1842 (for all newbies, 1842 is the name of a bar in the Masquerade hotel. First floor, red disco balls line the hallway it's on) and arrive no later than 10 p.m. IMPORTANT: do not verbally spread this event to anyone else. Not unless they're in the same show (refer to post title).

"Bay."

I jump at my nickname and turn around to my tense-faced brother. Usually he wears mirth like another layer of skin. Always friendly. Constantly smiling.

Then he sees me upset, in any way, and he stiffens to rigid attention. Like he's a soldier reporting for duty.

Black hair cut short, he runs a hand over his head, and I watch as he assesses my features for answers. We tell each other almost everything, so he was the first to hear about my plan to beg Human Resources one last time tonight.

Now he'll be the first to hear how poorly it went.

I open my mouth, but he speaks first.

"No," he groans, absorbing my dejection. "No, *no*. They can't just fine you a grand for doing nothing." Wearing a green V-neck, charcoal pants, and a spritz of cologne—which suggests a "night out" not confronting HR—he spins towards nowhere really. "I'm going to talk to these idiots."

"No you aren't," I tell him seriously.

Slowly, he faces me again.

I respect his great show of brotherly valor, but I'd *never* let Brenden sink his reputation or career. Mine is already bruised, so one more complaint from me won't make much of a difference.

"*Baylee*," he forces my name like I'm being unreasonable.

"Brenden," I shoot back. I may prefer to stand in the shadows over commanding the spotlight—I'm not loud or brash and I don't really like being the center of attention in my personal life—but that doesn't mean I don't have a backbone.

"You're my *little* sister," he argues.

I always tell him, *you're only one year older.*

He always replies, *a year is plenty of time.*

I don't have the heart for that banter. Honestly, I'm too upset about the situation, and even if I bottle most of the sorrow, it still enlarges a hollow pit inside of me.

A cavernous hole that I have no idea how to fill.

"So I'm your little sister," I say, shrugging tensely. "It won't change anything. Aerial Ethereal won't listen to anyone but themselves. You could even have evidence, and they'd still fine me. Can we please just *go?*" I wave him towards the cobblestone walkway.

Brenden lets out an incensed breath and then scans my wardrobe.

I threw on a red cotton dress for Infini's secret cast party. The outfit is simple like the rest of my wardrobe, and I didn't even bother fixing my hair. Long and loose curly strands mold my oval face and splay over my A-cups.

I'm not exactly slender like a contortionist or ballerina, but I'm not muscular and stalky like a typical gymnast either. I have wide hips like my Aunt Lucy and a flat chest like my mom. As a juggler, I have more leeway in *how* I look than other artists. I'm lucky in the sense that I only need to be fit and in shape.

Brenden shakes his head at my dress. "That thing is ancient."

"What? No it's not." I touch the short hem. "I bought it…two years ago, four years…" I stretch my mind. "Oh." I had this dress when I was *fourteen*, at least.

"Yeah. *Oh.*" He's not amused. "You should buy new clothes. If you're worried about money—"

"It's not that," I interject but then go quiet.

It's hard to part with things that still have a place in my life. If I'm not being forced to say *goodbye* to this dress and it still fits, then why wouldn't I just keep wearing it?

I touch the fabric, and I remember a moment with a boy I'm not supposed to name. I wore this dress when we were together, traipsing around Brooklyn on a brisk, fall day.

I try not to picture the moment. I try not to visualize him at all.

I can't start walking down a road that has an eighty-foot drop-off into a rocky ravine. There's only danger at the end of his name. At the end of *us*.

I have to remember this. Constantly.

Before Brenden offers to pay for a shopping spree or cover half of my fine, I speak up.

"I'm nineteen," I remind him, "and if I need a new dress, I can always buy it on my own." I also add, "Aunt Lucy sends me new clothes almost every month, so you *really* don't have to worry."

Our aunt is a brand & marketing executive for a major NYC and Philadelphia-based fashion company. She's at the very top of her career, but it wasn't always that way. When my parents died, a lot changed for my mom's little sister Lucy. At thirty, she paused her goals, moved to Vegas for us, and took her new role in our lives very seriously.

I love her more than she may even know.

Brenden stares at me for a long moment. Maybe he feels our past inside my words. Quietly, he says, "Let's go."

"IT'S DEAD IN HERE," I SAY TO BRENDEN.

We step inside 1842, a bar that resembles an old timey speakeasy: dark-green velvet booths, wooden high-top tables, and mood lighting thanks to gothic chandeliers.

It's almost completely empty. A bored bartender scrubs the already-shined counter.

Brenden smiles. "Pessimist."

"I'm just calling it how I see it."

He lifts up my wristwatch to my face. "We're also ten minutes early. Do you see that too?"

I shove his side, playfully enough that my lips start to rise with his. "You're annoying."

"You're more annoying," he teases and then nods towards the array of high-top tables.

I spot a very familiar person in the nearly-empty bar.

Zhen Li places little card holders on each table. The note reads: *infinite loophole*. I'm not surprised that Zhen, my brother's aerial straps partner, created the private Facebook group. Besides it being a very *Zhen* thing to do, I was there when it happened.

After two bottles of wine and wild theories about who our co-workers might be, Zhen whipped out his phone and concocted the bizarre plan.

And I like bizarre things.

So of course, I helped where I could. I spread the news about the Facebook group to two artists who we were sure would be shifted to Infini, and hopefully they told others about the secret party.

Zhen notices us and flashes a dazzling smile. He was born and raised in Beijing and started touring with Aerial Ethereal at fourteen. Now twenty-six, he has a lean build and dreamy, picturesque features that melt most of the females in AE. Sunglasses are perched on his head and push back his thick black hair.

Zhen jokes, "What do you think of the turnout?" His accent inflects his words.

"Horrible," I say seriously.

He smiles wider and then greets Brenden with a hand-grab and hug-pat. "About thirty-five joined the group," Zhen tells us.

My brows jump. "Almost half the cast?" I was expecting about ten people out of a cast of fifty. Maybe I am too pessimistic, but I've lost a lot in the span of seven years and met way more roadblocks than passageways.

Zhen tilts his head. "No hope."

Brenden chimes in, "Hopeless." Also tilting his head at me.

I take a seat on a stool while Zhen says something in Mandarin that probably means some form of *no hope* and Brenden mimics him perfectly.

They're way too in sync. On and off the stage.

Not to mention, Brenden switches to more languages that I don't know: Spanish, German, *Russian.*

I cringe at him. "It's less impressive when you do this every day."

My brother is a polyglot. Able to pick up languages fluently and effortlessly. Jealousy bites me. I still struggle with Russian, which floats around AE's gym hourly.

Granted, I'm not *hopeless.* In seven years, my Russian has improved, and I understand Patois, a dialect I hear mostly over the phone from my Jamaican grandparents. They immigrated to Brooklyn before they had my mom and Lucy, and even though my mom always had an American accent, her parent's lilt stayed.

"You mean *more* impressive," Brenden rephrases.

"No, I'm pretty sure I meant *less.*" I can't help but smile, especially as Zhen wiggles his brows, eyes pinging between us. He pretends like he's lost in the banter, but if anyone can keep up with a million different personalities and stay on course, it's Zhen.

Brenden backs up towards the bar. "Beer?" he asks my drink order. I may be underage, but fake IDs and saying *I'm an Aerial Ethereal artist at the Masquerade* goes a long way.

I hesitate though. Beer is my go-to, but after the meeting, I could use something stronger. "Whiskey straight."

Sympathy softens his gaze, and he nods before turning to Zhen.

"Pinot Noir," our friend says, and then he rests his forearms on my table. "It was that bad?"

It. Brenden must've told him about my Human Resources meeting. I'm not surprised since they're best friends. "HR won't budge."

He sighs sadly. "I'm sorry."

"The good news is that I at least found the box." Even if it was in the wrong room.

Zhen straightens up. "What was in it?"

Everything that means something to me. "All of my juggling equipment, Rudy—"

"Rudy?"

Brenden calls out, "The deformed cactus."

I look over my shoulder, seeing my brother leaning against the bar. Waiting for our drinks. "Rudy has *character*," I tell him. The pincushion succulent traveled from New York to Vegas, and on very, very rare occasions, a pink flower will bloom upon Rudy's bulbous build.

"That's what you call the wart-looking thing on its backend?"

I flip him off.

He air-catches my middle finger and pretends to toss it at Zhen.

Zhen chomps the air and swallows.

I give him a look. "Did you just eat my *fuck you*?"

"I did," he says, wiping the corners of his lips. "It was *quite* salty."

Brenden laughs, and I shake my head again, my smile returning. *Performers.* Dull isn't in their vocabulary.

"So the box contained your juggling clubs and Rudy," Zhen says.

"And my dad's books."

"You still have those?" Brenden asks, his voice tight.

I risk a peek at him, his face even tenser than his voice. Brenden has a hard time talking about our parents, but he hasn't erased their memory anymore than I have.

My gaze drops to his V-neck, and I spy lines of black ink against his warm brown skin. His tattoo is artsy topography of *Dad, Mom, Baylee* in the shape of a heart. It rests right over his actual heart.

Our parents died in a four car pile-up on a New York freeway. A fluke accident that involved a tractor-trailer popping its front wheels and spinning out of control.

My mom would've found light in the unpredictability of her fate.

My dad would've loved knowing he was right beside my mom when it happened.

About a year after they passed, I cried when I saw Brenden's tattoo. I was thirteen. He was fourteen. Then I punched my brother's arm and said, "I didn't die with them." Still, he included my name.

"It doesn't mean I don't love you too," he told me.

I'm nineteen now, and heaviness still clings to their memory. Sometimes it's a good nostalgic weight, but other times, it makes it hard to breathe.

I watch my brother collect a glass of wine, whiskey, and tequila.

"I kept the novels," I affirm as he sets our drinks on the table. "Do you remember *Two Summers of Rage & Delight?*"

Brenden lets out a short laugh while he squeezes lime into his drink, but I think he's too choked up to explain the memory to Zhen.

I sip my whiskey. "Brenden was six," I explain to our friend, "and he told our dad to rename his novel *Two Summers of Rashes & Doo-doo.*"

Zhen coughs on his wine and then starts laughing with my brother.

If it weren't up to his publisher, I think Neal Wright, New York novelist of contemporary literature, would've without a doubt titled his book Rashes & Doo-doo.

Just because he loved his kids that much.

I stare off and take a bigger swig. I find myself reminiscing way too often. Not just about my dad, but my mom—she's everywhere here. As a music composer for Aerial Ethereal, she still *lives* in the circus. In me.

Shit. My eyes water, and I wipe the creases. I sense the concern in their sudden silence, so I don't meet their gazes.

Thankfully, my phone pings.

"AE email notification," I tell them, and they start checking their phones.

Date: January 25th
Subject: First Practice - IMPORTANT
From: Geoffrey Lesage, Choreographer
CC: Baylee Wright, Brenden Wright, Dimitri Kotova, Zhen Li
Good Evening.

We're less than a month away from the first meeting / practice of Infini. I need you four to arrive **twenty minutes early**. You're the only artists that weren't recast in the recent shakeups—and there's a likelihood that you'll carry over bad habits from the previous choreography.

So I'd like to discuss my methods.

Also, if you think being an original Infini cast member carries prestige, think again. **<u>IT CARRIES A BURDEN</u>**. You're a burden to me and the clean slate that I asked Aerial Ethereal for. This is your opportunity to prove me wrong. Don't waste it.

Twenty minutes early.

No exceptions.

Geoffrey Lesage
Infini Choreographer
geoffreylesage@mailme.com

"He has a bad attitude," Brenden says, pocketing his cell.

Zhen swishes his wine. "And a love of caps-lock."

"He's supposed to be a genius," I remind them. "If he saves Infini from being retired, then his prickly personality will be worth it." I hate uttering the words *retired* in the same breath as Infini.

My heart, my soul—it's in this show and this show alone. I can't imagine losing it too. I'd do *anything* possible to save it from extinction. Including putting up with a stubborn choreographer.

Zhen fixes his sunglasses atop his head. "He's beyond prickly."

"Thorny, then," I offer.

"Only if you're referring to him being a thorn in our asses."

Brenden chugs his tequila and licks his lips. "A deep, *agonizing* thorn. He just told us we were burdens, and he hasn't even met us yet."

"And what a shame," Zhen adds. "We're very likable."

"The most likable." Brenden raises his glass. "Everyone likes us."

"If Aerial Ethereal had a congeniality award, they'd have to split it in half to give us both a piece." Zhen clinks his wine to Brenden's tequila.

I love bursting their bubble. "I doubt a congeniality award would go to two guys who occupied an eight-person booth at Angelo's. You let a family of six wait *two hours* to be seated."

Brenden shuffles beside Zhen, just so they can do this we're-older-than-you-and-staring-darkly-down-at-you thing. It's ineffective on me, and I usually just laugh in the end.

"She doesn't think we're likable," Brenden tells Zhen.

"Unbelievable," Zhen teases.

"You realize, Bay, that we've been eating our pre-show meals at that *booth* since we arrived in Vegas."

"It's tradition," Zhen confirms.

"You mean *superstition*." I laugh because eighty-five percent of the cast is superstitious in some way. Before a performance, one of the clowns eats ten green jelly beans and does five jumping jacks backstage.

"*And*," Brenden continues, "the restaurant gave us that booth. Now what do you have to say?"

"You tipped the hostess. If you're waiting for me to say you're the most likable in the entire universe—and to bow at your feet—it'll never happen." I like this back-and-forth too much to ever concede.

Zhen turns to Brenden. "Got to love your little sister. Always keeping our egos in check."

"There's a word for that," Brenden says, looking directly at me.

"What?" I wonder.

"*Prickly.*"

I shove his arm lightly while they both laugh. After a few moments, our humor dies out, and I notice something on my brother's mind, a darkness shadowing his face.

He actually acknowledges Zhen and physically blocks me out.

They start speaking in Mandarin, and I'm guessing their conversation is about me. The easiest way to make them switch to English is to try and change topics.

"Shouldn't everyone be here by now?" I ask, half expecting the door to whip open, but it stands still. I check my watch.

It's almost ten.

"Baylee," Zhen says, capturing my gaze. "Brenden thinks that Luka was the one who stole your box."

My jaw drops, and my heart palpitates and clenches. I haven't heard his name out of my brother's or Zhen's mouth in a long, long time.

"What?" I breathe.

Luka. Luka.

Luka.

His name blasts in my head like fireworks spelling out L.U.K.A.

It sends my pulse into a worse tailspin. I can't say anything more than *what*. I shouldn't feel all of this after years of silence.

Brenden clutches his glass tighter. "I'm not the only one who thinks it."

I frown at Zhen. "You too?"

"It makes the most sense. He has a history of stealing."

"*Useless* things," I emphasize, suddenly guarding someone I haven't seen in forever. Luka would've known how much that box meant to me. I truly believe this. For context, I add, "Aerial Ethereal gave him a warning for stealing a chess set when he was thirteen, and he didn't even play chess."

"Maybe he thought your box was *useless*," Brenden retorts. Off the hurt on my face, he says, "He's a bad guy. So why the hell are you defending him?"

Because he's not bad.

I'm not trying to support theft by defending Luka. I just wish I could tell Brenden that there's so much more complexity to Luka's issues. But I can't really talk about him.

I shouldn't even be having this conversation.

I shouldn't even be *thinking* about his name.

But in one moment, Brenden cracked the floodgates of my mind, and the surge of memories gushes through—I doubt I'll be able to stop them that easily.

Luka.

Luka.

I wonder if Brenden can tell I'm fixated on his name. On this "bad guy" who's not as bad as he seems.

When my brother heard that AE *nearly* suspended me for using cocaine (allegedly), he directed all of his anger towards the person he believed corrupted me. That hate hasn't extinguished.

It still boils in his eyes.

The worst part of everything: I can't tell my brother the truth. I risk the jobs of every minor in Aerial Ethereal, and so I have to lie to his face. Over and over.

Plainly, I say, "I just know he wouldn't steal my box."

"We've been living with him for three days," Zhen tells me, "and he's already stolen my carton of egg whites from the refrigerator."

I don't believe that, I want to say, but how can I know the truth? Years and a stringent contract have separated us, and maybe in that time Luka Kotova changed. Maybe he's less the boy I loved, and he's now become a man I'd hate.

No.

I don't want to believe it.

The thought alone hurts. I swallow and then sip my whiskey, the liquid burning my throat. I glance cautiously at my brother. "Did you… you didn't fight with him, did you?"

Brenden bears down on his teeth.

Last time Brenden and Luka spoke, fists were flying. My brother may be a couple inches shorter and a few pounds lighter, but he busted Luka's lip and left bruises.

Luka didn't even try to block him. It almost looked like he wanted to be hit.

Zhen pulled Brenden off of Luka, and Dimitri stepped in and grabbed the back of Luka's shirt. That was over four years ago, and ironically, now those four guys are roommates.

Whoever created the room assignments obviously has no clue about everyone's workplace rivalries and drama. They stuck me with Nikolai Kotova, his girlfriend, and his little sister. I've already endured the most awkward *hello* from Nikolai, and the coldest shoulder of all shoulders from Katya Kotova.

Brenden continues to silently glower.

"You're just going to let me guess whether you fought with him?" I question.

"You still like him?" he asks me point-blank.

"No," I say instantly, my face twisting. My pulse vibrating.

I feel hot all of a sudden.

Brenden nods, believing me *somewhat*. He still ends up sulking off to another table, and before Zhen joins him, he tells me that there's only been uncomfortable silence between Luka and Brenden. Nothing more.

I'm left alone.

I don't mind. By the time I order another whiskey and return to my high-top table, stool hard beneath my ass, the door blows open.

Zhen and Brenden do the meet-and-greeting. Both are incredibly welcoming to newcomers and old friends.

I stay put and just watch. My mom used to call me the *director of life*—someone who'd rather observe and take in the scene than be a part of it. The next year, I dressed up as a Hollywood director for Halloween, and my dad gave me his old Super 8 video camera and everything.

I was six.

In the bar, I spot three Asian girls, all extremely thin, and they speak to Zhen in Mandarin. I peg them as contortionists based on their builds. More artists of varying ethnicities and backgrounds flood inside.

The circus is made up of so many people and cultures. I love being here, and it makes me even more proud to be biracial and Jamaican.

As 1842 fills, I keep thinking about Luka. I heard rumors that he was transferring to Infini a while back, and I had trouble believing the news. I still can't understand *why?*

Why would Aerial Ethereal ever allow Luka to transfer to this show? The company has been hell-bent on separating us, which was why he ended up in Viva. Now, all of a sudden, our names are attached to the same cast sheet.

And he's rooming with my *brother.*

Someone I spend most of my free time with. I worry that I'll need to start avoiding Brenden in order to avoid Luka, and I don't want that.

Brenden is my go-to person in my life. He's the one I confide in— the one I text about my dating failures, the one who binge-watches Netflix shows with me, the one who has my back on hellish work days.

I wish I knew AE's reason for putting Luka in Infini, but I haven't figured it out yet.

And I *really* need to stop thinking about him.

I already feel myself whirling backwards in mindset. In thought. I need to just move forward with my life. I can't be yanked back to the past and to my choice. Because it hurts.

It hurts to touch, to think about—to relive. I don't go there.

It's pain that I'm not revisiting today. I try to cement this fact.

I scan my surroundings, and for whatever reason, my gaze plasters on a guy for two or three minutes. I've never seen him before, but plenty of the artists here are not only new to Infini but to Vegas. So it's not that he's *new* that entraps me.

Maybe it's because he's way past six-feet tall, a characteristic that really only fits Nikolai and Dimitri Kotova. I scrutinize him more. Broad-shouldered, dark brown hair cut short, gray eyes that sparkle, and a sculpted face—*he's a Kotova.*

He has to be.

Then his eyes lock onto mine.

Usually I'm so invisible that no one ever catches me staring. His lip tics upward, and he pushes away from the wall.

He's approaching me. It's most likely that he's a distant, *distant* cousin of Luka's, someone he's never met or even spoken to before.

I'm buzzed, I think as my fingers tingle against my second empty glass.

And the guy is at my table in a flash. Towering up above. He's white, dressed in a snug-fitting black shirt and black jeans.

"Can I get you another?" He nods to my drink.

I pause to consider his offer.

Where guys are concerned, I've made a pack with myself to *try* and not close off to any possibilities. I wouldn't actually pursue a Kotova romantically, but I don't want to make an excuse just to avoid *chatting* at a bar.

It's not like I'm not terrified or that everything works out in my favor. It doesn't, but I can't stop trying to open myself up just because I'm scared.

Take the risk.

I will.

If anything, it's what Luka and I were always good at. Until the very end, at least. When the risk was too great to take.

"Sure," I tell him. "Whiskey."

"Whiskey," he repeats with a smile. "I'll be right back."

ACT SIX
BAYLEE WRIGHT

Sitting on the stool opposite me, he slides over my whiskey. "Been in Vegas long?" he asks, his lilt clearly American. I'm not really surprised. Even though the Kotovas speak Russian fluently, the ones in his generation only have American accents.

I cup the new whiskey glass. "About three years. I'm a born and bred New Yorker."

He smiles into his swig of bottled beer, a dark IPA. "I can't remember much about New York. I was only three or four the last time I was there."

"It's *incredible*." My face is hot from the whiskey, and my buzzed-self (slowly creeping past buzzed), emphasizes more words than I normally would. "I first lived in Brooklyn. Then once my mom was hired for Aerial Ethereal's *Seraphine*, we moved to Manhattan." *I'm already oversharing*, I think, but I continue on. "I started juggling at six, trained by an artist from Seraphine. And later on, when Infini was being developed in New York, they hired me. My *first* time working in the circus—and it was *magical*. Once Infini moved to Vegas, I moved with it."

I become way too passionate about ordinary things most days, and it only intensifies when I drink. If I somehow switch to baseball, I'm going to send this guy fleeing.

In the next breath, I start talking about my mom being Jamaican-American, and I mention that she's black and my dad is white—and I use present tense for everything. I catch myself talking about them like they're still here, and that's when I shut up.

His gray eyes only on me, he seems partially interested and partially curious.

I decide to ask a question since I just spilled my guts. "Your specialty?"

"High-risk acrobatics," he says. "Aerialist. The normal."

The normal. For Kotovas, those are the staples. My discipline is more unusual.

"So what's the best part of New York?" he asks.

There's so much. I list out the street food, the nightlife, and then of course, I mention baseball. I go off about the New York Mets. So animated that I lean forward, elbows on the table.

"Mets fans have such *love* for baseball. It's like sitting in an audience that is completely and utterly *devoted* to this thing…this thing that gives people sheer happiness." I stare up at the ceiling for the precise words to what I feel. "Being in the stands at a Mets game is the closest thing to watching Infini live."

Luka once said that we'll never experience the magic of our own act from an audience's perspective. If we sat in the auditorium seats, we'd critique every little movement and cringe at what could've been better.

When I finish, he laughs. I can't tell if it's more mocking than amused. But I'm leaning towards *mocking*.

My passion ekes out of my face like an arrow pierced a floating balloon. "You think it's funny?" I say flatly and edge back from him.

"I've never heard anyone compare the arts to baseball. It's not my opinion." He swigs his beer, and his eyes drift down my body in a once-over.

"You disagree?" I realize. Which is fine, we can share opposing viewpoints.

"Baseball isn't the circus," he states like I never comprehended this simple fact. "There's really no comparison."

There is. I just made one, and I'm slightly irked that he's not considering even a morsel of what I said. Even if he disagrees with it.

Am I being too harsh? I don't know. At this point, I'd probably grab my drink and ditch my own table and him. I've done that in the past, but I'm trying to be *open* here. So I don't shut him down that quickly.

"Where are you from originally?" I ask.

"Nowhere and everywhere. The moment I was born in California, I started traveling the world," he explains. "My family moves with the circus, much more than you have, and I've been in touring shows all my life. Infini is actually my first resident show."

The first time he's in a place for longer than a few months. "That's a big change…" I trail off as his gaze veers past my frame and his posture straightens, almost like he just spotted a long-lost friend.

He's about to rise off his stool, but then he stays seated. And he glances at me. "This is my brother." He gestures to a tall figure that approaches our circular table.

I turn my head, and my lips part. I'm looking at him.

I'm not allowed—but I can't stop.

Luka?

It's Luka.

Luka Kotova.

My stomach drops as I stare directly at his angelic yet chiseled face. A face that can easily be called beautiful. I can't close my lips together. I'm in pure, cold shock. I haven't seen that face up-close in years.

And he's so much older.

Oh God. How much time did I miss?

My eyes begin to well, but I fight the emotion.

He's more a man than a teenage boy. His plain navy-blue shirt molds the ridges of his abs and biceps; his dark jeans fitting perfectly.

His mischievous yet charismatic eyes haven't touched my eyes in ages. And in one second—one overwhelming, soul-shattering moment—his grays flit over to me.

And his eyes hold my eyes.

We both inhale—and very deeply, Luka says, "We've met."

We've met.

Buried memories pummel me fast. I have a flash of New York. Where we ran across the city as kids. I always convinced him to go to the batting cages, and he'd pretend to be the announcer behind the fence while I struck the baseballs.

And then on our free days, he convinced me to play one-on-one basketball at a rundown court. I was awful, but I'd try to show off and spin the basketball on my finger. He'd grab the ball and dribble between my legs before doing layup after layup. Then he'd cheer, and I'd shove his arm.

Somehow we always ended up hugging.

I see Luka in my room at thirteen and fourteen. Depression and grief chained me to the mattress. The mornings I struggled, he'd crawl onto my bed, and we talked softly, quietly until I gathered the strength to rise.

In my living room, we danced to the beat of our emotion. Feelings strung in the air like a million neon lights. Soca music thrummed through my veins while he held my cheeks. And he kissed me. My first kiss.

My first love.

He's right here.

I look away quickly. My body stiffens like a wooden board. I wait for him to leave, but Luka takes a seat on a stool, much closer to me than his brother.

This can't be happening.

I just looked at him, and we're not allowed to *look.*

I glance over my shoulder, but I can't spot Brenden through the loud, packed bar. More than just Aerial Ethereal artists are here since 1842 is open to all hotel guests.

The cast part is *secret.*

Meaning the whole point is to go behind the company's back and figure out the cast sheet before they tell us. So no one here should be spying on Luka and me.

Still, it's been years.

Why is he coming near me now? Why is he willing to take this huge risk?

I look up at his brother. *His brother.* He says something to Luka in Russian.

I'd love to gauge Luka's reaction and read his expression, but I can't risk staring at him face-to-face again. It's too hard. It's too much.

And I'm afraid.

Luka sits as rigidly as me. "She doesn't understand Russian."

His brother makes a face like *so what?* "I was speaking to you."

"I don't care," Luka says, slight edge to his voice that's mistakable if you don't listen closely. Luka isn't usually confrontational. He'll help stop a fight before he starts one.

It clicks.

When Luka's family split up years ago (before I even met Luka) two brothers stayed with his parents: Peter and Sergei. Luka almost never harbors animosity for anyone besides the figureheads of Aerial Ethereal. I sense bad blood between them, and it's more alarming because of who Luka is.

Loving and very understanding of other people—and caring.

So caring.

Maybe he saw his brother chatting with me from across the bar, and he felt compelled to intervene.

I jump into their conversation and ask, "Peter?"

He peels his eyes off Luka. "Sergei." He's the first-born, I remember. Older than even Nikolai. Twenty-eight or twenty-nine? "And he's Luka Kotov."

"Kotov*a*," Luka corrects. Honestly, I don't know what's worse: the hostile tension laced between them or the thick, uncomfortable tension threaded between us.

"Not this again," Sergei mutters. "Our birth certificates don't really matter. We're Russian. We go by *Kotov*."

I understand what he's saying. Russian surnames change depending on masculine and feminine. Men drop the *a*, and women keep the *a* at the end. When the Kotova family immigrated to America, they had to choose between Kotova and Kotov for their documentation.

Obviously, they picked Kotova.

And every Kotova that I've ever come across has identified as just that. *Kotova*.

I remember Luka mentioning that his father upholds Russian customs more than others in their extended family, especially his mother who wanted to pick less traditional names for her children. Maybe their father had a greater influence on Sergei, and that's why he's so dead-set on *Kotov*.

"You can go by whatever the hell you want," Luka says. "I'm Russian-American. I'm a Kotova. I'll *always* be a Kotova."

"I should leave," I say aloud.

Sergei reaches out his hand. "No. Don't leave. We're fine." He means him and his brother. "Right?" he asks Luka.

They're anything but fine—but like I said, Luka won't be the first person to start a fight. So I'm not surprised by his response.

"Sure," Luka says. "Fine."

I sip my whiskey, and as Luka shifts on his stool, I'm overly aware of how close his shoulder is to my shoulder. I feel like he's watching me out of the corner of his eye.

He drops his hand off the table.

My arm falls to my side.

Do you still think about me?

Are you the same as you once were?

How much have we both changed?

Sergei speaks to his brother but gestures to me with his bottle of beer. "I was just talking to…" he trails off.

"You don't know her name?" Luka almost laughs. I listen keenly, wishing and hoping that I could hear his full laugh. *Don't stop.*

Keep going, Luka.

Sergei snaps at him in Russian, and Luka replies back in a smoother tone.

"What's her name then?" Sergei retorts like he's quizzing his brother.

Legally, he can't utter my name, so I'm about to cut in and say it.

I don't even open my mouth before he speaks.

"Baylee," Luka says aloud, and I swear he says my name from deep in his core. As if he's breathing out years of weighted silence. "Baylee Wright."

My stomach tosses in good and awful ways—we can't do this. I'm scared of the no minors policy. I'm scared of hurting other people because of our carelessness. I look over my shoulder again. No onlookers, right? No one will tell on us here?

Selfishly, a very big part of me hopes and wishes and *yearns* for this moment to extend. I don't want this to stop, and maybe that's why I stay seated. Maybe that's why I cling onto every second I can share with him.

Beneath the table, our fingers brush.

I inhale, a spark zipping up my veins. Our fingers try to grab hold stronger. Longer. We almost do.

"Baylee," Sergei says.

I retract my hand, our fingers breaking apart, and I cup my whiskey with both palms.

"You want Infini to go well?" Sergei asks me.

"Yeah." I nod, a little dizzy from drinking and from Luka. He ruffles in his jean's pocket for something, and then he places a handful of Jolly Ranchers on the table.

I'm a little worried he stole them, but I'm also used to Luka shoplifting candy and then sharing most of the loot.

He pushes the green apple towards me. My favorite flavor.

I pick up a piece while he unwraps a blue raspberry one.

Waving his bottle at me, Sergei tries to seize my attention again. When he's successful, he says, "Then you should tell my brother to start answering my *emails*."

I go cold. "He's ignoring you?" It's weird having to talk like Luka isn't right beside me, but it's not like him to carry a grudge like this. He loves everyone but the company hierarchy.

Maybe he's changed.

No. I still don't want to believe that yet.

He feels the same.

"For months he's been giving me the cold-shoulder," Sergei says. "And we're brothers. It's kind of unbelievable, right?" Whatever exists between them must be deep-seated.

And I can't side with Sergei like he wants me to. I'd defend Luka for millenniums. He's not just my secret ex-boyfriend. He's the boy who my dad called, "Poignant." Luka moved my father to near tears because…he was *there* for me.

For as long as I can remember, I have days where I just lie in bed, feeling weighed down, empty. My dad would nudge me to go to a Mets game, and the thought sounded worse than work. It seemed lifeless and then painful. All the things I love have felt *pointless* at some moment in time.

I hate the feeling. Because it's unshakable. It grips every bone in my body and tells me not to move, not to dance. Not to live.

That all joy is joyless. That all love is worthless.

That happiness is too far gone.

Before my parents passed, people would tell me "don't be sad" and "you have so much to be happy about"—and I did. Yet, my sadness doesn't listen to these pleas. There's not a switch that I can pull to turn it all off.

So my mom brought me to a doctor. I was diagnosed with clinical depression. I met Luka around the same time I began taking antidepressants. The pills help a lot now. It doesn't eliminate depression, but the medicine subdues these miserable feelings. Pushing them back into the crevices of my body and mind.

At first, way back then, the side-effects exacerbated my sad, disheartened thoughts and feelings. My dad was afraid of the warning label on the pills. *Suicidal thoughts in teens.*

At the beginning, it was hard.

Luka would come over while I lied on my couch, moping, and he'd lie on the other side, our legs tangled. We'd eat candy and popcorn, and he'd just keep me company. The kind of company I needed when I felt so completely hollow and alone inside.

My dad saw someone that was there for me in the simplest but most profound way.

Poignant.

"Why are you dragging her into this?" Luka asks his older brother. "You just met. You didn't even know her name."

"I like her," Sergei says, "more than I honestly like you right now." His glare grows hotter on his brother. "If you responded to me at all, you'd realize that we're supposed to be partners."

"What are you talking about?" Luka shakes his head.

"The Wheel of Death. It takes two people. Who'd you think you were working with?"

In my peripheral, I see Luka's jaw muscle tic.

"You're stuck with me whether you like it or not," Sergei continues. "We have to work together, and our act depends on *communication*." He finishes off his beer with a grimace. "At least be better than Timofei."

Oh shit.

Luka's back arches at the sound of his little brother. "What do you know about Timo?"

Sergei rips the label off the bottle. "He called me a traitor and said I wasn't to ever step into his room unless I wanted a broken kneecap."

"You're rooming with him?"

"Yeah." Sergei pauses. "He didn't tell you? I thought you were close." *They are.*

We're all silent. Even over the bar's loud commotion, I can hear the crinkle of the Jolly Rancher wrapper between Luka's fingers and the green apple one that I set down.

"Sweet children of mine, what the fuck are you doing?" Dimitri Kotova appears, and I go cold like solid ice. He's a part of Infini's cast, and he's most likely been inside the bar for a while now. I wonder how long he's been watching us.

"Talking," Luka rebuts and gestures from his chest to Sergei's. Emphasizing that the conversation is *not* between us. Dimitri is too loyal to his family to snitch on Luka to AE's figureheads.

So I try to keep calm about us breaking the contract as we sit next to each other. As we cast furtive glances. As we even speak.

Water bottle in hand, Dimitri sidles next to his cousin Sergei. One quick look, he studies the candy along the table, plus our stiff postures.

"Aren't you performing tonight?" I ask him, trying to sound casual and not tense.

Dimitri swishes his water bottle in affirmation, not drinking alcohol. He's in Aerial Ethereal's Amour along with Nikolai, Nik's girlfriend Thora, Timofei, and others. It's almost unheard of to pull double-duty in shows. To be in two at once.

Not only because of scheduling conflicts but because it's *tiring*. It's not that Dimitri is a scene-stealer or that they need him for gasps and awes.

It's more simple: Dimitri is really good at assisting the hardest apparatuses. He performs in large group acts, always ensuring that no one gets hurt on Russian swing and teeterboard, and in Infini, he has *always* assisted my juggling routines.

Dimitri is the one who throws me extra clubs and balls. We work well together, even if he's absolutely unequivocally crude. When I was thirteen, he called a corndog a fellatio stick. Which really, when you think about it, makes no sense.

"You're cool with Sergei?" Luka asks Dimitri. The air thickens, their familial divisions raw, like an open, infected wound.

Before he can reply, Sergei says, "Dimitri is mature."

I let out a laugh. I can't help it.

Sergei's brows knot at me, confused. Dimitri cocks his head in my direction, not surprised by my outburst.

"Sorry," I say into another muffled laugh. *Dimitri mature.* He may be older than us and professional when it matters, but he's been to jail for peeing on the street *three times*. And he constantly draws penises and balls on foggy locker room mirrors.

"Go ahead and laugh," Dimitri says, "at least I know which dicks I can and cannot touch."

Low blow. I'm used to them from him. I force a smile. "I didn't realize you planned on touching your cousin's dick."

Luka laughs under his breath, and my chest rises, lungs expanding. I made him laugh—and I want to hear him laugh again. And again.

Dimitri shakes his head at both of us like *knock it off.* He traveled down this disastrous road first by bringing up Luka's dick.

Now I'm really imagining his dick. What it used to look like—what it might look like now. Great. I need to stop. I know I need to stop, but it's like a snowball effect. I can't slow down enough to just…*leave* him. And this situation.

I can repeat *no minors policy* a million times, and it's not helping enough. It's not forcing me off my stool and through the exit.

I feel like a terrible person. Maybe I really am one.

Dimitri hasn't physically separated Luka and me yet, and maybe he's uncertain on what action to take since we've never been this close before. At least not after we signed those contracts. Almost five years ago.

Sergei's confusion escalates, and he suddenly motions between me and his little brother. "Are you two together?"

"No," we say in unison.

My bones ache; I'm so rigid.

"What are you drinking?" Dimitri asks me, grabbing my empty glass. He sniffs. "Alright, Baybay"—I hate when he calls me that, and unfortunately, he knows it—"you're cut off."

He likes to pretend he's my father and Luka's brother, but he's neither to us. He's his cousin and my co-worker friend.

For some reason, his words really rile me. It touches a deep place in my gut that was ready to enflame. In this moment, Dimitri represents Aerial Ethereal, those strict contracts, and every other hand that has clawed Luka and I apart.

On my stool, I spin more towards Dimitri—Luka looks at me. I feel him staring right in my direction.

"You can't tell me when to stop drinking. You can't order me around at all."

Dimitri raises his brows. "I think I can. I throw my balls, you catch my balls. That's how it works, Baybay."

Luka hates when Dimitri refers to them as *his balls* more than me. I usually don't care, but when he uses it as an attack, it's annoying.

So I'm not surprised when Luka retorts in Russian, right at Dimitri.

"Stay out of it," Dimitri tells Luka.

Before Luk replies, I say, "You're not my dad, Dimitri. I had *one*." They all hush and stare at me intently. My passion returns but in a more painful way. "His name was Neal *Wright* and he was a brilliant novelist, and not you or *anyone* could ever replace him."

At this, I stand off my stool. And I wobble. Luka reaches out to catch me, but I spin into someone else's chest.

My brother.

Shit.

Brenden holds me close and looks murderous, not just at Luka—but at all the Kotovas. Like they're an extension of Luka's bad influence on me.

"I'm leaving," I say to my brother, fisting the back of his shirt so my knees don't buckle.

Brenden points at Luka. "You owe her a grand."

"Stop," I force, about to break away from him now. I can't bring myself to meet Luka's eyes.

"What are you talking about?" Luka asks, sounding confused.

"You *stole* her box and then put it in another room."

Luka says, "You were fined?" I think he's asking me. *He's talking to me.* He shouldn't be…the contract…

A pit lowers in my stomach. I'm staring off at the wall—at the exit. *I'm leaving.* I try to pull away from my brother, but he clasps my hand like I need support.

I do, but not in the way he's providing. It's not his fault. He's doing what he thinks is right.

"I told you he did it," Brenden says to me.

Luka interjects, "What? *No.* No, I didn't steal anything of hers. I wouldn't…"

"Wait," Sergei chimes in. "What box are you talking about?"

My head whips up to Sergei. He's the only person still sitting, and behind him, Zhen starts to step on a tall stool to make an announcement.

"A cardboard box," I say.

"Her name was on it," Brenden adds.

"Right." Sergei nods in realization. "That was me."

What? I'm dumbfounded. Jaw unhinged, eyes big. He's not apologetic, but maybe because he's not aware of what happened.

"You stole her box?" Brenden is disbelieving. I think he wanted the thief to be Luka.

Zhen stands on a stool. "Infini artists!" he calls, barely catching anyone's attention.

"I was helping a cousin move, and I remember taking the wrong box. I thought I put it back in the right room. Didn't I?"

"At *midnight.*" I gape.

"You owe her a thousand bucks," Brenden says.

Sergei's eyes widen in shock, and he raises his hands. "No. I don't have that kind of money. Aerial Ethereal didn't even pay for my flight to the US."

"You think my little sister has an extra grand lying around?"

"Little sister," Sergei repeats under his breath, looking between us. "Right. I'm sorry, but I can't help her. It's not my problem."

Luka shakes his head repeatedly. Over and over.

"What?" Sergei snaps.

Luka fumes silently, trying not to start something. He starts to walk away.

Sergei hops off his stool and grabs Luka's shoulder. "No, what do you have to say? Tell me."

Luka faces him. "You don't want me to tell you what I think."

"I do. I just *asked.*"

Luka grimaces, features brutally pained. He runs a hand down his face like he hates feeling this, like he's trying to wipe it all off. I wince at the sight.

"Luka," Sergei growls.

"Nothing's ever your problem," Luka tells him. "Nothing's ever your responsibility—"

"Everyone!" Zhen shouts and snaps his fingers, wine in his other hand. "Look here!"

The bar quiets, just as Sergei snaps, "That's not true."

Luka's brows jump. "That's not true? You just told her *it's not my problem.*"

"It's not."

"Is that what you said when Mom and Dad asked you to take care of us?" Luka questions. "*It's not my problem.* You just shirked everything onto Nikolai without a second thought. I know you did. Look at your face. It says you don't care about anyone but yourself, which is fine. You don't care about me, and guess what, I don't give a fuck about *you.*"

It hurts.

Every word he says bleeds into the air.

"I was twenty-two," Sergei retorts.

"I was thirteen," Luka says with the shake of his head. "Timo was twelve, and you know, Kat, she was *ten.*" He stretches his arms. "I'm done." The bar is utterly quiet as Luka heads to the exit, but then he pauses and spins back again.

I can't read Sergei's expression. My vision not only blurs, but he keeps his emotions bottled.

Everyone in the bar stares at Luka, not Zhen.

"Don't you dare fuck with Timo," Luka says coldly. "Dimitri and whoever might be okay with you here, but I'm not. And that girl, right there"—he points at me but glares at Sergei—"is way too good for a piece of shit like you."

At this, Luka walks tensely out of the bar.

Leaving me iced-over and stunned. I don't attempt to follow him, even if I want to—because there are multiple men who'd physically restrain me from reaching Luka's side.

Zhen raises his wine glass and clears his throat. "Here's to a new season," he announces. "May we all work together and set aside our differences. Because…it might be the only way we can save Infini."

ACT SEVEN
LUKA KOTOVA

The elevator beeps.

I exit onto the lobby floor at 5:30 a.m.—and no one's out and about except for gamblers that can't quit and hotel employees. Quiet, mostly, I reach the enormous Dionysus fountain that parades over the entrance's revolving doors.

My little brother waits on the edge of the fountain. His dark hair is damp from a circuit workout before his actual practice in the performance gym.

I carry two plates of breakfast food over to Timo, and he plucks out his earbuds while I sit beside him.

His face lights up. "You didn't burn my pancakes. Miracles *do* happen."

I pass him the paper plate of egg-white oatmeal pancakes that I did almost burn. It's not a secret that I suck at cooking and baking, but Timo asked me to whip these up since he wanted to hit the gym early.

Usually we eat breakfast together in our suite, but we don't share one anymore. Our options are pretty pathetic. Hotel food is way too expensive to eat every single morning. So that's out.

Timo's room contains Sergei. Who we can't stand.

My room contains Brenden. Who I've successfully avoided since the secret cast party weeks ago. (I'm keeping it that way.)

And then Nikolai and Katya's suite also includes a girl I've promised I wouldn't touch. Promised I wouldn't *look* at—and I recognize, more than anyone can tell me, that I fractured these promises in one night.

In one impulsive moment.

I did it. I saw Sergei, of all people, speaking to the one girl I've never been able to truly forget. And something snapped in me. I just moved. I just walked over there and butted in—and you know what, I don't regret it.

I *looked* at Baylee. No one can even understand what that felt like. For my eyes to latch onto hers, for us to really see one another after years of avoidance.

It was like I'd just taken my first breath. Maybe I was dreaming. I don't even care if I imagined our fingers touching. Because it felt real to me.

Breaking a part of the contract and getting away with it—it fuels me.

In the worst way.

I *crave* to do it again, but I'm trying to honor her own feelings and wishes. I could tell she was scared, and I don't want to frighten her or push her.

So I hang back. I cross off her suite as an option, and I try to forget Baylee.

Every fucking day, I try.

As I eat, Timo watches me bite into my breakfast burrito, bacon and sausage spilling out onto my paper plate. In so many ways, we're different from each other.

He hesitates. "Please tell me you cooked my pancakes in another pan."

I wipe my mouth with a flimsy paper napkin. "No, but I cooked yours first." Timo has been vegetarian since we were little.

"In a clean pan? No judgment," he adds. "Just being careful."

"Clean," I say through a mouthful of food.

Then he starts cutting into his pancakes. I look around the lobby. I miss Katya. I've been in her suite less than usual because Baylee is there.

Likewise, I overheard Brenden complaining about nearly the same thing. To Zhen, he said that Bay won't come over our suite because of me, and he's spent less time with her recently.

"How's Kat?" I ask Timo.

"Unhappy. Like the rest of us." He adjusts his earbuds around his neck and picks up his plastic fork again. "I asked for a pay raise yesterday."

My brows lift, and I take another bite of my burrito. He's talked about approaching Aerial Ethereal for a raise before, but he's never taken the steps.

"What really irritates me," he says, "is not that they said *no*. It's that they still expect me to put in total, complete effort above everyone else while paying me as much as..." He glances hesitantly at me, not wanting to hurt my feelings.

His salary is identical to mine.

The thing is, I've been slapped on the wrist a million times. I've even been demoted, and only now that I've returned to Infini, my pay is higher. Timo is their real money-maker. Right alongside Nikolai, and yet, Nik is paid a lot more than him.

Timofei deserves a pay raise. I've been in the audience for Amour before, and *everyone* leaves talking about his performance. His talent can't be manufactured or taught. It's a hundred-percent natural and one-of-a-kind. Add in his disciplined work-ethic, and he should be the top-paid artist in Aerial Ethereal.

I nod in agreement. "It's bullshit," I mumble through a mouthful of egg and tortilla.

Timo gives me and my burrito a look.

I return the favor, my brows cinching at him.

"Don't you have your first formal practice in an hour?" he asks.

Today is the day.

The day that I have to stop avoiding Sergei. And whether intentional or unintentional, I'll most likely see Baylee again. (It's not a bad thing to anyone but Corporate.) Plus I have to greet a choreographer that has badgered the entire cast of Infini via email for weeks.

I'm looking forward to this like someone looks forward to a full-body wax.

I shrug at my brother. "So?" I give him a look that says: *I'm fine.*

His says: *I don't think you are.*

"I have everything under control," I tell him.

Timo knows I have a horrible diet. I ate an entire pepperoni pizza before conditioning last week. Zhen saw me and then a day later, he slipped a nutritional printout beneath my door.

I smoke. I drink.

I eat junk food. The best part: there is nothing that Corporate can do to stop me. Their Wellness Policy is all about maintaining certain body measurements and not taking any kind of performance drugs.

I've maintained the same body measurements for years.

I'm drug-free.

(Corporate can kiss my ass.)

"Is there anything I can do?" Timo asks.

"No," I say instantly.

He takes the hint and switches topics, talking about club-hopping this weekend. He always invites me, but I don't always join. When he parties, he's a firestorm. Lively and enthralling but completely uncontrollable. He rolls in around 4 or 5 a.m., still upbeat. Very few people can keep up with him.

And I'm not really one of those people, much to Nikolai's displeasure. He'd love for me to be Timo's 24/7 chaperone.

Finishing my burrito, I ball my soggy plate and free-throw it into a trash bin. Right when it lands perfectly, a familiar person pushes through the revolving door.

John Ruiz.

I know him well enough by now. Twenty-five, six-foot-something Colombian-American. Unshaven jaw, windswept brown hair, and a never-ending gruff expression. Like the universe just took a giant shit on his head.

Two coffee cups in hand, he makes his entrance into the Masquerade like he's being forced into a circle of hell.

Yet, I doubt he'd choose to be anywhere else but here.

"Seriously?" John stops a couple feet from us, dumbfounded. "Seriously. You're both *still* camping out in the lobby like vagrants when you have suites that cost five-hundred a night. Tell me, world, what is wrong with this picture?"

"Does the world ever respond to you?" Timo banters. "Or do you just get off hearing your own voice, old man?"

John stares blankly. "You think I like the sound of my voice? No. But I have to talk because people don't say what needs to be said."

Timo raises his brows. "That's really why?"

John looks fresh out of amusement. "Maybe if everyone practiced honesty, they wouldn't need me."

"The secret is out." Timo smiles. "You'll shut up if I say all the honest things on my mind."

"As delightful as you are, Timofei," he says dryly. "You're not the only human on this planet. I'm making up for *everyone*."

"So you're not shutting up anytime soon." Timo's face breaks into the brightest grin.

"Not a chance, babe."

At this, John passes Timo a coffee.

My brother is like a beam of light, and then John dips his head down to cup my brother's cheek. He kisses Timo on the lips, and he reciprocates the affection, only smiling more.

John mumbles a greeting against the kiss, and when they break apart, I notice the red flush on my brother's neck, completely taken by his boyfriend.

It makes my lips curve upward.

"Luka," John greets and sips his coffee. "Should I just expect you both to be sitting here a century from now? Decomposing. Archeologists digging up bones that they *really* didn't want to find."

He talks way too much for me.

Seriously *still* smiling, Timo eats the last of his pancakes and says, "It's complicated." My brother hands me the coffee cup, and I pop the lid. No whip cream, no cinnamon. John buys Timo's favorite soy cappuccino.

(It tastes like ass, but I'll still drink it.)

"Complicated? You're both avoiding siblings. It's not complicated."

"Have you met Sergei?" I ask John.

"Not yet." His face grows darker, more serious, and he eyes Timo, waiting for my brother to respond.

"I don't want you to meet him, man," Timo admits, standing with an empty plate in hand. "He's an unpleasant person."

"Most—no, *all* people are shit," John says. "The world is a terrible, disgusting place to live."

Timo gapes. "No wonder the world never responds to you."

John rolls his eyes dramatically, but they both smile at one another. "I want to meet your older brother."

"Even if I hate him?" Timo asks, throwing away his plate.

"*Especially* because you hate him." John reaches out and catches Timo's hand, tugging him to his chest.

I give them privacy by staring off at the entrance, the sky lightening. I chug the soy cappuccino, and I hear John ask about Timo's pay raise and the subsequent "I'm sorry, babe" after my brother explains the rejection. When I look up, Timo and John part—Timo headed for the gym, but John, for whatever reason, lingers by the fountain.

By me.

I'm not chatty like him. If he has something to say, he better say it.

His eyes drop to my cup. "Can you tell me why he gives you his coffee *every* morning?"

I know why. "Ask Timo." I rise to my feet, finishing the last drop and chucking it into the trash. I pick up my water bottle.

John is still here. "I did. Now I'm asking you."

Of course Timo didn't tell him the truth. Then John would stop bringing a second cup, which means that I'd stop getting a coffee every morning. (Even if it tastes like ass.)

"It's simple," I tell John, walking backwards towards the guest bathrooms. "Timo doesn't drink caffeine before practice."

John simultaneously sighs and rolls his eyes. "But you do?"

I extend my arms. "I'm not Timofei." Spinning on my heels, I leave John behind and head to the bathroom.

Timo has John. To turn to. To share his lousy day and news about his failed pay raise. Other than my siblings, I have no one.

(Again, don't pity me, *please.*)

I'm happy for Timo. I'm happy that Nikolai has Thora James. Instead of resenting them, I choose to nod and be grateful that people I care about can find their happily-ever-after.

Even if I know it'll never be me.

Seeing their love is the closest that I'll ever come to feeling it again. So I don't need to hide myself and pout. My stomach doesn't curdle, and my heart doesn't drop.

In the bathroom, I peek beneath the four blue stalls. No one is at the urinals or sink. The place is unoccupied, and so I slip into a stall.

I squat by the toilet and check my watch. About forty minutes until practice. I take one deep breath, and then I stick my finger down my throat.

I puke.

Everything appears in the toilet bowl. My throat scalds, the rising acid all familiar. I make sure that I vomit all the shit I've eaten. A minute later, I pause and try to poke at my esophagus, but nothing more comes out.

I spit a few times. And I suppress any guilt from this action. I'm fine.

Blowing out a breath, I stand, grab my water bottle, and chug. Hydrating.

Starting new.

ACT EIGHT
LUKA KOTOVA

Passing many sets of blue double doors—right outside of Aerial Ethereal's performance gym—I aim for the end of the long hallway. I always enter the last door.

It's as much superstition as it is procrastination.

I feel invisible.

No one notices me; no one really cares, not even as my torso and shoulders move to the beat of a song, blasting in my earbuds. My head bobs, and I lock eyes on the dead-end ahead of me, double doors to the left.

I see the wall and my lips lift. Quickly, I toss my gym bag aside and then I *sprint*. Straight at the ivory-painted concrete wall.

I run up it. Two huge steps, I gain height, and then I backflip.

Midair, I sense the double doors opening beside me, someone exiting the gym into the hallway. I land on my feet. Startled, I stagger backwards into the incomer.

Our shoulders collide.

"Fuck, sorry," I immediately apologize and stabilize my balance. I hold out my hands towards a guy I've never met, afraid I hurt him.

He fixes his gray blazer, his beady brown eyes narrowing at me. I sweep his features quickly: slicked-back ash-blond hair, goatee and slight mustache. Yeah, I've definitely never met this guy before. He can't be any older than thirty.

His mouth moves, and I realize that I can't hear him.

I pop out my earbuds. "Sorry. I didn't get that."

"*Your name*," he snaps.

I stiffen and eye his shirt beneath the blazer. No Aerial Ethereal paraphernalia. No sign that he's with Corporate. My guards still skyrocket. "Kotova," I answer.

"First name."

I shift my weight. "Luka."

"Luka," he repeats like he's filing this moment for *life*. "What does that say?" He points at a sign above the blue double doors behind him.

I don't have to look to read it. "*No running, tumbling, or acrobatics in the hallway.*" My face is stone. "Sorry." (I'm not sorry.)

His pinpointed gaze drops to my right leg. I wear white gym shorts over black compression shorts, but I'm positive he's not staring at my clothes.

"Problem?" I ask, my voice easygoing.

"Your tattoos." The dude gestures to the black ink that runs up my right leg, more designs beneath my shorts. Decorating my thigh.

My whole right leg is completely covered.

Most of the time, I forget I have tattoos. Especially since almost all of my cousins and siblings have them somewhere on their bodies.

Timo even has a tattoo on his ribs. Small script from the film *The Red Shoes*:

"Why do you want to dance?"
"Why do you want to live?"
"Well, I don't know why, er, but I must."
"That's my answer too."

My tattoos aren't as poetic. Since I was fourteen (young, but not to me, not in my world), I literally walked into the same shop and told the same artist, "Do what you want." He added more and more to my right leg, until I had to find a new artist in Vegas, and by eighteen, there was no room for more to be added. It's not really about *what* designs I have.

It's the moment. The time I went there. What I was feeling.

Who I was with.

A Cheshire Cat is inked on the back of my calf and I've never been a diehard *Alice in Wonderland* fan, but Bay was with me when I got it. Sat right beside me, cross-legged on a stool. She ate a beef patty from her favorite Jamaican restaurant, and she smiled when I looked over at her.

"Stop looking at me like that," she said, trying to stifle her smile. "You're hurting my face."

Lying on my side, I sat up more and kissed Baylee.

Her lips pulled beneath the kiss. "You're making it worse," she whispered.

I held her cheeks. "I wasn't trying to make it better."

She groaned into a wider smile. "You're awful."

My nose flares in the present. Here.

Now.

The memory gnaws at my gut, and I swallow hard and plant my gaze back on the goatee guy.

"What about my tattoos?" I ask as gently as I can.

"The last show you were in, did you cover them?"

(He has to be with Corporate.)

I shake my head. "Viva was fine with them." Though I was given *multiple* warnings to stop adding more, but I didn't listen. One of my cousins was suspended for filling out two sleeves, and now Aerial Ethereal tries to relegate him to the background.

"Buy flesh-toned makeup as soon as possible. You'll need to cover them for *every* live performance."

I have no reaction. It is what it is, so I just nod.

"And Luka? This will be the last time you break the rules." He motions towards the double doors. "After you."

Tensely, I grab my gym bag, my phone buzzing, and I look stone-cold ahead, not at him. Pushing into the noisy gym, I unbury my cell-phone from protein bars, extra clothes, IcyHot, and my water bottle.

As I head to the locker room, my gaze remains plastered on my phone. *What.*

Dazedly, I cram my bag into my assigned blue locker. One of my cousins says a greeting in Russian, and I just nod at him.

The email notification is from Marc Duval.

I click into it.

Date: February 15th
Subject: keep it professional
From: Marc Duval, Creative Director of Aerial Ethereal
Bcc: Luka Kotova, Baylee Wright

Luka & Baylee,

Because of certain underlying circumstances that we could not work around (i.e. casting you both in the same show), the company recognizes that you will be sharing space & time together.

Do not misinterpret this action. You are still to uphold the contracts to the best of your ability. Do not take this small amount of leash and run wild. You can speak to one another but **only about professional matters.**

Anything else is strictly forbidden. Remember there are two company members watching you. Remember what is at stake if you break the contracts.

Keep it professional.

Marc Duval
Creative Director of Aerial Ethereal
marcduval@aerialethereal.com

I can speak to Baylee.

I rest my palm on the cold locker, blown over.

I can speak to Baylee.

Like I care that there's a stipulation attached. *Professionalism.* It doesn't matter. The thought of being allowed to say *hi* knocks me forward. I can have a work friendship with Baylee.

I can look at her and not fear the "no minors policy"—I sit down. I have to sit down.

(Holy fuck.)

I put my hand to my mouth, overcome with too much at once.

And then Dimitri lets out a long groan, making sure his presence is known. I watch him slip around the corner into my row of lockers.

Drenched in sweat, he puts his foot on the bench and leans his weight on his knee.

I raise my brows. "What happened to you?"

"The motherfucking fart-face." He groans as he stretches his arms towards the ceiling. "New choreographer made the four OGs do burpees for twenty minutes." *OGs*—he means the original cast: Zhen, Dimitri, Brenden, and Baylee. "If we slowed down past his 'required tempo'—which was butt-ass impossible—we had to sprint the length of the gym twenty times."

It's not a small gym. It resides in the back lot of the Masquerade with eighty-foot ceilings, big enough to house all the apparatuses for each act.

I start imagining Baylee being pushed by the choreographer, and I tense up. I can't ask Dimitri how Baylee is. I can't even ask if she's okay.

I comb a hand through my hair. Trying not to picturing some new guy screaming at her to "run faster" or "push harder" while she's already giving her all. I know Baylee. I know that she hates being called out in front of people, for any reason: negative or positive.

"He also told me to *bulk down*." Dimitri glares. "I can do what I need to do at this size. I've done it for twenty-six years."

"Did you hear that?" Zhen quips from one row over. "Dimitri Kotova was six-foot-five in the womb."

Nikolai comes around the bend, rolled bandana wrapped around his forehead. "Did he have enough room in there for a double layout too?" he banters.

The *rare* time that I see my brother loosen up—it's with Dimitri or his girlfriend, Thora.

Dimitri hooks an arm around Nikolai's neck and purposefully wipes his sweat all over him.

I hate to ruin my brother's good mood. I normally wouldn't intentionally try, but I have to show him this. "Hey." I approach both of them.

They break apart. Towering over me.

Nik's face instantly becomes serious, tapping into his stern big brother side.

I flash them my email. "Okay?" I need them to not intervene if I talk to Baylee.

Dimitri just looks to my brother for how to react.

Nik hardly relaxes. "It's safer if you try not to talk to her." His gray eyes never soften.

I knew he'd tell me to *stay responsible* and *be serious* about what this means, but I'm not floating in some fantasy. I understand my fucked-up reality better than him. I'm the one living it.

"I just wanted you to know," I say easily and return to my locker, zipping my phone in my bag. When I pass them to leave the room, Nik clasps my shoulder.

I wait for him to say something.

He struggles to speak. To say what he feels. Lowly, almost beneath his breath, he tells me, "Don't hang yourself with the slack you've been given."

"I won't."

"I know you, Luk." He pauses. "I know that if someone gives you an inch, you'll go five feet."

"I *won't*." It's all I can tell him. If he doesn't believe me, then he doesn't believe me. There's not much else I can do. So I add, "I'm not a kid."

"I know that." He releases his clutch on me.

I don't let Nikolai trounce the fraction of good news. I pocket it. I carry it, and what should be happiness transforms into apprehension. Concern.

What do I even say?

Will she even want to speak to me?

Does she even like me anymore?

ACT NINE
LUKA KOTOVA

The gym is crammed, and it's not a typical gymnastics gymnasium. In the middle, Amour artists practice on a giant, intricate metal cube, teeterboard placed precariously beneath.

Timo effortlessly sprints across the metal rung that looks like adult jungle-gym bars. With a magnetic grin that ropes my gaze, he drops straight down.

And he grabs hold of a lower rung before hoisting his body into a handstand.

As I pass, it takes me a while to tear my attention off my brother. Other artists definitely have that issue, too. Staring. Gawking.

Wondering how the hell Timofei Kotova is so enthralling.

I pass another aerial apparatus. Scarlet silk is attached to the eighty-foot ceiling, and Nikolai clutches the fabric. His much shorter girlfriend already slices through the air, the silk intricately wound around her ankle.

Over in the far left, a trapeze is set up for Viva artists, mesh net secured underneath, and then I spot Kat towards one of the walls.

The Russian bar sits off to the side with our cousin Vitaly and a new guy who replaced my role in Viva. I used to be one of Katya's porters. I held one end of a bar similar to a balance beam while she performed a difficult routine on top.

What I love and miss most is working with my sister.

I notice that she hasn't started practicing yet. I don't have time to chat, but I call out, "Kat!" I already begin to wave before she turns her head.

I frown.

Is she wearing…? *She is.*

Kat wears pink lipstick, bright and overdrawn, and her black mascara and thick eyeliner darkens her eyes. I almost question whether it's stage makeup since it looks cartoonish, but no one else is wearing any. It has to be her choice. Still, she's *never* worn makeup at practice before.

That's not all.

She's dressed in a tiny sports bra and spandex. No shirt. My frown deepens. There's no way Nik saw her leave the suite.

Katya waves back like nothing's different.

"Fuck—" I walk straight into Brenden's drenched back, his shirt soaked through with sweat.

He shoots me a glare but says, "Zhen's leading the cast in stretching."

I nod, as tense as him. I try to push Katya out of my mind and take a seat on the blue mats. All fifty of us are situated in a jagged circle. A few cousins are between me and Sergei.

Zhen spreads his legs open and reaches forward.

We all follow suit, but I lift my head up.

Baylee.

She's directly across from me, only the empty middle of the circle separating us. I sweep her features more rapidly than I want or intend. More used to dodging her than staring.

Black spandex pants and a lime-green tank suction the slight curves of her body. Four thick but tight braids swoop down her head and are tied into a bun at her warm brown neck. Pretty and sporty. I remember she always used to wear this hairstyle for practices.

She tries to rub her damp forehead with her shoulder. Looking fatigued but still upright, she uses the short break to take it easy.

She's okay.

She's not hurt from being run-hard by the choreographer. I relax some, and as she leans into the stretch, her eyes slowly close in rest.

My lips begin to lift.

Baylee is confident and reserved. Quiet and passionate. I see all of what I remember.

She has an oval face that I loved holding between my hands. Rosewood-pink lips that I loved kissing. Thin yet strong arms that I used to intertwine with my brawn—and wide, curved hips that used to be beneath my straight.

She's undeniably beautiful. The kind of beauty that chokes me up, and I don't know how the whole world doesn't see what I see—how I'm not fighting every fucking person on the planet for the chance to even speak to her.

Way back when, I'd hold her tight in bed and tuck her firmly against my chest—she'd fall asleep in my clutch. And I'd stare out the window, right into the New York City landscape, and I thought *this is what I want forever.*

I want this and her.

Dreams.

They're fucking cruel.

Zhen reaches for his right leg. We all follow.

I keep staring. More than I would ever dare—all because of the email. Granting me extra room to move in a prison cell without windows. Without a door.

I notice Brenden sitting protectively next to Baylee, and just as he changes stretching positions, he catches me ogling his sister.

I absorb the threat in his eyes. He keeps glaring. Waiting for me to look away. But detaching is harder than I thought.

We all press our legs together, touching our toes, and Baylee turns her head a fraction. Enough to spy her brother's contempt. She follows the path of his piercing glare.

To *me.*

Her collarbones jut out in a strained breath, and she shakes her head at me like, *what are you doing?*

She hasn't read the email.

Or maybe she really doesn't want to risk anything concerning me. Maybe she's in agreement with Nik. My chest caves—*no.*

No, I'm not ready to accept it. I clutch tightly to what may be lost already, but I've always been unable to release my grip. Marc Duval made me believe that a future with Bay was hopeless, but he could *never* convince me that she didn't love me. That she didn't hurt just as badly when we were torn apart.

Brenden cranes his neck towards Zhen, giving me a moment to speak to Baylee. I mouth, *email.*

Her face scrunches, confused.

I lick my lips and mouth better, *email.*

Realization washes over her features, and she begins to stand, to retrieve her phone probably, but then a new voice pulls our gazes to the left.

"Infini artists."

(Fuck my life.)

Baylee sits back down, and my muscles constrict as the ash-blond goatee guy steps into the middle of the circle. The guy that I literally ran into. The one that chastised me.

The one that clearly disliked me.

I figure out who he has to be before he even introduces himself.

"Four of you have just met me, but to the rest," he tells us, clipboard tucked beneath his armpit, "I'm Geoffrey Lesage. Your new choreographer. For the entire season, you will listen to me. You will *respect* me. All without question or backtalk. No exceptions."

He purposefully hones in on me.

The cast definitely notices, some people whispering to each other. I bet Brenden is telling Baylee, *see, don't associate yourself with that.*

I screwed up in the hallway, but at this point, I don't really care. If Geoffrey has the power to demote me, then so be it. He demotes me. I've been there. I've done that. I live for the art and my family, and I doubt he has the authority to take *either* away from me.

I'm nonchalant. Calm. I drape my arm over my bent knee and everyone else pauses their stretches while Geoffrey appraises the whole cast.

My eyes flit to Bay. She keeps glancing in the direction of the locker room. Like she *really* wants to grab her phone to check her email.

She cares. I smile again.

She cares.

I nod to myself.

And then Geoffrey steals my attention. "There's no time for hugs and hand-shakes. I'm not your friend. I'm here to push you to *be* your very best, and it's your job to *give it* to an audience. Every time."

Some artists nod, but most of us stay still and just listen.

"To start, I'll read off the completed act list, and then we'll briefly discuss the narrative of Infini." He grips the clipboard, licks his finger, and flips a page. "Act list is as follows, including the participants. Listen closely for your name. Act one."

I stare off and absorb Infini's program:

Act 1: Dance & Floor Acrobatics (opening)
Act 2: Contortion
Act 3: Aerial Hoops
Act 4: Juggling
Act 5: Wheel of Death
(intermission)
Act 6: High-Risk Trampoline
Act 7: Clown Trio
Act 8: Aerial Straps Duo
Act 9: Hand-to-Hand Balancing
Act 10: Russian Swing (finale)

Geoffrey calls me out for four acts (1, 5, 6, and 10): the Opening Dance, Wheel of Death, High-Risk Trampoline, and Russian Swing. I expected to be a part of those. I even expected Bay to be called for Act 1 and Act 4: the opening and juggling.

What I didn't expect—what makes zero sense—is why Baylee is called for trampoline. Act 6.

Bay's eyes grow, mouth slowly falling. As stunned as her brother. As the rest of us. She's only ever participated in her juggling act and the opening.

But beyond that, trampoline is notoriously an all-Kotova act.

Chatter explodes, and Geoffrey doesn't take Marc's approach by shushing uneasy crowds with the raise of a hand.

He literally says, "Shut the hell up."

I can't even be surprised at this point.

The cast quiets, and Dimitri simmers silently, his face full of hard lines. He's a proponent of *you must give respect to earn respect.* Although Dimitri's definition of "respect" doesn't always equate to everyone else's.

"What'd I say before?" Geoffrey takes measured steps around the inner-circle, eyeing us. "You *listen* and you comply. No backtalk. We'll put on a great show if you accept these changes without falter and work your asses off."

I catch Baylee nodding in agreement, determination narrowing her eyes. She'd do anything for Infini's survival. I already know this.

"As of now, the narrative for Infini will not change, including stage decorations and original scores."

Baylee lets out an audible breath, and I realize now that she must've been worried about the fate of the music, all composed by her mom.

"Expect new costumes. Fittings will take place much later. The atrocious choreography is more pressing."

I can tell that several artists are biting their tongues.

"Someone stand up," Geoffrey says, "and briefly describe Infini's story to the newcomers."

At first no one offers. An awkward beat passes before Zhen rises to his feet.

Clearing his threat, Zhen explains, "The audience follows a girl just as she goes to sleep. The first five acts, she travels through an imaginative nightmare that tries to seduce her. After intermission, she reaches the dreamscape. The last five acts, she celebrates the *infinite* realms of enchantment and revelry. Where lastly, she wakes from bed." Zhen smiles. "The end."

We all clap. I whistle using my fingers.

Zhen takes a bow, and right as Geoffrey is about to speak, Zhen kindly translates his previous words in Mandarin for a group of new girls.

I've never seen Zhen rub anyone the wrong way, but Geoffrey huffs loudly, outwardly agitated. When Zhen finishes, Geoffrey shoots him a look and snaps, "You done now?"

Zhen nods, tensed.

Geoffrey tightens his grip on his clipboard. "How many of you can't speak English?" he asks.

Some artists mutter the question in different languages so others can understand. Besides Russian, I hear Japanese and Portuguese.

Slowly, artists begin to raise their hands. I count about fifteen out of fifty.

As I gauge Geoffrey's reaction, I get why Dimitri called him a fartface. His forehead crinkles, cheeks pulling upward, and his lip curls like he needs to take a really big shit.

But come on—Aerial Ethereal employs athletes and performers from all over the globe. This isn't a new development. Language barriers are common and expected. It's a part of our job, and our shows are better for hiring based on *talent*, not on whether we all know English.

Dimitri gestures towards the choreographer, and in Russian, he says, "*Welcome to the circus.*"

I laugh with all my cousins.

Geoffrey isn't amused. At all. "If you speak English, keep it in English unless you have to communicate with someone who can't understand."

Brenden rolls his eyes and leans into Baylee to whisper, probably voicing his irritation. He's good at speaking a lot of languages—I wouldn't forget how smart he is.

The choreographer continues scrutinizing each one of us.

I pull my arm over my chest in a stretch, and I try to recall Geoffrey's credentials. I looked them up once. He's from Montreal. Maybe. I think he previously worked with a full French cast, and this has to be different for him.

Especially since AE fired most of the translators this year, deeming them "unnecessary". Corporate tries to cut costs where they can.

(One day they're going to chop off their own fucking foot.)

Geoffrey straightens his blazer. "As most of you know, the part of The Girl was once played by Adelia." The Girl connects the whole story together, and she's basically the only performer who appears in every act. Even if she's just standing on stage left, reacting to the other acts in front of her.

Bay knew Adelia better than I did. I think she was in her thirties, and last I heard, she was transferred to Noctis, a touring show.

"This year, The Girl will be played by someone else. I'd like you all to welcome a familiar face." Geoffrey extends his arm towards the left, and our heads turn—*what?*

I know her.

Even before he says her name.

"Milla Baiul."

The little Ukrainian girl practically skips merrily into the center of the circle, hands cupped together. Light chestnut hair, sheet-straight, touches her waist. Milla is only eight, and she used to be a part of Viva. The show that I was in. Where Katya is now.

And Milla's parents perform on trapeze in Viva too.

Infini hasn't employed children this young since it moved to Vegas. We're all shocked.

Minors.

Minors.

Children. Dreams. I wonder if this is Marc Duval's way of showcasing the consequence that stops me from breaking the contract. That stops Bay from even looking at me.

The threat of the no minors policy is glaring us down.

I miss the applause for Milla, and Zhen makes room for her to join the circle. She drops down by his side.

"Now for the schedule," Geoffrey says, "you have exactly *sixty days* to master your acts, perform stage and costume rehearsals *flawlessly*. We will go live in two months. We've already started selling tickets, so there's absolutely no room for complaints."

Sixty days seems impossible. It'd be fine if these were minor tweaks to the set choreography, but he wants to trash half of what existed.

The tension is palpable. My muscles strain, and I try hard to reason with myself, to believe that I can do whatever he throws at me.

It's fine.

I'm fine.

Geoffrey circles us like a hawk. "There are two stages inside the Masquerade and three shows. The fact that Infini has its own stage is a *privilege* that none of you"—he waves his finger across us—"have earned yet. Prove to me that you deserve to be on that stage."

His motivational speech should encourage most of us, but my cousins look *incited*, not excited. Their arms are crossed. Glowering.

I raise my brows at my younger cousin Abram. When he catches my gaze, his angst-ridden features soften a little.

"I have a sheet for each act, describing what should be included in your routine," Geoffrey continues. "Today, I'll be walking around and working with each of you. You'll practice your individual acts *except* for those who are in High-Risk Trampoline. You all need to work together now. It has the most choreography changes."

I risk a glance at Baylee. Almost undetectable, fear crosses her face.

We accept a lot of changes every new season, but there are some that can completely knock you off your feet. For Bay, this has to be one of those.

(I'll help her.)

I'm allowed to do that, at least.

ACT TEN
BAYLEE WRIGHT

"You want me to what?" I had to have heard Geoffrey wrong. What he's asking—it's out of my wheelhouse. It's *impossible*. Sure, I'm equipped in basic tumbling, rhythmic gymnastics, and technical juggling, which involves instinct, balance, good hand-eye coordination, and lots of practice.

But the last time I jumped on a trampoline, I must've been nine or ten. All I did was a simple backflip and a toe-touch. I was the cute little kid that peopled "awed" at.

I'm not a cute little kid anymore. I can't get away with rudimentary skills.

On top of this news, I looked at my cellphone and read the email from Marc. I haven't seen Luka since, but I'm about to and my stomach keeps fluttering like I'm headed for a first date.

Which is so inaccurate.

I'm at work. Not a *date*. I wish my body would recognize that all Marc did was allow us to talk without punishment. And it feels…

There are no words.

We've never been given this much slack. I couldn't even pry my hand off my mouth while reading the email, too astonished. Too consumed by the idea of him talking to me. Of me talking to him.

It's the little things that I want. The little things that I'll never take for granted.

So I'm nervous about Luka. I'm nervous about being a part of *trampoline*. First day jitters are real and at a maximum right now.

Geoffrey barely glances at me as we walk towards the back room of AE's gym. The trampoline apparatus is too large to be set up in the main area, so it's relegated to a quieter, more private section.

"It's simple," Geoffrey says like I'm wasting his time asking again. "You're going to perform a variety of juggling tricks on the trampoline. Seven-ball backcrosses, one-handed patterns, fountains, cascades—all of that and more."

No, he *just said* that I'd be doing an eight-ball, seven-up pirouette *on someone else's shoulders*. What is an eight-ball, seven-up pirouette? I have eight juggling balls, at one point all seven are out of my hands, and I spin three-sixty degrees before catching the balls.

It's hard enough doing that on the ground. Let alone a trampoline. But sitting on someone else's shoulders? It means that they spin me. *We spin together.*

They control the rate in which I turn and catch. If I see something wrong with my tosses, I can't even spin slightly left or right to correct myself and grab the balls. I have to rely on someone else.

On a Kotova.

Because High-Risk Trampoline is traditionally all-male, all-Kotova. Eight of them, to be exact.

Luka.

Luka is one of them. I shut my eyes in a tight blink, trying not to think about him. Trying not to feel a thing.

Realizing I have nothing else to say, Geoffrey leaves my side and we enter the back room. I can't complain to the choreographer.

I'm sure he'd just tell me the colloquial, "The circus is about making the impossible *possible*. So do it."

Dimitri shuts the door behind me, and when I face the apparatus, my stomach nosedives. The monstrous trampoline is long enough that it'll stretch across the entire stage. Hoisted fifteen feet off the ground, four poles on each corner jut upwards.

The poles scare me.

About twenty feet above the trampoline's net, mini-trampolines are secured to the poles. Higher up, and I spot tiny black-metal platforms on those same four poles.

So one monstrous trampoline.

Four tinier trampolines.

Four pole platforms.

And a gray forty-foot back wall.

Since this act is part of the dreamscape, the back wall is usually painted periwinkle blue onstage, cotton fluff attached to resemble a *sky*. I remember the angelic costumes from New York: white spandex, shimmery gold detail. It made all the guys look like celestial gods.

I always thought Luka looked hot, and he was just a boy back then. *Stop thinking. About him.*

I drop my sports bag off my shoulder, juggling balls and clubs inside. All of the Kotovas already begin scaling the poles to reach the trampoline. Effortlessly, they use their hands and balls of their feet to shimmy up to the taut net.

Yeah…I don't know if I can do that. There aren't ladders. Seriously, the only way up is by one of four poles.

Geoffrey begins giving them direction, and I hang back and rummage in my sports bag. I hear him talk about *me*, and my neck heats.

"You'll be assisting Baylee with an eight-ball, seven-up pirouette, among other tricks. One ball falls, and the entire act will be ruined. You must work closely together…" he trails off. "Baylee, get up there."

Great.

I gather my red-and-orange stitched balls, four gripped in each hand, and I approach the apparatus. On the trampoline's taut surface, all eight of the Kotovas stand in a line.

Confident. Intimidating. Gray eyes radiating with charisma—I forget how magnetic they are together, side-by-side.

Even if I haven't spoken one-on-one to all of them, I know who they are. Dimitri and his two younger brothers: Anton and Robby. Then there's Luka and Sergei.

Plus twenty-five-year-old twins Matvei and Erik, and their younger brother Abram.

Don't look at Luka.

Don't look at Luka.

It's easier concentrating on work if I avoid, but it also heightens something inside of me. Tension? Nerves? All of the above?

"Dimitri," I call out the tallest and largest Kotova. "Catch." Easily, I throw each ball to Dimitri, and he collects them for me.

I sprint to the front-left metal pole, encased in a rubber material. I grip it and try to use my bicep and quad strength to scale this thing. Six feet up, I slip and slide down.

Ouch.

The rubber burns my palms, and I wipe my hands roughly on my thighs. "Baylee."

My stomach backflips at Luka's voice. I turn my head, just as he lies down and reaches over the metal frame of the trampoline. He extends two hands for me to grab hold.

I'm trying to restrain my emotion, but it barrels forward. Flooding me *full.* Luka's compassion softens his eyes, and he gestures me forward with both hands like, *it's okay.*

I nod as though saying: *I read the email.*

His nose flares a little, smothering his own sentiments, too.

I dazedly walk towards Luka Kotova. Like I'm the girl in Infini's dreamscape. Dimitri isn't yanking him away from me, and Geoffrey—I glance once at the choreographer. Impatient, he taps his foot repeatedly and points at Luka, telling me to hurry into his arms.

It reinforces the unbelievable notion—that this is allowed.

We're allowed to *touch*.

I blink, suppressing water that tries to well.

This is allowed.

It rattles my bones. I blow out a short breath, and Luka nods at me the closer I approach. I hate being the one that keeps everyone waiting. I hate being the one who consumes all the extra attention. A weird pit wedges between my ribs, so I pick up my pace.

I stand beneath Luka Kotova. Half his torso off the trampoline to grab me.

And despite all that we've been through—despite aching to just *look at him*, to take five-trillion years to absorb every detail of his features—there's no hesitation between us now. No pause or reluctance.

I jump as high as I can jump, and Luka seizes my wrists. Easily, he lifts me up, his muscles flexing. Biceps supremely sculpted, even more so than I recall from our past.

Wow.

He's older. I see how much older again.

I see how much time I missed.

My feet gracefully meet the trampoline, and his hands stay still on my wrists, warming me. Skin-to-skin. We breathe deeply. Inhaling raw breath.

I feverishly soak in his chiseled, charming features, afraid that this is the only time I have with him.

Afraid it'll all be taken away again.

He's beautiful. Inside. Outside. All of him.

His eyes dance across my face, as though he's remembering a thousand moments together. As though he's protecting this new memory from harm. From destruction and erasure. Luka licks his lips and then tries to draw me closer, towards his firm chest.

Dimitri grasps the back of his shirt and tugs him away from me. We're physically separated in probably a snap-second, even if it seemed longer.

I try to shake out my feelings, still dazed as Dimitri passes me the juggling balls.

Geoffrey points at the apparatus as he speaks. "For now, let's have Baylee sit on the back-left platform before we add her in."

How the hell do I get on the back-left platform? I think and then realize, *I jump.*

The Kotovas let me tackle this on my own and stand on the metal edge while loosely gripping the poles. With a big breath, I swallow my fear and begin to jump.

By the third jump, I gain so much height that my pulse races ahead of my thoughts. I feel like I'm taking way too long—when in reality, I'm probably not in the air for more than ten seconds.

I use my arms for balance. Higher and higher.

I'm supposed to just…step onto the little platform, mid-air. *Go for it*, I tell myself.

And I try.

My foot touches the lip of the platform, but I careen backwards. *Shit.* I slip and plummet downwards. My back hits the trampoline net and bounces me. I use my core strength to right myself upwards, but I aim towards a mini-net. *Shitshit.*

My shoulder touches the net, and I catapult off, barely able to hear Dimitri and a few others coaching me on where to go. What to do.

Somehow I land in the center of the trampoline again, and I kneel and force my body down to ground myself. Impeding all movement.

My heart is stuck in my throat. Anxiety burns me up, and I feel some Kotovas start to shift towards me. Including Luka. "I'm fine," I say, extending my arm so they'll stay put.

I'll try again. It's not like everyone succeeds the first time. Some do, but in most disciplines, practice is important. Whenever I try a new juggling trick, I still drop balls and clubs.

Ignore everyone.

I find a calm place inside, and I just jump and jump. Gaining enough height again, I don't rush myself this time. I bounce once more, and mid-air, I extend a leg to try and touch the tiny square platform.

I land fine, but my momentum pushes me forward. I run *into* the pole, and I wrap my arms around it (hands already full of juggling balls).

Stable.

I breathe heavily and rest my forehead on the pole, thankful that I made it to the platform. The first time is always the scariest. And sometimes the hardest.

When I sit, legs hanging off, everyone but Luka reroutes their attention. His gaze lingers on me for a long moment, as though to ensure I'm secure. That I'm okay. When he sees that I am, he focuses on his cousins and the choreographer.

I really enjoy this part. Observing the Kotovas in their intense training session. It's like witnessing each individual piece of an extraordinary puzzle. All before it's put together.

Now that I'm allowed, I mostly watch Luka. I find myself smiling way more than I ever would—and it's not a coy smile. It's a giddy, uncontrollable smile that has been locked away for years.

Luka propels himself at the back wall with one deep jump, and then he runs *up* the hard surface. Three cousins in tow. So swiftly, they land on top.

Naturally graceful, they may as well have wings.

Luka steps off the wall like it's nothing, but he physically *drops* from forty-feet.

I inhale strongly, even if he's done this a million times before. Dimitri stands close on the trampoline and digs his foot deep. So as Luka plummets, he hits the taut surface and soars straight up.

He does a quadruple back tuck over Matvei who performs a triple layout below. Luka also has enough air for a triple full (one back somersault with three twists). My view isn't of haphazard, awkward actions. These aren't a bunch of guys on a backyard trampoline flopping around.

Their lithe movements carry extreme precision. They call out to one another in Russian, making *eight* in-flight bodies look like ordered chaos. They're unequivocally picturesque slicing through air, and this is just practice.

Geoffrey stops them more than once and asks who can do what combination, and they all always raise their hands, their advanced skillsets the same.

"You two." From the ground, Geoffrey motions to Luka and Robby. "Full twisting triple backflip. Luka goes from the far left to right, and Robby crosses in the middle."

Panting, Robby rubs sweat off his brow. "We're doing the same thing?"

"Yes. *Listen.*" Geoffrey glares. "You cross like this." He just crosses his arms.

Abram rolls his eyes, but it's hard to frustrate Luka. He runs his hand through his soaked hair, and he nods a few times like he's ready to just go ahead and try it.

I wrap my arms around my stomach and lean forward. If this is timed wrong at all, Robby will crash into Luka, and it's not like a full twisting triple backflip is easy.

Luka is positioned at the far left, and Dimitri counts in Russian, ignoring the choreographer's earlier rule about speaking in English.

I chew my bottom lip, worried.

Dimitri shouts one last time, and Luka jumps and twists his body three-sixty-degrees. Now facing backwards, he performs rapid, technically perfect layouts across the trampoline, hands never touching the surface. Just feet.

Robby is coming at him.

My fingers touch my lips, just as he accelerates and passes his cousin in a split-second. Luka gains a lot of air at the end, and he finishes his last rotations, his triple backflip powerful.

And beautiful.

Then he lands on his feet, wobbling a little more than I think he'd like, but his tiny movement may be unnoticeable to an audience.

Geoffrey critiques them more than praises, and he has all the Kotovas perform a few skills again. Hopping on the available platforms. Flying at the mini-nets. Soaring up the wall. Thirty minutes tick by before I'm called on.

"Baylee, come down to the trampoline's base."

That means falling, but this is the fun part. I jump down, and all eight guys kill my momentum with their weight. I can't even figure out how, but they just did it.

Focused eyes on me, Geoffrey asks, "You expressed grief over which trick?" He can't remember because I didn't actually vocalize my concerns yet.

"The eight-ball, seven-up pirouette. Six-ball, six-up is more manageable to start." *Just saying.*

"We'll see. For now it's eight and seven." Geoffrey fingers his goatee before pointing at...*no.* "Sergei, lift her on your shoulders. You'll assist..."

I partially tune out the choreographer's instruction, my eyes narrowed on Luka's oldest brother. Sergei raises his squared head, shoulders pulled back. His whole authoritarian demeanor puts a weird taste in my mouth. He looks ready to order me around, as though I'm a prop to *his* act. In actuality, he's assisting my discipline just as much as I'm assisting his.

I don't have the heart to glance at Luka.

Those not participating position themselves on the metal frame and the platforms. I stand in the middle while Sergei approaches.

I expect him to say, *tell me when I should rotate.* Or *call out to me with commands.*

Instead, Sergei says, "I'll lift you and begin jumping. I'll spin after three counts."

"That's not how it works," I say. "Three seconds isn't enough time for seven balls to be airborne."

If he hears my opinion at all, he doesn't say.

Sergei just clasps me by the hips and hoists me on his shoulders. My body is completely rigid. Uncomfortable, for one. My legs drape down his chest, and he grips my calves and begins jumping without even the slightest pause or call-out.

I feel like I'm on a theme park ride that I didn't ask to be a part of, and it's made of a Russian man and hard muscle.

At least thirty-feet high, all eight balls still in my palms—I internally freak out. I don't trust Sergei with my life, and if he drops me, I could bounce and go flying at the back wall or the metal frame of the trampoline. Which is hard enough to crack a skull.

"Any day now." Geoffrey pressures me.

And it works. I concentrate on juggling.

Rather than simply tossing, I *push* the first two balls into the air so I don't fall backwards. I work in pairs, the balls soaring in a clean arc, and then Sergei rotates just as I launch the fifth and sixth balls.

Juggling is about timing. It's practically math, and when the timing is off, this happens.

The balls *fall.*

On the trampoline.

And they fling every direction thereafter.

It's less embarrassing than it is aggravating. I want to succeed badly, but I've never relied this heavily on someone else. *This is going to take a while.*

I must wear the dejection because Geoffrey snaps, "What's wrong?"

Catching my breath, I say, "I don't think this partnership is going to work out."

Sergei is not my favorite person ever, and he technically owes me a grand that he'll never pay—but I'm not unearthing my personal life at work.

"Fine, we'll try Dimitri."

Sergei switches out with Dimitri, and in another breath, I'm on Dimitri's shoulders and he tells me, "Throw my balls, Baybay."

Ignore.

I'm not in the mood for his jokes, and ignoring them is the easiest tactic here, especially in front of a choreographer.

As soon as Dimitri jumps, I have trouble concentrating on the trick. I'm thirty-feet up again, but I keep thinking about Dimitri losing his footing and then me falling and face-planting into a mound of hard muscle or metal.

I realize fast that the problem wasn't just Sergei.

It's me.

During the rotation, all the balls drop. I shake my head at Geoffrey. I try the trick with Erik and Robby to only meet the same failed result.

Off Robby's shoulders and firmly planted on the trampoline, I walk towards the metal frame, lungs ablaze. Because I know what I'm about to do.

Please let this work.

ACT ELEVEN
BAYLEE WRIGHT

I ask Geoffrey, "Can I try this with Luka?" I don't believe the outcome will change with anyone else.

Whether Marc Duval informed the choreographer about my history with Luka, I can't tell—but Geoffrey nods. He approves.

I don't question whether Luka will be upset at my proposal. He was the one that helped me earlier, so he should be okay with close contact at work.

I walk to the center of the trampoline, and Luka abandons his spot by the back-left pole to join me. Instantly, we lock eyes.

My lungs inflate, a thousand memories rushing towards me.

Dancing—God, we danced for long drawn-out hours.

Drum beats thumped and rumbled the ground beneath our feet, and club lights swept our limbs that tangled. That touched.

We blistered in rhythm.

My head lolled back, and his strong hands found my hips. Sweat built between us, and our bodies—we fit just right.

I try to bury this image with one large breath. I have to concentrate on my job. Not the past.

Not *us*.

Because there is no more *us*. There can never be an *us*. Just separate lonely entities.

What am I even thinking? I didn't keep tabs on Luka. He may not even be lonely. He may have a significant other. Like a friends-with-benefits or an actual girlfriend. I try desperately to block out these agonizing thoughts.

It shouldn't be this painful.

He was allowed to move on. We both were *ordered* to. I should be traveling forward like him, not barreling into the past.

Luka comes to a stop a foot from me. Not shying away, he drinks in my features and his grays tenderly stroke my cheeks, my lips and eyes.

Touch me. I inhale.

He inhales even more powerfully.

Touch me.

His right hand instinctively rises up. Towards my cheek.

I step forward.

He steps forward. Our legs collide, and then he hesitates. I hesitate. We remember where we are. Who watches. He's not able to touch me *that way*.

Luka tightens his hand in a fist before it drops to his side. His brows cinch, face pained, but I nod once in understanding. We're working. We can't really reconnect here.

We're not even allowed to reconnect outside of the gym. *This* work relationship is what we've been granted. It has to be enough.

My dry eyes burn like I need to release four-and-a-half years of pent-up emotion, but my body knows it can't.

Luka tries to smile, and then he dips his head to me. "Tell me what to do." *Work.*

Work.

So I explain the jugging trick in detail, and he asks a few questions about timing and jumping.

Cordial, easy enough.

After I answer, he nods and says, "Just squeeze your thighs when I need to rotate. If you want me to shift at all as I jump, dig your right heel in my chest to go right. Left to go left."

"That'll work." I like this system more than Dimitri's "call-out" method. I'm sometimes deep inside my head during routines that I forget to use my voice. Using my body should feel more natural.

Geoffrey shouts, "Any day now!"

Luka's lip quirks, almost laughing at the absurdity. It makes me less stressed, and then he takes two balls out of my hands.

"What are you doing?" I ask.

"You said six-ball, six-up was more manageable, so let's do six." He listened to me from earlier?

I try to restrain my smile. *You haven't changed, have you?*

Do you ever think of me?

Do you even still love me?

Or am I just a heartbreaking memory?

My own lips inch up but falter. "Luka Kotova, already testing the choreographer's limits."

"Yeah." Luka's smile brightens the angelic creases of his face. "Because he's not the juggler. You are." At this, he chucks the two extra balls at Dimitri, who easily catches both.

Now I'm left with six. Which will make our chance of success a lot greater.

Luka stares fixatedly down at me. "Ready?"

I nod, and in one sudden motion, he clutches my hips and lifts me onto his shoulders. I sit securely on Luka, three balls in each of my palms.

He grips my calves so I won't fly off of him.

Then he jumps, and the power of his muscles, his legs, funnels through his body and up into my limbs. I breathe controlled, easy breaths. Knowing he'd protect me before he'd drop me.

Twenty-feet high, I push the first pair of balls into the air. Then the second pair.

Four balls soar in a clean arc. I concentrate solely on my juggling props, not even sure how high we are or how many bounces we've completed—I just catch the balls and then rapidly push up one pair after the other.

All six balls soar out of my hands. High, *high* above me.

I squeeze my thighs.

Luka spins three-sixty, and I never take my eyes off the balls. I grab them as they fall, using one finger to clasp the third ball to my right palm.

He effortlessly deadens his momentum, and we come to a stop on the trampoline. I smile because it worked. It's also a better indication that the trick can be done.

From the floor, Geoffrey assesses us, fingers to his jaw. "It needs more polishing, and you have to increase the difficulty within sixty days. No exceptions."

My smile fades, and I just nod. I'm about to slide down Luka's shoulders, but he's already hoisting me off and placing me in front of him.

I want to peek at Luka, but I shouldn't tempt it. Should I? I hesitate. I waver. *Look at him.*

I give in, and I brave a glance backwards.

He's already staring at me. He's already smiling, and his lips only pull higher as our eyes meet again. *Are you single?*

Are you the same as you were?

I open my mouth to ask one of my many questions.

"Baylee, let's chitchat over here," Dimitri calls out.

I drop my gaze instantly, jostled back to reality. Dimitri motions me to the other side of the trampoline, and Robby and Abram "oooh" like I'm in trouble.

On my way there, I slyly flash them my middle finger, and they subsequently laugh, which I expected.

Dimitri meets me halfway, and seriousness drapes over us. He lowers his head, no one able to overhear. "I'm in a fucked-up spot here. I love that kid." He gestures with his head to Luka.

"I know," I say. "I'm not asking you to choose me over him…" Why does this feel like a second divorce all of a sudden? Like Luka and I are splitting up again and all the people that mean something to us have to choose sides?

We did that once, but Dimitri has always sat in the middle. He was the one person we both kept equally in our lives.

Dimitri cocks his head. "Outside of cousins and brothers, I've worked the longest, side-by-side with you. That makes you family to me."

I end up smiling a small smile, but whatever else he has to say, I sense that it's not good. So I speak hushed. "It's not your job to pull us away from each other. We're not putting you in that position." I think this is where his concern lies.

"I read the email."

Okay. "Then you know we're fine," I whisper, glancing at the other Kotovas. They all stand at the edge of the trampoline, talking with the choreographer. Luka hangs back and constantly looks over at me and Dimitri.

"*Fine?* You know what you two are? You're both floating in space in some made-up *Star Wars* galaxy," Dimitri says, "and for some reason, I've been tasked to rescue you two shitheads from further destruction.

So I'm here, telling you, to tone that shit down. Nik thinks it's better if you do too. So do it." He crosses his arms. "Simple as that."

Except… "We were *only* working."

"Eye-fucking isn't working. Neither is casual flirting or smiley flirting—which you two do."

I try not to freeze up. "Smiley flirting?"

"I'm not demonstrating."

"Why not?"

"You're like a sister to me, Baybay."

I cringe at him. "Brothers don't tell sisters to 'not suck their cousin's cock'—which you said, word-for-word, when I was *thirteen*."

"If only you both listened to me, you wouldn't be in this fucking mess." He checks over his shoulder and then drops his voice another octave. "He's a heartbeat away from tattooing your name on his ass."

I try not to smile too much at the *Center Stage* quote, but I have fond memories of seeing the movie with all the Kotovas when I was twelve. They all superstitiously watch the movie the last Wednesday of every month. The one time they skipped a viewing, a little cousin fell in a performance and fractured his skull.

"Got it?" he asks.

"Don't cross the line with Luka," I whisper. "It's been painfully clear from the beginning." I leave Dimitri's side and try to build an invisible boundary between me and Luk.

It hurts.

It always hurts. Especially when trust not only exists between us, but it flourishes, stronger and fuller than with anyone else.

ACT TWELVE
BAYLEE WRIGHT

Practice ends, and I open up my blue locker. Shower pipes groan through the cement walls, the locker room extremely full and the bathrooms in use. Most everyone keeps to themselves, coming down from the first exhausting day of the season.

I rummage through my gym bag—and I freeze.

What…is this? I frown and grab a thick white envelope that lies on my towel. I turn it over. Next to the seal, I detect the legible, unmistakable handwriting of Luka Kotova.

For all the birthdays I missed.

"What'd you do, Luk," I whisper to myself, my lungs burning up. Gently, I peel open the seal, and my thumb skims the edges of *cash*. Many, many bills. I don't even have to count to know there's exactly a grand here.

I rock back into the locker, my knees weak. My eyes burning.

I can't believe he did this.

Then again, I can. He'd give the shirt off his back to a homeless man. I know this, because he would do it *all* the time in New York. How many shoes did he kick off and hand to other people that needed them more?

In the same breath, he steals from stores too many times to count. Timo used to say that he has a Robin Hood complex, but we all know it's even more deep-seated. Rooted somewhere that Luka barely touches.

I fan the bills and shake my head. I can't accept a thousand dollars from Luka. No matter how sweet the sentiment. I wouldn't even accept money from my own brother. I smooth my lips together and close the flap of the envelope just as tenderly.

My pulse rushes forward. I have to find Luka.

So I peer down each row of lockers. *No. No.* I can't exactly ask anyone where he is. They'd question *why* I'm searching for him. I already overheard someone discussing our fake cocaine drama earlier today, and saying, "It must be so awkward for them to be working together."

Awkward, no.

Tense, definitely.

I'm used to discretion, and I keep up the secrecy as much as possible.

After more searching, I think he's either in the shower or already left the locker room.

Envelope still in hand, I pass the rows of lockers and head to a dark blue door that says *showers* in gold lettering. I push inside.

Taupe curtains enclose every individual shower stall. I scan the area, charcoal tiles wet beneath my sneakers.

Kotovas fill the space, chatting loudly in Russian, drying their hair with extra towels. Definitely semi-naked. I'm not fazed, and I don't see Luka among them.

I walk further inside and pass the ten sinks situated in the center. A couple girls use the mirrors and comb their wet hair. I spot Zhen at a sink. He puts in a new pair of contacts, oblivious to his surroundings and me.

I'm invisible.

A wanderer. Watcher. Attempting to be a *finder*.

Find him. I grip the money tighter and peer at the other side of the sinks. Closer to the group of Kotovas. They don't notice me either.

Steam builds and clams my skin. I waft the air, and as soon as my hand drops, a shower curtain whips open.

I'm motionless.

There he is.

Cotton towel tied low around his waist, his sculpted, partially naked body is in my direct view. He doesn't notice me yet.

I slowly skim him from head-to-toe. My lips part in heady desire that heats my skin more than the steam. I haven't felt this *ache* since we split up. I take a shallow breath, and I actually clench between my legs. Pulsating some.

I can't close my lips together. The instant arousal stuns me, but more than that, I'm hypnotized. By *him*. Beads of water roll down the ridges of his abs, his biceps cut without flexing.

His right leg is inked fully, more tattoos than I remember. And the muscles along his waist create a V-shape, pointing towards his package that's hidden behind a thin towel.

I can confidently say that he's not only attractive but that I'm *extremely* attracted to him. That hasn't changed. In fact, it feels stronger.

Just before I call out his name, Luka turns his head.

He catches my gaze, and he solidifies, his brows furrowing. His eyes flit to the envelope.

I say, "Can I…" *talk to you about non-work things?* I don't have to finish because he already nears me.

Pushing his wet hair out of his face, he nods to the envelope. "That's yours, Bay."

Bay. It's like no time has passed, but then it's like forever spans between us. Look at his body. It's changed. He's clearly *physically* different.

I'm different.

We've been separated for years.

I fight the emotion that tries to surge again, and I swallow hard. "It's yours." I hold the envelope out. "You know I can't accept it."

Predictably, Luka raises his hands. "I'm not taking it back."

"Yeah you are," I whisper since his group of cousins have quieted by the wall. "I'm returning it."

Luka crosses his arms, further proving that he won't reclaim the envelope.

For some reason, my lips start pulling *upwards.* "Stop."

He begins to smile off mine, and he nods at me again. "Stop what?"

"Stop being stubborn or I'll just throw this at your feet."

Luka stares intensely at me. *Into me.* Lightness, happiness floods my soul so abruptly, so quickly that I become overwhelmed.

I breathe, "Luka."

Love me.

His chest rises in a deep inhale, and then he reaches out and takes the envelope. During the exchange, his fingers stroke my hand, lovingly. Affectionately.

My neck warms, and much further down—I'm wet.

I know I'm wet.

Suddenly Matvei rips the towel off Luka's waist and snaps it against his toned ass. Buck-naked.

My eyes grow, mouth slowly dropping, and Luka, hardly surprised, flips off his snickering cousins with one hand and uses his other to *barely* shield his dick.

Luka catches me staring, and he laughs into a wide smile.

It's infectious, and my lips begin stretching again. *We're allowed to chat.* Professionally, but that word could be expanded to other topics. If I take the risk.

So I say, "Nice tattoos." His ink only reached his knee before, but now the new designs rise all the way up his right thigh.

It's incredibly hot.

"That's what you were staring at?" he teases.

I'd shove his arm if I could touch him. In the past, he'd probably pull me into his chest right after and squeeze me in the tightest, warmest hug.

Tension keeps us apart. "Mmhmm," I say, not able to play into his words as much as I want to.

His smile vanishes, and he nods understandingly. We're both frowning now, and it hurts. God, it hurts so badly.

I start walking backwards to the exit, and I say, "I'll see you around… co-worker."

His eyes smile more than his lips. "See you, Bay."

We can do this.

I hope.

ACT THIRTEEN
BAYLEE WRIGHT

I finally have a use for my floral-patterned, blank journal, a well-meaning 19th birthday present from my grandparents. Maybe they figured I'd take after my dad, but I couldn't think of anything to write until now.

I make a list.

And I write slowly like the ink is made of my blood and these words are oath. Shedding my feelings on paper kind of feels that permanent.

"How's the dating going?" my aunt asks via video chat. My laptop is propped on my pillow, and I sit cross-legged on my bottom bunk, journal on my thigh.

I talk to Aunt Lucy about three times a week, and I've kept her in the loop about my dating life and about me trying not to close myself off to guys.

I pause writing at her question, and immediately, I think of Luka. We've kept it professional in the gym, but every single day, the underlying tension mounts greater and stronger. And it was already unbearable to begin with.

"At the moment," I say, "dating is non-existent. I barely have time to eat lunch on weekdays."

In the square video box, Aunt Lucy lounges on her suede couch, already in white designer pajamas, makeup off, and her hair is in beautiful micro braids splayed on her shoulder. It's late Saturday night for her, but evening in Vegas. She may be an on-the-go, thirty-five-year-old New Yorker, but she relaxes better than me.

Evidence: I can see myself in that little rectangle in the upper-right hand corner of the screen. My back is achingly straight tonight.

Staring at myself a little more, I know I'm a mixture of my mom and dad. My warm, medium-brown skin is a product of my dad's fair and my mom's dark brown. I have my mom's flat chest, full lips, and her rich brown eyes. From my dad, I have his tiny dimples and long neck. My parents aren't here, but every time I look in the mirror, small things remind me of them.

"No more online dating then?" Aunt Lucy asks. "You could always sit at a bar and wait for Mr. Right to buy you a drink." She smiles into her sip of hot chocolate. She always says that she has an abnormal craving for marshmallows, and not just because she's four-months pregnant.

Online dating. I sucked at it.

I gave up when I learned it's all about *numbers*. The more people you meet for a first date, the more likely you'll find a perfect match. But I don't have that much time for a numbers game, and I'm not lucky enough to be an exception.

I twirl my pen. "If I sat at a bar, chances are, my Mr. Right would be buying a drink for the girl on the other side of me." I hesitate to say more because I'm not alone. I share a suite with Nikolai, Thora, and Katya, but a bedroom and bunk bed solely with Katya, Luka's sixteen-year-old sister.

I glance to the left.

At our wooden desk, Katya has her nose practically pressed to her own laptop. Cosmetics are spread out beside a tiny mirror. I think she's watching makeup tutorials. I don't ask. I've been trying to give Katya space.

I eye our cramped room, something that I'm sure resembles a dorm. Katya already decorated the walls with Aerial Ethereal posters, and her feather boas and knock-off purses are draped over the posts of our bunk bed.

We haven't really spoken at all. Long, *long* ago, I used to be friends with Katya. To be in Luk's life means to be in Timo and Kat's—it's just how it is. Whenever we went to Coney Island, we used to ditch the guys and play carnival games together.

We had one goal: to win a green stuffed dinosaur that we named Marvin. We won him a year later, and we joked about having joint custody. He stayed with me four days out of the week. Katya for three.

Then I got into trouble with Luka, signed the contracts, and abruptly stopped speaking to or even *seeing* him. Not long after, Katya confronted me by the gym's water fountain. I was just fourteen.

She was twelve, and she tried sucking down her tears. Physically sniffing until they submerged. "Why did you two have to do that?" Her voice nearly split. "You really couldn't stay away from drugs?"

I shrugged, too distraught to speak.

Katya frowned. "Luka said that you're not friends anymore."

I nodded.

"This isn't fair." She nearly burst into tears. "You're my first friend that's a girl. We're…we're friends, and you…" She took a breath. "You have to make up with him."

"I can't," I said softly.

"Why not?" Her features cracked.

"I just can't."

"Not even for me?" Katya bit her bottom lip.

I knew I couldn't stay friends with Katya. She was so attached to Luka. They're inseparable. It was like asking Luka to be friends with my brother *and* avoid me—it'd never work.

I ripped off a Band-Aid by blurting out, "I can't be friends with you either. Your whole family is a bad influence…" I couldn't finish. Tears leaked out of her eyes, and I broke my heart and hers.

Later that day, I found our stuffed dinosaur at my door with a note that said, *you can have Marvin. I'm a bad influence anyway.*

I couldn't even bear to look at that dinosaur, but I also couldn't bear to throw him away. I crammed Marvin in a cardboard box, and he's now collecting dust in our shared closet.

I try to let our last interaction from the past drift away, and my aunt's voice draws my attention to the computer.

"What happened to 'putting yourself out there' and not being pessimistic about *love*?" she asks.

I clutch my journal tight and think, *that's exactly what I'm about to do.* "Is that how you met Devon?" I wonder. "You just sat at a bar and waited for him?" It seems like a one-in-a-million likelihood.

"Yes," my aunt says into a growing grin, an awful liar.

"You're terrible."

"She is." Devon pops his head into the frame, his smile brighter than hers. He's tall, black, a New York attorney, and Lucy's doting husband of three years. "We met in the line of Superheroes & Scones, and she approached *me*."

"Get out of here." Laughing, she elbows him out of the frame. "And I only talked to you first because I wanted to know why a man your age was holding three Storm plushies."

"For my nieces!" I hear him off-screen.

Aunt Lucy rolls her eyes but sets them back on me. "You're deflecting again."

"I'm not," I say seriously. "I like hearing about you." *More than I like talking about myself.* And I'd rather not stress my aunt out with my life. She's pregnant. Unloading any kind of grief onto her shoulders won't do any good. "How long will you get for maternity leave?"

I feel her assessing me. "A lot longer than most. A perk of working for a company owned by a feminist." Barely pausing, she asks, "What've you been writing?"

I go still. In the video screen, she can see my pen but not the journal. "Just…a list of things I need to fix and work on."

"Like…?"

"I can't really say." I peek at Katya again. She's slumped forward, face in her hand. She looks upset at something.

My aunt takes the hint about the list, but she's not finished prying. "And Luka?"

I jolt. "What?" My neck instantly heats. "What about him?"

Severity shrouds her usually sweet-natured face. "I talked to Brenden yesterday. He said you're working with him."

"Who's Luka?" Devon asks from off-screen.

Her eyes flicker to him. "No one, baby." To me, she adds, "*No one,* right?"

A lump lodges in my throat. "Yeah…yeah, he's just a co-worker." I understand her concern. Like Nikolai and Dimitri, she sees him as a youthful fling—someone I dated and got into trouble with. He's a kid that used to make me happy. A long-ago memory.

No one worth risking a career over.

No one worth risking the dreams of other children.

He's no one.

I open my mouth, and I ache to shake my head. To say, *he's so much more than no one.* How can I explain this to my aunt? She'll say that I'm in love with the idea. The fantasy.

Not reality.

But she's not here. She has no idea how much I trust Luka with my body, my heart—my life.

Katya suddenly sniffles. She's crying? I'm staring at the back of her head, so I can't tell for certain.

"I have to go," I say to my aunt.

With casual goodbyes, we log off, and I pop out my earbuds. Swinging my legs off the bed, I sit on the very edge. I hate that I hesitate to approach or even call out her name, but I do.

I shouldn't tear open a friendship that we closed poorly and painfully. I should leave her alone.

Marc's email must've shattered more than one fortification in my mind—because I stand up. When before, I would've never even *chanced* nearing Kat.

I set my journal on my bed and reach our desk.

She startles at my presence and quickly shields her face with her long straight hair.

A YouTube makeup tutorial plays from her laptop. I watch a vlogger showcase a compact of highlighter or blush. I can't really discern which.

"What do you want?" she asks uneasily.

To rewind time and never have to hurt you. I examine her spread of cosmetics, which must've cost a ton of money. She may've even tapped into her savings.

"What?" she asks just as cautiously.

I pick up a tube of lipstick. "I always thought you'd stay sporty with me." I try to smile, but it won't form. We both believed intense makeup was a hassle. All I use: eyeliner, lipstick, and concealer, just to hide zits.

"People change." Her tone is soft and morose.

People change. I didn't just miss Luka's life. I missed my friend grow older.

And it's not like I collect a million friends either. The tiny handful that I made from the past few years have *all* transferred to touring shows. I'm left with my brother and Zhen.

I miss having girls around me, but really, I miss Katya.

I set the lipstick down. "You really want to wear all of this?"

Katya takes a breath. "*Yes,*" she combats.

My defenses don't skyrocket. I lean against the desk. "Nikolai?" I'm guessing he's already been on her case. "Did he tell you to return it all?"

"Yeah." Katya slumps forward. "I thought if I'd buy the best stuff it'd make me look less like a clown, but then I figured out that, *no, I just paint on makeup like a literal clown.*"

I get it.

We all have to do our own costume makeup, and we can't choose the design either. AE gives us a detailed picture of the colors, strokes, blends, shapes—all around our neck, eyes, and lips. Those Aerial Ethereal classes teaching us how to shade and shadow were my *least* favorite.

I was awful at first. Plus costume makeup is so much different than one coat of lipstick. It's drastic and extreme lines that pop your features. All so the person in the very back row can see some facial detail.

Katya tucks a strand of hair behind her ear. "I suck at everything the first thousand times I do it, and I swear Nik would be great at cat-eyeliner on his first go-around. He's better than average at *everything.*"

It's why we never let her brothers try to win Marvin for us. They would've succeeded in less than half the time, and the point wasn't just to get the stuffed dinosaur. It was to prove that we didn't need a boy to validate what we always believed: that we had the power to do *anything* we wanted ourselves.

I hope she never lost that after she lost me.

I bend to the laptop and click into another makeup tutorial. "Yeah, well, we don't need Nik."

"We?" She's skeptical.

I glance over my shoulder at Kat.

Thick, blocky eyeliner shrinks her usually big eyes, doing the inverse of what she probably wants. Dark-red, blunt lip-liner makes her mouth look cartoonish, and pink blush streaks her cheekbones, very over-drawn like stage makeup.

I can't tell if I'd be able to do any better. "I'm still Sporty Spice," I say, noting how we used to both be the same Spice Girl together. We liked sharing the title. We liked sharing a lot of our things, actually. "But if you want to be Posh, I can try to help."

"Why?" she asks, eyes watering.

I shrug, searching for words that I'm allowed to say. "Because I…" *miss you.* "…because we're suitemates and roommates."

"Right…" She nods to herself and tucks another piece of hair behind her ear.

I click into a smoky eye and bold lip tutorial. We watch the video together, not all of the tension has been expunged. Our past still stretches uncomfortably between us.

"You can sit down," Katya offers a minute later. She scoots and gives me room on the same chair.

I take a seat next to her, and she plucks out a makeup wipe to clean her face.

"Why are there so many steps?" I mutter and rewind thirty seconds. "It's like they're setting us up to fail."

"Conspiracies I can get behind." I rewind again, and midway through the video, I peek at Kat out of the corner of my eye.

She peeks at me.

In New York, I became close to Katya around the time that my parents passed away. She was a girl who grew up without a mother figure, and I'd just lost mine. We bonded, not because of Luka, but because we needed someone who understood what we missed.

I'm not her mom. She's not mine. We just fill this warm place of empathy that no one else can touch or reach, and I want to be allowed to return. I want to laugh about how awful we are at makeup and try hard to make my friend the best Posh Spice she can be.

I vacillate between *cans* and *cants*—then suddenly I hear music from the living room. My thoughts torpedo, and I stiffen and look at the closed door.

It's not just any music.

I shut my eyes, soaking in my *favorite* music and my current favorite singer. Nori Amada's "Losing It" plays and floods me with raw energy and vigor. Even on my bluest days, her music can stir something deep inside of me.

Most soca can, the contemporary Caribbean genre affectionately known as *the soul of calypso*. Really, it's an evolution of calypso, invented by Garfield Blackman (a.k.a Lord Shorty) who feared the disappearance of the genre as reggae was rising. Soca was a way of popularizing calypso again.

I like thinking of soca as lively with energetic tempos and melodies, creating this upbeat rhythm with steel drums, horns and trumpets, keyboards and synths. It's music that immediately makes people want to stand up and dance.

It originated in Trinidad and Tobago, but soca has since spread throughout the Caribbean. My mom had so much fondness for it. On Sunday mornings, Joyce Wright would put Winston Soso's "I Don't Mind" on her record player. She'd push the kitchen table aside, and she'd dance with her son and daughter.

With Brenden and me.

At the stove, Neal Wright would whip up grilled cheese and watch us. Love behind his black-rimmed glasses.

"He saw your Nori Amada poster," Katya suddenly says.

My eyes snap open. "Who?" *But I know.* I think I knew from the start.

"Luka," Kat says. "You should go. He's trying to draw you out." She shakes her head. "He's so obvious. He's such a dork."

I'm smiling. I can't stop smiling. I agree; he's way too thoughtful. Too ridiculous. Too much of everything I love. *Oh God.* My stomach overturns, nervous.

And my lips falter at the thought of being caught by Marc's two company spies. Even if it seems unlikely.

I say, "I can't..."

Katya elbows me.

I elbow back.

"Stand up," she tells me. "Remember how much you really liked him." *That's not hard.* "And if you can find it in your heart, try to be friends with him again?" She smiles morosely at that idea, not believing it'll ever happen either. "He's not bad. I promise. He's *the best* ever."

I know.

"If you can't be friends with me, at least...for Luka." She has to look away from me, her eyes glassing.

I want that more than she can ever know.

So I stand up.

I follow my instinct which travels towards the music. Towards Luka.

And the consequences fade to the background.

ACT FOURTEEN
BAYLEE WRIGHT

I open my bedroom door to the unknown.

Music grows louder, and Luka—I see him instantly. He rummages through cupboards in the kitchenette while dancing to Nori Amada's song.

Luka's body absorbs the beat like he's a visceral extension of the music, his rhythm natural and the kind most would envy.

It's mesmerizing and tempts me to join. To dance right alongside him.

If we didn't have those contracts over our heads, I'd already be in his arms.

Luka flips a glass in his hand, and I near the bar counter. As soon as I put my knee to the stool and elbows to the counter, he sees me fully. And his drop-dead gorgeous smile stretches across his angelic face.

I smile off of his smile and try to suppress the giddy-factor, which is *way* too high. "You shouldn't look at me like that."

"Why not?" He sets the glass aside and edges close. Placing his palms on the counter, his hands are right beside my forearms. An inch or so away, and the hairs on my neck rise, apprehensive but eager. *So eager.*

His chest rises in a deep inhale.

My lungs expand just as much. "What would your girlfriend think?" Yeah, I just threw that out there, and I have no regrets. My curiosity is winning out.

Luka searches my gaze for more. Answers to why I'd ask this. Wondering if I care about him completely, entirely, *wholeheartedly.*

I do. I wish I didn't.

I wish I could let go. Because an underlying pain sits beneath every word. Every glance. The pain of knowing nothing can truly happen.

Knowing there is no *us* at the end of the desire and the longing.

Luka leans closer to whisper, "I don't have a girlfriend."

"Friends-with-benefits," I add.

"None of those either."

I nod a few times, my eyes burning as I restrain so many sentiments at once. "I should go." I step off the stool and head towards…well, nowhere yet.

Luka sprints over and blocks my path. "Wait, Bay."

I'm rigid. Uncertain.

He reaches a hand out to me but wavers too. His arm drops. "We're allowed to be friends."

"At work." We're not exactly *at* work right now.

Luka runs his fingers through his hair, and then we both go completely still. Not because someone entered the suite. But because the song changes to the *score* of Infini.

My mom's music.

Luka licks his lips. "It's on shuffle. That wasn't intentional, I promise."

I believe him, and I listen to the one drop drum beat and snares that hark back to rocksteady, a genre that originated in Jamaica, the predecessor of reggae. I even pick out a little bit of soca. Infini's score isn't exclusively Caribbean—there's some American jazz and Latin influences—but I think the soul is Jamaican.

Just like my mom.

I shift my weight, and I try to shake off every sentimental and emotional feeling that wrings the air. *Stay professional.* "Do you know why AE cast you in Infini?" Why would they ever give us room to move towards one another?

It's dangerous.

Luka shakes his head. "No clue."

Our eyes graze each other again. Head-to-toe. We unconsciously inch closer. Our fingers toy with the idea of actually touching. Outside of work. *We're outside of work.*

He dips his head, really looking at me. *Into me.* And as he opens his mouth to speak, the suite door blows open.

And we blow apart.

I act like I'm headed to the fridge.

Luka acknowledges his older brother who enters. "Hey, Nik…I needed to ask you about dinner."

I avoid Nikolai, grab a protein bar, and I aim for my bedroom. All the while, I sense the heat of Nik's gaze scouring me up and down.

"You couldn't text me?" Nikolai questions.

"No," Luka says firmly. "Don't spin this into something it's not, *please.*"

At this, I disappear into my bedroom, shutting the door closed. Not flooded with relief. If anything, my stomach hurts. My heart hurts.

And I'm more conflicted than before.

ACT FIFTEEN
LUKA KOTOVA

"Stop making this personal," I say calmly on my way out of the gym, showered and bag slung over my shoulder. I just had a brutal twelve-hour practice with Sergei on the Wheel of Death, and the last thing I want to do is start a pointless fight.

Sergei keeps my stride as I push through a set of blue double doors. "You're the one who made it personal."

I wish the doors would hit him in the face, but I spin around, just as the doors shut and enclose us in the long hallway.

"How?" I question with a shrug. "I did *everything* you asked me to do."

I'm abnormally agreeable when it comes to work. I don't roll my eyes. I don't sigh heavily or pull passive aggressive bullshit. I just do my job and I leave.

Since Sergei has been performing on the Wheel of Death for the past ten years—and it's a fairly new discipline for me—he has more experience. So he has to order me around, and I put up with his know-it-all attitude and constant reminder that "if you're not concentrating, you're going to get hurt. And that's on you."

(Thanks for the tip.)

Sergei blocks me from walking. "Seven practices in, I give you instructions and you only reply *okay*."

"And?" That's not me being personal.

"And if I were anyone else, you'd be more vocal. I'm tired of the one-word responses."

I almost feel bad for him. "Yeah, *no*." I shake my head and adjust my grip on my gym bag. "I don't do the whole let's-chat-about-every-little-thought-we've-ever-had bit."

Sergei crosses his arms, disbelieving.

"You don't know me, dude." Something raw enflames at the cold fact. "You could be Nik or Dimitri and I'd respond the same way at practice." He's asking me to be someone else, and I'm not playing that game to appease him or anyone.

He gets *me*.

Whether he likes me or not, I couldn't care less.

"I'd appreciate more enthusiasm then."

Off his harsh expression, I can tell that he's testing me. Silently, he's saying, *if this isn't personal, then you'll be happy like you would be with anyone else.*

I force a genuine-looking smile and push past him. I don't turn back.

Not even as he yells at me in Russian, and I don't care to listen. He's already ruined the allure of an apparatus for me.

Before he showed up, I was honestly excited about Wheel of Death. The forty-foot apparatus is one of the biggest in Aerial Ethereal. Two large hoops are connected together by a space frame beam, and with momentum, the structure rotates like a pendulum.

During the act, I run on the inside of a hoop, sometimes on the outside, while Sergei stays in sync with me on the other.

I first saw the Wheel of Death when I was about four or five, and I always thought it resembled two humongous hamster wheels. Men sprinted in the hoops, and once they started doing flips inside and outside, the wheel growing in speed, I thought it looked awesome. And later, *dangerous*.

Years went by and Sergei was chosen for the act. At one point, so was Timo, and I never thought I'd get the chance.

Of course, once I finally do, I'm paired with the only artist in the company that I literally can't stand. His voice is like balling up aluminum foil next to my eardrum. If I could, I'd tune him out every practice.

Barely five feet down the hallway, I run into commotion that looks more fun than hanging around Sergei.

Artists linger outside the glass door of a Corporate office. Show posters hang on the plastered walls, and the artists press up against them, spying into the glass.

No one stands in direct view of the office.

I sidle next to Dimitri from the right side, and he cranes his neck towards the door.

"What's up?" I ask him, but he's too consumed by the drama. Laughter is caught in about fourteen throats.

I'm curious.

And unafraid.

It makes for a bad combination. I step in front of the glass door on impulse. Now in direct view of…Geoffrey Lesage. I eye him while he fixates on the new items at his desk.

He picks up a leather ball gag and glares at a neon-pink dildo. My lips pull upward at the blonde blowup sex doll sitting on his office chair.

Dimitri grins and whispers, "And here I was about to call today miserable. Little did I know we'd be given such a precious gift."

I laugh as Geoffrey drops the ball gag and snags a piece of paper from a cardboard box. The big bold letters read: **RELAX**.

"Priceless," Brenden says into a bright smile.

I just notice Baylee's brother pressed to the wall beneath a Celeste poster. Zhen and Baylee are huddled with him, all three unable to contain their laughter.

I can't stop watching Baylee.

Cheeks big and dimpling, eyes lit up, she *laughs* through her body. Arms shaking, limbs quaking. She always used to do this thing in a laughing fit—she'd cover her face with two hands, not because she wanted it to stop. Because it was so overwhelming.

Because the emotion was almost too personal for anyone to see.

On stage, she'll give her all, but real life isn't a performance. She doesn't have to be an open book to everyone. Just like I don't.

I wait for her hands to fly upwards.

"Shit, he's coming!" someone shouts and rips into the moment.

It's a mad dash.

People zip back into the gym, sprinting through sets of blue double doors, and just as I turn, I hear Geoffrey.

"Don't move! You seven!"

Slowly, I rotate to meet his flushed face, cross. Full of indignation. He waves an accusatory finger at the seven of us closest to the office. "Names. Each of you. *Now.*"

He met us ten days ago, and I know he memorized our names. He's just dramatic.

His pinched glare lands on me first. (Let's just say he's not *shocked* that I'm here.)

"Luka Kotova," I announce easily.

"Dimitri Kotova," my older cousin says, still grinning. Unable to mask his joy.

Geoffrey jabs a finger towards another artist.

"Baylee Wright."

My stomach drops, and her brown eyes flit to me, cautious. Features tight. In the past few years, I've been in trouble with Corporate a lot (for stealing), but not with her attached. This'll be the first time since we signed our contracts, and I have no idea what to expect.

Maybe they won't even bat an eye. Maybe they're opening the door to our prison cells.

Maybe they're waiting for us to walk through, just to slug us in the face.

I do something I probably shouldn't.

I nod to her like *it's okay. I'm here for you.* I wish I could hug her. I wish I could just hold her hand. Something.

Anything.

"Brenden Wright." He shifts warily as he says his name.

"Zhen Li."

This—the blow-up doll, ball gag, dildo joke—it's not something those two would ever construct. Zhen and Brenden are like the unofficial welcoming committee of Aerial Ethereal. Corporate has even sent them on luxury trips, just to convince patrons to shill out thousands of dollars to AE.

I don't pull my gaze off Baylee, and she lifts hers to the ceiling, collarbones jutted out like she's caging a pained breath.

I adjust my gym bag which feels like a million pounds now.

"Sergei Kotov."

My head swerves to my older brother, but he's only the sixth person in the hallway. The seventh is blocked by Geoffrey's wiry body.

He sidesteps and my face falls further.

No.

"Thora James."

Muscular shoulders and a short stature, Nik's twenty-two-year-old girlfriend stands at five-foot-two, her dirty-blonde hair wet from a shower. She's dressed down in a baggy Ohio State shirt, a college that she dropped out of to pursue her aerialist dreams.

It's not like she was given a job at AE for talent alone. She worked hard, and as a lead in Amour, she doesn't need to get in *any* kind of trouble.

Thora looks around uneasily, stapled papers in hand. "I'm not really sure what's going on. I was just stopping by to drop off some forms…" Her almost black eyes dart around the hallway. "I mean, I can come back later…" She starts stepping backwards.

"*Don't*," Geoffrey snaps, finger aimed at her forehead.

Thora tries to freeze, but papers fall out of her hand, and nervously, she trips over her own feet to collect them.

Dimitri laughs, but it dies as Geoffrey verbally scolds him. I don't listen.

I bend down and help Thora collect her forms. I barely glance at the papers, but I do catch the word *Wellness Policy*. The forms must be normal and routine.

"Thanks," she whispers to me. We stand up at the same time.

Geoffrey addresses us. "Congratulations, the seven of you will be signed up for a *sexual harassment* seminar tonight. You'll be emailed the location and time. It's mandatory, so don't even contemplate skipping." Storming back into his office, he slams the door.

Thora frowns. "Who was that?" She looks to me for answers, but Dimitri's mouth is bigger than mine.

"A man who can't take a joke," Dimitri says.

Zhen picks up his Nike gym bag. "Maybe because it wasn't funny, Dimitri."

Dimitri cocks his head. "I saw you laughing."

"*Everyone* was laughing," Brenden cuts in, "but the humor kind of dies when we're the ones getting into trouble for a prank we didn't start."

Dimitri scoffs. "Don't know what you're talking about—it's still fucking funny."

These arguments happen about every hour in our suite, and I stay out of it. Dimitri likes to hear his own voice, and Zhen has known him way too long for any real fight to start. He'll pull Brenden out of the crossfire after a while, and it'll all simmer down until it heats up again.

By now, it's just ordinary.

Sergei steps forward. "Let's just end this. Whoever set up the joke, go confess." He wants someone to fall on a proverbial sword so he doesn't have to go to the sexual harassment seminar.

(Predictable.)

No one speaks at first.

So I say the logical thing, "It could've been someone who fled into the gym." I know a handful of cousins who would've put a dildo in Geoffrey's office.

"Or it could be *you*," Brenden retorts.

It stings, but our history together has always been strange. I can't touch it now. I don't want to, but I remember how moral he is. It's a *good* quality. Something I admire. He started a petition when he was sixteen to have equal pay for all minors. The girls had a lower salary than the boys.

He helped get his sister, and mine, a pay raise.

And there I was stealing a souvenir cup and three bags of Cheetos.

I stuff my hands in my pockets. "It's not me," I say coolly, knowing why he'd believe it was.

"You could be lying."

"Yeah, I'm not."

"What about Dimitri?" Baylee asks, steering the attention off me.

(Thank you, Bay.)

"Not me, Baybay." Dimitri walks backwards towards the elevators. "This is someone else's *genius* handiwork."

I watch him leave with Sergei, and Brenden and Zhen speak in Mandarin before following in tow. The only way out are those elevators.

Baylee is slower to exit. We barely speak at work unless it's necessary, and we haven't even tried to talk as frankly as we did in her suite. I worry that I might've scared her back then.

Her body is rigid, eyes pinned ahead. If she looks at me, it means she still cares about the possibility of us.

It means there's something still worth fighting for.

It's what I think. I stare intently, hoping. Praying she'll glance back. She passes me, staggering slightly.

(Come on, Bay. Don't give up on me. Don't give up on us.)

My stomach knots, and I fixate on her back as she leaves. Is it wishful thinking? Am I just dreaming—believing we could have something real outside of the gym?

She waits at the elevators, says something to her brother, and in the briefest moment, her head turns. Her eyes touch mine, and my lips begin to rise.

Hers pull up too. In a small, heartfelt smile.

"Okay, I'm…" Thora's confusion steals part of my attention, then all of it as Baylee disappears onto the elevator.

I help her out. "That was Infini's new choreographer. Let's just say I could cough and he'd glare."

Thora winces. "That bad?"

"Oh yeah."

"He might not last long." Always the optimist.

"Maybe." In my world, bad things don't disappear. They fester and extend for *years*.

Thora wears concern and sympathy, but her eyes are on the double doors. "He's not going to be happy." In the tiny squared window, I just barely distinguish Nikolai.

He ties up the aerial silk so no one slips on the fabric, finished for the day.

She's right. Nik will be pissed and agitated that some choreographer—on a different show—just sentenced his girlfriend and siblings to a sexual harassment seminar. And there's nothing that he can do about it.

He won't pull strings for this. My brother saves his influence for much bigger, more serious issues.

"You know," I say, swinging my head towards Thora, "besides you, there's not much that makes Nik happy. So it'll be like any other day." I don't think people remind her enough how much she's affected my brother. How much joy she brings him.

Before Thora, Nikolai just swam through the motions of life, living dully day by day, sacrificing everything for Timo, Kat, and me. Then he started falling for Thora, and I saw him smile for no reason at all. I saw him *breathe* wholly and freely, and it'd been some of the best days of my life.

For once, my brother finally got something good.

Thora scowls. She's so laidback and down-to-Earth that her "resting bitch face" or RBF (as she calls it) throws me off a lot. She's not mad, but really, she looks it.

She shakes her head at me. "I'm not the only happy thing in his life…he loves you. And Timo and Katya."

I shrug because I recognize that Nik loves us. I see that in everything he's done for us, but I can't say that I've made him happy. I've disappointed him, caused him anxiety and restless nights. I wasn't what he needed.

Guilt hurts like twenty knives in my gut, and I laugh into a weak smile. I don't have the strength to wrench out the blades. So I feel them.

(Every fucking day.)

Thora is about to reply, but Nik pushes aggressively through the double doors. Cellphone in hand, he aims for *me*. Gray eyes zeroed in, single-minded.

"What?" I ask, knowing it's nothing good.

"Timo just lost *nine-hundred* dollars on roulette," he says. "I need you to go to the casino and talk to him because I'm not getting through."

I frown. "He was just here. I saw him like ten minutes ago."

"Then it took him less than five minutes to lose nine-hundred bucks." Nik's muscles are hard as rock, more tensed than me. "Five more minutes and he'll be down another grand. *Go.*"

"Okay, okay." Gym bag on my shoulder, I turn but hesitate. "I can't promise I'll be able to tear him away." I couldn't last time, but Nik knows this. "When Timo's down, he just says he's going to win it all back."

"But he'll listen to you over me," Nikolai rebuts.

I'm the good cop to Nik's bad cop. In one breath, we're co-parents. I'm the consoling *mother* figure, who hugs a crestfallen Katya. Who soothes a heartbroken Timo. And then in another breath, Nikolai is scolding me, and I'm back to being a child in his eyes.

(Our relationship is weird.)

"Okay, I'll try." Before I turn around, he speaks again.

"And I need you to take Katya to the gynecologist. She has an appointment next month, or the month after—I'll text you the date and time."

My face scrunches. "Since when does she need to go to the gynecologist?" I shake my head. "She's not…" *having sex.* I just see Kat as a little girl. She's not having sex. She's not…even dating. Right?

I remember how she called herself a *woman*, and then the makeup, needing to keep things private from Timo and me and—*shit.*

Katya is getting older.

She could definitely be having sex. Or at least, acting on romantic feelings and desires. I don't want to think about it.

"She needs to go," Nik explains. "She told me that most girls go by the age of fifteen." He expels a heavy breath, and he glances at Thora for confirmation.

"I mean…some, not all…" Thora shrugs. "It just depends."

"On what?" I ask.

"On whether you're having complications, or want to be more informed, or are sexually active—"

"She's not," Nikolai says like it has to be a fact.

"Is it so bad?" Thora wonders. "Timo said he lost his virginity at fourteen. Just because she's a girl…" she trails off at the thickening tension.

Nik and I exchange a look, both of us knowing Thora is right, but our feelings don't waver. Double standards exist, and I know we're at fault for perpetuating them. My huge extended family bubble-wraps Katya because we're all afraid. We know men.

We know *Vegas*.

I think we'd just rather Katya stay young forever.

Lingering for a short second, I ask Nik, "Why aren't you taking Kat to the doctor?"

"Because I have a show, and I'm sure she'd rather you do it."

(True.)

My brother must assess Thora's features because he states, "Something happened."

She lets out a breath. "You're not going to believe it."

I check my emails on my way out. The seminar is scheduled for 7 p.m. Thirty minutes from now. I realize that I'm going to have to choose between the seminar and my little brother.

Really, the choice isn't hard at all.

ACT SIXTEEN
BAYLEE WRIGHT

The Masquerade uses their third-floor conference rooms for banquets, family reunions, conventions, and apparently sexual harassment seminars, set-up purely for the seven of us.

We've been sitting on uncomfortable fold-out chairs, facing a blank projector screen, for about an hour now. Geoffrey emailed and said the lecturer was running late. And apparently so is Luka.

"It's all a lie," Zhen theorizes between Brenden and me.

"Geoffrey wants us to sit in silence," Brenden agrees.

"We're in time-out."

"No one is coming."

I stand up, needing to walk around and to mentally separate myself from Brenden and Zhen.

My temples pound and my stomach growls. None of us had time to grab food, and it's already 8 p.m.

I did spare a second to snatch my journal from my bunk.

Even though I'm slightly terrified, I'm giving my list to Luka tonight. No welching. No backing out at last minute. I've cemented my decision in my mind.

My palms sweat the longer he's absent. I slide down the gold wallpaper and sit on the cream carpet, journal clutched tight. I worry that Luka won't show up and it's some grand sign from the universe. Telling me that I'm not supposed to reach out to him.

Yelling at me to *stop*.

I swallow hard and observe my surroundings. Sergei sleeps upright on his chair next to a preoccupied Dimitri who texts on his phone.

Thora reads a paranormal romance novel, and her scowl withdraws when she casts smiles to the door. In the squared window, I spot the outline of her tall boyfriend pacing back and forth. Nikolai has been outside for five minutes, waiting for this to end too.

"Maybe we should feel badly," Zhen suddenly says from the front row. "We laughed at something inappropriate. We embarrassed our choreographer."

Dimitri pockets his cell. "You better be joking."

"I'm not." Zhen turns partially around. "I can't expect you to understand, but we are in the wrong. Whether we put together the prank or not."

Brenden thinks about this. "Zhen's probably right."

Dimitri leans back. "And what's that supposed to mean, Zhen? *I can't understand?* Understand what? Sexual harassment? If this is about Baylee's juggling balls, we've been here. She doesn't care what I call them. I *asked.*"

I don't want to take sides in fights that have already ended years ago. Or at least, they were supposed to end.

"This seminar could help everyone," Thora chimes in, trying to mediate. "I mean, it could be fun? Who knows…?"

Dimitri gives her a once-over. "Fun? Does the chair and the floor excite you too?"

"Dimitri," Zhen says with the shake of his head.

"I said *excite*, not arouse." Dimitri outstretches his arms, but off of Zhen's stone-cold disapproval, his defenses lower. "Fine. I'll take the seminar seriously."

"Thank you."

My mind reels, and from the floor, I end up saying, "You know who should've been called into one of these seminars? Kirk Evans."

The second I let loose Kirk's name, Luka saunters inside the conference room. He carries three to-go bags with a bright red *Retrograde* logo, an Elvis-themed diner inside the Masquerade.

"Who's Kirk Evans?" Sergei yawns, waking up.

Luka holds my gaze as he nears the cluster of metal chairs. So much is buried beneath that single look—I can't even uncover all the sentiments. My chest falls in a shallow breath.

"A *dick*," Dimitri says curtly.

"What'd he do?" Thora asks. She's really new to AE and hasn't been around for the huge drama.

Luka is almost invisible to everyone. He sets down two to-go bags on an empty chair. I have trouble watching anyone else but him.

As the air conditioning kicks in, Brenden zips up his windbreaker, and he answers, "Kirk 'jokingly' opened shower curtains on girls."

"No," Sergei says, disbelieving.

"Yeah." Brenden nods. "And he thought it'd be funny to slap all of their asses before opening night."

Including mine.

Luka looks at me again. Noticing me staring. He actually…he starts to walk over. I sit up straighter, knees bent.

Thora scowls. "Kirk was fired then?"

The room tenses.

"No," Zhen replies. "He was transferred to Montreal."

"Last I heard," Brenden says, "he got a raise."

Aerial Ethereal might've done little to nothing, but Kirk did get decked in the face—by none other than Dimitri Kotova. He doesn't unearth that fact. He's competitive when it comes to Nikolai, but with other things, Dimitri doesn't really ask for praise.

A few feet away from me, Luka glances back at the others. "Hey, I brought food."

Dimitri reaches for a bag. "Thank God."

Brenden glares. "Stolen?"

"Greasy?" Zhen wonders, plucking a second bag.

"Receipt's inside, and it's mostly grilled chicken and vegetables."

If he were *anyone* else, Brenden would immediately say *thank you* but a painful, awkward second passes. Luka doesn't acknowledge me until Zhen hands Brenden a to-go container and inspects the contents. My brother finally nods to Luka in appreciation.

Just like that, they all start eating and their irritations about Luka's tardiness vanishes. His generosity goes a long way.

I'd say it was all a ploy, but he probably would've brought food regardless of being late.

Without a word, like this is as common as any other day, Luka sits right beside me.

Knees bent, leaning against the wall. We're so close that I see the rise and fall of his chest when he breathes.

I inhale. His shampoo must be citrusy, but he smells mostly like peppermint candy. It's a scent that I want to lean into, but I'm afraid to risk it in front of Dimitri.

His cousin is eyeing us a little, but he's mostly busy eating.

I watch Luka open his paper to-go bag. He pulls out candy boxes of Swedish Fish, Hot Tamales, and then a can of original Pringles. Lastly, he hands a plastic container to me.

I put my journal on my lap and grip the container. Snapping the lid open, my heart skips.

He bought me a grilled cheese.

I'm floored for a second. That he remembered how much I like grilled cheese, especially after my dad died. That he thought about me when he ordered.

My throat closes. I don't think I'll ever find someone like him. The thought devastates me, but I'm also just happy to have this moment. *Torn.* I wonder if I'll always be torn when I'm near him now.

"Thanks," I say quietly.

Luka nods and pops a can of Fizz Life. Gently, he tilts his head towards me and speaks hushed so no one else can hear. "You'll tell me if I overstep or anything? The line's kind of…fuzzy." The intensity of his gray eyes pummel me. It's like he's asking if I'm okay with him moving closer in my life or if it's too uncomfortable for me. Wondering if I'm scared.

I am scared.

I'm terrified, but I want more of him. *So much.* "Yeah," I say, breathless. "Actually, I need to ask you—"

"Hey, you two," Dimitri calls us out loudly and makes a gesture that means *separate.*

All eyes plaster onto us, and the chatter dies down. I reluctantly pick myself off the floor and carry my grilled cheese and journal.

Luka follows.

When I sink beside my brother, he shakes his head at me.

"What?" I whisper with a shrug. I could cry. I'm just…I hate this. I hate lying to Brenden, and I hate that he believes the *worst* about Luka. To the point where I can't even sit next to him without seeming weak and disloyal.

I lose my appetite, shutting my plastic container.

"What's going on there?" Sergei motions between Luka and me with a fork. The chairs aren't really even in rows anymore; we all sit in jagged lines, faced towards one another.

"Nothing," Luka and I say in unison.

Sergei's brows jump. "Sounds like *something* to me." He aggravatingly digs into his chicken. Maybe he's remembering that Luka called him a piece of shit while defending me.

"If no one's going to say it, I will," Brenden starts.

My eyes widen. "*No*, Brenden."

"*Yes*," he retorts. "Do you even remember what happened, Bay?" His voice is soft but also condescending.

"Yeah, I do. I lived it." My neck heats at all the pierced gazes on me. I don't like this. I don't want to do this. "Please, Brenden, *stop*."

He does stop out of respect for me, but Sergei apparently wants to *guess* now. "You two had a falling out?" Sergei speculates. "You got in trouble somehow?"

Luka shakes Hot Tamales into his mouth, not saying a word. Looking nonchalant about everything, but his muscles are flexed.

"No one's going to say anything?" Sergei questions like we're all acting suspicious.

Thora raises her hands. "I'm new. I mean, sort of."

"What were you doing with all those forms anyway?" Brenden asks, finding a way to dodge the subject.

Thank you.

"I just completed the Wellness Program," she says. "Technically I did a short version *before* I first auditioned, but I didn't land the job back then. Since they hired me on, they wanted a full physical." Thora drums her paperback and adds, "Oh, I'm all clear. In case you were curious or whatever…" She trails off and makes a face like she sucks at talking.

When we first met, I thought she disliked me, but she shook my hand for an awkward beat too long, actually admitted to being kind of awkward, and said she has RBF. Then Thora asked if I needed anything from the drugstore. She was about to make a quick stop for bathroom essentials.

She also tripped on her way out.

In a one-second meeting, I determined that I liked Nikolai's girlfriend—maybe even more than I like Nik.

Sergei kicks the leg of Luka's chair, stealing his attention. "Honesty is important between partners." Great, he's back to our secret. "So what's going on here?" He gestures again. From me to Luka. From Luka to me.

Luka looks to Dimitri.

Sergei glowers. "Why are you turning to him?"

"Cool it, Serg," Dimitri says huskily.

"That's my brother, not yours." Sergei stabs his fork in his chicken breast. "Don't tell me to *cool it.*"

"Stop," Luka breathes.

No one hears him.

"I've been nothing but nice to you," Dimitri growls. "Don't start with me."

"You're petty. You've always been that way," Sergei says like it's written in stone, but it's not. "You're still bitter that I nicknamed Nikolai the God of Russia, and it caught on. Or is it deeper? Is it that, as hard as you try, you'll never measure up to him or to me?"

Dimitri looks murderous, face blood-red. Two controlled breaths later, he growls, "I don't fight with family. So either you find Oz and grow a motherfucking brain or I'm leaving you with your stupid thoughts."

"It hurts because I'm right," Sergei says pointedly.

Dimitri kicks off his chair, and it folds into itself. "Sorry, Zhen. I'm not sticking around for this shit show." He picks up his water bottle and glances at Luka. "You're on your own, kid."

He's been on his own. It's not like Dimitri offers security all the time. It's mostly an illusion. It exists in theory, but not reality. Not when Luka has needed it.

The door slams closed.

Dimitri is gone, and in his absence, the room weighs down like a hundred tons. I feel Luka eyeing me and my untouched food. He'd normally lean on the legs of his chair, hike his feet up on another seat—but he's too uncomfortable. Like me.

Sergei won't stop digging. "Why is it a secret?"

Luka explodes. "We got caught, okay! Leave it *alone.*" He rocks forward, elbows on his knees.

My stomach cramps. *You can't tell him the truth.*

You can't tell him the truth.

No one can know.

Sergei frowns. "Not until you tell me—"

"Cocaine." Luka glares. "*Stop* pressing."

I try to let out a breath.

"Cocaine? You can't do *drugs*, Luka." Sergei goes off on a tirade, yelling at Luka about the consequences of cocaine use. Upset about our past that's an utter lie.

Luka buries his face in his hands.

Sergei has reason to be concerned. Drugs are a serious issue—one that we both disliked using as a front. Back then, we felt like we had no choice.

The long-winded rant ends when the lecturer arrives. Toting a briefcase, the mousy man apologizes for being late and struts to the front of the conference room. He's not alone.

Dimitri returns and plops down on a front seat, arms crossed. I'm not that surprised. This is a mandatory AE function, and he made a promise to Zhen to take the seminar to heart. The good inside of Dimitri can outweigh his short temper.

I have so much trouble paying attention.

I zone out most of the seminar. Even when the lecturer hands us packets to fill out, I forget to write my name in one of the blanks. He reminds me when I turn it in.

Officially, I'm in the worst kind of trance. I feel inside-out and winded. I try to eat my grilled cheese, but it goes down like a lump.

"You're all free to leave," the lecturer tells us.

I check the time on my cell. It's already 10 p.m. and everyone files out quickly. I move so slowly it's almost annoying in my head, but my body and mind don't seem to be in sync.

"You coming with?" Brenden asks me, just as I exit onto the third-floor lounge area: couches, a coffee bar—that sort of thing.

I rest against the wall. "Where are you going?"

Zhen already strolls to the gold elevators.

The concern on my brother's face could fill the Pacific Ocean. "To the suites."

I'm afraid if I go to bed at this very moment, I'll never want to get up. "Later. I think I'll get a coffee or something first."

"I can stay. If you need company—"

"No, it's okay." I really don't want to be alone, but I can't look at Brenden right now without seeing the lie I told him years ago. "You go on without me."

Brenden hesitates, conflicted, but after a long moment, he leaves for the elevators.

I clutch my journal to my chest, and when I glance to the right—I spot Luka at a brass water fountain. He pretends to take a sip, but he's clearly watching my brother depart.

When Brenden slips inside the elevator, Luka straightens up and heads over to me.

He sees my expression. Sees my sadness and pain.

His stride is unwavering. Strong and certain. I need him. And I can't fake it anymore. I can't act like I don't miss him. I can't act like he's meant *nothing* to me these past four years.

My heart is hollow in his absence. I feel despair.

He approaches me, no reservations.

No reluctance. He's a foot away, and my chest collapses as his hands rise—he touches me.

Luka *holds* my cheeks, my face, and his body heat warms every inch of me. I clutch his waist and look up.

Luka dips his head down, our breaths trapped. Our lips a kiss away. Deeply, he whispers, "Let me take you somewhere, please." *Please.*

Hold me.

Touch me.

Kiss me. I ache to bridge the space between us, but we can't kiss in *this* hotel. Being this close, we're already risking more than we ever have.

I nod more than once, and his hand falls to my hand, interlacing our fingers. Tenderly and discreetly, he kisses the top of my hand, and then he leads me out of the hotel.

I'm in a daze again.

This time, I feel like I'm dreaming.

ACT SEVENTEEN
LUKA KOTOVA

I choose a diner off the strip, a place I'm sure no artists or employees of Aerial Ethereal will be. It has a total of three Yelp reviews, all of which are two stars. The service apparently sucks, and one woman found a spider in her eggs.

We're not going for the service or the food, so I don't really care. I could've picked an alleyway, and it'd be just the same to me.

In the back of a yellow cab, we sit side-by-side. Vegas lights dance across Baylee's features as the car bumps along the city street. I can see the weight of our past bear on her chest. I can see the emotion tunnel its way forward in her eyes—because I *feel it all* inside of me.

It's nearly five years of silence. Of avoidance. Of not being able to talk about our love and our lives. It's *everything* piled a million feet high. And then falling straight down on top of us.

Baylee unzips her wrist wallet and then quickly zips it back up, hands shaking.

My next step is instinct. Impulse, just like before in the hotel. I drape my arm over Bay's shoulders and clutch her tight.

Closer. Firmer, and I feel her try to breathe deeper.

She eases back and rests her head against the crook of my neck, and I wrap my other arm around her tense frame. Holding her as protectively, as warmly, as I can.

Bay grips my arms like she'll descend into darkness if she lets go, and we stare straight ahead. A raw wound still exists in us, healed crudely, and for a long while, the stitches have slowly been breaking apart.

We had *no* closure. There was no time to talk or say goodbye. Our relationship was just over in a gut-wrenching second.

"I'm sorry," I whisper. "I'm so sorry, Bay."

She lifts her head, and she nods a few times before shrugging. "Me too." Her voice cracks.

I cup her cheek, our eyes reddening, and she clasps my wrist like it's too much. Our faces contort—this indescribable pain gnaws at us. There's a lot unsaid that we need to talk about—a lot we have to finally get out. At first, I don't even know where to start.

Then I do.

Assure of myself.

"I still love you," I say strongly. "There was never a moment I didn't."

Her chest lifts in a deep breath, and she starts to shake her head, almost in disbelief. Bay stops herself midway, and she says, "I think I love you."

I actually smile. "You *think*?"

Her eyes pool, but she rubs them before any tears fall. "I *do* know, but it's been four years, Luka."

"Five," I correct.

"Somewhere in between," she nods. "And I'm *terrified.*" Her whole face warps as she fights tears, and I hug her to my chest while her hands cover her face.

"It's okay." I kiss the top of her head, my stomach overturning—my body stringent. I understand. "It's the idea of us, right?"

She's scared that we only love the idea of one another. That we've changed, and we have *no clue* if we're good for each other now like we were back then.

Bay nods again, and after collecting herself, she sits up much straighter.

Away from me.

I feel as sick as she looks. This shouldn't be that hard, but there's so much—so much that we can't *do* because of the contracts. What are we striving towards if we can't ever be together?

I see that hopelessness cloud her eyes, and I want to prove her wrong. To show her that we're meant to be *together.*

Even if it means toying with a punishment much bigger than us.

ACT EIGHTEEN
BAYLEE WRIGHT

I'm incredibly nervous. More nervous than every first date I've ever been on. Usually I can articulate myself fine, but I feel like I'm one second away from stumbling over my words and feelings.

I sit tensely across from Luka in a tattered booth of an alien-themed diner. Stuffing peeks out of the ripped, midnight-blue vinyl seats, and UFO cardboard cutouts swing from stained ceiling tiles.

I kind of love how odd it is.

The sole waitress took our drink order and has been chatting up the only other customer, a mustached man at the bar. She's not really attentive towards Luka and me, which gives us more privacy.

I observe Luka, mostly. He stacks all the sugar packets together, a cigarette between his fingers. He hasn't lit it yet, but I think he wants to. I don't mind if he smokes in front of me; I never really have. But maybe he's not sure if that part of me has changed.

His eyes flit up to mine, a charismatic smile twinkling in them. "You still do that thing."

"What thing?" I almost smile off of his, but instead, I spin a silver ring on my pinky finger, anxious.

"Watch your surroundings. In this case, *me*." Luka stares so deep into me. As though he's reaching for the person I am—or rather, the young girl I was. The girl he knew.

I stop fiddling with my ring. "Would you rather stay invisible?"

His smile envelops his whole face. "I want to be seen by you. Everyone else, it doesn't really matter to me."

I bring my foot to the seat, knee bent. It's getting hard to look at him directly. Partially because we've been forbidden to stare at each other for years—and partially because he's so much older. And hotter. I didn't think that'd be possible.

As his smile slowly fades, the weight of everything we lost compounds and stretches taut between us.

"You look older," I say the obvious—but I'm not taking it back.

"So do you." He skims me.

I skim him, the table separating us.

Both of us wondering what else is different. What stayed the same. My style hasn't really altered. Outside of work, I wear a pair of spandex pants and a long-sleeved Nike top.

He's similarly dressed down like he used to be: jeans and a plain navy tee.

Luka runs a hand through his tousled, dark brown hair. Troubled lines form across his forehead, and then he eyes my floral-printed journal that I set by the salt shaker.

He hasn't asked what it is, and I haven't surfaced *the list* yet.

Luka nods to me. "Maybe we should start at what you planned to say."

"Back at the hotel?" I just remember being cut off mid-sentence.

"Yeah." He leans back, but then leans forward. "Or, you know, we can talk about how you are." The intensity in his gaze speaks that question: *how are you doing, Bay?*

"How I am," I repeat, thinking for a hot moment. I watch his fingers pause on the sugar packets. "It really depends on what area. Like work?"

"I work with you." Luka begins to smile again. "I know how you are at work."

"Then personal, health, financial, romantic—"

"All of it," he interjects and spreads his hands out. Sitting close, I wonder if he wishes the table disappeared.

I lean back—almost afraid of taking the risk. He's always been the one to plunge first. I rest my arms loosely on my knee. *All of it.* "I want to know the same about you."

"Trust me, my life has been boring."

"You're so far from boring, it's ridiculous." I smile off of his smile again. It seems so unbelievable how easily he can flood me with warmth, but reality claws behind us. Ready to tear us apart, and my smile lasts two-point-two seconds before deteriorating completely.

Luka checks his canvas wristwatch. "Practice is at five a.m."

"And?" Is he…saying what I think he's saying?

"And we have six hours until then." *Yep, he is.* "Want to pull an all-nighter with me, krasavitsa?"

I try to stifle my reaction at krasavitsa. It means *beautiful* in Russian. "Stop," I say into *another* smile.

"What should I stop, krasavitsa?" he teases. The old term of endearment seriously does a number on me.

I put my hand to my face to hide this uncontrollable giddiness— that I've only felt from him. "You're terrible."

He laughs into the most gorgeous smile. This is where he'd hug me. Kiss me.

As our cold reality bites us, the lightheartedness drops very abruptly. We're not those young kids anymore. Being careless and fun on our free days.

He's not dribbling a basketball between my legs and taunting me to steal it. I'm not whacking my bat at machine-sputtering balls while he announces, "Bases are loaded. She's 5-and-0. No one can strike out the indomitable, undefeatable Baylee Wright," all behind the fence. He's not hollering baseball chants like "pitcher's gotta big butt"—and I'm not buckled over laughing with my face in my hands.

New York with Luka—it seems like ages ago. Like a different lifetime.

Our gazes search one another. For hope that I'm not sure exists.

I cut into the silence first. "Is it sad that six hours seems too short?"

"It feels like five minutes," he agrees.

I pile a few sugar packets onto his, and I think aloud, "Marc always said that we were lucky. We got what no one else did." *A second chance.* "We're greedy, aren't we?" Just being here, we're taking advantage of the system when they ordered us not to.

Guilt wedges into me.

But not enough to leave this booth. Does that make me a terrible person?

The chiseled lines of his face overtake the angelic. "We've been selfless for five years, and Corporate is the one that put us in the same show together."

"Corporate," I repeat, the word carrying so much weight.

Luka Kotova is the only one that calls Aerial Ethereal by that generic name. It was always his way of bastardizing a company that set rules he said he could never tolerate.

The familiarity is like stepping into an ice bath. Waking me up to the past and present. Now it's my turn to stare straight into him.

And I say, "That hasn't changed."

He tries to edge closer, but with the table—it's impossible.

I notice the cigarette in his fingers. "You can light it. I'm not grossed out by smoking."

Stiffly, he procures a tiny box of matches from his pocket. After lighting the cigarette and blowing smoke upwards, he says, "What's with the journal?"

I straighten up. "It actually ties into one of the areas I mentioned before."

He scans me, head-to-waist, like the answer is written on my body. "Which area?"

"Romantic…" I trail off as the waitress returns with our coffees. "Thank you," I say and she asks if we're ready to order.

Luka flips open his plastic menu and spontaneously chooses the first thing he sees. He used to do this all the time.

My lips almost pull upward because I love that he still does.

"The extraterrestrial experience," he tells the waitress.

"I'm good with a coffee," I say, and as she leaves, I lean over the table and peer at his menu. We both read the description of the food called *extraterrestrial experience*, and I start laughing loudly.

"Fuck," he laughs with me. He just ordered a deep-fried Moon Pie.

"I know you'll still eat it." I laugh harder, not wanting to lean back just yet.

"Will I?" he teases. "I could be a picky eater now, and you wouldn't know it." He meant it to be lighthearted, especially since I've seen him eat the same stuff he used to: candy, pizza, huge hamburgers, you name it—all in the past ten days. But an undercurrent of sadness clings to his statement.

"That's true." I lower my ass to the seat.

"That was stupid. I'm the same," he says, more serious. "I *promise*, I'm the same."

He's had nearly half a decade without me. After what happened to us, how could we both be the same? Parts of us did change, but if I could choose anyone to let discover me and for me to be able to discover them, I'd choose Luka.

So I pick up my journal. With a deep breath, I start, "You were my first *everything*. And then, it just…ended."

"You were my first too," he reminds me.

This is going to hurt. "Did you have a second?" I ask outright.

Luka leans back like he got kicked in the stomach. He snuffs out his cigarette in an alien-head ashtray, and then he rakes another hand through his hair.

Yes, his silence says. *He did.*

My limbs are achingly strict.

"A third? A fourth?" I pause for him to interject, and my throat nearly swells closed. "A fifth? A sixth—"

"It was five *years*." He shakes his head repeatedly. "I didn't think I'd ever be able to look at you or even say your name. If I knew we'd be here, right now, I'd have…" he trails off, because it's too painful to rewrite history like that.

"I'm not admonishing you."

"Admonishing." He laughs into a smile. We shouldn't be able to go from severity to mirth this quickly, but we do. We did.

All the time.

I try to restrain another smile, and then I groan because it won't stop growing.

"You still look at that thesaurus, don't you?" he asks, good memories illuminating his features. We both sucked at Aerial Ethereal's version of high school English, and they gave us thesauruses because we kept reusing the same words in essays. I was actually more interested in mine than Luka ever thought I'd be.

"I like looking at your doodles," I say seriously. He drew all over the margins of mine. Mostly of stick figures doing cartwheels and backflips. Some of us holding hands.

Sappy teenage moments that I wouldn't even consider erasing.

"You'll have to show me them sometime." He glances over his shoulder like he gathers his thoughts or strength, and when he looks back, his face is stoic but still breakable. "Did you have a second?"

"I tried dating. A lot in the past couple of years."

He cringes like it's hard to hear.

I know the feeling. I open my journal so I can explain better.

Luka shifts in the booth, and his gaze narrows at the frosted window. A green neon sign blinks *open* from inside. "Did you fall in love?"

That's what he's really worried about? If I fell in love? "No," I whisper. "Did you?"

"No," he says. "You're the only one." He licks his lips. "You're single?"

I nod.

"No friends-with-benefits?" he asks what I asked him in my suite.

"None."

He tries to relax, and he glances at my journal, noticing my handwriting. It's not a funny list.

It's not a joke or surface-level emotions. What I wrote is intimate. It's something I haven't even shared with Aunt Lucy. And I definitely wouldn't show this to Brenden.

My stomach clenches. I'm really scared, but I don't want to back out. "I meant to show this to you earlier today, but you were late and things just spiraled in a weird direction."

"I was trying to get my brother off the roulette table."

"Timo?"

"Yeah." Luka nods. "I pulled him away when he was four-hundred down."

"Ouch."

"It's not the worst," he tells me.

It's just another indication that I haven't been fully a part of his life recently. *I want to be.* I want to be so badly, and I ache for him to be a part of mine again.

My list inside the journal is a step towards something more. It's opening a door that's been slammed shut. It's not exactly *hope* since the contracts still remain fixed, but it's a hand reaching out to him.

Luka fiddles with the sugar packets. "What is it? The journal, I mean."

"It's a list." It needs more context so I add, "I've wanted to move forward, but every time I try, I just…something happens. I'm having trouble in an area—"

"Romantic," he states.

"Yeah…" I draw out the word to bide my time. "And I think you can help me fix it. You may be able to, you might not. It just feels like my only shot at healing. So I can move on."

"Move on from me?" he asks tightly.

"I don't know, maybe." I would've said *yes* before this season. Before the Infini shakeups. But I feel myself clinging to him more now than ever. "Can you just…?" I hand him the journal, my pulse out of control.

I sweat and overthink. And I scrutinize his focused eyes as they absorb my list.

ACT NINETEEN
LUKA KOTOVA

I raise the journal higher and nearly smile at her handwriting. It's always had character. Some letters swoop and pull together, connected but not cursive. Other letters stand on their own. Beautiful like her.

I have no theories about what this list could be, but a chill bites my neck—and I find myself reading slowly.

I lost my parents at 12. I lost you at 14. Maybe this isn't something you can help me with. Maybe it is. I'd be remiss not to try. (My dad would like that word "remiss"—it's in the summary of his novel

Bones Against Bones. You also drew a carrot next to it in my thesaurus. No reason why. You just did it. I miss being random with you.)

I pause here and glance up at Bay.

We were just talking about her thesaurus, and she'd written about it here—who knows how many days ago.

Our lives have been circling back to one another. To these *moments*. Not temporary like the throw of a boomerang. Not flashy enough to be fireworks, but we're something subtle—yet bigger. Greater.

Infinite.

Baylee holds my gaze, and I see a pain in hers that says she's still terrified.

"You look scared," I say.

She makes a face at me.

I make one at her. "Come on, I can tell."

She shrugs, tense. "What I wrote is heavy and it's not like we've been…" She gestures from her chest to mine.

"Communicating?"

Bay nods. "We just started talking outside of work."

"Right…" I wish we could erase all the years of silence. Replace them with actual memories of us together. So my name doesn't sit side-by-side with her parents, in a pool of everything she lost. More than anything, I want to return to what we were. To be here for her.

To give her what she needs.

But it's not real. Because "giving myself" means breaking the contract even more, which I'm not sure she's willing to do. Me—I'd do just about anything at this point.

(I realize I'm reckless like that.)

I return to her list.

We ended things abruptly (no breakup, no closure, nothing) and ever since, physical intimacy has been difficult for me. This is a more detailed list of what I'm having trouble with:

1. <u>any over-the-clothes touching</u>: every time I've done this with another guy, I feel really numb.

2. <u>all kissing</u>: refer to explanation #1.

3. <u>skin-to-skin contact</u>: I've been called a wooden board and a corpse by two different guys.

4. <u>oral (giving & receiving)</u>: I freeze up. Every. Single. Time.

5. <u>sex</u>: refer to explanation #4. I haven't been able to go this far with anyone else but you. Honestly, every time I try, it just feels like I'm betraying the memory of you (and I know that's so inaccurate and weird—we're not together). But I'm still holding onto you, and I have to figure out how to let go emotionally. I eventually want to be able to have sex again. I can't cling onto you forever.

I can't.

I reread the entire list three more times. My muscles strain, burning up—and the only time I move is to lean back, stunned silent.

She's still holding onto me.

All this time—I had no clue. I didn't even recognize the impact it'd have to leave Baylee the day after we screwed behind a costume rack. Without ever talking to her. We should have had time to discuss *us*.

Everything physical we had was layered in emotion. She was fourteen. I was only a year older, but we'd lost our virginities a year beforehand. We were both anxious, nervous, excited, so many sentiments pooling together as we fooled around, but I did everything I could to make her comfortable.

On a rare day her brother was gone, we had sex in her bedroom. I lit candles and put on a playlist of her favorites and mine. I can still see her escalating smile when "Hold Me Tight" by Johnny Nash started playing.

In our extraordinarily abnormal lives, that night was the most typical teenage experience we've *ever* had.

After that, it became hard to find locations to have sex. We didn't own cars. (Still don't.) Our places were almost always occupied, bedrooms shared, and so we chose riskier spots like the elevators, the hotel guest bathrooms, the seemingly empty backstage.

It'd all been good up until we got caught.

I put my hand to my mouth, thinking.

She can't move on physically until she moves on emotionally…is that it?

(Corporate did this.) I blame AE for not giving us a chance to have closure. Four-and-a-half years ago, I pleaded to talk to her. To end this cleanly.

I look up just as Baylee sips her coffee. She's watching my hands as I flip through the rest of the journal. The pages are blank except for this one. I close the journal but keep it near me.

I have so much to say, but I choose to start with this. "These 'two different guys' that called you a corpse—they can go fuck themselves."

"Funny," she says, corner of her lip rising, "that's exactly what I told them."

"You didn't," I say, knowing her.

"No, but believe me, I was put-off. I physically kicked the second guy out of my bed."

Good. "Kick his dick or balls?"

"I was an inch away. No one was more pissed than me."

"I don't know. I'm *pretty* pissed right now." I never envisioned Baylee with another guy. I could've, but I tried not to torment myself like that. Not even when I saw her with Sergei at the bar.

Now I'm thinking about her in bed with a bunch of pricks—it's as horrible as I thought it'd be. (I don't suggest this for anyone who has an ex.)

I literally can't stop shaking my head. It's like I have a neck spasm, and now I'm grimacing at the ceiling. *Fuckfuck.*

I reopen the journal.

She watches.

With knotted brows, I reread everything. *She's only had sex with me.* If I were another guy, it'd probably make me feel great, but since I've slept with other women—I just feel like an asshole. And terrible.

I feel terrible.

I risk a glance at Bay, but she's unzipping her wrist wallet and inspecting the contents.

"I finished," I say.

"I saw." She looks up. "You still weirded out?"

"I wasn't ever." But we're both sitting uncomfortably straight again. I know what the list boils down to, and it kills me that she's struggled for this long. "How can I help?" (I want to help.)

Before she can respond, the waitress carries out my plate of fried Moon Pie. We don't order anymore food.

I stab a fork into my discolored "extraterrestrial experience" and marshmallow oozes. I take a bite. It's burnt and tastes like canola oil and *soot*.

Still, I eat another piece.

Baylee finishes off her coffee. "My original plan was to talk with you about your experiences. How you were able to move on, how you got over me—"

"I didn't get over you," I interject, mauling the Moon Pie with my fork.

"Luka." Baylee shrugs at me. "Don't make me say it."

I lean forward. "*Emotionally* I didn't get over you."

"I'm not talking about emotionally. I mean *physically*." She eases forward too, elbows on the table. "Do you really want me to say it outright?"

"Yeah."

"You *fucked* other girls."

We both wear a pained expression. A thousand arrows pierce and plunge into my chest—but I force myself to stay close, not recoiling. Not rocking back.

I stay right here. "We were apart for five years. I didn't think I'd ever be with you. And I never…" I take a breath. "They were all one-night stands, Bay. I never even *dated* another girl. You could've had a boyfriend…"

"I didn't…it didn't work out like that," she says. "Sure, I dated, but none stuck. I tried casual sex, but it didn't happen either."

(I realize that.) "Okay, do you think…are you saying that I don't love you as much because I didn't wait around?" I shake my head vigorously again. "This isn't a reflection of my love for you, Baylee. It's *not*."

"Hey, I know it's not." She drops her leg to the ground and scoots even closer to the table. As close as me. "I remember what you told me when I was thirteen, right after I asked if you knew what to do."

She means in terms of sex.

I can't recall exactly what I said, but thick nostalgia hangs in the air. "What'd I say?"

"You told me that you knew more about sex when you were *seven* than you did math or science. Not because you experienced it but because you were surrounded by men who constantly talked about 'fucking' and 'masturbating.'"

My older cousins: too many to name. My older brothers: Sergei, Nikolai, Peter. It suddenly reminds me that I did grow up with Sergei. More than just his absence shaped me, and I didn't really recognize it.

I listen closely as she continues, "You were raised seeing sex as an act of pleasure. Like momentary fun. *Love* wasn't a requirement. So I understand." She exhales. "I just want to know how you do it. How do you shut off the emotional aspect in order to just get physical?"

"You want me to visually describe all of my one-night stands?" I go numb.

She sits more stiffly. "Not all of them—please, don't give me an exact number."

If she can't even stomach that, then how would this ever work? I can't even fathom sharing the details with her. I want to scrub them all right now, and she's asking me to push them to the forefront.

I shake my head over and over. "I want to help, not cause you more pain." She deserves to be unburdened by our past, but this'll make her freeze-up more.

And I'm not even touching the fact that helping her means she'll be having sex with other guys. *She should be able to*, the moral part of me screeches. *She deserves to be free of me.*

The selfish part of me yells and shouts to hold on for dear fucking life. I already gave Baylee up once. I don't want to lose her again.

She leans back, dejected. "It was a long shot anyway."

My mind speeds through our history, and I dump out a container of toothpicks, slowly pocketing them. "Look, you don't need to be fixed.

It's okay if you can't separate the emotional from the physical. Both ways are fine, and neither is wrong."

She nods once and then hesitates, contemplating. "Maybe I shouldn't do it like you then, but in order to do it my way, I need to figure out how to get over you emotionally. That way I can form an emotional connection to someone else and eventually be physical with them."

I have no idea how to do that. My emotions are still completely tied around her. I'm no sooner ready to let go than she is. But really, I want to help as much as I can.

A thought pops into my head.

"You could just need closure," I say. "Like a redo."

Her brows spike. "With you?"

"Yeah, with me." I give her a look and upright the empty toothpick holder. "Who else?"

"We can't touch." She stares off, remembering earlier at the hotel, the cab. Where I did actually touch her. More than Corporate says I'm allowed to.

I take my cell out of my pocket and set it down. "It's not going off. No one's scolding us by email." I lean forward for the thousandth time. "I can touch you—outside of the Masquerade, we can do anything we want. We've just never tried." There's the risk of being caught, but it lessens outside of the hotel.

We're older.

We have more ways to evade Corporate's vigilant gaze than we did before. More freedoms. Simple ones: I don't have a curfew set by Nikolai. She doesn't room with her brother anymore.

Baylee rotates her empty coffee cup, deep in thought.

"Hey," I whisper, "it's up to you, krasavitsa."

She may not be ready to mess with Corporate again, not after we were burned. Since this is our first long conversation, I don't know where her head is at. She was only initially seeking a *talk* about her list and my experiences. I pushed things further.

I always do. Nikolai was right. Give me an inch, I go five feet.

I'm okay with that. (Chastise me. Sue me. I don't care.)

Bay looks up. "Let me get this straight."

"Okay."

"You want to go through my list and *physically* redo everything with me?"

"Yeah," I say, absolutely serious.

"That really seems counter-intuitive." She eyes me. "Sleep with you to get over you?"

Yeah. It's dumb.

I think we're both fighting for a way to see each other more. *I'm* definitely fighting for a way. It's a narrow path, but I'll gladly cross it. "It's an ending. Something you didn't get before."

She stares off for a moment and says, "And maybe…maybe the sex and being with you will be different."

"Different how?" I ask, nerves infiltrating.

"Well, the last time we were together, we were young. Maybe it's all in our heads, right?" She winces at this thought. "Maybe time has changed us, and we're not good together anymore. We'll never know unless we try again. And then I can move on…"

Chills snake up my spine. I want to defend *us,* but in the same breath, she's throwing out a rope to this half-brained idea. The only idea that'll push us towards seeing each other outside of work. And watching her, I'm not even sure she believes we've changed that much.

She adds, "We'll put a close to *us.* That way I can finally have sex with other guys."

Pain flares in my gray eyes. "Or you could just be with me." I'm a dreamer.

She's a realist, even when it hurts. "So we'll be together in secret forever. And you'll never be able to kiss me in public. No one will know we're married, and when I get pregnant, I'll have to tell people the baby belongs to some no-named guy that looks strangely like *you.*"

"I'm already getting you pregnant?" I tease.

She rolls her eyes, but her face slowly morphs into a smile. "You're unbelievable." At this point, I'd usually pull her body against mine.

It's killing me not to touch her—not to do something *more*. I want Baylee Wright. No limitations.

No one controlling us.

I want to push the table away and fuck her how she should be fucked. Until her legs quake and her mouth parts and a moan escapes. I want to give her that.

Not some other dude. *Me.*

I nod to Bay. "Do you have a synonym for unbelievable?"

She raises her brows, acting all grave and poised.

I smile. "I bet you're missing your thesaurus right about now, huh?"

She throws a sugar packet at me, and we both start laughing. Bay is almost always serious, which I love because it makes breaking her New Yorker cool-as-steel attitude more fun and worthwhile.

But tension soon replaces our laughter, and we're back to the list.

Even if we quit our jobs, Marc would still enforce the no minors policy. There are no clear answers. There are just risks we can take and safe places we can hide. One is dull, the other is *full.* Of love, of life.

Our future, together, may be a dangerous mystery, but we can start somewhere.

I catch her gaze. "Let's just try to work on your list," I tell Bay, my old best friend, my ex-girlfriend—she meant the entire universe to me. She still does.

"Say we do this," she says, "and we basically perform my list together. When does it end?"

If the point is to bring closure to each act, there's only one answer to that. "When we finish all the numbers on your list." Then it's over.

I try to push this part, this fact, so far back in my head.

She's thinking hard.

"Okay?" I ask, but right as I do, my phone vibrates on the table. Her cell buzzes in her wrist wallet.

We both tense.

ACT TWENTY
BAYLEE WRIGHT

I check my phone and see a new group text. Involving me, Luka, and the sender.

Before I can even read the message, Luka's phone goes haywire, buzzing and vibrating incessantly. He can't click into the texts fast enough.

Luka curses in Russian and shoots up, dialing a number.

"What's wrong? Is it Timo?" It's what always happened in New York. He'd wander off wherever his heart took him, and the Kotovas would send out a mass S.O.S. to hunt for Timofei. On occasion, I'd join the search party.

"No, it's Kat." He puts his phone to his ear, hand on his head and he starts speaking hurried Russian.

Quickly, I stand and unzip my wallet, about to fish out some cash for the Moon Pie and coffee. Then I freeze at the sight of my cell screen. "Wait, Luka."

I pick up my phone. The sender in the three-way group text—it's Katya.

What should I do?!?!?!!! I heard Dimitri + Nik talking in the living room, and D was saying how he hasn't seen Luk since that seminar thing. D asked about Baylee's whereabouts. N said he didn't know but he'd ask me. They seemed mad, and I don't want to rat you out, Luk. So I hid in the closet, and now N thinks I'm missing.

WHAT DO I DO?!? – Katya

"Bay," Luka says, eyes pooled with concern. "What is it?"

"Katya sent us a group text." I show him my phone since her text might be stacked beneath his cousins' and brothers' panicked messages.

Luka reads rapidly, and then he puts his phone back to his ear. I can't understand all of the Russian, but as soon as he hangs up, he fills me in. "I told Erik I'd call her favorite restaurant, see if she's there."

A lie, obviously. "You realize that you're simultaneously loyal *and* disloyal."

"You realize my little sister has your new phone number when I don't even have it."

I shake my head. "Not the point."

"It's my point." His smile fades quickly, the buzzing reigniting.

I cup my phone, about to text Katya back. "We can't rope her into this."

"She's already in it." Luka holds out his hand towards my phone like *I'll take care of it.* "The three of us—me, Katya, Timo—we cover for each other all the time."

I have plenty of these memories. When I was thirteen, we all snuck out for ice cream at 3 a.m. and ate freezer-burned popsicles from a 24-hour convenience store.

Three nights later, Timo went alone to that same convenience store. When his family tried to find him, Luka lied to Nik about Timo's whereabouts, but Luka caught up to his little brother and joined him. So he'd be safe.

"But you all don't lie for each other if it's serious," I say, also remembering that he's ratted Timo out to Nikolai before. Concerned about Timo's late-night club-hopping.

Likewise, I was around when Timofei told Nik that Luka stole from an Aerial Ethereal office. Just an ugly paperweight, but Luk was pushing it too far. I was as worried as his family, and he tried really hard to stop stealing after that.

He didn't always succeed.

"Yeah," Luka says as he texts his sister, "but Kat won't see you and me as a bad thing."

I nod, knowing that she wants us all to be friends again.

My phone buzzes.

Rose Calloway would know what to do — Katya

I've seen Katya watch a few old reruns of *Princesses of Philly*, a cancelled reality show that starred the infamous Calloway sisters and their men. It aired when I was split apart from Luka.

"Rose Calloway is her favorite," I realize, somewhat downtrodden. Because when we were younger, I would've pegged her as a Daisy Calloway fan. But Rose is basically the equivalent to Posh Spice. Always chic-looking, a fashion designer, ice-cold but tough-as-nails.

"Yeah, don't get her started on PoPhilly," Luka says. "She'll literally discuss the 'dichotomy' of Connor Cobalt and Scott Van Wright for hours."

I almost gag at that name *Scott Van Wright*. "Don't say his last name."

"Why not?" Luka looks up.

"I don't want to hear you say my last name with *Scott Van* attached." He's disgusting and a villain masquerading as a romantic love interest for Rose when she *clearly* had feelings for Connor. "I'd rather the name be synonymous with Neal & Joyce Wright."

His gaze softens and he nods, but he's hung up on something because he keeps staring at me.

"What?"

Luka sends a text and pockets his phone. "You watch *Princesses of Philly*?"

My cell buzzes. "Everyone does."

I quickly read the text.

Unhide and tell Nik you just came back from dinner at Retrograde with me. And I got stuck talking to a girl (not Bay) at the bar. Sound good? — Luka

A girl.

Not me.

An imaginary scenario shouldn't put a bad taste in my mouth, but picturing him chatting up another girl at a bar—who could be Mrs. Right—feels awful.

Katya replies with a thumbs-up emoji.

Luka's brows furrow. "You didn't used to like watching TV or reading *Celebrity Crush* magazines."

He thinks I've changed.

I slowly pull out my five-dollar bill, trying to figure out how to approach this conversation. "I tried a lot of things after we…ended."

"But TV?" He digs into his pocket and pulls out his wallet. "You used to cry at the detergent commercials."

"They were emotionally manipulative."

"Bay," he says like *I know you. I was with you.*

I can't exactly stand my ground when past evidence has shown that television doesn't help my depression. It doesn't always make it worse, but it hasn't been my greatest outlet either.

Listening to music helps more. And being with people. Even if "being" is just lying together. Somewhere, anywhere. A park, a bench, the floor.

"Depression doesn't just go away," I tell Luka. "What'd you think— we broke up and I'd be *happy?*"

"Come on."

"No," I say, defenses rising. I exit the booth, the waitress and mustached man nowhere in sight. We're alone here. "You were gone, Luk, and I had to figure out how to cope without feeling like the world was pointless. So I watched some television, and I *liked* it."

"Oh yeah?" He throws down cash. "How'd it go afterwards? Screen is black. It's quiet. You're alone in your bed. What'd you feel then?"

Fine. I felt fine, and I'm allowed to watch television if I want to— but this is deeper than all of that. "You don't have to worry," I say. "It's not your job or burden—"

"Come on," he repeats, like I'm punching him in the heart. "Don't push me away now, *please.*"

I take a deeper breath, about to toss my own money down.

"Let me pay," he insists.

I hesitate.

"Please."

"Okay." I leave the booth, and as he follows behind, I decide to spin around. To confront him.

But I collide straight into his chest. My heartbeat is stuck in my throat, and Luka clasps my shoulders to steady me.

Our eyes descend each other in a boiling wave.

Then he drops his hands, much faster than I truly want. Distance separates us, this sliver of space that I want to close. If I listen to my heart at all, I know what I need to do.

"Okay," I say again, but this one has so much more meaning.

"Okay…" He scrutinizes me head-to-toe. "Okay to the list?"

I haven't agreed to his proposal yet, but the answer is right here. I'm irritated at an imaginary girl and an imaginary *chat* between her and Luka. It's obvious.

I need him. Whether it's closure or something else, I don't know. But I'm ready to take the risk.

I nod confidently. "Yeah, the list."

"Okay," he says, more assured, his lips beginning to rise.

"Now what?" I wonder.

Luka skims me again but then he nods to the door. "I'll call a cab. We need to get back to the Masquerade before Nik and Dimitri catch on, but tomorrow, the next day, we can figure it out."

"Okay," I say, feeling awkward all of a sudden. Like this just turned into a first date—*wait*, he paid for me. Was this actually a first date in his eyes?

It's all I can think about when he holds open the door for me.

I step onto the concrete sidewalk, the night sky dark. In fact, the whole street is nearly pitch-black except for a dim street lamp nearby. We're in a lifeless part of town.

We move closer to the lamp for light. Further away from the diner. A red brick wall is behind us—what looks like the side of an abandoned mattress factory.

I glance at Luka more than a few times. He's mostly nonchalant as he calls us a cab. Casual and cool, but he's almost always that way. I can't gauge his feelings.

I wonder if his stomach is fluttering like mine. I'm nervous again, but a more excited-nervous than before.

"I can take the bus," I offer. "It'll be cheaper, and that way we won't arrive at the Masquerade at the same time." *We're doing this.* Being together secretly.

This time, for the list.

Luka shakes his head. "I'll just pay for the cab fare and get dropped off at the Bellagio."

"That wasn't…" I take a breath, my nerves jumbling my words. More clearly, I say, "I didn't mean for you to pay."

"Don't worry about it." Pocketing his phone, he faces me, his back to the street.

"We'll split it then." I put my stamp on that, and before he protests, I add, "Did you see the Mets last year? They were *so* solid." I make a batting motion. I doubt he's kept up.

Luka hasn't been the biggest baseball fan, but in New York, he used to go to Mets games for me.

"Tied for second in their division, right?" Before I show surprise, he continues, "Send some of that luck to my team, please." He means basketball. I already know which team before he says it—the same way that I'm realizing he knew mine. "I'm in literal pain watching the Knicks."

They only won one game in February. I don't like basketball, but I always check the scores of the Knicks. It's one of the only ways I can picture Luka, even when I should've been forgetting him.

We both held on.

That's a real fact now. It nearly overwhelms me, but I take a deep breath.

"I saw their February scores," I tell him. "Terrible."

Luka smiles and teases, "Don't hold back on what you think."

"I won't," I say with a grin.

He takes a step closer, and our chests rise at the exact same time. A blip of Luka from the locker room flashes in my head. His large hand barely covering his package, his washboard abs and lean muscles, and the cascade of tattoos up his right leg. To his thigh.

I rub my lips together, trying not to appear hot and bothered. *Play it cool.* "You still like Broadways?" I wonder, wanting to know everything about twenty-year-old Luka.

"Oh yeah."

"*Rent* still your favorite?" I loosely stretch my arm. Acting as normal as possible.

"No." Another step closer.

I try to mask my disappointment. Now I know how it felt when he learned I like watching TV. "*Chicago* then," I guess.

Luka nods, moving closer.

My pulse thumps, and my body throbs, sensitive spots awakening that have been dormant for ages. His muscles flex like he's experiencing a similar reaction, and he's still at least five feet away from me.

The intensity of the moment, the tension that strings us together, engulfs me in a hot second. My gaze falls to the concrete.

"How's Rudy?" he asks.

My chest swells. "Alive," I say as I look up.

His soul-bearing eyes touch mine, knowingly. Years blaze through us. The week my parents passed away, Luka Kotova gave me Rudy. I was crying about how ridiculous it was that everyone kept bringing *flowers* when those just die, too.

That very afternoon, a bulbous slightly lumpy cactus showed up on my coffee table.

And Luka said, "That won't die. It'll probably outlive us all."

"And it has character," I said tearfully. We were all about things that had "character"—because life contained *more* that way. We weren't sure what "more" meant—what it was. But we always sought after its existence.

"It has character," he nodded. "What's it named?"

Rudy's name was completely and utterly *random*. And he's still alive today.

Luka nears, four feet away.

Three feet.

Two.

He reaches out and clasps my hand. Already drawing me to his body. "Come here," he says softly, and a magnetic force pulls us together. Bodies melded.

And his lips touch my lips, kissing me with years' long pent-up emotion. His hands encasing my soft cheeks, drawing me as close as can be, and my pulse speeds. The deep force of the kiss says, *I missed you.*

I love you.

I burst, lighting up. And I reciprocate with the same desperate aggression. Our tongues tangle like they remember where they once were. Natural and scorching.

I grip his shoulders tight, and his hands clutch my head, my waist, with masculine energy that turns me on to the millionth degree.

My hips bow towards his body, and he pushes me closer by pressing on the small of my back. Glued together, he drives another kiss deeper, further.

Luka breaks apart, just to breathe, "I'm picking you up." His lips brush my ear. "And spreading your legs wide open." Before I register, he hoists me effortlessly to his waist, my legs stretched apart around him.

A noise tickles my throat.

Luka used to call out what he was going to do to me, before he actually did it. I liked hearing him unflinchingly say *I'm putting my hard cock inside of you.*

He was confident back then, but he's ten times that now.

My lips sting and swell beneath the spine-tingling force of our kisses, and my legs wrapped around him, I pulse and pulse. Dizzying, I run my palms down his back, our lips never breaking.

He walks forward with me in his embrace.

My back strikes the brick wall with a gentle *thud.* Letting me catch my breath, Luka sucks the nape of my neck, hard and so sensitive—a moan escapes my lips.

I shudder against his build, and he presses his weight completely to me. The force is *amazing.* His hand returns to my cheek, and as I pant, he looks deep into me. His eyes caressing mine.

He's fucking me with his gaze. It's honestly so powerful and intimate that my head tries to loll backwards—and it hits brick.

Luka breathes shallow breaths with a rising grin. And then he kisses me, tenderly this time, and he whispers, "That was number two on your list." *Kissing.*

I think about the list's stipulations. "Does that mean it's the last kiss?"

"No," he murmurs. "We can do everything again."

But the list has an ending. We'll get our closure. On our terms. "Just until the list is completed," I state and breathe heavy, fisting his shirt, scared to let go.

Our noses brush as he dips his head lower. "Exactly." We're about to kiss again, but the cab's headlights glare, and a beam of light sweeps our bodies.

He eases back, and I drop down off of him. I'm tense.

He's tense.

I'm also more aroused than I've been in years. A sheen of sweat coats our skin, and the chilly night pricks my neck. Yet, I burn up from the moment.

I expect a wedge to drive us apart, but we're clinging to one another as long as we can. In secret. I hug him around the waist, and he hooks his arm around my shoulders, bringing me even closer and kissing the top of my head.

He also used to do that all the time as we evaded AE employees. A warm side-hug and a head kiss. While we walked and talked. Everywhere we went.

And I miss falling asleep in his arms.

We have to go. But I never want this night to end. Once we reach the Vegas strip, reality looms, and in time, we'll have to fully separate and act like nothing happened here.

I try to remember the good. I try to hang on.

I'll see Luka again. Not just as co-workers, but as something more.

ACT TWENTY-ONE
LUKA KOTOVA

February in Vegas on a Friday afternoon. It's weirdly hot outside, and less strangely, overcrowded.

We're given an hour lunch break from practice, and I push through the throngs of tourists taking selfies.

Of course they choose to congregate around the Masquerade's street entrance. It's known for its mammoth marble replica of a regal ball. People can walk through the legs of marble masked men and women.

I duck beneath a selfie stick and spot Bay by the curb. Staring at the vast row of food trucks. I begin to smile.

Food trucks only stop by the Masquerade on the last Friday of every month, and I haven't been in the past. Always avoiding her. But I'm done with avoidance.

For once, I'm getting what I want.

After we kissed outside the diner, we agreed to keep it professional for a few days. Just to throw off any suspicion. We're not actively trying to be caught, but that cautiousness lessens today. Earlier, I texted her about grabbing lunch.

It went something like this.

Me: Lunch?

Baylee: it's food truck day. I can't miss it.

Me: so then food trucks.

Baylee: it's right outside the hotel. Unless you're okay with that.

Me: I'm okay with that.

If someone sees us, we can blame "coincidence" and that we just happened to want the same food. We're still co-workers.

This whole plan is going to work.

It *has* to work.

I approach Baylee, and she catches my gaze. Her lips partially upturn, sunlight glittering her brown eyes. Her sporty braids are a little bit frizzy (adorably so), both of us beat from six hours of morning practice. I notice an icepack melting in her hand.

I edge as close as I can, my fingers brushing hers. In deep Russian, I whisper, "*Hello, beautiful*," and smile into my words.

Baylee tries to suppress her own grin, smoothing her lips together. Then she covers her mouth with her fingers. How she looks—giddy, *overwhelmed*—I feel it too. My body lightens like I'm floating. For fuck's sake, it's a better feeling than actually flying forty-feet in the air.

I don't know how that's possible.

Love is strange and weird and unpredictable—and that's probably why I'm drawn to it.

To her.

Baylee drops her hand to gesture at me. "You have to pause *this* for at least one more minute."

She means me flirting. "Why?"

"Because this is serious." Baylee isn't referring to us. "I have fifty choices"—she motions to the long line of food trucks—"and I only ever make this choice once a month. It's not like New York where, *bam*, there's street food. Turn left, oh, a food truck. Here, outside of the Masquerade, *this is it*."

"The food truck apocalypse."

"That's dramatic," she says seriously.

And then we both burst into laughter, knowing her passionate declarations are more theatrical than my words.

As our humor weakens, I ask, "Which food truck are you thinking?"

"I don't know." Baylee cranes her head—and winces, freezing in place.

I grimace and watch her place the icepack on her neck. (What happened?)

"Most of the trucks are new," she says, "but there are some old standbys that are good."

"Let's try something new." I hone in on her neck, concerned. Practice for Infini has been hellish. (I'm not exaggerating.)

My calves, knees, quads, triceps, and the rest of my muscles throb and burn. Purple bruises dot my legs and torso.

In a cast of 50 artists, we've already gone through three boxes of Kinesio tape. It helps lessen pain, inflammation, prevents further injury, and reduces lactic acid buildup. We're *all* physically feeling the stress of Geoffrey's impossible demands.

And I worry about Baylee.

When I'm on the Russian swing or Wheel of Death, she's going over her solo juggling act. We're not always together in the gym.

I barely saw her today, so I don't know what caused the pain in her neck. If she got seriously hurt or what.

"This way," Baylee says, leading us down the street. Shaded by the trucks' overhangs, I spin my blue hat, wearing the rim backwards, and I chew a "stolen" toothpick (they were basically free).

Bay stops to study the menu of a falafel truck.

"Did you pull a muscle today?" I ask, about to touch her hand that's on the ice—but a cook yells out of a nearby taco truck.

"ONE TACO, ONE HALF-OFF! Step up! Come get 'em! If you don't trust me, trust Loren Hale!" He raises a framed photo of Loren Hale eating from that very food truck.

(It goes without saying, Loren Hale is the famous twenty-something fiancé to Lily Calloway: the shy, sex addict Calloway sister. Both starred on *Princesses of Philly*.)

Baylee deeply considers the taco truck now.

I toss my toothpick aside. "He's your favorite?" I start smiling.

She shoots me a look like *you're so wrong*.

"Loren *I'm-going-to-kill-you-with-five-words* Hale does it for you, huh?"

Baylee gapes. "You just made him sound like a murderer."

"Burst your image of him? No more hearts around his name. No more Baylee + Loren—"

"He's not even my type."

"You have a type?" I didn't know this. "It's *me*, right?"

She pushes my arm lightly but keeps quiet, killing me with suspense. I'm more ripped than Loren Hale. I have darker hair, and we're around the same height, I think.

His cheekbones are sharper. Some parts of my face are softer, and if I remember correctly, he has no tattoos.

Baylee starts laughing.

"What?"

"You're agonizing over this, aren't you?"

"No," I lie. "I'm cool." I outstretch my arms.

She places her palm on my chest—and my whole body stirs. The simple touch almost hardens me. My muscles contract.

And Baylee tells me, "I don't believe you."

I wrap my arms around her shoulders, caught up in the moment. (If anyone plans to tattle on us to Corporate for *hugging*, fuck you.) "Then I don't believe you actually have a type," I breathe.

Her eyes dance along my features, down my body. My hand rises to the back of her head, and she holds onto my waist.

Subconsciously, we sway to music that has only ever existed between us.

I dip my head and pull her against my chest, and my lips—meet her palm. *Fuck.*

Baylee stopped the kiss, and quickly, her hand falls. She glances over her shoulder, casts a fearful look at me, and then steps backwards. But not that far back.

"I forgot," I say honestly. *I forgot where we are.* Just down the street from the Masquerade. "I'm sorry."

"It's okay." She eyes my lips. "So you know, I wanted it too." Bay shrugs like it's just not in the cards for us.

"Okay." At least I'm not reading her body language wrong. I take off my hat and comb my hand through my hair before putting it back on. To cut the tension, I ask, "What is your type, seriously?"

She shrugs again. "Someone who really cares about me and who excites me." She shakes her head in thought. "In my life, I don't know anyone who does that but you." With another strong headshake, she tries to stifle a wince while adjusting the ice.

I cringe. "Bay."

"It's fine…" she trails off, spotting something down the strip.

I watch her eyes grow in excitement.

"No way," she breathes and immediately clasps my hand. We start sprinting side-by-side, our fingers laced.

Our smiles burst.

I feel fifteen again. Running across a city next to Baylee Wright. I feel alive.

Like this is where I'm *meant* to be. Nowhere else.

Only with her.

Baylee skids to a halt at a bright yellow truck. *Jamaican Cuisine* scrawled in green paint. As we slip into the long line, she explains, "They haven't had a Caribbean truck in *four* months."

"Bastards."

Bay smiles and adjusts her icepack, inadvertently drawing my attention to her neck. "I strained it," she admits and turns completely. Her back faces me so I can take a look.

I finally touch her hand that's on the ice. "Doing what?"

"5-club backcrosses."

My brows jump. I picture Bay launching clubs from behind her back, straight into the air. I lower her hand to inspect the strain. "Did the club land on your neck?" I worry.

Juggling is dangerous. Mostly because of the props. When we were younger, I helped bandage her hands. Flat rings sliced up her nails and skin between her fingers. She also broke her toe that same year. Club dropped on her foot.

She said she was distracted, and she had reason to be. It was the year her parents passed away, and she still had to perform in Infini. Grief, broken toe, and all.

The show must go on.

(It seems like a cute phrase until you have bronchitis and you'd rather face-plant on a couch than lift your two-hundred pound cousin on your shoulders—or juggle candlesticks while balancing on two legs of a rickety chair. True story from Luka and Baylee, the early years.)

"I just pulled a muscle," Baylee assures me.

"Hold still."

Baylee nods before going stationary.

I knead the base of her neck with my fingers, alleviating tension in her muscles, and her shoulders lower significantly. Relaxing.

Bay leans her back against my chest, and her hand creeps up my thigh.

Our breaths deepen. I wrap my left arm around her abdomen, holding her against me. Keeping her close. As the food truck line moves, we walk forward but never detach from each other.

Can we explain this embrace to Corporate?

I don't know.

I don't know, but right now, I'm banking on the fact that no one sees us.

Baylee shifts my hand to the nape of her neck. "Right there."

I massage the spot, adding deeper pressure, and she oozes against my body. The corners of my lips pull upward. "You're easy to please."

She stiffens. "Tell that to all the other guys."

All the other guys. "Sure, give me their names and cell numbers. I'll track them down."

Baylee steps away, just to turn and face me. Head tilted.

I clutch her waist, drawing her back to my chest. "Put two shit emojis next to the ones that called you a corpse." My voice is easygoing, not malicious or sharp.

"No." Bay tries hard not to smile. "Be serious."

"I'm completely, heartbreakingly serious. If you can't be with me, I'm going to interview all the assholes who have a shot with you."

"Really?" Her lips try desperately not to lift.

The food line moves. I step forward and walk her backwards. "You don't think I will?"

"You don't even do small talk. You usually toss a peppermint at people and walk away."

"Tell me that's not better than a *how are you?*"

She smiles into a head-shake. "So not the point."

"It's definitely *a* point."

My arms return to her shoulders.

And her arms snake around my waist. "You'd really interview potential boyfriends of mine?" Her face scrunches at the thought. "What would you even ask them?"

I raise my brows. "Boyfriend*s*? As in plural?"

"I heard it's better to date around."

"From who?"

"*Cosmopolitan.* Aunt Lucy. *Friends,* the television show."

I've seen a few episodes because of Katya. My brows furrow. "Pretty sure Rachel and Ross were meant to be together *from the start.*"

"Pretty sure they had to date around in order to realize that they were meant to be together."

My head spins. "They're not even close to being us. You know that?" We've always had feelings for each other. We didn't willingly break apart. Someone ripped her out of my arms. It's not like we chose to move on. We had to.

We *have* to.

Eventually.

"I know. God, I know." She sighs a heavy breath.

What would I ask her potential boyfriends? "You know what I'd ask them?"

"What?" she wonders, understanding the shift in topic.

"I'd ask them if they love you. And if they hesitate to say *yes,* even for a second, I'd tell them to get a life somewhere far, *far* away from you."

Baylee inhales and rises on her toes, her hand crawling up my back. "I think…"

"Yeah?" I whisper, both of us eyeing each other's lips.

Affection flows through her features. I see the *I love you* before she starts to say, "I—"

"What'd you two like?" the food truck dude asks.

We flinch and break apart. Baylee rotates fully and my hands drop from her shoulders.

We've made it to the front of the line. We both swallow at the same time.

While she scrutinizes the menu, I check our surroundings. No one looks familiar to me. No Aerial Ethereal employees. Just some bickering families and couples with strollers and crying babies.

I glance back at the menu that consists of jerk wings, oxtail, curry chicken, rice and peas, fried plantains, and chicken, beef, and veggie patties.

She acts like it's a tough choice, but she's the kind of person that tries the same exact food in different locations. I know her decision before she says it.

"A beef patty," Baylee orders, already fishing out some money. "Oh and…curry chicken with rice and peas, fried plantains. Two orders of those." She's stocking up her fridge for later.

When she finishes, the cook acknowledges me.

I ask Bay, "What's your second choice to eat for lunch?"

"Jerk wings."

"I'll take the jerk wings," I tell the guy, handing him my cash before Baylee pays.

She doesn't protest, probably not wanting to hold up the line. We stand off to the side while they prepare our order, and I immediately read her features that say: *you can't keep paying for me.*

"You can't keep paying for me," she says matter-of-factly, slipping her cash back in her wrist wallet.

"Look, we're technically not together."

"Right," she says, "you just made my point."

"*But,*" I continue. "You gotta wait for my but, Bay."

She gives me a look. "Did you just make a pun?"

"Did I?" I give her the same face.

She laughs and then groans at the sound and rolls her eyes at herself. "That wasn't even funny."

I stuff my hands in the pockets of my black sweatpants; my casual attitude a trait I can't shake. "Some part of you thought it was."

"The part that's infatuated with you," she says, blasé.

I raise my brows. "A lot of my body parts are just as infatuated with you."

She begins to smile. "One starts with a C, right?"

"Or a D," I tease.

"P."

"See, we can spell."

"Yeah," she says, "screw our tutors who wrote *poor language skills* in our tenth grade report cards."

I laugh at the memory, but the noise fades fast as she waves her wallet.

"Tell me your *but*," she says.

"But," I start again and then pause. I don't even know what I planned to say. I confront facts: I'm not with Baylee. I have to let her go at the end of this.

And I have to accept that.

Even if it hurts.

"But…?" She frowns. "You okay? Luka?"

I force a weak smile. "We'll split the bill next time. Sound good?"

Baylee doesn't prod about my change of heart. She just nods and then shrugs. "Yeah. Sounds like a plan."

After we grab our food order, we stroll down the strip. No destination in mind.

I carry my jerk wings, eating and walking, and Baylee has a to-go bag hooked on her arm, all the extra food for later in Styrofoam containers. But she holds her beef patty, a golden pastry shaped like a squared crescent. Meat stuffed inside.

She groans in disappointment after taking a bite. "Shit."

"Air patty?" I guess since I've seen that expression *many* times before.

"Yeah." She flashes me the inside of the patty. I see only a small dollop of beef. "It's like roulette trying to get a beef patty that's actually full of meat."

"The risk of ordering the same thing everywhere, you're going to be disappointed at least nine times out of ten."

"You think it's boring, but it's as fun as spontaneously ordering food."

"Evidence?"

She raises the beef patty towards me. "This beef patty. It may've let me down, but I've uncovered a huge mystery about how it would've tasted in comparison to all the others I've ever eaten. *That* is exciting."

I believe her because she says every word like it lives in the core of her heart. "Where does your millionth patty rank?"

"Low to mid-tier." Baylee takes another bite. "Crust is really good." She holds the patty out towards me.

I take a bite. It's one of the better ones I've tried. I share a few jerk wings with Bay, which is why I picked her second food choice.

"How's your aunt?" I ask.

"Happily married and in a successful career," Baylee says, licking her fingers and tossing a bone back in the tray. "Also, very pregnant."

"Wow." I'm actually surprised. I forgot that people aren't stagnant. That in five years, people do *really* move on, even if we haven't. "She still hate me?"

"Aunt Lucy didn't hate you." Baylee passes the beef patty to me. "Trade?"

I nod and give her the tray of wings. "There's no chance she liked me after we were caught though." Her entire family thought were just best friends, not also boyfriend-girlfriend and having sex.

Bay shrugs. "She doesn't like you, but only because she thought we were temporary."

"Yeah." I understand.

"My parents always liked you. Do you remember that breakfast where they invited you for ackee and saltfish?"

"I wouldn't forget that." I remember the moment really well. I didn't know her parents for long, but at the kitchen table, her mom would discuss music of all genres for *hours*, and she'd recount all of Baylee's embarrassing childhood stories. Most about toddler Baylee dancing without a diaper and accidentally peeing on the floor.

Bay claims she had an aversion to public toilets as a kid, and her mom loved to joke about it. I think she knew that Baylee wouldn't be embarrassed. The stories only made her daughter laugh, which made me smile wider.

Her mother was fun and protective and *lively*. Baylee used to say that her mom, she wasn't just the life of the party—she was the heart.

And we'd play Trivial Pursuit before dinner. Brenden won every time. I lost a lot, but her dad—he'd come in last place on purpose. I was sure he knew who the author of *War and Peace* was, but he didn't want me to feel badly for coming up short.

He's someone I'd be proud to have as a father, so I know why Baylee cherishes the hell out of him.

Baylee balls up the thin napkin. "I like those memories."

"Me too." I felt so a part of her world. Sometimes, painfully so.

I remember how her aunt invited me over for the same meal after Baylee's parents passed away. Lucy didn't ever learn how to cook ackee and saltfish like Bay's mom. I sat at a table with Zhen, Brenden, and Baylee—and the silent consensus was that it tasted nothing like the traditional Jamaican dish.

Lucy cried while eating and apologized profusely for being a bad stand-in for their mom. It was one of the most gut-wrenching things I've witnessed in my life.

Yet, I remember Baylee and Brenden assuring their aunt that it was okay. That she tried, and they loved her for trying.

We stop at a crosswalk, a red handprint flashing on the pole, and we dump our trash in a nearby bin. I think about offering to hold her to-go bag of curry chicken and rice, but I hesitate.

Because I'm not her boyfriend. (I hate it.)

"How much do you talk to your parents?" she asks.

It wasn't a lot when I first met Baylee. It's even less now.

We forget to cross at the light, and we end up lingering by the entrance to an Urban Outfitters, our hands brushing. I catch hers and hold strong.

"I call my parents maybe a few times a year, more if they're already talking with Nik and he passes me the phone." Our eyes meet. "It is what it is." I shake my head. "I'm not even friends with all of my cousins." There are too many. And I realize, a cousin isn't equivalent to a mother and a father, but my parents never really got to know me.

Not even when they were around.

It's easy lumping them into the distant-cousin category.

"I remember," she says. "One time you forgot one of your cousins was lactose intolerant when you suggested ice cream, but you always said that some cousins you loved like siblings."

(Dimitri.) "Yeah. That hasn't changed."

Baylee's gaze drifts to the right, and she abruptly straightens up, eyes widening in alarm.

ACT TWENTY-TWO
LUKA KOTOVA

"Luka, go—*go*." She starts to shove me away, but then she changes her mind and pulls me into the Urban Outfitters, the door shutting behind us.

Inside, we weave between jewelry stands and racks of purposefully ripped denim jeans. Her grip on my hand tightens, beyond panicked.

"Bay—"

"Shh." She puts her finger to her lips and then slightly crouches behind the window-front manikins.

I follow suit and through the glass, I spot what she saw.

My stomach drops.

Vince, an older dark-haired AE employee, the one who caught us almost five years ago—he stands authoritatively on the sidewalk, dressed in a suit jacket and white tee. I always thought he looked like Nicholas Cage, and he's not alone.

He speaks rapidly to Geoffrey Lesage, the young choreographer.

"Geoffrey shouldn't be with Vince," Baylee says. "They're not even in the same department." Vince is the head of marketing.

It seems weird. I can't hear or read their lips, but Vince has several disgruntled lines on his forehead. Clearly, he's not happy.

Geoffrey points at the store.

We duck behind the manikin's platform.

Baylee drops to her ass and shields her face. "Shit. *Shit.*"

"They didn't see us," I try to assure her. "It's okay." I'm squatting and I'd reach out and hold Baylee, but that's the issue right now. *Us.* Being close.

She exhales heavily. "What if they did see, Luka?" She tries to peer at the glass door without breaching the top of the manikin's platform.

"They would've already rushed in here and caught us," I whisper. "Look, we're not even positive Geoffrey is aware of our past." He always seemed oblivious. Case in point: he let us partner up on the trampoline.

Baylee stares off as she says, "He was with Vince."

I see where she's mentally headed. Marc Duval claimed that there were *two* AE employees informed about our contracts and watching us, just in case we broke them. We practically knew one had to be Vince. And now she's thinking the second is Geoffrey.

She's forgetting something.

"Geoffrey can't be watching us. He's *new*, Bay."

"There are shakeups every season." Her hand is on her forehead, stunned at this scenario. "What if the person who was watching us left Vegas, and Marc needed someone *new* to keep an eye on us? Geoffrey would be the perfect person. He's around us more than any other company member."

It makes sense.

I just don't want to accept that Corporate is that close, still breathing down our necks. "Then it's a good thing," I say, trying to hang onto the positives. "We know *exactly* who to watch out for."

Baylee nods to herself and then tries to peek over the platform but she hesitates. "I'm scared." Her voice spikes. "Luk."

I reach out and clasp her hand and squeeze. "I'm not going to abandon you at the end of this. Hey, Baylee, look"—I cup her cheek, and her widened gaze meets my calm—"I'm here for you. You're not alone in this."

Baylee leans towards me, and I wrap my arm around her shoulders, careful of her neck. Pulling her close, I kiss the top of her head.

"You know what's strange?" she says softly, glancing once to her right. We're secluded from most of the shoppers, and I don't see Geoffrey or Vince nearby.

"What's strange?"

She looks to me. "I feel the safest in your arms, but in reality, it's the most dangerous place to be."

I wear a weak smile. "Being with me is a dream."

"The best dream," she says confidently.

For the sake of our reality, I remain alert, and I risk a glance above the platform. I don't see anyone from Corporate.

"It looks like they left."

She tugs me down when I take too long, and anxiety surfaces in her features.

"I'll go out first," I whisper, "and head back to the hotel. I'll text you if the street looks completely clear. You can leave whenever you want after me." I know it'll give her peace of mind if we split apart here.

"I want to see you again," she says, so assured that I don't even ask if she's certain.

"I'll text you a time and location for tonight."

She starts smiling off my smile. "Okay." Fear lowers her lips, but I squeeze her hand one more time before I let go entirely.

Then I rise to my feet. I have trouble tearing my gaze off of hers, all the way to the door. I push outside, people meandering down the Vegas strip.

Cars honking.

Life moving quickly.

I look left and right down the long stretch of sidewalk. No Corporate in my view. And I text Baylee as I leave.

All clear. 10 p.m. Meet me in the lobby at Two Kings Hotel. See you later, krasavitsa.

ACT TWENTY-THREE
BAYLEE WRIGHT

*S*tuck in an agonizingly slow cab, I check the time on my phone again. Two minutes past 10 p.m.—*casually late.*

That's not bad, right? I'll start panicking when it hits fifteen minutes.

My curls hang loosely against my chest, and I fix the buckle to my red high heels that match the prettiest and newest dress I own: a rose-red strapless cocktail number. The fabric hugs my hips and pushes up what little cleavage I have.

Luka never said if this was fancy or a really laidback outing, but we can barely find a moment to spare outside of the Masquerade together. At least not without being interrupted. So I'm taking advantage of the moment and dressing up for once.

The cab halts by a curb, and the rich, glittering purple words *2 Kings* stands out amongst surrounding neon signage and flashing billboards. I've never been here, but I'm sure Luka has casino-hopped with Timo before.

10:12 p.m.

I pay my fare, exit the cab, and carry my silver clutch as I push through the revolving doors. The lobby is the casino floor, boisterous with multicolored slots and gamblers. Packed tight.

I'm not out of place. The average age is young. About twenties to mid-thirties, and most are dressed like they're ready to hit the nightclubs.

I look up as I walk further inside, *thousands* of crystal chandeliers hang from the ceiling. Modern with a regal touch—it's breathtaking.

"Baylee."

My gaze falls, straight ahead, just as Luka rises off a velvet bar stool. My lips part at how utterly *gorgeous* he is in formalwear.

Black slacks fit him perfectly, and his white button-down contrasts his dark hair but brings out his emotive gray eyes. His hair is slightly wet. Like he didn't have time to dry the strands.

His hot gaze travels down my body in an intoxicating once-over, his desire so apparent. My neck instantly heats.

I can't contain a smile as we near one another, my pulse pounding. "Hey," I say, my voice more breathy than I intend.

He clutches my hip and whispers, "You look gorgeous."

Butterflies. I feel them tenfold. "Funny," I say seriously, "I was going to say the same about you."

"Gorgeous?" His lips stretch.

I go off of impulse. *Feeling.* I touch his cheek with a tender hand, and our gazes devour one another. My fingers trace the hard, dominant line of his shaven jaw, and I intake the soft, virtuousness around his eyes.

"Yeah," I breathe, "*gorgeous.*"

Luka shifts my hand towards his lips, places a warm kiss on my palm, and then threads our fingers together. He nods towards the elevators. "You can say no, but I got us a room for the night."

My new overwhelming smile, I try to tame a bit more. "I'm not going to say no." There's no practice tomorrow. It's our one free day this week, and I already texted Brenden that I was going to watch Netflix alone tonight.

I'm ready for Luka to *really* touch me. So ready that I'm wearing pink lacy underwear instead of my usual cotton.

Luka smiles a captivating, panty-dropping smile. "This way." He takes charge, guiding me to the elevators, our hands never separating.

We slide into an elevator that quickly compacts with other twenty-somethings, chatting loudly. He pushes the 25 button and slips further back with me. As the doors shut, I scoot closer to Luka, and he leans his arm against the wall-mirror.

He catches me staring at him, and the corners of his lips lift again.

"Your hair is wet," I say. "Did you leave fast?"

He sighs at a recent memory. "You don't want to know."

"Now I really do." The elevator jerks to a stop, letting off only one person on the fourth floor. This may take a while. Now that I'm with him, I don't mind at all.

"I couldn't get in the bathroom until ten minutes before I left."

"Why?"

He lowers his voice. "Dimitri was jerking off."

I cringe, not wanting to picture Dimitri masturbating.

"Exactly why I didn't want to tell you."

"You didn't see him, did you?" I wonder, too curious not to ask.

"No. I have seen too much of my cousins, but that's not something I've ever stumbled in on."

Tenth floor. His hand slips around my waist, to my lower back. I'm nervously stiff, so I try to bring up casual conversation again. "Have you ever walked in on someone having sex?"

"Oh yeah."

My mouth falls. This must be a Vegas thing because it never happened to him in New York. "Who?"

"Erik, Robby, Timofei. All different occasions. I didn't mean to see them. They were fucking in the living room of their suite, and I wasn't always alone when I went inside."

"What did you do?"

"I walked right out."

I nod. "Smart."

He starts laughing.

"What?" My smile grows.

Sixteenth floor. "That's literally the first time I've been called *smart* with zero sarcasm. Thank you, Bay."

"Anytime." I smooth my lips together, restraining my smile some.

Nineteenth floor, the elevator almost empties. We're left with two couples in matching tuxes and shimmery gold gowns.

We go silent, but his eyes practically undress me. I breathe shallowly, and his hand descends to my ass. My body curves towards him, wanting his whole build to press up against me. I imagine the power, the strength and force—and my knees feel weak and my skin bare.

His other hand travels discreetly up my hip. Then he brings me close, pretending to hug me, but really his hand is making a scorching trail up to my chest.

"One," he whispers against my ear. *One: over-the-clothes touching.*

He memorized my list.

I feel wet and hot all over. But I'm more rigid than I want to be. "I'm nervous," I admit in a soft breath.

He draws back, just to study my expression, and I have trouble making direct eye contact. I watch the two couples leave on the twenty-second floor.

The doors close.

We're alone, and the elevator ascends.

"I'll take care of you," he assures me. "You tell me to stop, at any point, and I'll stop."

"I don't want you to stop. I'm just overwhelmed." I haven't been this consumed by someone. It's more than just being physically attracted to each other. It's knowing him. Loving who he is.

And him loving who I am.

He nods. "Just remember to breathe, and you'll be fine."

"Planning to steal my breath away?"

His hands return to my hips as he whispers, "Caught me."

I grip his button-down. Our bodies aching to meld together, but we wait. And the elevators spring open. Our floor.

Luka walks me backwards. His large hands sear through my dress. We enter the *empty* carpeted hallway, chandeliers dangling in a long row.

I pop a button of his shirt. His palm runs up the curve of my body, veering to my boobs again. No bra, his thumb skims my hardened nipple, fabric of my dress keeping his skin from my skin.

I quiver from the drawn-out sexual tension, my lips parting in a heady breath. I undo his shirt halfway.

His clutch strengthens on my body, and his left hand descends my hipbone…lower and lower. Reaching the hem of my dress, he pulls the fabric up, just slightly and his hand moves to my bare, inner-thigh.

Oh God. I have to hang onto his biceps, throbbing. I'm throbbing for him to push his cock *hard* inside of me and pump and pump.

And Luka says, "I'm going to kiss the fuck out of you."

I almost fall against him, but he has me. Pulls me against his body. Seizes me completely. His hand to the back of my head, he kisses me so passionately that a noise catches my throat. I grasp his neck for support as the kiss drives deeper.

He cups my heat—and I'm so soaked. His fingers skim my panties between my legs. I shudder against him. Where the hell are we?

I'm barely coherent to see.

A hallway.

An empty hallway, thankfully.

I kiss back. Just as hungrily. Our tongues dancing together. My hips arch towards his cock.

"Up," he says in one breath. He hoists me, my legs wrapping around his waist. One hand on my ass, the other free, he takes out his keycard while we're lip-locked.

Door open.

He carries me inside and kicks the door closed.

Then Luka sets me on my feet and spins me around, seamlessly pulling my back to his chest.

I catch my breath and digest my new surroundings: a king-sized bed with a wine-red comforter, a sleek dresser with a TV on top, a sultry velvet chaise, and drawn curtains to reveal tinted glass and a view of gleaming sin city.

While I lean against him, Luka kisses the base of my neck, and as he hits a bundle of nerves, a gasp breaches my lips, my hand searches for support. I end up clutching his muscular thigh.

His other palm roams my body, toying with my sensitive nipples. It feels amazing. I'm lit up, and we're just on *number one* of my list.

I ache for more. I'm so afraid that we'll be cut off and interrupted again. Yet, I like each lengthy step, the moment stretched like a taut rubber band, readying to snap into a body-shaking climax.

While my back is right up against his chest, he does something that he knows I love. Luka wraps both of his arms around me. One snakes around my collarbones, the other around my abdomen. His embrace firm and incredibly loving. I'm vulnerable as he clutches me this strongly, but I still have control—and I trust him entirely.

Wholeheartedly.

"Tighter," I whisper.

He strengthens the force of his hold on me. The muscles of his biceps cut in sharp lines, and my head lolls back while his lips burn hot trails up my neck.

His mouth finds mine, kissing me upside-down, and I feel his smile. In a short breath, he whispers, "*Two*."

Two: all kissing.

I reach up and run my fingers through the back of his hair. Especially as he dips his head down again and kisses me languidly, extending the force. I grind my ass, my body digging deeper against *his* body, even if there's no more space. *So close.*

His lips break from mine, a grunt in his throat. He starts walking forward, and of course, I go with him. Not detaching. He guides us to the window, and my palms hit the glass.

"*Three*," he says deeply.

Three: skin-to-skin contact.

I tremble in anticipation of what's to come. *OhGod.* "Luka," I cry out his name, and I don't wait for him to unzip me. I spin around on him and fist his shirt.

Luka kisses me roughly, full-forced again. I kiss back. Feverishly, he rolls up the bottom of my dress to my hipbones. Exposing my panties.

I bite his lip.

He nips mine, and I finish unbuttoning his shirt. He tosses it aside, bare-chested—his sculpted abs in direct view, and then he undoes his slacks. Stepping out of them, I see the outline of his cock in his dark-blue boxer-briefs, rock hard and long.

Swiftly and skillfully, he unzips me in one quick stroke, and my dress falls to the floor. Luka draws me against his chest like a dance move, and he murmurs, "*Three*, again."

A sheen of sweat already coats our skin, and even more heat gathers. My flesh tingles, and my hands explore his body as vigorously as he rediscovers mine. Practically naked, my laced panties leave nothing to the imagination.

His forehead touches mine, staring deep into me. "You're going up again."

"Why?" I breathe, wanting to hear him say it.

His lip almost quirks. "I want to feel your pussy against me."

I pulse and pulse, and without falter, he lifts me up, my legs spreading open and then gripping tight around his waist. He pushes me closer, and I arch towards him, gasping aloud.

Luka holds my ass but his other hand strikes the window. Pressed there. "Bay," he nearly groans out. My limbs shake.

"Luka." I wrap my arms around his shoulders, eye-level with him.

He seizes my gaze, staring straight into me again, and he rubs the inside of my thigh, inching to my panties.

Instead of letting my shoulders touch the window to brace me, he uses the strength of his left arm to keep me hoisted around him. He still cups my ass, and his more dominant hand—his right hand—finds the most sensitive place.

His fingers graze my swollen clit through my panties, and I curse beneath my breath, my veins on fire—the feeling *incredible*. Mind-numbing. And I never tear from his gaze.

Luka shifts the fabric of my panties so he meets flesh. Our eye-contact is just as intense, and I inhale a sharp breath as he adds friction, rubbing—*OhGod.*

OhGod.

He's a statue that I tremble against, and he only clutches stronger. I can't imagine breaking off the way he's looking at me. It fuels me. Lights my core in a thousand extraordinary colors.

He pushes two fingers into me, and I can't pick my mouth up, too overcome. I blaze head-to-toe from the force between my legs. Feeling *full.*

Luka speeds up.

High-pitched noises fly out of my mouth—I almost shut my eyes. *Look at him.* I stare right at him. God, look at him.

His gaze consumes me whole.

I hit a peak, pulsing around his fingers, and I buck against Luka. He retracts his hand and holds me so tight to his body. I moan softly into his neck. Hands in his hair.

Don't let me go.

Don't let me go.

And then my phone rings.

I lift my head slightly. Dazed. Luka glances around, but I pant, "It sounds like…my ringtone."

He brings me to the bed and sets me on the edge. "Do you want me to—"

"No," I cut him off. "Just…leave it." If I answer the phone or look at the caller, *this* could end. I don't want reality to catch up to us yet.

Luka listens, but he does return to his slacks. He digs in his pocket and procures a condom. I swallow, realizing that this is happening.

Tonight.

As he approaches the bed, he assesses my rigid posture and expression. "If you want to go slower—"

"It's been four years—"

"Five."

"I don't think it can go slower than that," I finish my thought. "I want *this*. I want you. I'm just kind of nervous because I haven't had sex in a long time." *Unlike you.*

He understands. "That's the point of all of this, right? The list."

"Yeah," I nod, but we both go quiet, heaviness tensing the air. If we could, we'd be together. I think we're both well aware of this fact by now. I scoot towards the headboard, my cell ringing out to silence.

Luka bends down and picks up his own fallen phone. He puts on a playlist of music, and the old song "Stand By Me" by Ben E. King starts playing.

I immediately smile. "You're too much."

He laughs. "Compliments from Baylee Wright. I'll take them all."

My heart is full.

As Luka towers at the edge of the bed, I eye the tattoos that cover his right leg, disappearing up the hem of his boxer-briefs. I spot a tiny river otter from afar. It's random.

All random.

Unabashed, he lowers his boxer-briefs and frees his erection. Stepping out of his underwear, he opens the condom package and then effortlessly slides it on.

I was with him when he actually struggled at that, and now he does it easily. And his dick is bigger, which shouldn't be surprising that he hit a growth spurt. It's been obvious that he's not a fifteen-year-old boy anymore.

I just soak in the differences. The similarities.

And I'm more satisfied with this new chapter of our lives. If I could rewind time, I'd be with him in that gap of separation, but since I can't, I hang onto the present.

I crawl beneath the red covers, and the mattress undulates with his weight. Right beside me, he slips under them too, and I peel my panties off my ankles.

Naked.

We're both naked.

I lie down, head on the pillow. I feel like this is my first time again. I'm just as nervous. It really is a giant redo of our last experience together. Caught behind a costume rack. *Horrible.*

We ended things one-hundred percent terribly.

Bracing his hand beside my head—and keeping his weight off of me—Luka is above my body, and he uses his knee to break apart my locked legs. Spreading them wide open.

Then he kisses my nose, causing me to smile.

"What are you scared of?" he asks quietly.

I think. And I realize that I don't have the same fears as I did years ago. "I'm afraid of loving it too much," I tell him.

His brows furrow. "Why?"

"Because it's going to end. Someday. One day."

Luka can't promise that it won't end, but his lips meet mine in a full-bodied kiss that lifts my chest up against his. Breathing life into me.

I clutch his biceps, my body reawakening. My ankle rubs his leg, and our tongues tangle. He clasps my cheek with one hand, and when he edges back, our eyes possess each other.

Very tenderly, Luka says, "All I know is what I feel. And I'm *in* love with you, Bay. Right now. Not just five years ago—but here, today. Yesterday. Tomorrow. It's forever kind of love, and I'm not letting go. I can't let go."

Tears crease the corners of my eyes, and I nod in affirmation, in agreement. Too overcome to speak aloud. I touch my eyes with my finger, and he rubs an escaped tear with his thumb.

I love him beyond recognition. Beyond perception. I love him so *fully* that it hurts.

I mouth, *I love you*, and he soaks up the words before he kisses me again. And again. Deeper. Stronger. We wrap up in each other's limbs, heat brewing.

He pulls me further beneath him so we're in perfect alignment, and he whispers, "*Five.*"

Five: sex. He skips number four on my list. Maybe purposefully leaving oral for another time. Because once we do everything on the list, we're over.

Luka seizes my gaze while he lifts up my hips, just slightly, and inch-by-inch, he slowly fills me. The hairs rise on my arms, his unhurried, agonizing pace striking all of my nerves. I shudder and my legs unconsciously twitch.

I clutch his toned ass that flexes as he thrusts harder into me. *OhGod.* He starts rocking in and out, and I swear, I see stars. My eyes nearly roll back, breath lodged in my throat.

Luka cups my face and kisses me, forcing me to breathe properly. It's one of the kindest efforts ever given to me in bed.

I appreciate it, so much so that I grind forward. He meets me, pushing deeper. I moan against his lips, and he smiles—before a grunt catches his throat, aroused. So aroused.

I try to hang onto his body, my limbs tensing up and aching to hit a climax and fall slack. *I'm so full.*

Luka never stops the momentum. Our friction builds more sweat, and he suddenly lifts me up in his arms.

I'm on his lap, my arms draped around his shoulders. Our eyes lock, and gripping my hips, he moves me up and down his shaft.

"Luka," I cry out, the feelings in my body and heart welling my eyes.

His glass, too, and he presses his forehead to mine, holding the back of my neck with one hand.

My nails dig into his shoulder. "I don't want to come. Not yet, *not yet,*" I say in rapid breaths.

Luka kisses me and whispers, "You're going to come, and it won't be the last time, Bay." But he doesn't specify whether it'll be from him or someone else.

One more push in and out, and my vision blackens, my body shaking, and my lips part for the millionth time, no noise able to escape. I clench around him, and he reaches an orgasm just as powerful, his body rocking forward. He holds me.

He's always holding me.

As light returns, I blink—slowly descending this high. We both breathe heavily, and I rest my forehead on his shoulder, my body weakening to mush. I have no energy to lift myself off his cock.

And then my phone rings *again.*

I stiffen.

He glances over his shoulder, my cell vibrating on the carpet.

Do we look? Do we ruin this? I hesitate. "If it's serious, your phone would be going off too, right?" I ask him.

"Yeah." He nods, combing back his damp hair. I feel like he's trying to assure himself. "We're good." No sooner does he finish, and his phone pings with a notification, either text or email or social media. I don't know which.

I freeze more.

"Ignore that," he tells me, but my ringer dies out only to start up again. He sighs, resigned and frustrated.

We both know we can't really ignore it any longer. I rise to my knees, and Luka pulls out.

I slide off the bed, cold air chilling my bare skin. I shiver but hurry to find my phone, buried in my clutch.

The moment I clasp my cell, the ring ends.

Three missed calls from… "It's my aunt," I tell Luka and immediately return her call, worried that something happened to the baby. Her due date is still far away.

I press my phone to my ear, shivering more.

Luka tosses me a hotel robe and adjusts the air conditioner. I watch him also simultaneously slip on boxer-briefs and check his phone— multitasking too well. We both have good hand-eye coordination, but he can't juggle more than four balls at once.

I like having a leg up on him somewhere.

He also can't spin a basketball on his finger for more than two seconds. That, I won't ever let him live down.

I put on the soft cotton robe, knotting the ties around my waist, and then the phone line clicks.

"There you are," Aunt Lucy says, voice more tight than usual.

"Is everything okay?" I sit on the edge of the bed.

"You tell me."

I don't understand her vagueness at all. "What do you mean?" I look up as Luka flashes me his cellphone screen.

Are you with my sister? Be honest. — Brenden

Luka shakes his head like he has no clue what to say, and he takes a seat next to me, hunched forward, hand on his mouth in thought.

Why wouldn't Brenden just text me?

Maybe he's afraid I'll lie to him. I don't want that type of relationship with my brother, but I feel boxed in. I'm barred from giving him the truth by Aerial Ethereal, so I *have* to lie.

"How are you doing?" Aunt Lucy clarifies. It must be hellishly late on the east coast, so I don't know why this question would warrant multiple late-night calls.

"Are you okay?" I ask her, trying to make sure of this. "The baby—"

"Is fine. I called about you." She must shift her phone because her voice is muffled and I hear chatter in the background. Clearer, she says, "Devon says hello."

"Hi, Devon." I swallow. "I'm fine too."

"Really?"

"*Really.*"

"Because your brother thinks you're using cocaine again, and between you and me—we both know that you never started, so tell me what's really going on."

My face falls. "Why would he think that?"

Next to me, Luka flashes his cell again.

I'm not trying to grill you. I'm worried about Bay. She's been acting off lately. Text me back. – Brenden

"Apparently you've been standoffish at work towards him," Aunt Lucy says, "and every time he asks if you'd like to hang out, you say you'd rather be alone."

I pause and decide to tell a partial truth. "I'm just stressed out. Infini's new choreographer is really demanding, and I haven't felt social lately. It's *nothing* to worry about. I'll talk to Brenden tomorrow and tell him that."

Aunt Lucy is quiet.

My stomach is in my throat.

Luka is typing on his phone, forming a response to Brenden.

"Aunt Lucy?" I say.

"Are you still taking your antidepressants?"

"*Yes*," I say firmly. "I haven't had a really bad low in a while."

Luka's eyes flit to me for the briefest second. His concern is noted, too.

She lets out a strained breath. "You're not skirting around the truth because I'm pregnant, right? Because that's *not* right. I'm able to handle your emotions and mine because I care about you. And you're *my* responsibility. Understand?"

I smile faintly. "You're going to be a great mom."

Her voice softens. "Thank you, but talk to me."

"I've been honest," I say.

"Will you FaceTime me?"

Right now? My eyes widen as I look around the hotel room. Sheets tangled, covers askew, and clothes litter the floor. "I'll FaceTime tomorrow," I say. "I promise."

Aunt Lucy hesitates but then says, "Tomorrow. I'm setting a reminder on my phone."

"Okay. I love you."

"I love you too."

I almost smile as we hang up, but Luka presses *send* on a text that I start reading.

I don't know anything. Sorry, dude. — Luka

I give him a look. "That's your response?"

"We literally exchanged numbers two days ago, only because I left my keycard and got locked out of the suite. I'm not exactly your brother's best friend."

Correction: they've never been friends. Friendly, maybe. But in New York, all invites from both sides were rejected.

"He's going to text you back," I tell him.

Luka rereads the text and shakes his head.

"If you read your message a certain way, it comes across dry and rude."

Luka laughs.

"I'm not kidding." I groan because now I'm smiling. "Luka."

He extends his arm. "I'm not sarcastic." His humored smile shouldn't be that beautiful or contagious, but it is. A hundred percent.

"Brenden doesn't know you that well."

On cue, Luka's phone pings in his palm.

Are you fucking with me? – Brenden

Luka hands me the phone. "You text him back."

"As you?" This is a bad idea. But we're full of those.

"Yeah."

I start typing, trying to figure out what to say to my older brother as Luka. This is bad. Bad, bad, *bad.* "We're going to hell for this," I tell Luka.

His lips stretch. "At least we'll be together."

I lean into him, and he wraps his arm around my shoulders, kissing the top of my head like usual. The tension lessens in my limbs, and I breathe easier. "There." Pressing *send*, I flash the phone at him.

Luka reads my message.

I'm being truthful. I really have no idea where she is. If I hear from her, I'll let you know. Thanks :)

Luka tilts his head at a me. "A smiley face?"

"What? It's *nice* and a tone indicator."

He shakes his head again and starts laughing, which causes me to laugh just as much. The noises cease the moment another *ping* resounds, his phone in my hand.

The text isn't from Brenden.

Come dance with me at Hex!! I'll be there at 1 :DD — Timo

I wonder how many people have been texting Luka tonight.
Luka sees the message from his little brother. "I'll reply back later."
Another text.
Ok — Brenden
That's better than before, at least.
Luka stands and gestures to the bathroom, where he's headed, but before he leaves, he says, "You can look at my messages."
"Are you sure?"
"I can tell you're curious."
I am curious, but I'm afraid I'll see something I won't want to know.
"Okay," is all I say before he disappears. I waver but then tap into his feed of text messages from the top senders.

Timo's going to Hex tonight. Can you keep an eye on him? — Nik

How do you have a fake ID and I don't have one? :(— Katya

The next thread is from earlier tonight, so Luka has already replied.

Send me a pic of your blind date — Dimitri
No. — Luka
She that ugly? — Dimitri
stfu — Luka
Someone needs to get laid. — Dimitri

It's normal. Nik being concerned and asking Luka for help. Katya getting older. Dimitri being crude. I like that he let me see his family-life.

When Luka returns, I use the bathroom and then we order room service: creamy pasta, which I only eat when I don't have practice the next day, and a bottle of whiskey.

I curl up against him on the bed, and we spend the next couple of hours eating, drinking (a lot), laughing (even more), and watching old reruns of *Princesses of Philly*.

"Wait, *shh*," I say as one of the most climactic scenes of PoPhilly appears on screen. I lie against Luka's chest, and he leans against the headboard, his arm draped over my shoulder, and we both sip our fourth—fifth or sixth glass of whiskey?

I don't know.

Maybe less, maybe more. Who's counting?

Luka is smiling, near-laughter. Where I'm a passionate-talker drunk, he's a happy drunk.

On-screen, an altercation breaks out between Loren Hale's half-brother and the youngest Calloway sister's model boyfriend.

Punches are thrown, and then Julian, the boyfriend, touches his swollen eye and glares at Daisy Calloway, his young *teenage* girlfriend. But Julian and Daisy are no longer together, for obvious reasons.

"You're just going to f**king stand there?!" Julian yells at her.

"What do you want from me?" Daisy Calloway looks petrified of her own boyfriend.

Watching the show, Luka grows more serious, his lips down-turning. "I really hope this is all staged."

I know what he means. I want to reach through the television and protect Daisy Calloway.

Julian retorts, "For you to give me back *months* of my life that I wasted with you, you stupid c**t."

"Jesus," Luka mutters like he's never seen the episode before, but this scene is still hard to watch the tenth time. I lower the volume. And he suddenly says, "I'm terrified of my sister growing up."

"Technically she's already grown up."

Luka looks down at me. "You know she's been saving up her money for something—and I don't even know what it is."

"Makeup," I say.

"What?" He scrunches his face, but smiles wide.

I sip my whiskey and laugh off his smile. "You know makeup is *really* expensive."

"Why?"

"I don't know." I kind of slur. I can't believe I'm slurring, but then I can. "I guess it costs a lot to produce and package eye shadow and lipstick—"

He laughs. "No, Bay, why is she spending all this money on *makeup*?"

I shrug. "She's figuring out who she is, and she wants to be more Posh-like."

Luka nods, comprehending it now. "I guess it's better than what I thought."

"Which was?"

"She was saving up for a plane ticket to see our parents."

I don't see why that's bad, and he must read my expression because he adds, "According to Nik, they really don't want to see any of us since we'd have to take days off work. *Be professional.*"

The way he says *be professional*, I have a feeling he's mimicking his father.

His phone suddenly chimes. Mine buzzes.

We search in the depths of the twisted sheets and covers, and I finally find my phone the same time as him.

Email notification.

We both read silently.

Date: February 28th
Subject: MANDATORY PRACTICE TOMORROW
From: GeoffreyLesage, Choreographer
Bcc: Baylee Wright, *and other undisclosed recipients*

Infini Artists:

I was not impressed by your clear lack of motivation today. No more lunch breaks. You don't have tomorrow off. In fact, there are no free days from here on out. Be on Infini's stage at 5 a.m. sharp tomorrow. **<u>No exceptions.</u>**

Geoffrey Lesage
Infini Choreographer
geoffreylesage@mailme.com

Holy shit.

It's already 3 a.m.

We have practice in *two* hours.

"Fuck," Luka curses. *Fuck* feels like an understatement. I'm drunk. I ate heavy food, and chances are, more than half of Infini's cast is completely and totally wasted.

ACT TWENTY-FOUR
BAYLEE WRIGHT

"What *the hell* was that shit-show?" Geoffrey nearly yells, shutting off the opening score to Infini before it plays through.

Dripping in sweat, 47 hung-over artists—including me—are scattered across the stage of a beautiful globe auditorium dedicated to Infini.

We've performed the opening dance and acrobatic sequence *fifteen* times already. I also have to juggle eight clubs, so I'm desperately trying not to drop one. My head pounds like a jackhammer lives inside my eardrums. I breathe deeply through my nose, and sweat continuously slides down my temples.

Everyone looks just as awful.

Most of the Kotovas are crouched with hands on their heads to keep from puking. Across the stage from me, Luka kneels and concentrates on one spot of the floor.

Beside me, Brenden shuts his eyes from the glaring lights and sways close to Zhen, who wears dark Ray Ban sunglasses for the same reason my brother won't open his eyes.

I already told Brenden that I was drinking whiskey alone in my room, which spiked his worry, but at least he didn't think I was with Luka.

Geoffrey scrutinizes us from the midnight-blue velveteen seats down below. This auditorium is identical to the one Amour and Viva share except for the color of the chairs (theirs are *red*) and the max occupancy.

Their auditorium is intimate and small.

Infini's is grandiose and way too big. We have double the amount of seats that we need to fill. Which means double the pressure.

Brenden opens one eye to look at the trio of women sitting comfortably in the front row. He sways towards me and whispers, "I wish I were a clown."

They're exempt from Geoffrey's commands because they're not on stage during the opening number.

I whisper back, "You're not funny enough to be a clown."

Zhen laughs beneath his breath.

Brenden nudges me, his lips rising. I nudge back. He forgave me for being standoffish about an hour into practice. Nothing mends tiny spats faster than shared misery.

"*Again*," Geoffrey emphasizes. "This time try to look less dead in the eyes." I'm surprised he hasn't found a whistle yet.

We all sluggishly move in the wings, hidden from view while Milla, the little Ukrainian girl, remains center-stage. She's the first person the audience sees, and as my mom's score starts playing, I inhale deeply and nod my head, listening for my cue.

I'm next.

The second person on stage is me. I walk and juggle all eight clubs around Milla.

"Look alive!" Geoffrey shouts.

I try to emote, but nausea brews viciously. I perform various tricks, catching and tossing clubs *high* and fast. It's more subconscious. Like typing on a computer or driving. So I don't have to think a lot, but I'm leaning backwards more than I like.

Honestly, as soon as Luka, Robby, and Abram do full twisting triple layouts in sync onto the stage, followed by *so many* Kotovas—it's all a blur around me. Ordered chaos. Handstands on top of another person's shoulders. Acrobatic floor work. Dancing to the rhythmic drum beat.

Everyone claps twice.

I spin three-sixty. My stomach hates me. I catch a club. Toss. Catch. *Clap. Clap.*

I spin again and join the dance sequence *while* juggling. Brenden slips on the sweaty stage but catches himself.

Clap. Clap.

I'm going to throw up.

Anton bumps into Sergei on accident, and the music screeches to a halt. We all skid to a stop too, and I lose control of a club. It clatters on the stage, the noise echoing and basically broadcasting my failure. *Thank you for that.*

I feel too many eyes on me.

"Bucket!" Dimitri shouts from stage right. Grabbing a tin pail, he slides it across the stage. It reaches his little brother, Anton, who immediately vomits into it.

Collective, nauseated groans ring out. I have to squat and set down my clubs. My hand is on my mouth. *Don't gag.*

Don't gag.

I risk a glance at Luka, the length of the stage separating us again. He watches me, breathing as heavily as all the Kotovas, mostly from their athletic performance.

Don't gag.

Erik joins Anton, retching in a second bucket.

I gag.

Luka's eyes grow in concern.

Swallow. I swallow puke in my throat, and my brother crouches beside me, a hand on my shoulder.

"Don't think about it," Brenden coaches in a whisper.

It'd be easier if I didn't hear a chorus of vomiting. I keep my hand firmly planted to my mouth, and Geoffrey climbs onto the stage. We all tense as he struts around us and surveys our clearly hung-over state.

"*Embarrassing,*" he says with a curled lip, wearing a black blazer on top of an '90s concert tee. Giving away his age. "Am I wasting my time? Do you not even *care* about your own jobs? Really, what am I doing here?"

Many noses flare, suppressing irritation. No one back-talks, knowing AE hierarchy, and I bite down, also submerging more nausea.

Infini's fate means *everything* to me, but we had no time to prepare for this practice. I don't want to believe that today's fuck-ups will jeopardize the future of the show.

While Geoffrey pauses, *six* more artists retreat to buckets and backstage. Puking.

"For Christ's sake," Geoffrey says, shaking his head. "*Again.*"

We can't.

No one moves.

"Did you not hear me?" Geoffrey asks, his wild enraged eyes perusing us.

Zhen speaks for the cast, our unofficial captain. "Essential artists in the dance sequence are currently indisposed." It's the nice way of saying *their heads are in puke buckets.*

I wait for Geoffrey to call off practice, but I'm expecting too much.

"You'll improvise," he says. "That's what you do when someone falls ill, is it not?"

"Yes, but we never lose this many cast members at once."

"There's a first for everything. *Again!*"

We reluctantly stand and restart the opening. I gather my clubs. I try so hard to stifle nausea that my eyes burn and well. Once more, it's all a blur.

I'm on stage juggling. Everyone performs around me.

Clap. Clap.

I spin too slowly, and a club nearly crashes down on my head. I dodge just in time, the club striking the floor, and I *run* to the side of the stage. Finding an already-filled puke bucket, I vomit up brown whiskey and pasta.

The music cuts off for the umpteenth time.

"Get it all out," Geoffrey hollers at hopefully more than just me. "When you're done purging your apathy, *line up.*"

I wish I listened to Luka and threw up before practice, but I didn't want to encourage bulimia, which he has always struggled with. For as long as I've known him, he's gone through phases of fighting against it and letting it control him.

Until this morning, I had no idea where he was mentally in the spectrum of combatting and giving in.

But he stuck his middle finger down his throat without any hesitation.

I wipe my lips with the back of my hand, pausing for a moment, and I rotate slightly to see the jagged line of artists who are currently "composed" enough to stand.

Drenched in sweat, Luka, Dimitri, Sergei, Zhen, Brenden, amongst others line up—and a lot more kneel off to the side, sick.

My brother and Luka watch me, their heads turned while everyone else stares at the velveteen seats. And then they acknowledge each other with weird grimaces. I don't have the energy to care about their clashing feelings right now, but Luka needs to stand down if we're going to keep our hook-ups secret.

Thankfully, Luka backs off, tearing his gaze away from me.

I rise to my feet, hunched over. Hand on my hip. I make sure I don't have a second wave before I join the line. I avoid the middle and slip into the right side, hoping to hide from Geoffrey.

A good chunk of the cast is still missing, and the choreographer paces the length of our uneven line. He eyes each one of us up and down.

"You." Geoffrey stops and points.

I go rigid.

For some unearthly reason, he picks *me* out of the line and gestures for me to approach him.

I near the choreographer.

"Can you roll up your sleeves?" he asks me.

This is strange. "Yeah?"

"Do it."

I roll up the sleeves of my black Adidas shirt, and he inspects my arms. I glance back at Brenden, and he mouths, *what the fuck*, at me. I shake my head once, just as confused.

I've never seen the Kotovas so on edge either. Half of them are whispering, probably in Russian.

Geoffrey tries to peer at my shoulder blades, but I can't exactly *roll* the fabric off that part of my body. "Are you wearing a sports bra?"

"You're not allowed to ask that," Dimitri, of all people, interjects.

There's an audible inhale from *many* of us.

"I would know," Dimitri adds, "I attended a sexual harassment seminar."

There's a collective laugh, but the noise sputters out at Geoffrey's glower. "If I want to hear from you, Dimitri, I'll call on you. Otherwise, *shut up.*"

I wince at that exchange.

Dimitri grimaces and forces a *fuck you* smile—but he remains quiet.

Geoffrey faces me, waiting for a response.

"I am wearing a sports bra," I confirm.

"Take off your shirt."

Whoa.

Out of the corner of my eye, I see Luka stepping forward, but Dimitri yanks him forcefully back. My brother similarly tries to intervene, but Zhen is speaking to him.

We all have to choose our battles, and this feels insignificant since I don't mind taking off my shirt. I've worked out in just a sports bra before, but if I felt uncomfortable, it'd be a different story. Because I'd definitely refuse his request.

I pull my sopping shirt off my head, and he examines my back, nodding to himself.

"I thought I saw old burn marks on your arms and shoulders yesterday but I wasn't sure. Now I am." Geoffrey motions for me to put my shirt back on. I tug it over my head as he says, "No one mentioned that you've juggled fire before."

Great. I see the interest in his eye. "I stopped juggling fire when I was fourteen."

"Why?"

I'm scared to say the truth. I know what his response will be. "It no longer fit the choreography."

"The *choreography*. You mean the *boring*, soulless routine that once existed before I arrived?" That's exactly why I should've lied, but maybe a tiny part of me agrees with him.

"What other high-risk juggling can you do?"

I'm quiet, hands on my hips. Almost winded.

"Don't make me examine your scars next."

I'm afraid. He's already one-hundred percent going to add fire to the routine. Which is fine. It'll add the "awe" factor that might help Infini. I'm definitely okay with that.

But I can't tell him that I can juggle machetes.

He'll without a doubt incorporate it within the choreography, and even with blunted edges, they're *too* dangerous for the kind of complex tricks I perform. I'm worried that if I tell him "I can juggle humongous-as-fuck knives" and then put my foot down, he'll fire me and find someone who *can* do it.

I slowly shake my head. "Nothing else."

"Nothing else?" He looks disbelieving.

"Why would I lie?" I say.

"Laziness."

I stare up at the eighty-foot ceiling, suppressing the urge to roll my eyes.

"Here's an ultimatum," he begins. *No.* I feel sick again, but for a completely different reason. "If I ask the veteran staff about your various props and they list off a high-risk one—you're fired. Or you can tell me the prop now and you'll have a choice."

Choices.

This one has to be less painful than Marc Duval's choice four-and-a-half years ago.

"What choice?" I ask.

"You'll either perform with the high-risk prop *or* you'll prove to me that you don't want to—by holding plank for three hours on this stage."

A three-hour plank? My whole face falls, unknowing whether or not I have the strength for that.

"How badly do you want to omit the prop? How much iron-will do you have?"

Strangely, his words bolster fight in me. I nod over and over.

"No, Baylee," Brenden calls out, his voice sharp with worry.

Only one choice lets me off the hook. There's no way the staff won't tell Geoffrey the truth. He may even be able to look in AE's artist database and see my specific skills.

"I'll ask you again," Geoffrey says, ignoring my brother's outburst. "What other high-risk juggling can you do?"

"Machetes."

Geoffrey claps his hands, grinning. "*That* will grab an audience's attention."

I look back at the line and almost everyone has their palms to their head. Luka is squatting, his face in his hands.

It's okay. I want to tell him.

Brenden can't meet my eyes, but he looks sick to his stomach.

I focus on Geoffrey. "Where do you want me to plank? Off to the side—"

"Right here." He points at my feet. Where I stand. Front and center. I hate being the center of attention like this, but it's over. I can't exactly rip the spotlight off anymore.

I lower to my forearms and use my core to hoist my body up, my toes on the ground in a push-up position. I hold this pose, my muscles already burning.

And then something happens.

Luka breaks the jagged line by walking forward. I arch my neck to see him fully, and without any hesitation, he comes in-line with me and easily lowers to a plank position. My lips part, stunned and overwhelmed.

He's doing this with me.

Luka turns his head to meet my gaze. So much love and encouragement stares back at me.

Sweat drips down our temples and the bridge of our noses, and not long after Luka's demonstration, Brenden leaves the line to join us. He sets his forearms on the ground, his determination pouring through me.

I love my brother so much.

One beat later, there's a mass rush forward of Russian men.

Every *single* Kotova drops down to plank position. It builds an even greater fire beneath me. The last time I had all the Kotovas on my side, I was best friends with Luka. I lost all of that when we got in trouble.

I forgot how powerful their solidarity feels.

Ten minutes in, and the entire cast of Infini is holding plank. Even the clowns.

"Camaraderie!" Geoffrey shouts. "This is what I like to see! This is what I *want*. Give me that fighting spirit every minute, *every day*."

It's not as easy as it looks, and I only wonder if there'll be more tests after this one. And worse: what happens if we fail?

ACT TWENTY-FIVE
LUKA KOTOVA

"**Y**ou can blame being late on me," I tell Sergei, an offer I shouldn't even consider—but I let it out almost subconsciously.

"I was going to," Sergei says while we ride down the Masquerade's elevator to the lobby. We were supposed to be at Retrograde, the Elvis-themed diner, about twenty minutes ago. He adds, "You're the one who couldn't land a triple-sault today."

I'm not reigniting a pointless argument. Geoffrey quickened the tempo of the music for Wheel of Death—and we're only thirty-one days away from the premiere. These little changes affect the whole routine, and I lose *time* for extra rotations in the air.

I feel like I can't keep up with the music anymore, and I've never had that problem. Rhythm—it's one of the few skills I actually excel at.

Sergei keeps glancing at me. Waiting for me to reply.

I unwrap a peppermint from my pocket. I already offered him one to break the ice, and he said *no thanks* before I could toss it to him.

I haven't hung out with Sergei outside of work yet, and now we're about to have a dinner with immediate family only: Sergei, Nikolai, me, Timofei, and Katya.

(It's going to be awkward as fuck.)

Our dark hair is wet from quick showers, and I half-expected Sergei to dress in sportswear like me: black Under Armour pants, a plain blue tee. Instead, he wears a Metallica T-shirt with black jeans.

Metallica. As in, the heavy metal band. I'm still shocked.

If I try to understand my twenty-eight-year-old brother, then that means I care about him—and I don't want to care right now.

Sergei exhales a tense breath.

I frown as he wipes his clammy palms on his thighs. "You're nervous?" (So much for not caring.)

His eyes flit to me. "Yeah. I haven't been making any ground with Timofei, but he probably told you."

I nod. Timo still isn't welcoming Sergei at all.

The grudge is simple and also explains my reservations with Sergei. Our history: we believed for the longest time that Nikolai was forced to take care of the three of us. Not even a year ago, we learned that when our immediate family split up, the only ones given a *choice* between a touring show or a resident show were the three oldest sons: Sergei, Nikolai, and Peter.

Sergei and Peter chose to travel the world with our parents.

Nikolai chose to stay with us. To become our guardian.

Their choices are loaded with emotion and feeling that none of us can separate out. Sergei decided to leave us and also let his younger brother carry a massive responsibility alone.

I think about how different my life would've been if Sergei chose us and New York. I wouldn't have filled the co-parent role with Nik part of the time. I doubt I'd be the same person I am today—and isn't that bizarre? That one person's choice can drastically change the outcome of multiple lives.

Maybe even the foundation of *who I am.*

It makes me think of my decision in Marc Duval's office. If I quit AE and gave up my family back then, Kat and Timo—they'd be affected more than I can even process. But I thought about them.

I chose *them.*

And look, I'm not trying to blame Sergei for how I turned out and my own issues—I wouldn't. I just think he has a lot to prove to Timo. To Katya. To me. And I can't lead him there.

I don't know the path to redemption. I've barely even cracked the door.

"Katya has been ignoring me," Sergei mentions, the elevator still descending. "Nikolai said to try English instead of Russian, but she won't reply in any language."

Kat and Timo offer a lot of love if you're on their side. To be against them, it'd be a fucking nightmare. I can't imagine it. Nik can probably relate more, but I'd hate for that to be me.

"They'll come around," I end up saying, wrapping him up in a fantasy. I like making people feel good, and the truth is cold. It could take them *years* to accept Sergei into their lives. It'll take me less, even if he agitates me. Even if I can't stand to be around him or listen to his voice.

I'll be cool with him in a couple months. I already know this about myself.

I already feel it happening.

Sergei exhales. "I hope so."

I suck on a peppermint. "Why are you telling me this anyway?"

His gray eyes, identical to mine, flit to me again. "Nik told me 'while everyone loves Timo, Luka loves everyone else.' I thought you'd care."

What shocks me more: that Nikolai knows me *this* well or that Sergei looks to me to help bridge the divide in our family?

I'm all out of answers.

SERGEI AND I WALK DOWN THE SINGLE AISLE OF

red vinyl booths and a bar counter with retro stools. The diner is small and open-faced to the casino floor, so I easily spot my family in the back. And chances are, they've already spotted us.

Timo slides out of a circular corner booth, his effervescent grin on me. He used blue glitter to line the bottom of his eyes, and he pinned a tiny disco ball to his leather jacket. "We waited for you to order food," he says as I greet him with a hug.

"Thanks, dude." I slide in next to Kat.

She scoots a glass-bottled soda to me. "We got you a Fizz."

I reach into my pocket and slyly hand her a packet of Starbursts. (Yeah, I have to do this beneath the table like it's a drug deal. Nik lectures me every time I supply her candy because she's prone to cavities.)

Timo takes a seat beside me—all without acknowledging Sergei, who loiters uncomfortably. An awkward second ticks by before he slips into the booth next to Nik. Knowing how much Sergei wants to mend things, I almost feel badly by the cold-shoulders.

Nik clears his throat, his terrible attempt at breaking the tension. "I ordered you water," he tells Sergei.

In Russian, he replies, "*Thank you.*"

Now that they're side-by-side, I realize Sergei looks young: clean-shaven, hair short. In contrast, Nikolai appears older: unshaven jaw, dark hair long enough to curl around his ears. Nik also sits like he has a stick up his ass.

I smile. It's just who he is. Twenty-six going on seventy-five. Life aged him—*we* aged him. My lips falter, and I take a swig of Fizz and check my cell.

I miss Baylee.

With *fire* being added to her juggling act, the tempo change in mine, and Infini's premiere in sight, we haven't had time to see each other outside of the Masquerade. Not since Two Kings. We would be with each other more if we snuck around somewhere in the hotel, but it's clearly more dangerous.

Which is why I asked her in text: *you up for meeting in the hotel, krasavitsa?*

It's her choice, but it's been a few hours and she still hasn't replied.

I push the thoughts back.

Timo hums a song and taps his drink. He beams at me, and I drum the table to the tune. Kat clinks my bottle with a fork—

"Stop," Nik says.

Timo sing-songs, "Someone sucks the fun out of everyone."

I laugh with Kat, but the humor ends when Timo expels a resigned breath, giving into Nik's request.

"What are we supposed to talk about?" Timo asks. "The weather?" He leans forward. "I heard it's nighttime." He wears real enthusiasm. "Such a revelation. *Night.*"

Sergei rolls his eyes.

"You don't like the night?" Timo asks, his grin turning bitter. "That's too bad."

"Why?" Sergei says

Timo swings his head to me. "I own the night."

Smiling, I put my arm around his shoulder and nod to him. "From two to five a.m."

"Damn right." He mimes grabbing a star from the sky.

We all laugh, except for Nik and Sergei, and thick silence returns even faster. I drop my arm off my little brother, and Sergei eyes me like *help me out, man.*

He hasn't given me a reason to help him, and yet, I'm going to. "Have you met John yet?" I ask Sergei. Instantly, I regret it.

Timo rocks backwards like I sucker-punched him. I hold my breath, my muscles flexed, hurting just as much. I shake my head at Timo and mouth, *what?*

"Who's John?" Sergei asks.

Timo shoots me a pointed look like *that's what*. I didn't know he hasn't even mentioned John Ruiz to Sergei.

Nikolai explains, "Timo's boyfriend."

Sergei looks confused at Timo. "Why didn't you tell me that you have a boyfriend?"

"Thanks, Luka," Timo says, upset.

"I'm sorry," I whisper.

Sergei sets his arms on the table, inching closer. "What am I missing here?" Silence. "I already know you're gay, Timo. When you were a little kid, you asked me to help you come out to the family. We baked a cake and had a party. Don't you remember?"

Timo nods, eyes glassing. "I remember." He produces a pained smile. "I also remember being *devastated* when I thought you were forced on a touring show. Because you"—he points at Sergei and takes a short breath—"*you* meant everything to me."

I look down.

Timo confided in Sergei the way I'd guess most sons would confide in fathers.

In New York, my little brother used to tell me, *I wish the company picked Sergei instead of Nikolai to live with us.* He believed Nik hated being our guardian—mostly, I think Timo imagined Sergei would've loved it more.

But Nikolai was the one who chose us. And Nik never wanted Sergei and Peter to be viewed as villains in our eyes, so he kept this fact hidden until it came out on its own.

It's why I undeniably *love* Nik. I respect him more than I respect any other man on this planet. If he needs me to help, I'll be there. No matter where *there* is.

Sergei leans back, submerging his emotion. "I was twenty-two. I chose my career."

Timo's face twists. "If I was given the choice to leave for higher pay or to stay here—I'd choose to stay with my brothers and sister."

"I wasn't alone. Peter left too."

"Peter who?" Timo says. Pretending to forget our twenty-four-year-old brother.

Nik puts a hand to his face, one second from groaning. He sees the fast decline of this conversation like I do.

"You can't resent me forever," Sergei says, almost pleadingly.

Timo stares sadly at Sergei. "I don't resent you. I'm just giving you exactly what you chose. Your career. Not me, not *my* life. And John Ruiz is the biggest part of my world."

The waitress steps in at this, and we tensely order from the menu. I pick something called *the kitchen sink*: a double cheeseburger, fried egg, bacon, tomato, onion, and green pepper. I'm also given a disapproving glare from both of my older brothers.

As soon as the waitress leaves, Sergei says to me, "You have practice tomorrow morning."

"Yeah," I say casually, "I'm aware of my schedule."

Nikolai pinches his eyes and whispers to Sergei in Russian, but I can't hear. I wonder if he's saying something like: *see what I've been having to deal with.*

Guilt knots my stomach. "I'm twenty," I say easily. "Please, back off."

No one says a thing, and the tension only strengthens. Everyone is looking at me.

"I'm fine," I tell them. "I have everything under control." I flip my cellphone in my hand and comb a hand through my hair.

Nikolai veers onto Katya. "How's your new porter?" (He means the dude that replaced me in the Russian bar act for Viva.)

Katya sips her pint of root beer.

Nik stares darkly and disapprovingly. "We talked about this, Katya. You said you'd make an effort."

"I said that I'd be nice. I'm nice."

He snaps in Russian, *"You're being rude."*

Katya sighs, and her eyes soften on Sergei but she speaks to the whole table. "My new porter is infatuated with Rachel Bevens, the Olympic-gymnast-turned-trapeze-artist—you know her?"

We all nod.

She twirls her straw. "He ogled her from halfway across the gym, and then they started talking, which was more like shouting, about butt glue of all things."

Nik's features darken. "What is this about?"

Timo smiles. "Katya has a crush on her porter."

"*No,*" Katya says adamantly to Timo. "I would've said something. I told you when I had a crush on Teddy—"

"Teddy?" Nik asks.

"A waiter at Imperial," Timo says, naming an expensive restaurant on the rooftop of the Masquerade.

I frown. "Wait, was this recent?" She never told me.

"A week ago," she says and shrugs like, *we haven't seen each other much.* I hate that.

Sergei clutches his water. "I still don't understand the significance of Rachel and your porter." He returns to the main subject.

I'm just as lost—and worried because she's hiding something. Her eyes dart around the diner before landing on Nik.

"I was doing a full-in full-out," she says slowly, "and he was so caught up in butt glue and Rachel that he shifted…well, he moved the beam too far to the left."

"What?!" we all yell, causing half the diner to flinch and glance at us.

"I recovered!" She raises her hands. "Calm down. One foot reached the bar and slowed my momentum. Then I kind of…"

"You kind of what?" Nik snaps, his anger directed at the porter. Not her.

Katya makes a motion with her hand that looks a lot like a body-flop. My eyes widen. "Onto the bar?"

"Yeah."

I sway back, pummeled. I can't look at her—or anyone. I stare haunted at the table, and Nik starts asking about her ribs. Sergei mentions the hospital for X-rays; AE will pay for it.

"Luk," she whispers, ignoring Nik and Sergei. "It's not your fault."

If I stayed as her porter in Viva, this wouldn't have happened. I have distractions more weighted than flirting about butt glue, but my personal life has *never* compromised my work. I've been drilled since birth about safety inside the gym and on stage.

It is my fault.

She's lucky she can even walk—in fact, Nik asks her if she can.

"You saw me walking here," she says with a tone like *you're being dramatic.*

"Do you have a bruise?" I ask my little sister.

"No."

She's lying. I can just tell. I've known her for too long. Spent too many hours around her at work, at home. "Can you show me?" I ask nicely enough that she lifts up the corner of her purple sweater, knowing Sergei and Nikolai can't see from behind the table.

I expel a pained breath. Dark yellow and purplish blemishes surround her ribs like marker bleeding into a paper towel. Only it's her skin. It looks *excruciating.* She should've immediately contacted Corporate, but Nik will be the one to say so.

My eyes lift to hers.

Katya raises her chin like she's tough, and I remember her saying, *I'm a woman.* Getting older shouldn't be about ignoring pain and emotion—but who am I to talk. I've shoved mine in drawers.

Nik never cries.

Sergei bottles his feelings.

And Timo will explode all at once.

Performing on stage is the one cathartic release we all share, and maybe it's too late for some of us to let go off stage, but Kat is still finding herself.

I hug my sister, careful of her ribs, and I whisper in her ear, "I love you, Kat. Tell me next time?"

She sniffs and nods, and I lean back as she rubs her watery eyes.

A half-wall separates us from the casino floor, and Timo must notice someone familiar by the slots because he stands up slightly on the seats. Cupping his hands around his mouth, he starts shouting, "Looking good, Thora James..." His voice teeters off, his face falling.

Something's wrong with Thora.

Katya and I slide up against the half-wall. Peering over, I spot the short blonde by a slot machine about twenty feet away. Face splotched—crying.

She's crying hard.

Nikolai sees and his demeanor changes to fierce urgency. Not even waiting for Sergei to let him out of the booth, my brother hurdles the wall and rushes to his girlfriend's side.

"Do you know what's wrong?" Sergei asks us, and we all shake our heads and watch.

Because of their noticeable height difference (six-five to five-two), he has to squat down to be eye-level.

From two booths over, I hear a person whisper, "Look, *look*. See how short she is compared to him?"

"Oh my God—and he's really built."

"Imagine them in bed."

"*Ouch*. I would not want *that* inside of me if I were her size."

I'm irritated, but Nik would kill me if I confronted hotel guests. Nik and Thora deal with worse when we go out. A drunk guy tried to fight Nik by insulting Thora, saying how "stretched out" she must be.

(People are fucking ridiculous.)

"I can't hear Thora," Katya says. "Can you hear anything?" She looks back at me.

"No." I see Thora's lips moving, but her voice is drowned by pinging of slot machines and waitresses yelling food orders to cooks.

Thora sees us and tries to rub her bloodshot eyes—Nik looks back, and then he turns his body to block our view of his girlfriend.

"You think he'll tell us what's wrong?" Timo asks.

"No," I say, knowing Nik likes to keep his personal life private. But it doesn't always mean it stays that way.

My phone buzzes on the table. Sitting back, I grab my cell before anyone can read the screen.

Out to dinner with my brother, so not tonight. But yeah, let's meet in the hotel sometime :) — Baylee

My lips rise and I type back: I like your smile.
Her next text is quick.

Where's yours? — Baylee

I reply back with five emojis.
They're all hearts.
A second passes before my phone buzzes again, but when it does, my smile expands.

I love you too. — Baylee

"Who's the girl?" Sergei asks—at first I think he's talking to Timo or Katya but they're still watching Nik and Thora.

And his gray eyes are on me.

"What are you talking about?" I pocket my phone.

"The look on your face while you were texting," he clarifies.

I shrug. "She's just a girl." It underscores every ounce of what she means to me, and I feel like I'm betraying her by calling her that—I don't even know what *just a girl* is.

Maybe he's recalling how I stepped forward on stage and held plank beside Baylee first. We all lasted the three hours, thank God. Maybe he's thinking of how I defended her. How we "did cocaine" in the past.

Maybe he's about to chew me out.

He wouldn't be the first or the second or the motherfucking *third*.

I wait.

I wait for it. (Come on, Sergei. Chastise me, too.)

"I'm starting to think," he says lowly so only I can hear, "that I don't really understand you."

I nod slowly.

Too stunned to do anything else.

Sergei looks at Timo and Kat. At Nik and Thora. And I think he's realizing, for the first time, just how much he truly missed.

ACT TWENTY-SIX
LUKA KOTOVA

"Stop! Stop!" our choreographer yells.

Inside the performance gym, I deaden my momentum on the trampoline, Bay on my shoulders. I clutch her legs, and she catches her last ball on its descent.

She can now successfully perform an eight-ball, seven-up pirouette while sitting on my shoulders, so I have no clue why he shut off the music at this spot.

My brother and six cousins come to a full stop on the net, just as perplexed.

Baylee leans her head down to me, and I look up. "Did I screw up?" she asks, wiping her forehead with the back of her hand, four balls gripped methodically in her palm. "I didn't, right?"

"No," I assure her. "It felt good."

She nods but starts smiling as my own lips rise. I'd kiss her if I could, and I really don't want to set her down yet. I run my hands discreetly up her legs, and she unconsciously tightens her thighs around my neck.

I shut my eyes in a tight blink, just for a split-second. My muscles flex, cock aching to harden.

The past two days we've been meeting in the Masquerade's twelfth floor maid's closet. (I stole the keys.) We make out but we also talk a lot. I caught her up on my family issues, and she caught me up on her brother. Who's stressed about his own act.

Geoffrey just trashed the new aerial straps choreography that Zhen and Brenden learned. Baylee said that Geoffrey called it "lackluster" and now they have to start from scratch *again*. With less than thirty days until the premiere.

There is a chance that aerial straps could be pulled off the program completely.

Baylee's lips lower, and I see that she's worried our act will have a similar fate as her brother's.

"All nine of you," Geoffrey calls, "come down here."

Gently, I hoist Baylee off my shoulders, setting her feet on the net, and I hold her hips while we wait for my cousins to descend the poles to the ground. She almost leans back into my chest, but she catches herself and straightens up.

I stand beside Bay, waiting for a free pole. Our hands skim, pass each other by, brush again—and I don't even realize I'm holding her hand until I feel her quickened pulse against mine.

We separate almost instantly. "Do you need help?" I ask as she clasps the pole.

"No, I'm okay." She drops down, better at this than when we first started.

When we're all on the ground, Geoffrey tells us to form a horizontal line. This can't be good.

We all stand stiffly, my hands clasped in front of me, and I try not to think about the last time we were in a horizontal line.

How he almost forced Baylee to start training with *machetes*.

I can't think about it. I've never been in a blackout rage, but that might push me somewhere I shouldn't be.

Geoffrey paces the length of the line, clipboard beneath his arm. "There is a reason you're all called an *artist* and not just an athlete. Your job is more than just juggling tricks and technical gymnastics. You. Must. *Emote*." He grips the air like he's trying to wrench our hearts out of our ribcages.

My family has never struggled when it comes to acting.

Which is probably why Dimitri back-talks. "Your point?"

Geoffrey walks backwards and stops in front of my older cousin. Right beside me. "You think you've given enough to this performance?"

"When the curtains are drawn, we give our all," Dimitri professes. "You don't have to concern yourself with this."

"I don't want what you've always done, and I don't care if it was good enough last season or for another show. I want unexplored, *untapped* passion." Geoffrey eyes each one of us. "You've all done acting warm-ups with the troupe."

It's not a question. On Wednesday mornings, all the AE artists form a circle in the performance gym, and we do silly and fun exercises. Like pretending to be a teapot or tossing an imaginary ball to one another. Sometimes we freestyle dance in the center.

Those mornings bond us together and create an uninhibited, non-judgmental atmosphere. It's why I love my job.

We're all family at the end of day.

Even those of us with different last names.

Pacing again, Geoffrey tells us, "Now you're going to do my acting exercise. And I'm going to pull something *new* out of you."

Half of my cousins roll their eyes. Baylee shifts her weight. I lean back on my heels, nonchalant.

I catch Baylee's gaze and smile, which upturns her lips for the briefest second.

"When I stand in front of you," Geoffrey says, "you must share an excruciating moment in your life—and don't say the words like you're reading from someone else's diary. Claim it. Use it. *Feel it.*"

Abram mutters, "No exceptions."

I laugh.

Geoffrey zeroes in on me. (Yeah, I'm still smiling—but not dryly or in defiance.) The choreographer inches towards me, and Baylee almost clasps my hand. I hook one finger with hers.

And then Sergei steps forward, obstructing the choreographer's path.

"You want to go first?" Geoffrey asks.

"Yes."

I stare fixatedly, never thinking Sergei would do that for me.

Geoffrey faces my oldest brother. "Go."

Sergei, with all his stoicism, takes one breath, and pain grips his eyes in ways he's never displayed before. "I hurt my brothers and sister."

"How?" Geoffrey prods.

"I left them when they needed me," Sergei says. "And I didn't even hesitate."

I stare off. I don't want to care right now.

I don't want to care.

But the impact behind his words rip through me, *he didn't even hesitate.* He didn't even think about us in his decision. He couldn't have.

I hurt more for Timo. That would've gutted him, and I'm never repeating it. (No fucking way.)

Baylee squeezes my hand, but she has to let go as Geoffrey glances at us.

He saunters down the line. Attention hot on me like a million spotlights. Before he reaches my place, Dimitri steps forward.

I expected that one.

"Dimitri," Geoffrey says. "Go."

He runs his tongue over his teeth before he lets out, "I was *in* love with my best friend's girlfriend. Now ex-girlfriend. Tatyana."

I didn't know he actually loved Tatyana. By the shock on his brothers' faces, neither did Robby or Anton.

"I not only had to watch Tatyana be with him—knowing she'd never love me—but I watched her break her leg and leave permanently for Russia." He has to pause here, his nose flaring. "So I lost a friend too."

Geoffrey scrutinizes his features for an extended moment. "You're holding back."

"I'm *not*," Dimitri growls, his chest puffed out in offense.

"That's better." Geoffrey nods once and then eyes me. Again.

Baylee is about to step forward to the left of me, but I clench her tank and pull her back. Geoffrey will reach me no matter what. She doesn't need to go before me.

Geoffrey faces me. "Luka."

(What's up, Geoffrey? Relax, dude.) I think of the sex doll in his office, and I try hard not to smile.

"Go."

I unbury a raw place inside of me—just through my eyes. "When I was young, my girlfriend *died*." I let out a heart-breaking breath, and I think I would've gotten away with it if Abram and Robby didn't lean forward with shit-eating grins.

Geoffrey eyes them, brows furrowed. "You're lying?"

"I spoke figuratively."

My younger cousins laugh.

I can't help it—I smile.

Geoffrey steps forward, only a foot from my face. I remain calm and cup my hands in front of me again. He searches my eyes feverishly for *truth*, I'm guessing.

I am full of truths and heartache and pain.

Half belongs to people I care about. Me hurting for them. And the half that belongs to me, I'm not allowed to express.

If he's aware of my past with Baylee, then he already knows this, but he still seems oblivious. Even if we caught him chatting with Vince one time.

"Are you ever angry?" he asks me.

"What?"

"Do you *ever* get angry?" he wonders. "I've seen these ones"—he gestures to my cousins—"argue and become frustrated, but you…you just let everything roll off your shoulders."

Is he serious? "Can I ask why you're saying this like it's a character flaw?"

"I want *feeling*. What makes you tick?"

(Motherfucking Corporate.) I shrug. "I don't know." He's literally staring me dead in the eyes like we're in a Western and he's about to draw a gun from his holster and shoot me.

"I'm glaring at you, and you're relaxed."

"You don't scare me."

"I don't?"

"No," I say just as casually. I seriously believe Geoffrey wants to provoke me into a fight right now.

Dimitri, Sergei, Matvei, and Erik—the oldest four—turn towards me in anticipation of something that I don't even want to happen. I'm not even tensed up. If I touch our choreographer, I could be fired on spot.

I see Baylee out of the corner of my eye. She's trying to angle her body to catch his attention and draw his interest off of me.

I angle my back to her. Hiding her from his sight.

Geoffrey follows my shift. Still right up in my face. (His goatee is ugly, in case you were wondering.) "When's the last time you sobbed?" he asks.

"I don't remember," I say the truth.

"When's the last time you jerked off?"

"You *can't* ask him that," Baylee says passionately, pretty much pissed off for me.

Geoffrey barely acknowledges her. "I just did. Does it make you upset?" he asks *me*.

"Yesterday," I answer his previous question. "And no."

"What were you thinking about?"

I almost laugh. It's absurd how much I can't actually say because of Corporate, which he works for. Irony. I think that term fits here. The answer, of course, is Baylee Wright. I imagined wrapping my arms around her waist and chest from behind. Then I bent her over a bed and pushed into her pussy.

She came instantly.

"Don't laugh," Geoffrey says. "Don't smile. I want severity."

Severity. "Fine," I say, suppressing my humor. "But asking me what I jerk off to isn't exactly serious."

"You have a sister? Don't you?" (Welcome to the worst segue in the history of segues.)

I'm already feeling overprotective of Katya. I took her to the ER with Nik, and the doctor said if she came down any harder on the beam, she would've fractured three ribs. Luckily they were just severely bruised.

Geoffrey snaps, "It's not a hard question. Do you have a sister?"

I immediately glance at Dimitri—who's scrutinizing the choreographer with narrowed eyes.

"Don't look at him. Look at me."

I obey.

Geoffrey smiles. "There's a glare."

If he wants me to glower like I'm seconds from ripping out his large intestines, I can do that, easily. Anger just leads nowhere good. I've been the angst-ridden fifteen-year-old banging at Corporate's brick walls until my fists bloodied. I don't do that anymore.

"Tell an excruciating moment," he says, "that involves your sister."

"No," I say like someone would say *yes*. No harshness.

"No?"

"No," I say just as simply.

His nose is one centimeter from touching mine. (I'm not exaggerating.) "Then I'll list out various scenarios involving your sister that *will* bring something out of you."

I blink a few times, and he studies the way I literally process two aggressively painful situations. I lick my lips and breathe, "Stop." It slipped.

"I didn't catch that."

My nose flares, and I blink rapidly before I rake my fingers through my hair. *I'm in control.* (Am I in control?)

"Lay *off* of him," Baylee interjects, trying to side-step around me, but I block her again. "Luka."

"I'm fine."

"No, you're not."

"He's not?" Geoffrey tilts his head at me, almost challengingly.

"My sister is a minor," I suddenly inform him.

Geoffrey actually flinches.

(Yeah, fuck off.)

I am compacting too much shit I'm not supposed to say and feel into drawers and (parentheticals) that my heart pounds at an abnormal speed.

"If you're not willing to participate, then you're officially out of this act," he threatens.

"I am participating," I say. (You just don't like my responses.)

"A story about your sister—"

"I was *ten*," I retort, stepping towards him, hands cupped behind my back. *Can't touch him.* He's forced to back up so our noses don't hit. "In Minnesota for the month. I stole a pair of sunglasses and gave them to my sister. Thought it'd be nice. She wanted a pair. Store clerk saw, called the cops—couldn't get ahold of Mom and Dad." I grimace out my feelings. "No matter how many times I told the cops that I stole the sunglasses, they didn't believe me. They just kept scolding my sister. Who was *little* and sobbing on the ground."

"More," he says.

"What more?" My voice nearly shakes in ire. I think of Baylee and me. How we always search for *more*—it's not a feeling you can capture. It's intangible. Unquantifiable.

I'm not giving him what I can't even give myself.

"Why do you steal?" he asks.

Not, why *did* you steal. Why *do* you steal. As though he knows it's ongoing. It's never left. A demon in my drawer.

Rumors. People talk about me. I know.

I'm tense. On edge. But I'm quiet. So quiet that Geoffrey does something—he swiftly steps at me, our noses hitting and he fists my shirt.

(I'm not kidding.)

(I'm still not exaggerating.)

I shove him with two forceful palms to his chest, and as he stumbles back, almost tripping on his ass, all four of my cousins swarm me. Yanking me back.

"Stop," I tell them, my right arm raised. "I'm cool, dude." Erik is wrestling with my fucking arm for no reason, and Dimitri grips my shirt so tight, the collar digs into my neck.

Here's the thing: when people think you're a doormat, they try extra hard to walk all over you. Then they get surprised when you fight back.

Bay knows what it feels like, too. We're the ones minding our own business in a corner quietly, and then someone comes over and tries to poke at us.

This is what happens.

Every time.

I rip out of my cousins' protective hold. They're saving me from being fired, just in case I go at him again.

"Take a break in the locker room," Sergei suggests, his tone unreadable.

I nod, and on my way out of the gym's backroom, I hear Geoffrey speak to my brother. "If he's not willing to be vulnerable and honest in front of nine people, how can I expect him to be in front of three-thousand, twice a night?"

"Was that not vulnerable enough for you?"

"No. He's still holding back."

ACT TWENTY-SEVEN
LUKA KOTOVA

In the locker room, I sit on a bench across from my blue locker, my water bottle in hand. Pretty much alone for a half hour until I hear footsteps around the corner.

Baylee appears, and my lips begin to rise. She leans her hip on a metal locker and digests my smile. "You're not even a little nervous that I just sought you out at work?"

"No." I stand and put my water away. "I just figured you snuck off without anyone seeing."

Baylee straightens up as I near. "I did." She gestures with her head towards the entrance. "The whole gym is obsessed with celebrity gossip. Thought I'd find you while they're preoccupied." She touches her shoe to mine. "See how you're doing."

I watch her cast a furtive glance over her shoulder. She's taking a huge risk being here right now. Sure, we can say it's for "work" but the Corporate spy is more likely to catch us here than a maid's closet.

I nod towards the showers.

She relaxes at the suggestion, and I interlace our fingers, leading her deeper into the locker room. We push through a door, and our shoes hit damp tile.

It's empty. I pass the middle row of sinks and choose the very last shower stall. Whipping open the curtain, we step into the tiny "undressing" area with two ledges to set towels and toiletries. A second curtain conceals the actual shower.

Hidden, we instantly hug. My arms curve around her shoulders, and I pull her as close to my chest as I can. Her arms wrap around my waist, her heartbeat thudding hard against my body.

We sway like we're dancing.

I breathe deeply and drift back, just enough for her brown eyes, full of empathy and fear, to meet mine. "I'm okay," I say.

"He's trying to break you," she says matter-of-factly, trying not to hurt from it. "It's awful."

I cup her cheeks. "He *won't* break me."

Baylee inhales a strong breath and then groans softly in frustration. "I didn't think he was this malicious."

My brows jump. "Bay, he forced you to take your shirt off and boxed you into a three-hour plank. What'd you think, he was being *nice* then?"

Her eyes flit to the curtain before speaking hushed. "His intentions made sense to me. His job is to make Infini more exciting, and high-risk juggling has a wow factor. But singling you out and trying to *purposefully* incite you because you're laidback compared to your cousins—what even is that besides cruel?"

I ask because I have to be sure, "The story about my sister, I said it with emotion?"

"*Yes*," she whispers adamantly. "More than Sergei's. It's almost like Geoffrey thinks you have some sort of magical compartment of *pain* that you can tap into, and it'll cause audiences to cry in adoration."

I have a compartment of pain, but if I open it, I'll be too fucked-up to even get on stage. She knows this. It's why she's afraid he'll break me.

"In short," Baylee whispers, "he's a diabolical moron."

I speak quietly too. "I still can't believe you're just now horrified. Should I feel honored or concerned?" I smile at the look she gives me, her seriousness never waning. "Come here, krasavitsa." Edging close, the curves of her hips meld against the ridges of my body.

She looks up. "You know I'm here for you, Luka." We used to always have each other's back. When she was depressed, I was there. When I felt like things were spiraling out of my control, she was there. Our mental issues predate our friendship. They existed when we were together.

They persisted when we separated.

And they're here right now. Living inside of us. They will rise and fade but never truly go away. There is no quick-fix or cure—but we deal. Every day, we silently *deal* with it, but facing our demons with support has always been easier than facing them alone.

"I *see* it," I say wholeheartedly. I nod to her. "I *feel* it. You don't even have to say it, Bay."

She swallows, this small thread of hurt still strung between us— because we can't do or say any of this out in the open.

I rest my forehead to hers; I hold the back of her head. She grips my waist, and I can hear her shallow breath. I slip my other hand up her tank top, our bodies grinding instinctively together.

My lips descend to hers, and a breath away, I whisper, "I know how hard you've been fucked before."

Her lips part, and she makes an involuntary noise, like a breathy moan. The sound alone fists my shaft and strokes up and down. My muscles flex, and instead of kissing Bay, I spin her around and clutch her back to my chest.

My arm around her abdomen, other one around her breasts. Pressed this close, she can feel my erection against her, and she curses beneath her breath, *panting* already.

I suck the nape of her neck, and she shudders in my arms. My muscles constrict, and I harden even more. Without letting go of Baylee, I walk through the next curtain. Into the actual shower. She moves with me, and I only take my hand off Bay to close the curtain.

My lips against her ear, I whisper, "In a minute, you'll be fucked harder than you've ever been fucked before. My *cock*"—I have to hold her tighter as she trembles more forcefully—"will be buried so deep inside of you, you'll cry at the feeling of being completely, entirely full."

"Luka," she says into another breathy noise.

My nose flares, and I release my grip around her waist and put her palms against the shower wall. She turns her head slightly—I turn her head more with two fingers, and our lips meet, kissing hard and rough and urgent. Like this could all end.

At any moment.

It could be all over again.

I deepen the kiss, and Baylee digs her ass into me—I yank down her sports leggings, and she steps out.

I peel off my shirt, her shirt and bra—my shorts and compression shorts. Both of us naked, my arm snakes around her hip, and my hand dips between her legs. *She's beautiful.* Every curve. Every straight line and mound—I love every inch of this girl.

Baylee leans her weight back against me, trusting me. Letting go of the wall.

I kiss her neck, a grunt in my throat, and I rub her clit while I hold her back against my body. Baylee's head lolls to my chest, eyes shut in pure arousal. Mouth agape.

In my arms, she has no problem getting off. She's not numb or frozen in fear. But that's only because she's emotionally connected to me. She's hasn't let go, and this list is making it even harder to do that.

I know now—or maybe I've known all along—that we're just using the list as an excuse to be together. To see each other. Neither of us will bring up the fact that it's not working. Neither of us will admit the truth.

Because then it ends.

I cover her mouth with my palm. Her noises raspier and louder as my fingers speed up and pulse inside of her. *So fucking wet.*

She turns her head left and right, overwhelmed. I smile, my heart rate elevating and sweat building just as much on my body as hers. Baylee arches in an orgasm, her moan vibrating against my hand. I suck the base of her neck, and she careens forward, her entire body quivering.

My cock is throbbing, too intensely. I flex my core to keep from coming.

"Shit," she cries, water creasing her eyes from the climax. She clutches onto my wrist between her legs.

"You're okay," I breathe in her ear. "You're okay." I cup her pussy and then wrap my other arm around her collarbones. Baylee shuts her eyes, coming down with heavy breaths.

With every muscle fiber, every burning nerve in my veins—I *crave* to go down on Baylee. More than she can probably fathom, but I'm not touching *number four* on her list. Once I do, it's all over.

Our ending will be crueler than Geoffrey could ever be to us. There is no happy ending, so I'm staying in the middle for as long as humanly possible.

Baylee's head swerves, finding my lips, and we kiss slower. Sensual. I spin her around fully and cup her face. Since she's on birth control, I don't worry about a condom.

I draw her even closer, and I hike her left leg around my waist. I'm about to lift her up by the hips, but she presses her forehead to my chest and mutters, "Wait wait."

I wait, at first thinking she needs to catch her breath, but gradually, she slides her arms beneath mine, hugging me. Her cheek to my chest.

Bay.

I drop her leg so I can wrap my arms around her again. I watch her eyes close, and she relaxes before grinding up against me. I can't explain what that was. It's happened a million times before. When I was young, I used to think every girl needed this skintight affection.

(They don't. Everyone is different.)

"Ready?" I whisper in her ear.

She nods.

Easily, I lift Bay, clutching her hips, and our eyes lock while I lower her onto my erection. Warmth cocoons my cock like a closed fist—my eyes nearly roll back. *Yes...* She inhales a sharp breath and cries out, not too loudly.

I use my arms to raise her up and down my shaft. Slow at first. Baylee's fingers dig into my shoulder as she pants for deeper breaths. Our gazes don't detach, and I speed up in an instant—unknowing how much time we have before people fill the locker room.

Fuck...fuck. I ram so hard and quick into Bay that I brace her shoulders to the wall and rest my forearm beside her head. My muscles constricting. Scalding. Flexing. All to drive my cock deeper, farther, *harder* into Baylee.

On another plane of existence, *fuck.* A guttural sound scratches my throat, but I force it down and cover her mouth as she cries out again. I seize her gaze, desire blanketing my entire being. She trembles, thighs vibrating against me.

Fuckfuckfuck. I lift my hand off her mouth, kissing her passionately, and then she has to turn her head, about to come.

"Luka," she says into the softest, most vulnerable cry.

Lit on fire, I hold her cheek and caress her skin with my thumb. "You're coming," I whisper against her lips, only speeding up the friction.

I'm so far inside this girl.

My eyes roll and I shut them and hit a peak with Bay. My body rocking forward. She clenches around my cock, fingernails dug in my back, and eyes tightened closed.

With a heavy breath, I milk the climax, pumping in and out on a slow descent. Coming down, Baylee hugs onto my neck, and I carefully pull out but keep her hoisted around my waist.

That's when a door creaks, proceeded by the *slam* as it shuts.

We both tense and don't dare make a move.

Someone's here.

I strain my ears and catch two audible voices. A girl. And a guy.

Baylee stares wide-eyed at our closed shower curtain. Footsteps near. The voices escalate, growing close. I feel her pulse race.

I strengthen my grip, one hand beneath her thigh, my other arm around her back—pressing her body firmly to my chest, and her breathing steadies.

I listen intently, my gaze fixed on the motionless curtain.

"AE's doctors did their own tests, and this…is happening."

I know that voice.

It's Thora James.

"Myshka—" Nikolai starts to say *little mouse* in Russian, his husky voice tender for his girlfriend.

Thora interjects, "You said that you'd leave the choice up to me, and you'd support me no matter what—but you already know what I'm going to say, don't you? You knew what I'd choose."

"Yes."

I frown, hearing the emotion in my brother's voice.

Thora takes an audible breath. "You think I'm idealistic?"

"*Brave*," he says deeply.

In a short pause, I picture her wiping tears and my brother hugging his girlfriend. As they speak more hushed, I turn my head slightly towards the curtain. Trying to hear every word.

"I decided," Thora breathes, "that life has always been unpredictable. I came here for the slim chance to be in the circus, and what I got was the most unbelievable dream job—and *you*. How we react to life's curveballs is what defines us. I can put my job on hold while I'm…" Her voice breaks, but in Thora James' fashion, her optimism blooms in place of fear. "I might be ordinary and average, but I'm capable of anything if I just believe in myself. And I do. I can do this, Nik."

"*We*," Nik says. "The responsibility of a baby is not all on you, myshka. This is ours."

My jaw unhinges.

Thora is pregnant.

I exchange a stunned look with Bay. Being pregnant in this profession—it's like sustaining an injury with a year-long recovery. It means being benched for a whole season with no guarantee that you'll land a contract for the next.

"The other thing I have to say," Thora tells him so quietly I almost miss it, "you're not going to like."

I can almost *feel* my brother tense up.

"The higher-ups in AE, I don't even know their names, already created a timeline and schedule for me. I didn't meet them, but their assistants relayed the info. They said that while I'm unable to perform, aerial silk will be shelved—"

"I don't care," Nik says. He performs aerial silk, so he'll be relegated to group acts only. "I *wouldn't* care about that."

"That's not it," Thora says. "They want me—*us*, to finish out March."

My stomach drops.

Baylee looks incensed and confused, and she mouths to me, *they can't do that.*

It sounds like Corporate just did.

"You're *pregnant*," Nik growls under his breath, his voice rattling in rage. "You can't perform. It's too dangerous."

"They said since I'm only six-weeks, I can go until the end of March."

I try to count in my head, but Nik already has the numbers. "It's only March 17th, Thora. There's two weeks left—you *can't*. I know you believe you *can*, but this shouldn't be on the table at all. I'm talking to Kavich."

He's the lead director for Amour.

"You can try," she says softly, "but they told me that more critics were coming in March—and they need aerial silk in the program. If I don't do this, they said that they wouldn't pay me for the two months I've been in Amour. And they kind of hinted that I wouldn't have a job to return to."

She means *threatened*.

(Fuck Corporate.)

"They're trying to take advantage of you. They have to pay you; it's in your contact—"

Thora cuts in as he gets heated, "I know. I already called my parents. I asked them if they knew any lawyers that could read over my contract."

Baylee gives me a look like she's about to sneeze. She pinches her nose, and I try to bring her head to the crook of my shoulder.

She sneezes, and in Thora and Nik's abrupt silence, the sound muffles—but not a hundred-percent.

We cage our breaths. Rigid. Staring at the curtain. They drop their voices to inaudible whispers, and their footsteps near.

Closer.

Closer.

Curtain hooks scratch the metal pole, plastic fabric whipping to the side. It's not ours. It's to the left of us.

Their paranoia radiates as strong as our panic.

And then they whisper and begin to retreat. Leaving the showers.

Look, I don't feel like we dodged a bullet. We're gripping fiercely, *ragingly*, onto an unconquerable mountainside—and instead of falling, I just learned that my brother is climbing nearly the same one.

ACT TWENTY-EIGHT
LUKA KOTOVA

On the indoor cobblestone walk, I pass a Masquerade gift shop—and then I skid to a stop for no apparent reason. A family of four rolls their suitcases past me to the elevators, and I turn my head, staring down the gift shop's glass walls and door.

Pressure, like three-tons of weight, bears on my chest. I uncoil my earbuds that are wrapped around my phone and stick them in. I play "Time" by Jungle and nod my head to the beat, moving forward. Onto the casino floor.

I try to breathe. I blink a few times and switch to my Broadway playlist. I try to loosen up.

Not even a minute later, I stop again.

I look back, rubbing my lips. The weight isn't gone. Something itches at me. Like a bug stuck in my eardrum. I need to do it.

I need to do it.

Fuck it.

I rotate and aim for the gift shop. Popping my earbuds out, I shove my phone in the pocket of my navy gym pants.

Inside the tiny gift shop, the twenty-something blonde employee flips through a magazine and welcomes an old couple behind me.

I'm invisible as I peruse racks of snacks and essentials like batteries and toothbrushes. Knowing where the security cameras are positioned, I set my back to them and act like I'm examining the ingredients of Chex Mix. I'm actually pocketing three packs of spearmint gum and orange Tic Tacs.

I'm not afraid.

I'm not even out of breath. It took me years to understand what I'm searching for, and it's not the excitement or adrenaline rush. It's this next part.

I turn around, and as I leave the store, I look back just once. The blonde employee smiles brightly at the old woman, and I think, *I got out unscathed.* Relief floods me.

Fills me.

Weight lifts off of me for this moment, and I breathe deeply.

And I smile, unwrapping and popping a piece of gum in my mouth. Ignoring the guilt.

Not many people are congesting the casino, especially for a Saturday afternoon. I saunter further through the rows of slots and velvet-topped tables. Looking for my little brother.

I spot Timo at a blackjack table in what's considered the "party pit"—but it's not as rowdy as it could be. As I sidle up to the empty stools, I catch Timo's attention.

Even though he wears workout gear, he's in full costume makeup for Amour tonight: a black streak across his gray eyes, dark shadow enhancing his cheekbones, and silver shimmer lining his features.

With his hair slicked back, he should appear menacing, but his partial smile carries more light than a person's full-blown grin.

I nod in greeting, but I don't sit down like him.

Timo gives me one look that says: *don't bring up Sergei.*

Mine says: *I won't.*

"You've both fallen one-too-many-times on your heads, right?" That's John. From behind the card table, dressed in a dealer's black tux and gold bowtie, his eyes ping from me to Timo. "It's the only explanation. *People*, real life, breathing people—"

Timo grins. "Why do you always have to leave out ghosts, man?"

John cocks his head but steps over Timo's comment, "People shouldn't be able to communicate by eyesight like that. It's unsettling. It's an evolutionary malady. One step too far for humanity."

I think this is John's long-winded way of saying Timo and I are "creepily" close.

My brother's smile brightens. "You think I'm evolved, John?"

"I think you're killing humanity, and you're killing me. As we speak." Despite appearing surly, John never breaks my brother's gaze.

They're flirting. It's obvious to me.

From other slots and tables, people watch Timofei as he radiates pure energy that's almost indescribable. And he's just sitting down. It lifts my chest, and I start to smile for no reason.

John is just as entranced, though he doesn't let on as strongly as others.

"I'm that powerful in your eyes," Timo teases.

John glares at the ceiling with an expression that's best described as "I hate the fucking world and its incompetent subjects"—and I've actually heard him say that exact phrase before.

"Don't worry, John," Timo says, "I'll bring you back to life after I kill you."

John shakes his head once. "Don't try and you can't. In this ghastly overpopulated universe, the dead stay dead and the living stay shittily living…." His voice drifts with his eyes. "Luka, take a seat."

I sit before I follow his gaze to a drunk cluster of thirty-something guys in nice suits. Their gold-plated watches seem expensive.

"They don't tip," John says to me, "and they've been throwing down ten-grand a hand. They smell like a rotten ham sandwich and menthol—oh, and they're fucking clumsy."

Timo leans into me. "They spilled bourbon on his table last night."

"I hate people," John finishes, which makes no sense since he's a service worker. He's *paid* to put a smile on his face and chat-up strangers. He rarely does the former, but he's way too proficient at the latter.

As the drunk guys look to John's table, I kick up my legs on all of the empty stools. Stretching out. They're too plastered to be offended, and they stumble and holler their way to baccarat.

A few of our young cousins pass, no older than ten, and they all say hi to Timofei. Spinning on his stool, he slings his arm over their shoulders, and he compliments them in Russian. Makes them feel better about themselves—I can tell.

They light up, and by the time they leave, they're all smiling. In a better mood.

Happy.

Timo makes people happy. (Me included.)

"ID," John tells me.

I smile while I chew my gum and pass him my fake ID. Many times, he's mentioned that his pit boss is watching, but management knows we're underage—and they still let us drink and gamble.

(Perks of being a Kotova.)

The Masquerade profits a lot off of my family's talent. I'm talking millions of dollars that we rack in with every show, and the hotel has become known for Infini and Viva and now Amour. People stay here *especially* for the circus.

So yeah, management looks the other way when I drink a beer, dance in a club, or sit at a blackjack table. Why shouldn't they?

The Masquerade is worth 5 billion.

Aerial Ethereal is worth 2 billion.

And I'm just an artist. On the low rung of the Corporate ladder. They all bathe in their wealth, and I'm on stage, working my ass off for the art.

For that final applause. For my family.

I watch John inspect my ID. Really, I think he just likes reminding us that we're not special.

He takes longer than usual. "Something wrong?" I ask.

Timo says, "The old man probably needs his glasses."

John rolls his eyes but hangs onto my ID. "Play a few rounds and then I'll return this to you." He slips my ID in his back pocket. I don't understand what he's getting at.

"Luk has early-evening practice," Timo says and spins more towards the table. "I'm betting five-hundred."

John feeds a deck of cards in an automatic shuffler. "As your dealer, I advise you to bet less."

Timo almost laughs. "How do you still have a job here?"

"It's advice I only give to people I can't stand."

"So everyone."

"*You,*" he corrects.

Timo leans forward. "I'm up two-hundred, and this is my last hand before I leave for work. I've made worst decisions." He gestures to him. "Like dating you."

It's supposed to be a joke, but John is the one with the insults while Timo exultantly chases after him, like a firefly in a storm cloud.

John looks more concerned than hurt. "You think I like nagging you, babe? I don't—I'd rather eat my left foot."

Timo opens his mouth to say something, but he hesitates and checks the time on his phone. "I have to go warm-up for the show anyway." Standing off the stool, he avoids John's gaze and they don't kiss like usual.

I'm about to follow my little brother to make sure he's okay.

"I have your ID," John suddenly tells me—and now I realize why he held onto it. He wants to keep *me* here after Timo leaves. With twelve-hour practices every single day, it's not like I've been accessible lately. Today is just different. Our practice times were shifted for a Corporate luncheon, all to schmooze investors.

I wasn't invited. (I'm still Corporate's Least Favorite.)

Standing, I reach out for my ID and watch my brother vanish towards Amour's globe auditorium.

John doesn't even reach into his pocket. "Can you sit?"

I take a seat and face him. "But I'm not playing." I don't like wasting money gambling.

John nods understandingly, and for once, he's *quiet*.

I laugh into a smile.

He scowls. "What?"

"You're nervous, dude." I lean back on two legs of my stool. Balancing. "It's alright. You can talk about Timo. I'm not going to snitch if it's serious. It can stay between us."

John glances at his pit boss before shuffling the cards again. "I couldn't be more opposite from your brother if I actually tried—and I don't try. Trying is for idealists and romantics."

I worry this is about Timo's lack of relationship experience. He mentioned that John only does monogamous relationships, something my little brother knows nothing about. This is his first.

"When I'm stressed, I let it permeate because misery should be felt by all," John tells me. "It keeps people grounded. Life sucks, don't enjoy it."

I almost smile again. His pessimism is somehow engaging, which is why he's one of the most liked dealers in all of the Masquerade.

John stacks casino chips. "When Timo is stressed, he holds it all in and gambles. He's been at my table *four* times just today, and not because he wants to see my face—which I'm sure is part of it, but not all of it." He flips a red $5 chip between his fingers, and his eyes finally lift to me.

I see his unease. "What are you getting at?"

"His stress originates from *Sergei*. He's been going out of his way to keep me separated from your older brother, and he's been obsessing over the joint birthday party next week."

Katya and Nikolai. Their birthdays are one day apart, and we're supposed to celebrate at The Red Death on Saturday, Nik's favorite nightclub.

Sergei will definitely be there.

So will John.

He adds, "This familial whatever-you-want-to-call-it: dispute, drama, headache—it's making Timo sick."

Chewing my gum slower, I fall onto all four legs of the stool and sit forward. Careful not to touch the tabletop. "Look, I know all of this. I don't give Timo money when he gambles. I don't rag on him except when he overdoes it."

His dark brows furrow. "I'm not sure you're hearing what I'm saying." He thinks I haven't comprehended the severity of the situation.

"No, I am," I say, self-assured. "You're telling me that my brother has a *serious* issue. Mind you, it's taken you a thousand extra words to come to a point I've been aware of forever. You're also going to ask for my help because I'm the closest person to Timo, and you're not sure how to intervene without overstepping."

John skims me up and down. Like he's never truly seen me before. I listen when people talk. It shouldn't be such a fucking revelation.

I rip open another piece of gum. "You can ask."

"I'm going to run into Sergei next Saturday. That's not a question. It's a fact, and I need to know how I should react."

I smile while I pop spearmint in my mouth. "You want me to tell you how you should feel?" I shake my head. "Dude, the minute you see Sergei, you're going to feel what you feel, and there's no shutting that off."

"I can program my feelings."

"If that were true, wouldn't you be less…?" I gesture at him.

His dark scowl never changes shape. "I like the way I am. I prefer it. The sun is annoying. Smiles are ridiculous, and happiness is for fools." He says that, but John is also full of contradictions. I never take all of his words at face value.

"Okay, without my opinion, how would you react to Sergei if you saw him right now? I'll tell you if it's a good way to go."

John stares at the ceiling like it has personally accosted him. "Let's see what I know about Sergei. One"—he counts off his fingers—"he's the cause of my boyfriend's daily distress. Which should be enough for me to hate the fuck out of him. But life just has to be more complicated than that. Two: he's the older brother of Nikolai, who I initially didn't gel with at all. Do I expect Sergei to be antagonistic or affable towards me? I have no answer."

I'm about to interject, but John isn't finished.

"Three"—he raises three fingers—"beneath everything, I see that Timo loves Sergei, but I don't know how much love is left after what he did."

I realize that Timo must've filled John in on the bad blood. "Is that it?" I wonder.

"I could go to one-hundred, but I'll stop there for the sake of my own sanity." He motions to me. "So what is Sergei really like?"

I shake my head with a weak laugh. "A know-it-all. Rigid in thought. If he has an idea, his is the best one. Sometimes it's like speaking to a brick wall, and not the kind you can knock down."

"So he's like Nikolai."

"No," I say quickly. "To me, he's nothing like Nikolai." I lick my dry lips. "Nik is humble and protective. When Nik clashed with you in the past—it's because he was guarding Timo. Sergei has *no clue*…" My throat closes, choked for a second.

I feel John staring at me darkly and intently. "No clue about what?"

"Sergei hasn't been here," I say strongly. "Not in New York, not in Nevada. He missed all the terrible shit we dealt with."

John pauses for less than a second. "There's a high probability that I will flat-out hate Sergei on the spot."

"You can't be a dick to Sergei just because Timo is on the outs with him. You also can't be too friendly because Timo will feel like you're not on his side. Stay somewhere in the middle."

John sighs into an exasperated groan. "What's in the middle of being dickish and nice-ish?" He rubs his unshaven jaw. "Nothing. It's just a void."

"Try not to glare at him," I suggest while I stand up and outstretch my palm for my ID. "Sergei likes *enthusiasm*."

"Fucking A," John says flatly and puts my ID in my palm. Before I move, he asks, "Will you be at the birthday party next week?"

I frown, confused. "Yeah. Why wouldn't I be?"

John lifts his brows at me like it's obvious. "I consider The Red Death my third or fourth home, and every Saturday night, regardless of special occasions, Kotovas swarm the place like locusts. No offense."

"None taken."

"But weirdly, I think I've seen you there twice…maybe three times. If that. You're not going there tonight, are you?"

"No."

"But next week—"

"I'll be there." I pocket my ID.

"Why exactly don't you hang out with the Kotovas at The Red Death every week?" he asks point-blank.

It's simple. "We all weren't allowed to go to The Red Death until we turned seventeen—Nik's rule. I turned seventeen, and I promised Kat that I wouldn't ditch her every week. That I'd wait for her to reach my age." I give him the same look he gave me. Like it's obvious. "Most Saturday nights, I go to Verona with Katya."

Verona is the Masquerade's throwback dance club. They play eighties and nineties music. It's tamer than The Red Death, but still fun.

John tilts his head. "And here, I thought you were a Kotova sellout."

My lips upturn. "Circus is family."

The love we carry for each other is the strongest and most vulnerable place in us all.

ACT TWENTY-NINE
LUKA KOTOVA

*I*n my suite, I have one hand on the fridge handle and I text using my other.

> Do you need ice for your burn? I can bring some over.

I send the message to Baylee. I'll be in her suite because everyone's eventually congregating there for Nik and Katya. All before we leave for the party tonight.

I check the oven clock. It's only 8:00 p.m.—still early.

I mouth the lyrics to "ABC Café / Red & Black" from Les Misérables that blasts in my ears, my headphone's cord tangled around my cell.

Incoming text.

You know you can't. — Baylee

Just tell me if you have ice in your freezer's tray. I type and send it, refusing to pretend like I don't care about Bay. I'd *care* as just co-workers. (We're more than that, but still, no one can know.)

She majorly burned her forearm juggling fire at practice this morning and had to see AE's on-call docs.

I reread my text and then send a heart emoji.

With my elbow, I rub off water that drips down my temples. I should've towel-tried my hair better after my shower. I face the fridge in just charcoal-gray boxer-briefs. Still getting ready.

I scan the fridge's contents for any food without *Brenden* or *Zhen* written on it.

My phone buzzes.

:(— Baylee

I frown, my stomach dropping. *Sad?* I send.

Yeah. I feel like sleeping ... or just talking to you. Do you think we can hang out at The Red Death in front of everyone? Or is that too much? (no ice) — Baylee

Someone suddenly rips my earbud out.

I flinch and my head swerves to my right. Brenden stands a foot from me, and I instantly lower my cell, hiding the screen from his view.

Brenden sighs like he's annoyed at the annoyance he feels for me. "I called your name five times."

"Sorry," I say casually. "I couldn't hear you." My muscles constrict. Unsure of where this is headed. We've successfully avoided each other for months.

If I'm in our kitchen, he turns the other way.

If he's in our living room, I dip out of the suite entirely.

Beneath an unzipped windbreaker, he's shirtless, and I immediately spot the letters *Baylee* inked with *Mom* and *Dad* over his heart.

I try not to forget how much he means to Bay, and how much she means to him.

"Are you done?" He gestures to the fridge.

"No, but you can go." I step back, but he's already shaking his head.

"You can go first." He motions and then crosses his arms over his chest.

The exchange is more awkward than it even seems. We're both uneasy, and we're just standing in the tiny kitchenette opposite a refrigerator.

Quickly, I scour the shelves and realize that I need to go grocery shopping.

I find a jar of dill pickles. Dimitri's food, but he won't care.

Brenden stares at me weirdly as I exit with the pickles. He hangs onto the fridge door and watches me unscrew them and search for a fork in the drawers.

"What are you looking for, man?" he asks.

"A fork."

"No, I mean *food*." Brenden points at fridge shelves. "I was going to make myself a sandwich." He pauses. "If you want one, I have more cheddar and turkey. Wheat bread, though. And it's all organic."

I'm caught off guard by the offer and a little on edge. Still, I nod. "Yeah, sure." I nod again. "Thanks."

Brenden pulls out cheese, turkey, and mustard, and then he points to the cupboard. I follow the silent direction and grab the loaf of wheat bread.

When we collect plates and silverware, we run into each other and awkwardly side-step. Then tensely, we both start making our sandwiches. Side-by-side on the same counter.

For as many moments I shared with the Wright family, there's not one stretch of memory where Brenden and I bonded. We were nothing stronger than acquaintances. Not friends. Not enemies until after I got Bay in trouble.

A quiet, invisible divide has always separated us.

Brenden is bookish and intellectual. When we were being tutored, we shared the same table in a hotel conference room. At sixteen, he aced every school exam that I failed. He worked hard for his grades and his physical victories, and he saw me leaning back on my chair, listening to music. Staring out the window.

I wonder if he looked at me and thought that I had it easy. I was a Kotova. Born into a legacy more sturdy and predictable than his life would eventually be.

I wonder if he looked at me and thought Baylee deserved a better friend. Someone smarter. Someone less reckless and wild. Because I ran with his sister to vast unexplored places. In a city more new to me than to her.

And even when I remembered to ask, he never wanted to come along.

In the kitchen, Brenden meticulously spreads mustard on one slice of wheat bread while I just throw cheese down on mine.

The air strains the longer we share company, and I feel something brewing.

My cell vibrates on the counter. I try not to grab it too fast, but I'm also worried he'll see the sender on the screen. Discreetly, I check the text.

Are you okay? Usually you reply faster... — Baylee

I text quickly: I'm talking to your brother (and yes to hanging out at the club. I'd risk more than that)

After I send the message, I glance at Brenden. He looks at me with an unreadable expression. I set my phone on the counter and reach for the turkey, but I realize it's in his hand. Not purposefully since he hasn't put meat on his sandwich yet.

But he's still staring at me.

(It's nothing.)

I believe it's nothing.

I try to believe, at least.

"Something wrong?" I ask just as the main door opens.

Zhen crests the doorway and then skids to a stop. His confused and slightly alarmed eyes dart between Brenden and me. "…is everything okay?" he asks Brenden. I hear, *do you need me to stay?*, beneath his words.

"I'm fine," Brenden says.

Frazzled, Zhen spins on his heels and leaves through the same door. He looks back once before shutting it closed.

I rotate my taut shoulders and hold his gaze.

"Tell me you're not texting my little sister," he says, freezing my muscles. "Tell me I'm just *imagining* this nightmare in my head with you at the center."

"I'm not texting her," I lie in one breath.

Brenden gauges my features and then shakes his head. "I don't trust you. I don't think I *ever* trusted you." His jaw tightens and he caps the mustard.

"I'm not texting Baylee," I repeat, suppressing all of my emotion. Numb—I want to be numb. I want to not fucking care, but Brenden is Baylee's rock. He's her world. Her brother, her heart.

Slowly, he rotates to face me. "Show me your phone then."

I rest my elbow on the counter and grab my phone, but I don't pass it to him. I open my mouth and expect to let out a million excuses— but I say, "I love her."

His nose flares, jaw muscle clenching. Trying just as hard to trounce uncomfortable sentiments.

"I'm in love with Baylee," I say again, my heart on fire.

"I heard you," he says flatly.

I breathe deeply through my nose, and I rake my fingers across my damp hair. I thought it'd change something if he knew, but it only makes it worse. A rumor about "my love" for Baylee can't spread through the troupe. It'll somehow reach Marc Duval.

The no minors policy will be enforced.

We'll probably be fired.

So I backtrack. "Just as friends," I clarify. "She doesn't know either. I've never told her."

He processes this. Staring me dead in the eyes. "But you text."

"About work. Sometimes about Katya. It's my sister's birthday today—that's what the text was about." (I'm sorry. I'm so fucking sorry.) Lying to Brenden feels equivalent to ripping at his relationship with his sister. I don't want to touch it with malicious hands.

Brenden scrutinizes me, discomfort mounting between us, and I can't tell what he believes. He might not even be sure himself. "Katya's turning seventeen, right?" he asks.

And I immediately regret bringing up Katya.

"Yeah." I screw on the pickle jar for something to do. "She's seventeen today."

Brenden nods. "You know what I remember?" He leans slightly on the counter, angled more towards me. "She's little. Like this high." He motions to the counter's ledge. "Ten or eleven? We were conditioning for Infini, and Katya accidentally slid down the climbing rope. Burned her palms badly."

I remember this, but I don't add to the memory. I just listen.

"Before she even thought about crying, you were there. You blew on her hands and then lifted her onto your back. You were silly enough that she started laughing, and you found the nearest first-aid kit and bandaged her palms."

A chill slips down my neck. I see where he's going. I can share a story in the same vein as that one, only replacing me and my sister with Brenden and his.

Bay was almost inconsolable when their parents passed, and Brenden was the one who made sure she had a dress for the funeral. The one who accompanied her to the doctor for checkups. The one who kept her upright when she wanted to sink low.

I understand more than I want to.

Baylee and Katya aren't alike, but our relationships with our sisters are similar. Mirrored. Almost identical. He played the brother and the friend and the parent to Baylee. Just like I did to Katya.

Just like I do.

"How you treated your sister—that's what I liked most about you," Brenden tells me. "And then you screwed over mine, and I thought, *fuck this guy.*" He glowers and grimaces.

I go cold.

He nods to me. "So I want to know how you'd feel."

I dread the next moment. "If what?"

"If your little sister met a guy that got her into hard drugs. That steals on the regular. He's been to jail for theft, and he's a stain on the company that she's employed by—how would you feel if he came into her life and tore at her career and everything she's worked so goddamn hard for? How would you feel then?"

(Heartbroken. Worried. Protective.)

My eyes burn, and I nod more than once before I say, "I'm sorry."

"Tell that to her."

"I already have."

He shelters his feelings. And then he faces the counter and finishes putting together his sandwich. The air is even tighter than before.

"I would never wish ill on anyone," Brenden tells me, "especially not Katya, but I hope you realize something."

I place a slice of bread on top of my sandwich and cut it in half. He waits for me to ask, and I finally do. "What?"

"Being a Kotova doesn't make your little sister immune to bad guys. Some prick can come into her life and completely unhinge it—and then you'll stand there and you'll look him in the eye." His gaze latches onto mine. "And you'll think, *fuck this guy.*"

I feel like I'm seven billion tons of brick.

Brenden take his sandwich to the couch, and then I stare off at the wall, his words echoing shrilly in my head.

Stomach coiling, I grab my phone and text Bay.

Has my sister opened her birthday present from me yet? I send, and she replies back fast.

Not yet — Baylee

I stare off again. My gift was a bad idea.
And I'm going to take it back.

ACT THIRTY
BAYLEE WRIGHT

"I've fortunately and *unfortunately* known him since I was twelve," I explain to the girls in my bedroom while shaking out a dry tube of mascara. We're all in bathrobes, our hair twisted out of our faces while we get ready for the club tonight.

I sit beside Thora on the floor, tiny mirrors propped up. One of my legs is outstretched and the other tucked beneath my ass. And I try *really* hard not to think about my texts or Luka and my brother chatting right now. My phone, I've set aside to ignore that stress for a second.

"Emphasis on unfortunate," Katya agrees, seated at the desk chair.

The last girl here, I just met about an hour ago. She's friends with Thora, and also John Ruiz's twenty-three-year-old cousin.

Camila Ruiz draws the most even cat-eyeliner on Katya's lids. Substantially more skilled at makeup than both of us. We couldn't even do a halfway-decent smoky eye after two hours of trying.

"Why unfortunate?" Camila asks.

I blow a clump of mascara off my brush. "Besides the fact that Dimitri has a hundred different names for a vagina?" I say seriously.

"And he calls tampons string peens and spirit sticks," Katya adds.

"He'll also talk about his magic dick at some point."

Katya nods. "And if you're above eighteen and not related to him, he'll hit on you." She opens an eye and looks at the short blonde beside me. "Thora knows."

Thora grabs a makeup wipe. "Yeah, it wasn't…good."

Camila smiles and quips, "Unfortunately."

She's better at banter than Thora, but I think Thora would say that most people are superior than her in that area.

I go still while I watch Thora rub costume makeup residue off her eyes, the silver streaks from her performance earlier tonight. She hasn't missed a single Amour show, and I can't believe that AE is making her perform aerial silk while she's pregnant. It's *unfathomable* to me.

My heart hurts for Thora. Because I know what it's like to be boxed into a contract and dark threats. It's a terrible, powerless feeling. I can't ask if she's okay or reach out since she still hasn't announced her pregnancy to the troupe.

She also doesn't know that Luka and I overheard the news, but I think she's aware of my suspicion. I've seen her rush to our suite bathroom, her face pallid with nausea.

"Pick a color, birthday girl." Camila raises four tubes of lipstick to Katya. I think we can all tell Katya is debating what's the "right" color.

Kat studies the tubes and then Camila, who's already finished her own makeup: bright magenta lipstick, neon-yellow eye shadow against her brown skin that's golden in the lamplight. Camila wears striking and bold shades that most wouldn't pick.

"What should I choose?" Katya asks.

"What are you wearing?" Camila wonders.

"I don't know yet. Can you help?" she asks me and Thora and points to our shared closet. I already have her outfit covered, but it's a huge surprise. Thankfully Thora is in on it.

"Definitely," Thora says as we both stand. Keeping the birthday surprise alive, we pretend to search through the closet.

Thora plucks out a short emerald dress of mine, and my eyes grow in horror as she displays it to Kat. "What about this?"

I try to stifle a cringe. *Don't cringe.* That dress—it's six years old. I had *sex* in it. With Katya's older brother.

Kat tilts her head. "Is it too plain?"

"Yeah," I say. "Really plain. You can do better." I snatch the dress from Thora, and she mouths, *what?*

Not able to tell her the full truth, I lean close and our arms touch as I whisper, "I had sex in this."

Thora puckers her lips like *ohhh.* And she returns the dress. "I won't suggest anything else," she whispers. "We'll tell her to open your gift soon, and I think Luka's too. He wrote *don't show Nik* on the envelope."

I smile just hearing Luka's name. I'm not sure why he texted me earlier about his gift to Kat. I think she'll be over-the-moon when she sees it.

Thora slides hangers from left to right. "And then her cousins should've picked out jewelry."

We're very different—me and Thora. I see how badly she wants situations to work out in everyone's favor, but I've been on the opposite side of luck too much to believe in real *good* fortune.

I whisper, "You're way too optimistic about the Kotovas." In New York, they always purchased one large ticket item for Kat's birthday. Usually it's superfluous and something they can use. Like a dirt bike.

And golf clubs.

"Katya said the same thing," Thora tells me. "I gave them a list though, and I wrote down which stores to visit. If they can't follow that, then…" She scowls, an intentional scowl. Not just RBF.

"If they screw up, it's their fault," I whisper, "and Katya appreciates us just being here." But I understand wanting to give Katya more. Especially when she asks for so little.

As slowly as I've crept back into Luka's life, I've been sliding into Kat's too. At night, we lie on our bunks and chat for hours about nothing and everything. Baseball and PoPhilly and fashion, my interests and hers. But there's an underlying fear that it'll all come crashing down.

One day. One moment.

That's all it took the first time.

"You don't have to overthink," Camila tells Kat, waving the lipsticks hypnotically from side-to-side. "What speaks to you?"

Katya sighs sadly. "I don't know."

"You like glitter," Thora says. "Don't you?"

I nod in agreement. Katya has tons of feather boas, most coated with glitter.

Camila rummages in a makeup pouch. "I can highlight your cheekbones with glitter."

Katya tucks a flyaway hair behind her ear. "Isn't glitter juvenile?"

"Not really, and even if people think it, so what? I was bartending yesterday and some guy said that my green lipstick looked like a Fruit Roll-Up."

"What'd you do?" Katya wonders.

"I told him *no free shots for you*, and I applied an extra coat of lipstick in front of his face." Camila procures a tube of silver glitter highlighter. "Look up."

Kat lifts her face higher. "Would you've done that, Baylee?" She's always remembering that I exist in the room when, to most people, I just fade into the background.

"I'm not that outspoken to strangers unless I've had about three shots." I shrug. "I probably would've just glared, taken my drink, and walked away."

Thora leans on the closet door frame. "I think I would've stumbled over my words and then waited for the awkward reply."

Katya ponders this.

I hope she sees that she doesn't have to be Camila or any of the Calloway sisters. Or me or Thora. She can just be Katya Kotova. Whoever that girl ends up being, I'm glad I'm here to witness. I really don't want to miss that too.

I pretend to examine a new romper that Katya bought. "Where do you bartend?" I ask Camila.

"The Red Death. I'll be there tonight. Can't pass up the tips if I'm hanging around there anyway. Plus I can dole out more free drinks." She bites the end of her makeup brush and bobby-pins Katya's flyaways.

"How haven't you met Dimitri?" I ask since the Kotovas flock The Red Death every Saturday night. Dimitri was only initially brought up because Thora asked about my forearm burn. It turned into an explanation about Dimitri tossing me clubs. The burn wasn't his fault, but he also accidentally singed his neck lighting my prop on fire this morning.

Camila releases the brush from between her teeth. "I generally try to stay away from Kotovas because half of them are shitty tippers—no offense," she says to Katya.

She laughs. "I bet it's Abram. He's *so* cheap. He won't ever pay for cab fares."

This is really true.

"Could be," Camila says. "I don't know their names. What does he look like?"

Katya tries to describe him, and I put the romper back on the hook. Thora mouths, *where are the gifts?* I gesture with my head to a drawer, and Thora casually approaches the dresser.

"The only Kotova guy I really know is Timo," Camila says, "and that's mostly because he's been crashing at my cuz's apartment."

"He's trying to avoid Sergei," Katya tells us. "It's kind of complicated." She says this sort of tensely and morosely, like she can't explain more. None of us delve into the subject, but Thora and I know bad blood exists.

I abandon the closet, a heaviness inside my body that I can't kick. It lingers quietly and silently. Even when I don't mention it.

There's no source, but lying on the floor or bed and *sinking* seems too nice right now. I hope music will lift my spirits so I fiddle with Katya's digital stereo on her desk, right beside her makeup spread.

"Who's your favorite?" Camila asks me.

"Favorite Kotova guy?" I follow her train of thought and click into a soca playlist Katya created. A Nori Amada song floods the bedroom, the tempo upbeat and lively. I smile more.

"Yep. Which guy?"

And my smile flat-lines, eyes growing as I contemplate *no* great answer. Katya frowns deeply at me, Camila brushing highlighter on her cheekbones.

"It's apparent. Right?" Katya asks me.

It is. I just don't know if I'm allowed to spread this news. Katya is the best secret-keeper, but she has no idea why Luka and I are so private about our mere friendship.

My shoulders bind. "Yeah." I have to say his name. "It's Luka."

It's always been Luka.

"Luka," Camila muses. "I think John has mentioned him. What does he look like?"

I rub my lips together, thinking before I speak. "Tall-ish. Not Nikolai's height, but tall for an acrobat. Dark hair that's between short and long, and the Kotova gray eyes." I pause. "Pale, clean-shaven." I look faraway, picturing Luka standing at Two Kings. Waiting for me to near. "His features are frozen between youth and maturity, and he's so welcoming. That one frame at the end of *Titanic*, where Leonardo

DiCaprio extends a hand to Kate Winslet—that's Luka. Charming and kind inside silence." I begin to smile. "He's the one sitting on the armrest of a couch, trying to make you smile when you're sad."

I'm lost in my head, and when I break from this warm reverie, I realize all three girls are staring knowingly at me.

I straighten up. "We used to be really good friends."

"Best friends," Katya clarifies. "Luk always called you his *best*." She nods at me like I deserve that title, but it hurts to think that we can't even be called *friends* now.

Just co-workers. Always co-workers.

I stare at the carpet, my stomach clenching.

Camila twists the lid on her highlighter. "You really weren't together? Like boyfriend-girlfriend? Friends-with-benefits? Nothing?"

"No," I lie and try to subtly deflect. "I can tell you which Kotovas are single, if you're looking." I'll selfishly omit Luka off that list.

"Not looking." Camila dusts extra glitter over Katya's eyelids. "I'm actually seeing someone."

"What…when?" Thora asks, collecting the purple-wrapped wardrobe box from the drawer and an envelope.

"Last night. Craig apologized for being standoffish, and then we had makeup sex."

By the shock on Thora's face, I feel like this isn't a good thing.

Thora frowns. "What happened to not touching his dick with a forty-foot pole?"

"He's the only dick I've ever touched," Camila says honestly. "He's my first *everything*, and I can't give up on him yet."

I empathize with that currently, but not the standoffish part. "What'd he do?" I ask.

Thora and Camila exchange a heated look. I sense that Camila would rather tell a half-truth but Thora isn't an advocate.

"We have a very passionate relationship," Camila explains vaguely.

Thora is upset, but she keeps quiet.

"You and Craig are on-again-off-again?" I realize.

"More *on* than off, but for about three years. I was nineteen when I randomly met him. I was eating off the strip at a little café with family, and Craig and I were both waiting for the tiny restroom to free-up. We started talking and instantly clicked." She uncaps a burgundy lipstick and asks Katya. "Yes? No?"

Katya smiles. "It's pretty."

And then the loudest, most raucous clamor enters the suite. Rowdy footsteps and too many Russian words and phrases to untangle. We all pause and look at the bedroom door, but no one pounds the wood or slips inside.

"Damn," Camila whispers, her honey-brown eyes alight in shock. "Is that all of 'em?"

"Probably," Katya says in a louder voice. "Unless they're my brothers, they won't come in here. So they won't bother you." She has a rule about "no cousins" allowed in her bedroom, and they all respect her wishes.

We flinch at the sound of glass shattering, and I roll my eyes. I'm afraid for Rudy. Seriously, I left my potted cactus on the coffee table in the living room and there's a chance someone will knock him over *on purpose.*

Guys, in a huge pack, are idiots. Not all the time, but most of the time, it's true.

I'd go save Rudy, but running into a huge hoard of Kotovas is never a good idea. There will be teasing. Inappropriate jokes in Russian and English. If they know you're cool with it, they'll even pick you up and throw you over their shoulder.

I'm not cool with it, but Dimitri will mime the gesture to try and piss me off. I don't get angry that easily, so it's a futile mission.

Camila finishes Katya's makeup: dark smoky purple, sparkly gray, and shimmery silver. Her orb-like eyes appear less youthful and more sultry. Even with all the glitter.

Katya can't stop grinning at her features in the mirror. "Thank you." She's about to cry.

Camila hugs her tight. "I can always show you some tricks and tips when we have more time."

"That'd be amazing."

I jump at another crash, followed by *cheering* and laughter. "Shit." I expel a breath, hoping Rudy is in one piece. Their noise drowns out the soca music—that's how boisterous they are.

Returning to my seat on the floor, I apply ruby red lipstick.

"They're probably trying to slap Nik's ass," Katya tells us. "They always do this two days in a row since we celebrate both of our birthdays on *my* actual birthday." Nikolai turned twenty-seven yesterday.

Camila presses her ear to the door and listens but also whispers to us, "I'm close to my family, but there's enough girls to offset the rampant testosterone. John is the one with all brothers…" she trails off and her jaw drops. "Oh my God." She makes a face that sits between humor and *what the fuck?* "They really love the word *tits*."

I shake my head with a wince. "I don't know why they can't call them nipples."

"Or nips," Camila adds.

"Boobs," Katya chimes in, carefully opening the envelope.

Thora stares at the ceiling for a good response. "Breasts?"

We all laugh with Thora, and then Camila goes quiet, trying to hear through the door again. "Wait," she says, "they said *Baylee*."

Do I want to know?

Kind of. *Maybe.*

Okay, yeah I do.

"Someone mentioned 'tits' and your name together," Camila says and pauses to listen more. "*Rude*, what the hell."

I already know, and I don't care. "They talk about which girls have 'small tits' all the time. I'm on the list." I have A-cups. It's not a secret, and this list isn't glamorized. It's a "meh, don't touch that" list. I couldn't care less about their fantasies.

"Let's talk about their dicks," Camila says, crossing her arms. "Which one has a small wiener? I'll yell it."

I'm all about ribbing Dimitri. So I say, "Dimitri has the *tiniest* dick."

Camila grabs the doorknob, but before she opens it, she asks Katya, "If I just stick my head out, will they come in here?"

"Nope. They're not allowed." Katya unfurls Luka's letter and the actual gift falls to her feet.

"Perfect." Camila cracks open the door, not enough to be seen but to be heard, and she yells at the top of her lungs, "DIMITRI HAS THE TINIEST DICK!" Then she slams the door shut.

We all burst out laughing. I lie on my back, my stomach rising and falling and I have to cover my face with my hands—my smile hurts.

I hear the commotion outside. Russian curses and then in English, a lot of them shout, "Who was that?! Who is that?"

I roll on my side, a laughing cramp forming. And then slowly, my humor wanes and my smile softens. I see Katya reading Luka's letter.

Love in her glassy eyes, she tries to suppress waterworks because of her makeup. She delicately picks up the fallen item.

An ID.

"What's that?" Camila asks.

Katya flashes the present. "Luka got me a fake ID. It has my own picture and everything."

"Cool brother," Camila says, and her eyes flit to me with a smile. Like she knows I feel something at the mention of his name. How can she know for sure? I just met Camila.

My love for Luka can't be that obvious. Can it? We would've been caught from the start of the list.

Suddenly a few hard knocks rap the door. I flinch.

Camila backs up and plops down on my bottom bunk, sitting forward in intrigue.

"You're not allowed in here!" Katya calls out.

I strain my ears for the response.

ACT THIRTY-ONE
BAYLEE WRIGHT

"It's me, Kat!" *Luka.*

That was one-hundred percent Luka Kotova. I keep smoothing my lips together, and my arm loosely hangs onto my bent knee. Nervous-excited at even the *thought* of seeing him right now.

Katya springs off the desk chair and cracks the door. I piece apart the chaotic shouts. Most of them yell at Luka, "Who's in there, Luka?! Find out who! Who said Dimitri has a little cock?!"

Luka ignores his family like it's just any other day.

Katya speaks in Russian to her brother, and after a couple exchanged words, she opens the door wider and Luka slips inside. He kicks the door closed.

And his eyes instantly find me on the floor, his lips surely rising.

"You're Luka," Camila states.

Luka glances at Camila and nods.

She swings her head to me. "Accurate description. Spot on."

"What?" Luka smiles bigger at me.

I shrug, but I smile off of his as usual. "I described you to her."

His brows jump, his grin curving even higher. "You did?"

I nod and lose track of my next thought. I notice a baggie of ice in his left hand, along with a potted cactus. *Rudy.*

Before he nears me, he hugs Katya to his side and says *Happy Birthday, Katya* in Russian.

She hugs back and then rises and falls on her tiptoes excitedly. Speaking eagerly in the same language, I assume she's thanking him for the gift.

"You already opened it?" he asks in English, his voice tighter than normal.

"Was I not supposed to?"

My stomach nosedives like maybe I forgot to intervene. Quickly I double-check our text thread, but Luka never replied to my *not yet* answer. So whatever he planned, he didn't inform me.

"No, it's…" He stops himself as Katya's face falls, and he sweeps her makeup with deep, tormented thought. I seriously think he regrets gifting the fake ID.

Luk.

I wish I could hug him and remind him that his sister is older than she sometimes appears. She's *seventeen.*

She's tough-skinned and sweet-hearted.

And Kat has the *best* directional sense. Whenever I forgot where a really good food truck was located, she'd remember and tell me which block it was parked on. I'd trust Katya Kotova with my life, and usually Luka would too.

So what's his deal?

"Luka?" Katya's voice breaks a little.

"It's okay." He nods a couple times like he's trying to believe it. They share a look that I can't translate perfectly. If I had to try, I'd say it's Katya reassuring him that she's not naïve and she's allowed to grow older—and Luka trying to accept this fact.

Then Luka shakes the baggie of ice and gestures to me.

Katya smiles and nods like *go to her.*

I'm about to stand, but Luka already towers above me, dressed up in dark jeans and a white button-down. Squatting, he becomes eye-level with me. He passes me the ice but hangs onto my cactus.

I roll up the sleeve of my robe, genuinely scared about Rudy now. The ice touches my bandage, and my shoulders relax at the cold that soothes my second-degree burn.

I have no idea if the other girls are watching us. I'm concentrated on the potted succulent more than I probably should be.

"He's not in pieces?" I ask, seeing an intact ceramic pot.

"Still alive," Luka assures me. "He just has a little more character than before." He waits like he's ensuring I'll be okay with the incoming news.

My features plummet. "Who took a knife to Rudy?"

"I don't know," he breathes, not denying that someone cut my cactus.

My fingers touch the watery corners of my eyes, and I try to speak— to say something like: *it doesn't matter* or *it's just a cactus. It's just a thing.*

I must not believe those words because I can't find the strength to say them. I gather my thoughts, and softly, so only he can hear, I ask, "What kind of character?"

Luka reaches out to touch my cheek, but he stops short. Hesitating. He drops his hand, and my chest caves with his. *Hold me.*

Kiss me.

Luka licks his lips and then hands me the pot. "You have to turn it."

I rotate Rudy, and my face contorts.

The bulbous lump on Rudy's backside has been hacked off. I try to process this into an emotion other than *heavy* sadness. I keep swallowing and swallowing. I see no point in racing out to the living room and accusing every Kotova. It doesn't really matter who did it.

What's done is done. Yelling feels worthless.

Still, it hurts. "He looks awful," is all I can say. My nose runs before my eyes leak, and I wipe my upper-lip with my arm.

Luka can't hold back any longer. He wraps a strong, sturdy arm around my shoulders and draws me to his chest. I place Rudy down and clutch Luka's sides tightly.

Kiss me.

He kisses the top of my head. Taking the risk in front of the girls. Then he tugs my body even closer, and his heartbeat thuds right against mine.

My cheek to his collar, I eye the round cactus, and I think about how Luka found this pot in a chaotic living room full of men. And he knew to protect what was left of Rudy for me.

Immense, boundless affection swells inside my body, and I inhale a deeper breath than before. "Thank you," I say in a whisper.

Luka cups my cheek, not resisting anymore. Lips to my ear, he murmurs, "I'm here for you. Whatever you need, I'm here, Bay. It's not a dream. It's *real* life."

I try to believe in a reality where we can touch in front of people.

And hold one another.

It's happening right now.

It's happening.

I breathe easier, and I lift my head to see all three girls trying not to gawk. But they see us. Luka kneeling on the floor. Clasping my cheek with tenderness and care. Me gripping his waist like I'm afraid he'll leave soon.

I'm the first to reluctantly let go, and he slowly follows suit. His gaze travels with mine to Thora, Camila, and Katya. I don't know what to say, but I rise to my feet with Luka, our fingers the only part of us that consistently touch.

Camila is the only one who doesn't know the "cocaine" rumor, so I'm not surprised by her curiosity. "You're really *not* together?" she asks while untying her messy bun. Curly brown hair cascades down her chest.

"No," Luka and I say in unison.

He's less tense than me. Casual. At ease. He stuffs his hand in his jean's pocket. "We used to be best friends."

"Best friends who kiss, right?" She wears a teasing smile.

Katya, sitting cross-legged on her desk chair and clutching the wardrobe box, interjects, "They couldn't; Aerial Ethereal has a huge rule about minors not being allowed to date or hook up inside the company, and they were friends as teenagers."

Technically I'm still a teenager at nineteen, but thankfully an *adult* in the eyes of society.

Camila recoils. "What kind of rule is that?"

A terrible one.

Luka and I stay absolutely silent. Like our secret history is seconds from being broadcasted. In this room, no one knows that we've confronted this rule.

"It makes sense," Katya says. "They employ kids, and they want everyone underage to focus on the profession, not hooking up. It doesn't mean it doesn't happen in secret, but everyone who's been caught has been fired. So most don't even try."

Camila has her chin in her palm, looking between Luka and me. "Why'd you two stop being friends?"

I can't tell if she's connecting all of these tiny pieces together and finding the *real* picture that we've been sworn to hide forever.

I open my mouth, but I notice Katya pondering so hard that her brows pinch together. Just as I'm about to say our lie (*drugs*), she swivels on her chair to Luka.

"You two…you never secretly dated, did you?"

He has to lie.

He can't tell the truth.

Luka shields most of his heartbreak, but I see it shatter in the creases of his eyes. I know that pain. I feel it every single time I lie to Brenden.

Meeting Katya's gaze straight-on, he says, "Never. Baylee and I were only just friends. Nothing else" He goes even further. "I promise I would've told you…" *if he could have.*

It hurts to hear him lie to someone he loves.

Katya nods, believing him without falter. "That's what I thought."

Luka swings his head to Camila. "We stopped being friends when we were caught doing drugs."

"Wow." Camila has nothing else to add but that, and I try to compartmentalize my feelings. I pick up Rudy and place him on my windowsill. All the while, I feel the heat of Luka's gaze.

I nudge Katya's chair with my foot. "You can open your present from me."

Katya slips off a tiny card beneath the bow. Flipping the card, she laughs and flashes the script to everyone. I wrote: *For Posh Spice.*

Then she begins unwrapping the purple paper.

I still feel Luka staring at me. It makes me curious. I'm supposed to be the observer here.

Maybe he's wondering how I am. I take a breath, and I brave a glance his way.

Luka leans coolly against the wall, a Nova Vega show poster hung above his tousled dark hair. The longer I observe him, soaking up his features—his nonchalant, relaxed posture and radiant eyes—the more his lips upturn.

And then he mouths, *I love you.*

I feel my smile emerge, and I press my fingers to my lips. My eyes dart cautiously to the other girls, but their focus isn't on this captivating, heartbreakingly gorgeous guy.

Luka acts like he's invisible, but I see him. All of him.

His earnest grin grows brighter. Like a shooting star across blanketed, quiet night.

Katya gasps, and our gazes break.

She springs to her feet, eyes big. Tissue paper flutters to the floor, and a sequined, gunmetal gray dress is draped over her arm.

With shaking hands and fixated eyes, she reads a birthday card from the designer of that particular dress.

"What is it?" Camila asks.

Katya tries to play it cool, but she's almost hyperventilating. "Rose Calloway wrote me a birthday note. She's my…" *role model.* "She means so much to me." Katya sniffs loudly, stifling tears. "She wrote 'Katya, confidence starts within, and I believe this dress will help add fire to your strut. Be you. Be proud. Happy 17th Birthday, from one powerful woman to another.'" Kat looks to all of us. "Rose Calloway called me powerful."

We're all tearing up at Katya's reaction to that. She wafts her hand by her face. I can practically hear her *don't ruin your makeup* chant.

Katya sniffs again and then she wraps her arms around my shoulders. "Thanks, Baylee. This was…"

"You don't have to say." I hug back, my arms around her waist. "I know what it means to you." I wish I could've given her Marvin, but our stuffed dinosaur is part of a past that has no place for our future.

We're both grown. And moving somewhere else.

Somewhere new.

"Oh my God." Camila gapes at me as I split apart from Katya. "You know Rose Calloway?"

"No, my aunt does. She's the brand and marketing executive for Calloway Couture." Rose's fashion line. "But I've never met Rose Calloway."

It took a couple phone calls to Aunt Lucy. I asked her if I could have the most "glittery" Calloway Couture dress on the sale's rack. After I explained the gift, Aunt Lucy said, "I can do you better than that."

The note definitely outshined the dress.

Camila shakes her head in awe. "You're *two* degrees away from the Calloway sisters and their men." Her mouth drops further. "Do you know Ryke Meadows? Do you have his number? I'm not joking when I say this: he's my soul mate."

Luka listens like a fly on the wall, and I think I'm the only one that catches the amusement in his gray eyes.

Thora wads up tissue paper. "You'd dump Craig?"

"For Ryke Meadows, the holy grail of all rugged, daring, women-adoring-and-protecting *men*. I'd dump everyone for him."

Glass shatters outside, and someone shouts, "WHO SAID DIMITRI HAS A TINY DICK?!"

Camila cups her hands to her lips and yells, "THE TINIEST!"

Chatter explodes, and I mostly hear the name "LUKA!" among them. They really want Luka to relay an answer.

Grinning, Luka pops an orange Tic Tac in his mouth. When he notices me staring, I make a face at him. Almost like a serious pout.

He makes the same face back and then gestures me over.

I'm scared if I approach Luka, I'll just sink into his arms and look up for a kiss. And he'll say *yes* because it's too hard to say *no* now.

Our emotions are at an all-time high. It's safer staying away, even if I hate it.

So I mouth, *later*.

He nods, understanding.

Katya hugs her dress to her body. "I'd dump everyone for Connor Cobalt." Rose Calloway's husband.

"What?" Luka cringes.

Thora and Camila are smiling, and Katya gives her brother a look like *you'll never understand*. "Connor Cobalt is the smartest man on the planet," she reminds him.

His brows scrunch, and he shakes out another Tic Tac. "That's the only reason you like him?"

"I like that he's always well-dressed, and he respects Rose Calloway's opinion. And he's a *genius*," she emphasizes like this outweighs all.

Luka is fishing for something else. "That's it though? Nothing else?"

Katya is confused, and then realization hits her. Now she's the one cringing. "I didn't say anything about sex!"

His brows jump. "If you Wikipedia *Connor Cobalt*, his sexual preferences are *in* his bio."

"I was thinking it," Camila chimes in.

I'm stuck on the fact that Luka searched *Connor Cobalt* on the internet before. "Is he your favorite?" I tease Luka like he once teased me.

He instantly smiles at my question, remembering our food truck outing. I wish I could call it a *date*. "No," he says, "but I know who yours is."

"Who?" Katya asks me.

"Not Loren Hale," I announce.

Luka tilts his head at me. "Come on."

I give him a look, and then sigh into surrender. "I mean…if I *had* to choose, it probably would be him."

Luka grins like he caught me. Maybe he did. But if it was Loren Hale vs. Luka Kotova, there is no contest. There's only one man who completes me.

Thora asks, "In terms of Connor Cobalt's bio, are we talking about what I think we're talking about…?"

Katya sighs. "The fact that Connor Cobalt is into BDSM, yeah. And maybe I do prefer that."

Luka's face is frozen in shock, processing this at a snail's pace. I watch. Staring. I think he's not sure how he should react. If he should wince or smile or do nothing at all.

He asks, "Do you know what BDSM is?"

"I'm *seventeen*. God," she groans. "I know I look young and all of you baby me, but I'm aware of what's outside. I live in sin city. I've *met* working girls—I've been propositioned to be one, and I said *no*."

"I know," Luka says. "I was there."

"I'm reminding you." Katya huffs.

Camila leans forward. "Have you tried BDSM?" she asks her.

Luka immediately steps off the wall. "This is my cue to self-eject." His voice is easygoing, and he heads to the door.

Katya isn't hesitant to answer. "Not yet, but I've read scenes in one of Thora's books." Paranormal romance. Thora often lends them to Katya.

"They're good books," Thora says confidently. "I mean, solid stuff." She shakes her head at herself. She was doing really well there.

"*Very* solid," Camila quips. "I loved the one about the twelve-inch vampire cock."

I watch Luka pause by the door, more interested than he's letting on. People-watching is a serious form of entertainment of mine, so I understand the lingering.

"*The Forgotten Night*," Thora names the title. "It's in my top ten favorites, but not just because of the vampire dick. Though that's…"

"Hot," Camila finishes.

Thora looks grateful when Camila finds the words that are tangled in her head.

Luka nods to Camila and jokes, "Have you met Dimitri? Guy's massive."

Of course Luka puts a good word in for Dimitri. That's the opposite kind of relationship I have with his cousin.

"He's not that massive," I assure Camila. "He's *tiny*." I squish my fingers together to a microscopic size.

Luka laughs at me. "He's fucking huge."

I squish my fingers even closer.

"Which one of you has actually seen his dick?" Camila asks.

We both raise our hands.

"No you haven't," Luka laughs again, and we've somehow unconsciously stepped towards one another. We're only a few feet apart.

"I did. I swear." I can't stop smiling. Are we seriously bonding over Dimitri's dick? We're so bizarre. Weird. And I really love every second.

"He just whipped it out on you?" Luka questions, disbelieving and a little peeved, I think.

"He unabashedly let his towel drop in the locker room showers. I caught a glimpse in my peripheral." I motion to my eyes.

Luka grins, shaking his head. "That doesn't count."

I think about this. "It counts *somewhat*."

"Somewhat," he agrees.

To Camila, I say, "Trust me, you don't want to compliment Dimitri's penis. He'll think you're into him, and since you have a guy…"

"Good to know," she nods and then shouts again, "DIMITRI HAS A LITTLE WIENER!"

All the Kotova guys yell in unison, "LUKA!!"

Camila winces at him. "Sorry."

Luka looks the furthest from bothered. "I don't mind. I can keep your name a secret from my cousins; you never told me it anyway. No sweat." His gaze sweeps me head-to-toe, the once-over heating every inch of me, and then he returns to the door.

Katya splays her dress on the chair. "We'll be out soon."

Luka checks his watch and then casts one last glance back at me, as though cataloging my emotional state. My lips inch up, but I wish he could stay longer.

Luka nods to me like *we'll be together soon.*

At The Red Death.

He's the only thing I'm looking forward to tonight. Otherwise, I'd probably just curl up in bed.

ACT THIRTY-TWO
LUKA KOTOVA

After I leave Kat's bedroom and enter the living area, I'm swarmed and hounded by my cousins. All for answers about a girl who I'm pretty sure is Camila Ruiz.

Dimitri's *many* brothers zealously push my arms, pat my shoulders, and ask, "Who was she?! Who said that?!"

Bay was right about me being disloyal and loyal. I choose my sides wisely, and I'm not snitching on those girls.

I pop a piece of gum in my mouth with a grin full of mischief. "Who?"

They all groan and hook their arms around my shoulder, rubbing my head roughly. I laugh and shove them off, and not long after, I slide past all their bodies and they start hollering at Anton who fiddles with the music.

The suite is *crammed*. Shot glasses, whiskey and vodka bottles scatter every surface, and Erik plus his little brother Abram and seven other cousins carry a poorly wrapped present through the suite door. It looks heavy and about five-feet tall.

I have no clue what they bought for Kat, but she's going to hate it. Like every year, they're all looking forward to her huff and eye-roll.

I pick up a fallen trashcan, and as I pass Nik by the bar counter, I slap his ass. No reaction. He downs a shot of liquor and refills another.

He's more uptight than usual. And that's saying something.

Thing is, I know what's on his mind. Thora. The pregnancy. (Corporate being complete dicks.) I keep an eye on Nik and spit out my gum. I weave through bodies in the small kitchen space and find a bag of bite-sized pretzels.

Returning to my brother's side, I offer some, and after a reluctant pause, he fits his hand in the bag and eats.

"You okay?" I ask.

He fills another shot while he pops a pretzel in his mouth. "I've been better."

I don't want to pile more onto his shoulders, but if I don't warn him, he may upset Katya. "One of the girls did Kat's makeup," I say.

He slides me his shot and then fills another.

"She looks like she's in her twenties, and you know you can't tell her to wash it off. She's seventeen."

Nikolai is rigid, but then he nods, accepting this before his shocked-self says something he'll come to regret. Like *go wash your face, Katya.* "Most of us will keep an eye on her tonight."

I figured as much. We raise our shots, clink them together, and down them in unison. When we turn to face the couches, I spot Sergei by the floor-length window. Nighttime, the Vegas lights sparkle in the distance, and Sergei laughs with Matvei about something on their phones.

I hear his truth about choosing his career over us. Repeatedly on blast in my ears.

I didn't even hesitate.

I didn't even hesitate.

I'm not angry. Because I'm standing beside the selfless brother who thought about us in his choice. Who asked for nothing in return. I have Nikolai when I could've easily had no one.

I lean my head towards Nik. "For what it's worth," I say, "I'm glad you were the one who chose us."

Nikolai isn't surprised. "Because you dislike Serg."

"Because I love you."

He rests his hand on the back of my head, one gesture that says he feels the same about me. And I hear him breathe deeply, "It's worth a lot."

WHILE THE GIRLS FINISH GETTING DRESSED,

Timo and I guard Katya and Bay's bedroom door. Just so our cousins stop banging on the wood and screeching, "Who's in there?!"

In front of the door, we dance to a popular song, and I fit on my baseball cap backwards. Timo pushes up his gold Venetian mask to his head, twirling a scepter in his hand, and we both sing somewhat off-key. Our voices aren't that great, but we don't hold back.

Most of our cousins are playing beer pong, and Robby hands Timo a bottle of Fireball. My brother takes a swig, passes it to me; I take a swig, and then crack open the door and stick my arm through.

Baylee grabs the Fireball out of my hand. Just by touch, I can tell it's her. Our fingers hook for a second longer, before we have to let go. "Thanks," she says. I picture her smiling, and it's enough to make my lips upturn.

"Cool brother!" Camila calls out, not loud enough for everyone else to hear.

They shut the door.

Timo grabs hold of my shoulder, shakes me to the beat, and I feel *happy*. Which scares me more than usual. Every time I capture this kind of light, it sputters out and turns impossibly bleak.

No one says the truth. That at the end of every good moment, there's a bad one waiting.

Timo senses my slight change in demeanor. His feet fall flat, and he tosses me the scepter as he asks, "What's on your mind, brother?"

I pass the gold staff between my hands. Nikolai gifted him the scepter for his sixteenth birthday. "I just have a bad feeling."

I haven't *really* felt this way since the three of us were little kids. And one of the worst things happened…

(Don't make me say it. I can't touch it. I'm sorry.)

"About what?" Timo asks, his features still endlessly bright despite cradling worry.

I spin my hat but keep the rim backwards. "I don't know. It's probably nothing."

Timo bites his thumbnail, and I toss the scepter back. He grabs hold, and close enough to whisper, he quietly asks, "Can I tell you something? I've been keeping it in, and it's starting to get to me."

"Yeah."

"Katya thinks you're in love with Baylee. That you've *been* in love with her for years, and honestly, I think she's onto something here."

I open my mouth to deny on impulse, but he keeps talking fast, knowing I'd shut this conversation down early on.

"I mean, we all skirt around some stuff, but you refused to say her name like you were told not to—"

"Dude, stop—"

"There you go, clear as day." He shakes his head like he should've confronted me sooner. "I just don't understand what the big deal is? *Hey Jude, you love her, now go and get her.*" He points his scepter at the door beside us.

I try not to laugh. "It's not that…" *simple.* My smile vanishes in one instant. With one thought: the contracts.

The no minors policy.

Timo twirls the scepter, his eyes still twinkling. "You're hiding something."

I shake my head. "No."

"Okay truth," he says so quietly that only I could hear over the music. Then he leans against the door, and I lean beside him. Timo swings his head to me. "I've *never* believed that you got into cocaine. Not even on a spur of the moment. It'd make you feel…"

His gaze says: *out of control.*

I don't nod, but he's right. "So you just thought I lied?"

"I thought that you couldn't be honest, but one day you would be."

Today's not that day. Tomorrow's not it either. I can never be honest with my little brother. With my sister. The lie will always remain, and it eats at me more than Timo knows.

The door cracks, and the girls tell us that they're ready. Timo and I drop our conversation, and we step back so they can slip out.

Thora is the first to exit, wearing a low-cut silver dress, and immediately, she gapes at the five-foot gift, still wrapped and standing next to the television.

"What is that?" she asks Dimitri. "What happened to the list?"

Timo and I exchange a knowing smile.

"I wiped my ass with that list," Dimitri says crudely. "Do you want it back?" He jokingly digs into the pocket of his slacks.

Thora scowls darkly, but Nik is by her side, his hand on the small of her back. It's the first time I've seen him smile all night.

"Luka," Bay calls from inside her room. Sticking her hand out, she waves me over, and I'm there in a flash.

I peek into the barely ajar door, and I think I'm supposed to be fixated on Camila—who flings a fuzzy lilac blanket over her head—but I'm entrapped by Bay.

It's not just because of her sparkling halter dress that hugs her hips. Or the glittering red and pink sequins. It's not just her curly hair that's let loose, because she's also gorgeous tired and sweaty.

It's how she tilts her head and shrugs at me.

How she struggles to suppress an overwhelmed grin.

It's who she is.

I breathe deeply. She takes a bigger breath.

"Luka," Katya calls, breaking my trance. She waves a hand in my face. "Did you hear me?"

"What?" I blink a few times. "Sorry." My sister wears that Calloway Couture charcoal-colored dress, glitzy and shorter than I thought it'd be.

"Can you make sure no one hassles her?" She motions to Camila, who's hidden by the blanket.

"I have you covered, sister." That's Timo, poking his head inside the room from behind me. Beneath the blanket, Camila raises her hand and high-fives Timo.

"I'm heading out with her," Baylee tells me. "I'll meet everyone at the club."

I frown. "You sure?" I fight the urge to reach out and draw her to my chest. Maybe that's the problem.

Baylee shrugs. "We'll see each other, right?"

"Right."

"Then I'm sure."

Timo and Katya study my interaction with Baylee way too keenly, so I don't press onward or try to convince her to stay.

My brother and I back up, and together, Bay and Camila slip into the living area, and we walk them to the door while our cousins go wild, almost all of them shouting, "What's your name?!"

A few try to follow, but I push them back and Timo spins his scepter on them. "I'm the royal guard of the princess. Step back, you fiends." He hisses.

My smile explodes. It's impossible not to love Timofei.

Baylee disappears out the door faster than everyone probably realizes. She's invisible. Like me, but I see her.

I've always seen her.

Camila stops by the door frame, sticks her hand out of the blanket, and waves everyone goodbye. She puts her palm to her blanket-covered lips, miming a kiss.

"I love you, princess!" Dimitri shouts from the bar counter. "Thank you for calling my dick massive!"

"TINIEST!" she shouts before darting out of the suite. Timo and I hurriedly shut the door and block about five cousins from chasing after Camila and Bay.

"No," I repeat in a bored tone. "No." I push a few off, and they curse at me in Russian. I don't care.

In a split-second, they all forget about Camila. Their attention swerves onto Katya who comes out in full makeup and a long-sleeved, short dress with a plunged back.

The room falls so quiet that if I shut off the music, you could probably hear a pin drop. No one knows how to react. If they should compliment her or tell her to go change or feel wierded out. She's the *only* girl in this generation by blood. And there are very few marriages and even less current relationships.

It's different for everyone.

Before Katya gets frustrated or annoyed by the silent reaction, Timo and I start dancing our way over to her—which is more like jumping up and down to the beat of a new song. As soon as she sees us, her lips pull in a huge smile.

We reach Kat, and she starts jumping with Timo and me. We sing-song, "You're seventeen!" And she sing-songs back, "I'm seventeen!"

The music cuts off, but we're still jumping. Timo flashes Erik his middle finger for silencing us.

I laugh.

Kat laughs, and we only fall to our feet as the chatter escalates and our cousins start tearing at the wrapping paper of the gift they bought.

She already rolls her eyes. "You can open it."

Thora sidles to Katya and gives her a side-hug. "You look so pretty," she tells her, which I see makes her light up.

I nod. "You do, Kat."

"You really think so?" Her voice spikes in surprise, and I wonder… maybe none of us have ever told her how pretty she is. I know our mom never did.

"*Really*," I say.

"Thanks, Luk." Katya laughs at a thought. "You know the funny thing? I don't think I needed to hear it. I already believed it. Rose Calloway taught me that."

I smile and nod repeatedly.

"Oh my God," Katya groans at the sight of the unwrapped gift.

Dimitri motions to a giant gumball machine, and in Russian, he says, "*Happy Birthday, Katya.*" Our cousins already bombard the machine, and they bemoan at the realization of needing quarters to get a gumball.

I look to Katya. "It's better than the tennis rackets."

Timo spins his scepter. "And the Santa statue."

"Definitely ranks over the boys underwear," Kat says.

"I don't know," Timo says, "I took a pair of those."

"Me too," I laugh.

We bump fists, and Katya pushes us lightly. "Traitors."

We hook our arms around her, and Timo raises his scepter. "To the reddest death!"

Even though I'm smiling, even though everything seems upbeat, my bad feeling—it still hasn't vanished.

I'm usually afraid of so few things, but fear crawls towards me. I see it coming, and I don't know how to stop it.

ACT THIRTY-THREE
BAYLEE WRIGHT

The Red Death is the epitome of sultry Vegas nightlife. The Masquerade's most popular club is nearly pitch-black except for red strobe lights that sweep grinding, intoxicated bodies, and the sensual red bulbs above the packed bar, plus mandatory glow necklaces worn by all attendees.

I dance in a sweltering pit.

Last I knew, Kat and Thora were close by, but my senses are lost to the heady atmosphere and strong drum beats. Shutting my eyes, my limbs move in a natural rhythm. I feel more heavy than I like, but I don't stop dancing.

And then hands spindle down my hips from behind. My eyes snap open, but his lips already touch my ear. "It's me," he whispers deeply.

It's Luka.

My lungs expand.

It's Luka.

Our bodies never pause, never go motionless. We move in sync to the music, fitting perfectly.

My arm curves upwards around his neck, my fingers running through his hair, and his hand dives down my hipbone. Feeling each shift of my body, from side-to-side. We dance as one, and my skin tingles, sweat building between us, lit alive.

Burning up.

I tilt my head back, happy to risk this moment with Luk. Our unrestrained energy seeps into my veins and bursts.

Reminding me why I *love* to dance.

Why I unequivocally love him.

I look up at his features, illuminated by his blue glow necklace, and he stares back down at me, my face glowing with the same *blue*.

On impulse, he snaps off our necklaces. Shrouding us in the club's darkness, he drops his hand, glowing blue by our sides.

My back pressed up to his chest, our bodies are in equal rhythm.

And Luka—he never hesitates. Never falters. His lips meet mine, and he kisses me with a *powerful* insurgency of warmth.

His affection flames and dances inside of me.

I can't help but smile against his lips, and I feel his own appear as strongly. We kiss and dance, and something overpowers me just knowing we're *surrounded* by other people.

It almost feels like we're a real couple. Like he could be my boyfriend. I could be his girlfriend, and we're living inside a fairytale.

I clutch the back of his head for support as he deepens the kiss.

"GOD OF RUSSIA! GOD OF RUSSIA!"

We rip apart at the sudden chant, our feet falling flat. Stopping for the first time. And then a giant red spotlight glares down on us and our section of the club.

Our chests rise and fall heavily, and even though we've physically separated, our gazes stay latched. I'm scared to lose him in the massive crowds. I'm afraid to break apart.

I want him close.

Forever.

I wish it could be in the realm of possibility. I wipe sweat off my forehead with my arm, at least feeling lucky that Nikolai or Dimitri didn't catch us kissing.

"GOD OF RUSSIA!" the *Kotovas* still chant. They pat Nikolai on the shoulder and push him towards the center of the spotlight.

People start backing up to make Nikolai the sole bearer of attention. I follow suit with Luka, standing more on the outskirts of the red circle.

We fall even further into the shadows.

Our fingers brush, my nerves twitching in a good way, and with my other hand, I reach for my necklace.

"Let me," he says.

I nod and collect my hair over my shoulder. He snaps the plastic around my neck.

"Thanks," I whisper, not sure if he heard me over the music and chanting.

Luka thumbs the necklace for a second longer, and I see a sad thought cling to his gray eyes. I stare at his own blue glow necklace, and I wonder if any girls will try to hit on him.

I cringe at the possibility, but I know the glow necklaces signify relationship status.

Blue means single.

Green means taken.

Red means it's complicated.

I thought about choosing red, but I figured it'd prompt too many questions by Katya and Thora. Blue seemed safer.

I watch his features darken. "What?!" I ask him over the music.

Luka lowers his head and raises his voice. "I cut off a few guys from dancing with you! Sorry!" He's not sorry.

Neither am I. "I'm not here for other guys!" I shout back.

Luka smiles, so charismatic that I smile too. His hand tightens in mine, aching to pull me to his chest, but he glances at his cousins and the red spotlight.

Things are happening around us, and we're not noticing.

We're dangerously in our own world.

Reality catches up even more as Katya sidles close. "There you are," she says to both of us. She tied her hair into a high bun, and her blue glow necklace brightens her big eyes. "You're not missing it, right?" Katya asks and gestures to Nikolai.

"GOD OF RUSSIA! GOD OF RUSSIA!"

I've heard of this Red Death event enough to know that Nikolai isn't about to breakdance and this isn't special just because of his birthday.

Every Saturday night, Nikolai Kotova has an "after-show" for the crowds, mostly tourists and people staying in Vegas for only a few days. The Red Death promotes his theatrics—hence, the spotlight—because he packs the club.

I'm not sure if I should watch, but I can't lie: I've *always* been curious. I've heard mutterings about what Nik actually does, and I thought they seriously had to be rumors. Until Brenden confirmed that Nikolai tattooed a fork on a man's chest.

I jab my thumb towards the bar like *I'm headed over there.*

Luka raises his brows at me, smiling wide. "Come on, Bay! You want to see this!"

I give him a look. "No I don't!"

"I know you!" he has to shout over his cousins like me, but the music lowers for Nikolai.

I find myself stepping closer to Luk. "What do you know about me?!"

He nearly laughs. "You're a people-watcher. *This*"—he nods to the spotlight and his older brother—"is a spectator's heaven!"

Okay, he knows me. "Fine." I try hard not to smile.

"Come with me." He clasps my hand before I can protest, and he wraps an arm around his sister's shoulder, leading us to the front "row"—which is really the edge of the spotlight.

Our hands disentangle as soon as Nikolai saunters across the open space and eyes us. He carries a magnetic force that's simultaneously hard to meet and abandon. A green necklace swaths his rugged features, and he assesses the gathering, rapt audience with keenness.

"What'd I miss?! What'd I miss?!" Timo bounces up to his brother and sister, wedging himself on the other side of Katya.

"Nik's just starting," Katya tells him. "Thora!" She hugs onto the short blonde who slips into our group with a smile.

For the first time in years, I feel a part of what I once lost. I'm inside the depths of Luka's world. With his little sister and his little brother, who's my age. I'm witnessing more than most ever will or can, and he's letting me not only *see* but be here.

I smile, almost in disbelief that this isn't all a dream.

Luka catches my expression, and his face brightens in an indescribable, profound way. He wants me beside him. Just like I want him beside me.

More than anything.

"GOD OF RUSSIA!" Timo shouts, hands cupped to his mouth.

"He's ten feet away from you," John says behind his boyfriend, clutching Timo's waist. "Really, what's the point in shouting?"

Timo leans back against him. "I'm working out my lungs."

"Your lungs don't need a workout. They're fully-functioning every night you're with me."

Timo smiles like a five-thousand-watt bulb, his gold Venetian mask adding to his effervescence. I watch Luka grinning at his little brother, wholeheartedly happy for Timo.

Everyone will talk about Luka's generosity, but I always see his empathy surpassing everything else. It's his foundation. It's why he loves so strongly. Why he cares so deeply. It's why he can watch two people fall in love and not be weighed down by sadness.

I can be happy for Aunt Lucy and her husband. I can be happy for Luka's brothers, but I can't always separate what I lost from the love I witness.

It *hurts*. Plain and simple.

Luka notices me staring, and he puts two fingers to his upturned lips. As indiscreetly as possible, he rotates his fingers, imprinted with a kiss, and presses them to my own lips.

Quickly, I lower his hand, cast a glance at Nikolai whose back is to us and then his siblings who laugh amongst each other, not about us. That's when I realize I've been smiling this entire time.

Luka laughs, and he opens his mouth to speak—but Nikolai suddenly casts his attention onto our "row" of onlookers. And I go rigid.

Luka is a hundred-percent relaxed, hands stuffed in his slacks.

I don't know how because Nikolai keeps perusing us and Timo, Katya—Thora, too. Actually, Thora a lot. I spot the creases of Nik's mouth slightly lifting at the sight of his girlfriend.

She's smiling back at him.

"Can you unzip me?" Katya asks Thora. I know what this is about. Kat explained a little of it earlier, so I'm not surprised when Thora unquestioningly goes to unzip her dress.

"Wait a minute," John cuts in, flabbergasted. "She's not seriously undressing right here. Seriously. Seriously? Everyone." His eyes ping to all of us, but no one disapproves. "Why does no one else see what I see?"

Timo twirls his scepter. "Because we're not a hundred-and-fifty, old man."

John rolls his eyes. "Pick an age that actually exists."

Timo calls out loudly, "Two-hundred-and-fourteen!"

We all laugh, and John shakes his head. "I'm not even smiling on the inside."

"You can smile?" Timo says. "I thought John Ruiz droids were programmed with one setting."

I notice John giving Luka a look, and Luka shrugging in return. Then John tells his boyfriend, "You mean *truthfulness*."

"Grumpiness," Timo combats, pounding his scepter on the ground to the beat of the song.

John is entrapped by him. "I'm cheerful in my left pinky nail."

"Let me see." Timo inspects John's left pinky, and John's eyes smile more than his lips. He tilts Timo's chin up and kisses him strongly.

I just realize—Luka, he's tucking his shirt into his pants. Nikolai looks between Katya and Luka. "Who wants to go first?"

Katya steps out of her dress, spandex shorts and a spaghetti-strap tank top underneath. Workout gear. Thora helps unclip her heels.

"You're supposed to choose," Katya tells Nik pointedly. "You said you wouldn't go easy just because we're family, and I'm the girl."

My brows furrow at Luka.

He leans close and tries to explain quickly. "I promised Katya that I wouldn't take Nik's Saturday night bet until she did."

That's what they all call Nikolai's performance: a bet. In a lot of ways it is a bet, but Nikolai almost never loses.

Nikolai tilts his head at Katya. "People also don't usually come prepared." He motions to her workout gear.

"I wasn't going to flash the whole audience," Katya says. "And you're just worried I'm going to beat you, aren't you?"

Nikolai almost smiles, and he doesn't deflate her confidence. Instead he says, "I choose you." He asks her something in Russian, and she replies back with a nod.

He backs up into the center. Kat follows suit, but she makes sure that Thora is protecting her dress.

A server carrying a tray of shots enters the red spotlight, and everyone starts cheering. I clap, the energy wild and heady. My phone buzzes in my wrist wallet.

I unzip and try to keep watching.

Before they reach for the shots, Nikolai addresses the crowd while speaking to Kat. "Tell me your name," he says. "And speak loudly and clearly so everyone can hear."

She raises her chin. "Katya."

"Katya." Nikolai is full of charm, his on stage demeanor commanding everyone's attention so easily. "For everyone new, I'll explain the game. I bet Katya that she can't beat me in a handstand competition. Two-hands."

Katya crosses her arms. "Easy enough."

I squint at the bright screen of my phone.

Nikolai acknowledges the crowd again. "If you lose, I pierce or tattoo you, and I choose where and the design. If I lose, you can tattoo me. You choose where and whatever you like."

Katya is grinning from ear-to-ear like she's imagined those words and this moment forever. It must all be colloquial. Routine. What he says every Saturday night to random people and sometimes family members and friends.

I have something to tell you — Brenden

My lips part, unsure of where this is going. Kind of scared. I still don't know what Luka and Brenden talked about, but I type back: what is it? After I press *send*, I try not to let my curiosity consume me.

Nikolai angles towards his sister. "Tattoo or piercing? Your choice."

Katya thinks for a moment. She has a tattoo already, a cluster of little stars on her left shoulder blade. She told me that she got it inked last year at a shop with Luka and Timo.

"Piercing," she decides.

Nikolai nods and downs three shots in a row. He's been drinking all night, and Katya only takes one shot. Nikolai asks her something in Russian. I wish I knew what, and I must wear that on my face.

Luka whispers to me, "Nik asked her if she needs more time before they begin, and she says"—we watch her lips move and hear the Russian—"'I'm ready now.'"

They stand side-by-side, and after Nikolai counts to three, they place their hands on the floor and hoist their bodies into the air. Effortlessly.

Luka whistles with his fingers, and I clap while the crowds shout loudly.

"Kick his ass, Kat!" Timo yells.

"Go, Katya!" Thora cheers. "Go, Nikolai!" She's rooting for everyone to win.

Luka shouts, "Beat him, Kat!" Another long whistle. I missed that noise. I feel my smile and press my fingers to my lips.

My phone vibrates in my other palm.

Luka told me that he loves you. Crazy, right? – Brenden

My mouth drops at Luka.

His face falls at me. "What's wrong?" He sees my phone. "Is that your brother?"

"What were you two talking about?"

He licks his lips and leans close to say, "Sisters."

I spin the phone screen at him, so many emotions tumbling through me. Should I be angry or upset? Should I not care? I don't know at all. There's no precedent for anything like this.

Luka blinks a couple times, trying to wrack his brain for what to say. "We were talking about you and Katya, I promise. I only let that slip." He nods to the screen. "But…it changed nothing."

It changed something.

It means I have to lie *more* to Brenden. It hurts again.

I pass my phone in both hands, my eyes scald, and I end up typing quickly: yeah crazy.

I'm not sure he'll believe me.

I wouldn't believe me if our places were reversed.

A loud "awww" rings out, and our heads swerve to Katya, who fell to her knees. Nikolai stands on his feet and then helps her up. I zone out a little as Nik chooses her nose to pierce. I have a feeling he knew she'd want that place pierced anyway.

And yeah, he pierces her right *now*, right in the middle of the club. One of his cousins hands him a sterilized hollow needle, and a minute later she returns to our group with a glittering stud in her nose.

"Bay," Luka says, trying to grab my hand.

I shift away. "I'm okay." I just feel weird. Like a traitor to my family. Like maybe I should be with Brenden right now. Not here.

Not lying to my brother, who I love with *all* my heart. He's been struggling with the new choreography changes for aerial straps, and I haven't been around as much as I want to be.

I should back up, but I'm cemented to this place. My feet unmoving.

"Baylee." Luka reaches out to touch my cheek, but Nikolai faces him.

Luka and I jerk away from each other on instinct, and I avoid Nikolai's domineering and disapproving stare.

"I choose you," Nikolai tells Luka and motions him forward.

He reluctantly and painfully tears away from me.

ACT THIRTY-FOUR
LUKA KOTOVA

I can't even keep an eye on Baylee in the crowd. Nik watches me so fixatedly that I worry he's a fucking breath away from scolding me out loud.

Nikolai refrains from repeating the rules to the audience, and he asks me firmly, "Piercing or tattoo?"

"Tattoo."

A server brings out shots of tequila. Nik and I clink glasses before downing two each, and the air tenses more. I don't feel like he's on my side when it comes to Bay.

He never has been.

"One-handed handstand," he challenges me.

I nod, and he asks me if I'm okay in Russian. I just nod again. I don't try to pick apart his expression. I don't try to care about what he thinks of my irresponsibility and recklessness.

I go through the motions, and after he counts to three, I perform a one-handed handstand beside my brother.

(Don't hold your breath. I never win at these types of competitions.)

Like clockwork, I fall after a few minutes. I barely hear the *boos* from Timo and Katya. While Nik gathers the tattoo equipment, I search the audience with my gaze.

She's gone.

I sense it before I really confirm by sight.

She's not here.

"Lift up your shirt," Nikolai says, cutting into my trance.

I snap out of it and comply. I hear Timo say, "I bet a hundred bucks he inks a penis."

"Deal," Anton says.

"Good God, that's a losing bet," John says dryly.

Nikolai says under his breath to me, "I'm not inking a dick."

"Thank you," I say, wishing I could laugh at the absurdity, but my stomach is in knots.

"Stay still," he instructs.

"Okay." A chill runs down my spine. My body is screaming to run after her. Wherever she went, I want to be.

The tattoo gun buzzes, and Nik places the needle to my right ribs. "Be careful," he says lowly, and I know he's not talking about the ink.

He means *Baylee*. The contracts. The no minors policy. My own brother won't rat me out, but he'll caution until I stop.

"I am."

Nikolai looks disbelieving.

So I rephrase, "I'm trying."

"Try harder."

I can't even nod or respond. I'm frozen solid, and he's finished with the tattoo faster than I thought he'd be.

In tiny script, he wrote *circus is family*.

He bears the same words in the same place on his body. It means something to him.

And it means something to me.

I nod a couple times, and he touches the back of my head like earlier tonight.

Why do I still feel like he's my enemy?

WHEN I HEAD TO THE BAR WITH MY BROTHERS,

sister, and cousins, I spot Baylee sitting at a stool and chatting with Camila, who wears a red glow necklace like a crown.

They're both instantly distracted by the on-rush of Kotovas.

"Hey, cuz," Camila says to John, who claims a stool about two down from Baylee. She departs from Bay and starts taking a slew of drink orders.

Baylee turns slightly, and our eyes lock.

I quickly occupy a free stool to her left, the music blaring. "Are you okay?!" I ask at the same time she says, "What tattoo did you get?!"

I lift the corner of my shirt to show my ribs.

Her smile appears and vanishes rapidly. "Yeah, I'm okay!" She raises her cup to me, the liquid clear. It's water. I figured she wouldn't drink tonight. When she feels a lot more low than usual, she'll stay away from alcohol.

I scoot my stool closer, so we won't need to yell. Bay casts a cautious glance to my siblings. And cousins. They all fight about what to drink, and Katya, back in her Calloway Couture dress, rolls her eyes and spreads her arms out. Giving herself a small bubble of space.

Robby, Dimitri's younger brother, still bumps into her.

Baylee fixates on me again, and just as I'm about to ask another question, she says, "I invited Brenden here."

It makes sense. "Okay."

Baylee studies my reaction. "You'd really be okay with Brenden showing up?"

I nod, assured. "Yeah, Bay. He's your brother. I'm not trying to tear you two apart. I'd never do that." Does she really think I'd stoop that low? That I even have that in me?

"I know," she says, taking a large breath like the strain from earlier starts to alleviate. "What if it's awkward?"

"I can handle awkward." I begin to smile. "I'd handle anything for you."

Bay inhales strongly, eyes starting to glass, and a heartfelt, over-whelmed smile plays at her lips.

I want to reach out, but the bar, however dimly lit, is blanketed in a red hue from lights overhead. Making this area more visible than the rest of the club.

"Brenden actually can't come until later," she tells me. "Like a few hours from now."

"Why?"

"He's on a date. Tinder."

"Fun," I say easily.

Her brows rise in interest. "Luka Kotova has Tinder experience?"

I wince through my teeth. "Maybe."

She laughs once. "Me too. Only it went pretty much *nowhere*."

"Same." I nod, and Timo hands me a beer bottle. I say *thanks* in Russian, and then I'm met with Bay's disbelief.

"If sex is nowhere for you, what's somewhere?" she wonders.

"Emotion. *Love*." I stare straight into her. "You."

Baylee bunches up her face to keep from smiling. "Stop." She grins into a sip of water, and I smile into a swig of beer. She groans and touches her cheek.

"Naughty children of mine." Dimitri comes up behind us and hooks his muscular arms around our shoulders.

I face the bar at the same time as Baylee, and I take a larger swig of beer.

Dimitri drops his husky voice another octave. "You can pretend not to know each other, but I saw what I saw—and it looked a lot like *smiley* flirting to me. Which I advised Baylee against, but here we are."

Baylee shrugs. "It's hard taking the advice of someone who sings to their protein shakes."

I grin into another swig.

Dimitri says, "It gives my banana extra *pep*." We can't respond because he physically wedges his body between our stools, separating us now.

"Come on," I say to my cousin.

He cocks his head and nears my face. So only I can hear his next words. "History isn't repeating, little Kotova. I'm not screwing you two over." Determination hardens his already hard features, resolute with this idea.

That he won't be the cause of our demise again.

I didn't realize he still blamed himself for that night. If doing *something*, even separating us, makes him feel better, then I won't argue.

Baylee also resigns, shrugging like *it is what it is.*

Setting down my beer, I crack my knuckles and scan my surrounding family members. One person has been missing. It's why Timo sits carefree and untroubled on the bar, a whiskey-bourbon cocktail in hand, his laughter radiating.

"Where's Sergei?" I ask Dimitri, who tries to flag down the bartender. Camila raises a finger at him like *one second*, busy making a tequila sunrise for Thora. Though, I doubt she ordered it since she's pregnant, but Camila probably knows her friend's regular order.

"I don't keep tabs on Serg." Dimtiri cranes his neck over his shoulder, and asks Nikolai in Russian, "*Where's your brother?*"

Nikolai hangs back from the bar with Thora. She's turned into his chest more than usual, and her arms are curved around her stomach.

"Sergei," Nik says in English, assuming it's about our older brother.

"Yeah, the one who thinks you two are best friends and sip from the same straw," Dimitri retorts.

At work, Dimitri has been cordial with Sergei, and outside of work, they get along alright. They've argued a few times, and they've made up just as fast.

I sense something different here.

I grab my beer. "Jealous?"

"No," Dimitri denies, the same time Nik says, "Yes."

Dimitri glowers. "Being jealous of Sergei implies that he's your best friend. When I know that I am."

Nikolai rolls his eyes. "Just this morning you complained that he spent more time with me yesterday than you did."

"That's not jealousy," Dimitri growls. "That's *inequality*."

Baylee snorts into a laugh.

I smile wider, and Dimitri gives us both a look. Like we've chosen the enemy's side.

"I'm not Team Sergei," I assure him.

"Neither am I," Baylee says seriously.

Nikolai cuts in, "There aren't *teams*." He glares at Dimitri, wearing an expression that says: *don't add a greater divide in our family*.

Dimitri groans lowly but nods. "There aren't teams. Just assholes, bigger assholes, and slow-as-fuck bartenders playing favorites." He raises his voice. "How much do I need to tip to get a beer?!"

"A hundred bucks!" Camila yells back, but she's focusing only on John. If I strain my ears, I'd pick up the words, but I don't try.

Dimitri digs in his pocket for a wallet, and not far away, I spot my sister's disgruntlement at the pushing bodies. I act on impulse.

And I stand on the bar.

"No," Camila reprimands.

I swing my head back to her. "For Kat." The soft sides of my features allow me passageways to too much probably.

"One song," Camila says with a smile.

And I already reach out to my little sister.

Katya smiles big, and I help her up onto the bar.

Timo is beside us in less than a second, scepter in hand. As an upbeat Saint Motel song plays, the club's energy livens like fireworks blasting off in three-hundred-sixty degrees. The three of us dance with silly throwback moves: the windshield wiper, the sprinkler, checking out groceries.

I pull my baseball hat out of my back pocket and fit it on backwards. Timo tosses me the scepter. I spin it like a baton and then throw it to Kat.

She lip syncs into the staff, and Timo and I do a dance from *The Breakfast Club*, one of his favorite movies.

We all clap at a heavy drum beat, even Bay and my family down below.

I think I was worried for no reason.

I think the bad feeling is *me* being overly paranoid.

Because everything is great right now. We're all having a good time. That's what birthdays are about, right?

As the song changes, Camila lets Kat sit on the bar, and I drop onto my stool, catching Bay's rising smile before Dimitri's body blocks us again.

Timo stays standing and raises his glass of whiskey-bourbon. "Listen up!" he shouts jubilantly, stealing the attention of more than just our family and friends.

We all grab hold of our drinks.

Timo points his scepter at our sister. "To Katya Kotova."

Kat cups a vodka soda, her gaze lit up at Timo.

"I wouldn't choose any other sister but you. May your seventeenth be the *best* it could ever be." Everyone raises their drinks in agreement.

"Thanks, Timo," Kat breathes, eyes welling in happiness.

"And to Nikolai." Timo spins his scepter towards Nik.

I look back at my older, stoic brother who holds onto Timo's gaze. In the creases of Nik's no-nonsense demeanor, there's light. I can't say these two have always gotten along.

They haven't.

But some sort of peace hangs in the air.

Resolution between them. And love.

Timo says loudly and deeply, "You're the brother we all don't deserve, but I'm damn happy I have you. You're irreplaceable to us. I hope you know that."

Nikolai nods, telling him he feels the sentiment.

Timo raises his glass higher. "Happy Birthday to Nik and Kat…" His voice trails, and his eyes widen, lips down-turning at someone in the distance.

I can't see from the ground, but I know who it is.

Timo collects his thoughts and repeats the same phrase and cheers in Russian. Then we all drink. I already finished off my beer, so I set my bottle down and keep an eye on Timo.

He hops off the bar and then tries to stand behind John's stool, shielding his boyfriend from the incoming person.

Sergei.

My older brother squeezes between jam-packed bodies and somehow reaches the bar. Of course he chooses the only free stool, which happens to be in the middle of Baylee and John.

(I'm not happy.)

Timo tries to wedge himself between our older brother and John. The same tactic Dimitri is using towards Bay and me.

It literally only causes Sergei to focus entirely on Baylee.

I rest my elbow on the bar and peer beyond Dimitri, who's busy waving a hundred dollar bill at Camila. With the strobe lights, the music, and the chatter—the chaos should disorient me, but I hone in on Sergei.

"Can I buy you a whiskey?!" he asks Baylee over the commotion. I remove my hat, just to run my fingers through my hair.

"No thanks!" she shouts back.

Sergei scoots closer to Bay like I had done. "I always find you sitting alone."

(She's not alone.)

Baylee shrugs, tensed. "There's nothing wrong with that." She eyes his Black Sabbath T-shirt and the leather bracelets on his wrist. He's definitely dressed differently outside of work.

"Other than it being lonely."

Dimitri shifts forward, obstructing my view again. "Bartender girl, I have a hundred dollars for you!"

I grab his shoulder and pull him back slightly.

He doesn't even notice.

Baylee flashes her phone at Sergei. "I have baseball streaming to fight boredom. I'm good."

Sergei laughs. "Why even stay here if you're just watching baseball?"

Because she can. What other fucking reason does she need? I shake my head a couple times, my muscles more constricted than normal. Nik said there aren't teams concerning Sergei, but I instinctively feel *Team Baylee*. I can't help it.

Baylee shrugs again. "Says the guy who hates baseball. I don't think you'd understand."

Sergei goes quiet instead of becoming defensive like I assumed he'd be.

I edge forward more and wave my empty beer bottle at Sergei, catching his attention. "Where've you been?"

My brother rotates towards me. "Convincing Geoffrey to return our act's music to the original tempo."

My brows knot. "You didn't have to do that."

"Yes I did," he says. "You couldn't keep up."

I almost laugh, and my smile stretches very wide. It's ridiculous how easily he can blame me and think it's a constructive critique. I've been *trying*. I practice for twelve hours a day. I can do more within the fast tempo than I could days ago, and he missed a rotation in his triple-full yesterday.

So it's not all on me.

Baylee gives me a look like *is he for real?*

I nod in reply. He's a hundred-percent unaware of how people perceive him.

"It's not funny," Sergei tells me. "You need to take this seriously." And he's reading my expression incorrectly.

"I have been," I assure him. "I don't know what else to say, dude."

"You could say *thank you.*"

My brows jump. "Geoffrey really returned our act's music because you asked him nicely?" That's incredibly hard to believe.

"Yes," Sergei says like it's simple logic.

It's not.

I don't understand how that worked at all.

Dimitri leans forward, forcing me to edge back, and Camila Ruiz stands in front of him.

She splays out her palm for the money.

"Ah-ah-ah. Beer first." Dimitri wags a finger at the draft spouts.

Baylee is near laughter, and I understand why. Neither one of them have recognized each other yet.

Camila looks to Baylee and asks, "What?"

"No, no, no," Dimitri chimes in, putting his hand at Bay's face. "Ignore this one. She's purposefully trying to make me dehydrated."

"If only that were true," Baylee says into her sip of water.

Camila squints in the poor lighting and tries to scrutinize Dimitri. She stiffens at the sight of his neck. "Is that a burn mark?"

"Yes, Nancy Drew, now *beer.* Right there." He jabs another finger. "I'll make it easy: I don't even care what kind. Just give me something."

Camila smiles. "You're Dimitri."

I can see the gears clicking in his brain, processing her voice, maybe. And then he says, "Princess?"

Camila curtsies.

Simple as that, he forgets about his pursuit of beer. Dimitri grins and rests his elbows on the bar, leaning so far over. "You're obsessed with my cock."

"Tiny cock," she corrects.

"Whatever you like to call it, it's fine with me, princess."

Camila taps the red glow necklace on her head. *It's complicated* could mean anything, and Dimitri would hit on her even if the necklace represented *taken*.

"You know what the red one means?" he says.

Camila crosses her arms and waits for the punch line.

Dimitri straightens up. "It means you're confused until you've met me."

She stretches her hands on the bar, and confidently, she says, "Take a long look. Because that's all you're ever going to get." At this, Camila snatches his hundred-dollar bill and starts filling a pint of beer.

I pat his shoulder. Dimitri is the underdog, every which way you look, and I understand that more than I do a champion. I understand someone losing more than winning and fawning over people you can't have from afar.

Dimitri isn't pushy. When someone rejects him, he accepts this fact, but he still watches like maybe there's a hidden chance. A world in which he gets what he wants, too.

So I'm not even a little surprised that he hasn't peeled his gaze off Camila—or that he doesn't pressure her either. He just grins when she glances back at him.

Horns and trumpets suddenly blare through speakers, and multicolored lights flash. Girls in matching silver cocktail dresses parade into the club. Carrying baskets and bottles of booze.

John scoffs. "Not this stupid thing again. Why didn't you warn me?" He's asking Camila.

She slides the overflowing pint to Dimitri. "Because you still would've come and *complained* for a solid three hours beforehand. I was saving myself, cuz."

"What is it?" Baylee asks, just as the girls strut over to the bar. They pause to pour liquid in a few mouths, and then they reach into their baskets.

I can't see what they grab.

"It's a promo thing," Camila says. "The club offers free booze and a Vegas experience. People tell their friends, and then before you know it, we have a full house and I'm swamped at the bar with tips ranging from *best night of my life* to *I want to eat a tub of rocky road.*"

"Vegas experience?" John arches his brows. "That's what we're calling it now?" He doesn't see the girl with the basket behind him, or the others pouring shots into my cousins' mouths.

In one swift move, a girl procures a pink fuzzy *handcuff* from the basket and clips John's wrist to Timo's.

John gapes. "What." He looks personally affronted, and we're all laughing. Except for Timo, who's really trying to avoid Sergei. I think the handcuff situation makes it harder to keep John away from our older brother.

"Natalie," John says dryly, knowing the basket girl who works here. She high-fives Camila.

"I hate you all," John says. "Where's the key to this fucking atrocity?"

"There's never any keys," Camila reminds him. "That's the whole *fun*. If you understood that word, this would make more sense to you."

John cringes. "Whoever came up with this idea is a sadist."

"Don't diss my boss. She's the best." Camila tosses a dirty towel at John, and he dodges the rag.

Natalie digs in her basket for another handcuff. (Wait, *no.*) I rise halfway off my stool, but she's fast. In two movements, she cuffs Sergei to Baylee.

ACT THIRTY-FIVE
LUKA KOTOVA

I slowly sink back down, my face frozen in disbelief.

Baylee examines the cuff and tries to pry the metal open. I'm about to lean over and help, but Dimitri purposefully angles his body to cut me off, happily drinking a pint of beer, too.

I shake my head at him and fit my hat backwards again.

Dimitri offers his own beer to me. "Cheer up, buttercup."

I push the drink to his chest. "I don't want your beer. I want you to move slightly to the left."

"Not happening." He sips from his pint.

I rub my lips once and then press my chest up to the edge of the bar. Trying to peer at Sergei and Baylee again. They're turned towards each other.

I trust her.

I don't trust him.

I honestly don't really even know Sergei. Not beyond work.

"It matches your dress," he tells her.

I blink a few times, wondering if I heard him right.

(No, don't tell me my oldest brother is flirting with Bay. This isn't happening again.)

"What?" Baylee frowns, and he raises his arm, pink cuff attached. It's the same shade as her sequined dress.

Sergei adds, "Maybe the universe is telling us something that we haven't figured out yet."

(No. Just *no.*)

My eyes narrow at my brother, but he's so concentrated on Baylee that he hardly notices the rare glare that I burn into his skull.

Baylee leans back from him, but they're physically connected now. "The universe?" she repeats, skeptical.

"You know, *fate.*"

He's oblivious to what I feel for Baylee, and I can't even be shocked. It's not even the blue glow necklaces that make us difficult to read. (He's also, unfortunately, wearing a blue *I'm single* necklace.) It's that the dude wouldn't recognize a connection between *anyone* if it pressed up against his nose.

"Fate," she repeats the word with the shake of her head. "I think I'm the universe's reject. You should attach yourself with someone that has better luck than me."

I want to reach out and hold her hand.

But I can barely even see her past Dimitri's body.

She digs in her wrist wallet for something. Maybe to avoid his gaze that stays plastered onto her. Erik passes him a vodka soda, and I watch Sergei take a sip. Still eyeing Bay.

My nose flares, and Baylee glances over at me.

Dimitri side-steps before her gaze meets mine. I turn towards the bar, my face in my hands. I try to stifle a frustrated noise that scratches my throat.

Through the creases of my fingers, I see Camila passing me a shot of tequila.

I slide the shot back. "I didn't order this."

She smiles. "Free shots for glum-looking people."

John interjects, "How long have you had this policy? And why don't I have a free shot?"

I tune him out, and my muscles bind as Timo and Sergei exchange a look. Timo is trying to tell him: *don't speak to John.*

Sergei is confused as ever.

And Timo notices that our brother isn't registering the *hint*. I catch him biting his thumbnail to the bed. I rub my face a couple times, wincing. I'm wincing in concern and pain. Look, I have issues, and so does Timo.

(It's not that big of a secret by now.)

I can practically feel his weighted apprehension crawl up my back like an invisible monster. I hate this feeling. Just as much as he does.

"You're not glum-looking, cuz," Camila refutes. "*This*"—she makes a circular motion at John—"is the face of bitterness." She gestures to me. "*That* is the face of heartbreak." Camila is about to slide my shot back, but John steals the glass.

He downs the liquor in one gulp.

"Heartbreak?" Sergei laughs at me like it's a joke.

I can't even fake a smile right now. I glance back for Nikolai in all of this, but he's speaking to Thora a few feet away. She looks pale, and his features turn grave.

I try not to worry.

(Don't worry.)

When I rotate to the bar, I notice most eyes uncommonly on me. My muscles flex, and I spin my baseball cap forward so no one can read my expression. "I'm not heartbroken," I tell anyone who wants to hear.

"Please," Camila says, "I'm an expert on matters of the heart. I know things." She winks at Baylee.

I frown. There's no way Bay told her about *us* being exes or secretly something more. Camila must just be making assumptions.

John steals a second shot from Camila, his expression sour. "You've only been with *one* person," he announces, and Dimitri rocks back in shock. "That makes you an expert on Douchebag Dave and that's it."

John clearly hates her boyfriend. I wonder if Sergei is comprehending that exchange or if he's really that bad at subtext.

"Where's Douchebag Dave?" Dimitri asks. "Is he here? Tonight?" He's even more intrigued, looking around for this dude.

"His name is Craig," Camila says, "and *no*. You're never meeting him. No Kotova is."

Dimitri cocks his head. "You're anti-Kotova?"

(She wouldn't be the first. Some of us are annoying as fuck.)

"Today I've decided I'm anti-drama, which means I'm anti-Kotova. At least for the next half-century." She forces a smile at a customer at the end of the bar and waves.

"I'll wait for you, princess."

Camila actually smiles. I think she's surprised by her own reaction. Dimitri does well enough with women, but he also ends up with drinks thrown in his face as often as he gets a phone number. Sometimes those are the same girls.

I'm not the cock-blocker.

Bay is.

"Can you get Luka a beer?" she asks Camila.

My lips curve upward.

Dimitri looks at Baylee like she's causing him erectile distress.

Camila frowns at me. "Do you want a beer? I'm serious about those shots."

"By far the worst policy I've ever heard," John interjects. "Sad people don't need more liquor, let alone free liquor. Bitter people, on the other hand, could use some free shots."

"A beer is perfect," I say, and I sense Baylee's burgeoning smile not far from me.

Camila nods, looks between us with a knowing grin, and she searches for a bottle that matches my empty one.

I'd like to say it's all easygoing from here, but even with house music thumping, a really awkward silence starts stringing across the bar that begins with Kat, John, Timo, Sergei, Baylee, Dimtiri, and me—all in that order. Some of us sitting.

Others standing.

Sergei rotates on the stool and stares past Timo. "You're John?" Oxygen is vacuumed up. I thought this moment would be uncomfortable. Uneasy. And maybe more awkward than all else.

I didn't think it'd feel this unpredictable.

Like anything can happen.

Timo lifts his mask to his head, but John already rises from his stool.

His scowl dark, he outstretches his hand to Sergei. "I'm John Ruiz. Timo's boyfriend."

Sergei remembers that he's cuffed to Baylee, and he carefully stands without pulling her off the stool. But to give him more room to move, she stands too. The chain to their handcuffs isn't longer than a few inches.

They're literally *that* close. Her shoulders lock, uncomfortable, and she tries not to bump into his side.

I abandon my new beer and stand up too. Dimitri is distracted by Nik and Thora, and he ends up joining their deep conversation a few feet away.

Quickly, I come up behind Bay, my hands lightly on her hips. "You okay?" I ask in the pit of her ear before I step around her frame. I want to fucking hold her. Wrap her up in my arms.

Squeeze her tight.

Instead, we're left doing this.

Her fingers brush mine, and our pinkies hook for a brief second before falling to our sides. "Yeah." Bay lets out a deeper breath. "Do you have anything small or sharp to pick the lock?"

I dig in my pocket: gum, Tic Tacs, a few buttons, and actually something of use. I flash a safety pin to Bay, and she plucks it out of my fingers.

"Some hope exists after all," she says seriously.

I almost smile. (Luka Kotova: pockets full of *hope* and shit.)

Bay untwists the safety pin, and she elbows hair out of her face.

My eyes flit up to Timo, and my face falls. He bites his pinky nail, and now that we're all standing, he can't shield Sergei from John or vice versa. They're both taller than Timofei.

Sergei reaches out and shakes John's hand, cordial enough, but I study my little brother, his expression contorting like he teeters on the precipice of a cliff.

Timo.

(Look at me. Everything's going to be okay.)

His eyes dart to John and Sergei, and he says, "Great, you've met. Now never meet again."

Sergei sighs heavily. "You're being dramatic. We're getting along fine." He motions from his chest to John's. "It's not a big deal."

"It's a big deal to *me*." Timo touches his own chest.

My bad feeling—it's starting to catch up to me. I immediately walk forward. Towards Timo.

To reach him. And then Sergei extends his un-cuffed, free arm across my chest, stopping me next to him.

Like he needs me to be his advocate.

I glance back at Baylee, but she's urgently trying to pick her lock. I'm about to tell Sergei to let me through, but he speaks again.

"You're the only one with a problem, Timofei," Sergei nearly yells out of frustration. "Do you realize that?"

(No.)

Timo's face breaks into painful fragments. When people hurt him, it's not snuffing out a light. It's taking the heel of your foot and smashing a lantern to a million shards. You wonder how he can ever be lit again.

I duck beneath Sergei's arm, and I almost pass through—but I'm jerked back. Sergei fists my shirt, yanking me beside him.

"Stop, Serg." I push him once, my shirt out of his possession, and his eyes narrow and soften like *help me.*

I can't fucking help him be friends with Timo! I wish everyone would leave me out of this and just let me be there for my little brother.

I look back at him.

John has his arm draped around Timo, hugging him to his side, but Timo doesn't tear his shattered gaze off our oldest brother.

Sergei shifts his weight. "I didn't...I didn't mean it how you're taking it, Timo."

"How am I supposed to take it?"

"Realize that this could all be *fine* if you just got over it..." Sergei trails off again, starting to see that he's making it worse.

Timo instinctively turns into John's chest and tries to wrench his own wrist out of the cuff. He wants to leave.

"Babe, slow down. Stop, *breathe* for a second," John says, his voice hardening in concern, and then he glares at Sergei. "Don't put this all on him. He's entitled to his own feelings. He can be upset at you."

I don't reach Timo. Katya does. She rushes to our brother and tries to help unlock the handcuff, bobby pin in her fingers.

"I'll get you out. Don't worry, Timo," Kat says.

"It's been months!" Sergei yells, his frustration palpable.

I spin my baseball cap backwards. I'm on edge, nervous that both Sergei and John will start swinging, and right now they're literally attached to two people I love. They're not accidentally pulling them to the floor because they forget their surroundings.

I'm not letting that happen.

They take one step closer, and I slip between Sergei and John, extending my arms. My palms touch their chests, and I force them apart.

John yells, "I didn't realize agony had a fucking timeline!"

"He's not in agony!" Sergei grimaces at the thought.

"Stop!" I shout at them, but it's like no one hears me. I glance at Bay—her fearful eyes meet mine. I think she heard me, and she works faster, yanking at the cuff.

It's still locked.

"Shit," she says, but she tries to pick the lock again, still determined.

Sergei points at Timo with his free hand but yells at John, "He's giving me *no way* to fix it! I can do nothing but watch him hate me! You know what this is?!"

I shake my head at Sergei. "Don't go there, dude—"

"It's *life*!" John sneers, eyes blistering on Sergei. "Welcome to the real world where every shitty thing we do affects other people!"

"It's immature!" Sergei yells, and my chest collapses.

Timo is crying hearing what Sergei—the one person he wanted as a father figure—really thinks of him. Sergei doesn't respect his feelings.

People always say that: *get over it.* Why? So they can feel better about the hurt they caused?

Everyone heals at different rates. Some people need *time.* It sucks. It's frustrating, but our minds are more fragile than we like to believe.

(Than I like to believe.)

And I can't remember the last time I saw Timo sob this hard. He usually contains it all until one unintentional moment, and Sergei just kicked open Timo's floodgates.

Timo drops his scepter and covers his eyes with his free hand, and John points an antagonistic finger at Sergei. "Fuck you!"

"He's my little brother!"

"And you're hurting him!"

I shove them back as they wrestle closer. "STOP!" I yell.

Katya unlocks Timo's handcuff, squeezes him in a hug, and then she bounds over to Baylee, switching out the safety pin for the bobby pin to help.

Timo lifts his watery eyes to me as I push both guys apart, and he looks past tears. Numb. His heavy gaze rises to the ceiling.

I wonder if he's contemplating Sergei's words.

If he's questioning whether he's the root of the problem. Immature. And just a pain to us all.

I shake my head. Timo is a good person. He means everything to me.

To so many people.

I tune out Sergei and John. I drop my hands, and I beeline for my brother. He sees, and at nearly the same time, our arms wrap around each other. Clutching tight.

His speeding heartbeat pounds against my chest, and we don't let go.

Against his ear, I say, "I love you, Timo."

I can practically feel him shutting his eyes, blocking out the world around us. Our chests rise and fall heavily at the same pace, and softly, I hear him mutter, "I don't know what I'm doing anymore, Luk."

I whisper strongly, "You're living. That's all we can do." I don't think there are any real answers. Timo is the one who talks about sucking the marrow out of life.

He's the one who lives for every moment. I don't want him to stop now because he's questioning everything he is. His feelings. His hurt.

His maturity.

Timo is his own joy.

Isn't that enough?

I feel his pulse slow, and as we ease our heads back, I worry a fistfight broke out around us. What I find is…something different.

John and Sergei stand side-by-side, cooled down. Watching us. Their eyes are bloodshot, reddened—but they never fought.

Never threw a punch.

They're civil for Timo.

Baylee and Kat are still working on the handcuff. When Timo and I separate, John reaches his boyfriend and cups his cheeks, wiping his tears with his thumb. They whisper, John consoling Timo more, and I walk beyond them.

I pass Sergei, his nose flaring like he's trying to suppress emotion, and his gaze lands on mine, full of apologies.

I nod at him, accepting.

He takes a breath and glances at Timo whose head is buried in John's shoulder. As soon as I near Bay and Kat, they unlock her handcuff—and some random person immediately *bumps* into Baylee.

She stumbles backwards, her feet sliding out from beneath her, and my reflexes are quick, I reach out and clasp her hips. Holding her body like we were dancing and I just dipped her.

Baylee clutches my biceps, her collarbone jutting out as she catches her breath. "What…?"

I smile. "You're in my arms. That's what."

Her lips rise, and all the emotion we'd been suppressing starts overpowering me. It takes…everything in my body not to kiss Bay. Slowly, tensely, I lift her upright, and I can't stop. My lungs and heart thrash in my ribcage, screaming at me to do something more.

On instinct, my arms slide around her shoulders, drawing her so close.

She hugs my waist and presses her cheek to my chest.

Warmth bathes me, and I kiss the top of her head. I kiss her temple. I look down. She looks up, and I'm so fucking close to kissing her lips.

"You two."

We freeze.

That voice…I have to be dreaming, but I turn my head and a foot from my face is Geoffrey Lesage. In the red light, he appears more menacing, his judgmental, harsh glare set on me and Bay.

I'm about to ask what he's doing here, but Sergei must read my wide-eyed expression.

He quickly explains, "I invited Geoffrey. I thought it'd be a good idea to make amends outside of work since it's been tense inside." Sergei is rigid, actually noticing that this was a horrible idea.

Baylee and I haven't separated. Her fingers dig into my back, afraid that we were just caught breaking the contracts. But what are the chances that he's one of only two Corporate spies?

"I need to talk to you two," Geoffrey says sternly, "about *this*." He motions at the way we hold one another.

And before I can even comprehend the enormity of what's happened, Nikolai starts screaming, "Thora! THORA!"

We look behind us, and Nikolai has Thora in his arms, tapping her cheek repeatedly. His distress shrouded by his grim, take-charge demeanor.

She's passed out. Dimitri is on the phone, and I hear him say *ambulance*.

ACT THIRTY-SIX
BAYLEE WRIGHT

Here's something funny: Brenden calls me the pessimist, but I'm the one who sees the good in hospitals. Sure, sadness exists here, but people help other people here too. Brenden is the one who grows quiet and somber every time he steps into a waiting room.

I guess that's not really funny, but I've never been great at jokes anyway.

I try to think about this as I sit at the foot of Thora's hospital bed with Katya and Camila. She asked if the three of us could take a seat. We slipped in after Nikolai left, and there aren't any chairs in this enclave of the ER, mint-green curtains drawn shut for privacy.

So we chose the end of the stiff bed.

Thora looks less sickly than earlier, but tear tracks stain her splotchy cheeks. I notice that she keeps glancing at the hospital bracelet and her flimsy paper gown. Like she has trouble believing she's here.

We know what happened. Someone overheard an ER doctor. I think Robby, and he spread the news to every Kotova in the waiting room, which eventually reached us.

Camila stretches forward and holds her hand.

Thora's chin trembles, but she nods and says tearfully, "Thank you all…for being here." Her voice breaks.

We all scoot forward and hug Thora at the same time. There's not a dry eye right now. Everyone is dealt weird hands of life, and in another timeline, we could've been Thora. Maybe we still could be, and if I were in her place, I'd want Thora at the foot of my bed. And I'd want to know she cares about me.

That's all.

Just a little compassion.

When we retract a little, Katya curses under her breath. Our eyes veer to her. Mascara runs down her chin and drips onto the white hospital sheets.

I don't know why, but I laugh. Thora starts laughing, and not long after, so do Katya and Camila. I rub my face, makeup everywhere.

Camila's bold shadow is smeared across her eyes.

Thora laughs harder at Camila. "You need to take a picture. For once your makeup looks worse than mine." Then her face contorts and she shakes her head—we all go quiet again.

I have to ask. It's been plaguing me since we first heard the news. "Do you think you can sue Aerial Ethereal?"

Thora takes such a deep breath, it's not only audible but it inflates her whole chest. She sits up straighter like the weight lifted a fraction. "No…I know I can't."

"But…" I try to figure out how to mention that I knew she was pregnant. God, *was* pregnant. As in past tense. If it sits strangely with me, I can't imagine how odd it is for her.

She had eight weeks to become used to the idea of carrying a baby. Maybe she even started envisioning names or what he or she would look like.

Thora stares at me intently, and she nods like she understands what I mean to say. "The doctors said that the miscarriage didn't happen because I was doing aerial silk eight-weeks in. I was careful at my job, and I didn't ever sustain an injury."

I nod in reply.

"They said it was most likely mismatched chromosomes." She nods to herself more, fiddling with her fingers. "They said it's the cause of sixty-percent of miscarriages, and that I'll probably have no problem getting pregnant…next time."

Thora sighs out the tension in her bones, and she stares off at the wall. "I told Nik that…no matter how much the doctors tell me it's not my fault, I keep thinking I did something wrong to cause this. Like…I could've done something differently and I'd still be…" Her face twists in hurt.

"*No*," I say strongly. "Bad things—they happen for no reason, all the time." I think of my parents.

"It's not your fault," Katya chimes in.

"They're right," Camila says, squeezing Thora's hand.

Thora blows out a measured breath and then wipes her watery eyes. "I thought I'd be *relieved*. I thought Nik would too." She looks up at the ceiling. "I mean, AE is probably jumping for joy. I can now stay in Amour for the rest of the year and longer, if they renew my contract. I don't know, maybe they won't want to after all this…and I'm rambling. Nonsense. It's all nonsense, right?"

I nudge her lightly. "It's not nonsense. It's your life."

Thora blows out another breath. "I can do this," she mutters. "I can do this." I once asked Thora how she's able to be so positive.

She said that if she gave up on herself, then her biggest cheerleader would be gone, and she needs Thora James rooting her on in the stands.

It was inspiring.

And I slowly start to smile watching Thora motivate herself forward.

I wish I could find that inner-cheerleader.

I'm going to need Baylee Wright to buckle up soon. Geoffrey Lesage is waiting somewhere in the hospital, and when he confronts me and Luka, my whole world may change.

But right now, I think about Thora.

I listen as she tries to gather more words, more strength and courage in the face of heartbreak and pain. *We're here.* Girls bonded not by last name but random happenstance and choice.

And we're here for as long as she needs us.

ACT THIRTY-SEVEN
LUKA KOTOVA

No one's seen Nikolai since he left Thora so the girls could talk and comfort her, but after a three-minute search in the hospital, I find my brother. I just don't tell anyone else.

I enter a two-stall bathroom, empty except for Nikolai. He grips the sink basin, slightly hunched over. A rare sight for a guy who stands so erect you'd truly think someone shoved a stick up his ass from birth.

He barely acknowledges me. Barely moves.

I lock the door behind me, and Nik slowly turns on the faucet.

I'm not the best with words. I'm not the best at much, but family is all we have. And I have to be enough for him. Like he has to be enough for me.

His nose runs, and he wipes it with the back of his hand before splashing water at his face.

I take a step closer and stuff my hands in my pockets. "Dimitri texted. Said he heard the girls laughing. Like *good* laughter."

Nikolai tightens his eyes closed, his chest caving. And he clutches the sink's edges again.

I've never seen Nik cry.

I wouldn't be surprised if he never has.

He's used to being everyone's rock. He was next to Thora in the ambulance. At the hospital. By her bed. I saw a glimpse through the ER curtains, and he was holding her after the doctors explained the news. She cried into his shoulder, and even from my obscured view, he looked so torn up. Maybe Thora even saw him cry for the first time right then.

I can imagine him being vulnerable with her, easily.

Nikolai staggers slowly back from the sink and he drifts to the mirrored wall. His knees nearly give out, and he sits on the tiles, head hung. Arms draped on his bent legs.

I approach like a ghost and quietly sit next to him. And I say what I think he needs to hear. "It wasn't your fault."

His nose flares, and he shields his face with a shaking hand.

I wrap my arm around his broad shoulders. "There's nothing more you could've done. Nothing to prevent it or save her from this. You did *everything* you could." I feel him shudder, and I edge closer. He reaches out, his hand on my knee.

His grip is strong like he doesn't want me to leave. And I watch my selfless, stoic brother pinch his eyes and fight gut-wrenching tears. His face reddens, scrunched up.

His pain balls in my throat, and I rub his back. "She's going to be okay, Nik."

And then he drops his hand, and tears slip out of the corners of his bloodshot eyes. Mine burn and cloud.

After a few minutes of unleashing his emotion, he finds the strength to lift his head up, and he leans more against the mirror. I stare at the locked door with him.

Outside of that door, my life is about to become undone, and I can't tell him that I fucked up again. Irresponsible Luka Kotova. Letting down the people I love most. Repeating all of my mistakes, and still, I wouldn't change anything but being caught.

(I'm so sorry, Nik. You deserved a better brother than the one you got.)

ACT THIRTY-EIGHT
LUKA KOTOVA

"**B**aylee?" I say.

She looks numb, staring off as we stand in a tiny vending area within the hospital. One of the only secluded places Geoffrey could find after he corralled us in the hallway.

I didn't even have time to hug Bay before he said, "Don't touch."

I rake my fingers through my dark hair and then fit my baseball cap on backwards. I reach out to her, but she shakes her head once. "We can't."

Geoffrey will be back soon. He said to, "Wait here."

I have no idea what he's doing.

I rest my forearm against a Fizzle machine, and I'm turned towards her. "What can I do?" I want to fix this. I want to take her pain away. I'll feel better knowing she's alright. "Bay?"

"I don't know." She looks up, eyes welling.

My heart is being ripped to shreds.

She crosses her arms like she's trying to hug herself.

I reach out. "Let me, please. He's not back yet."

Baylee takes a breath, looks over her shoulder, and then she walks into my arms. I hug her so tight, and I feel her exhale just as I do.

Softly, she whispers, "I don't want this to be our last hug."

I shake my head, weight piling on my chest. Eyes burning. "It's not."

She doesn't believe me. I don't even believe me. "This hurts," she says. "God, this hurts."

I pull back some, and Baylee has her hand on her chest like it's her heart.

My hands slide up to her cheeks, and she feverishly traces all of my features. I try to engrain all of hers, just as urgently. Our eyes dancing.

And then we hear footsteps. The sound of metal scraping the floor. My hands fall, and we separate two feet which feels like ten thousand leagues.

Baylee presses the buttons to a snack machine, sadness blanketing her brown eyes. I feel like I've been kicked repeatedly. My whole body aches, and I keep rubbing my face, wishing I'd stop wincing soon.

When Geoffrey returns with two chairs, Bay actually sighs in relief at something to sit on and sink into.

"Sit," he orders.

She's already sitting, one leg tucked beneath her ass.

I take a seat and lean back some, my hands on my knees. "What is this about?" I speak first, knowing Baylee is quieter in these situations.

Geoffrey crosses his arms, his goatee a little fuzzier than yesterday, and his ash-blond hair is askew like he's been anxiously grabbing at it. I'm surprised he's not pacing in front of us, but he is trying to tower. Which is probably why he only brought two chairs.

It's working more than I want to admit.

"You know what it's about," Geoffrey snaps. "When I first signed onto Infini, I thought I'd be the reason this show *succeeds* for a decade longer. I thought I'd be the *hero*." He laughs like it was foolish. "Then I have a private meeting with Marc Duval. He tells me that through the transfer of a colleague, he needs someone new to be his *eyes* and *ears* towards two artists. I hesitate." Geoffrey holds up his hands. "It sounds like babysitting to me. I'm here to reinvigorate a dying show, that's all. Marc tells me that if I don't do this, I lose out on the Infini job and the biggest sum of money in my career."

I ball my baseball cap in my hands, listening and now knowing our far-fetched thought about Geoffrey is real. That he was told by Corporate to spy on us.

The no minors policy is coming.

Baylee stares so far off, wide-eyed; I worry. And I turn more towards her than to Geoffrey.

Our choreographer continues, "So I *agree* to make sure Luka and Baylee don't even sneeze on each other outside the gym unless it's about work. But let's be honest here, you're both *far* from professional at this point. Vince thought he spotted you on the strip during a lunch break. Did you know that?" He steps closer.

It forces me to crane my neck to look at him.

"Did you know that I also talked him out of entering the Urban Outfitters he was *sure* you were hiding in?"

Baylee snaps out of her stupor, and my brows furrow in confusion. We're both shaking our heads. Why would he help us?

"I also cancelled lunches. I thought you two would take the hint. Surely you both know what's at stake if I or Vince relay news about your *sex buddy* to Marc."

My jaw muscle tics, but I'm not back-talking right now. Not to prove a point that he couldn't give two shits about.

"Why didn't you tell on us?" Baylee asks with a shrug, face pained. "Why even pair me with Luka on the trampoline?"

"I'm here for *one* purpose." Geoffrey points at the ground. "For *Infini*. Not to babysit two stupid kids."

(Fuck you.)

Geoffrey looks to me. Like he's waiting for me to attack. Show some raw emotion.

When I give him none, he sneers at me, "Unbelievable." He crosses his arms again and scrutinizes Baylee. "I actually think you two have promise together on stage. You have real chemistry, and I took advantage of that for the betterment of the show. You know what I'm not willing to lose? My underage girl who will be kicked off Infini the *second* I go tattle to Marc. I need Milla. The show needs Milla, and the no minors policy is threatening the creative value and potential of Infini."

He's going to help us?

It's what I'm hearing.

He's not planning on running to Marc Duval.

I straighten up. "What do you want then?"

"I want a guarantee that you two won't ever be caught by Vince or Marc himself."

"Done," I say, but Baylee is holding her breath, more realistic while I try to dream about a happy ending in all of this.

Geoffrey chuckles at me. "That's funny that you think I trust you. You know you're in AE's artist database with everyone else? You want to know what a former choreographer wrote in your file? He typed: *will lie to protect other artists.* Here's what I'm going to write in yours." He mimes writing on the air. "*Nuisance, not worth the time or effort, soulless—*"

"Stop," Baylee interjects, setting a glare on him.

Geoffrey's brows spike, and he appraises us. "I asked around about you two...to your...aunt, was it?"

Baylee recoils. "You talked to my aunt?"

"About two weeks ago. I wanted to know if I could trust you two to stay separated. I didn't let her in on your current 'relationship' status, but I casually asked about your history together. She didn't give me much at first, just said you were best friends. Then I asked if she's ever seen Luka *yell*, and she said *yes*." Geoffrey tilts his head at me like he caught me in a lie.

(He didn't. Not really.)

I blink a long blink.

"She said that Baylee was upset one day, overslept, and you were defending her tardiness at practice to a staff member. You were suspended for two days. Your aunt warned me that you both used to try to fight each other's battles. One would fall, the other would scream. That sort of thing."

We're both eerily silent.

Baylee is scared. I can feel her stiffen beside me. Maybe she's afraid he's going to use this against us. I shake my head a couple times, and Geoffrey backs up, leaning against a Ziff machine full of sports drinks.

"You know what I believe?" he says. "I believe that you'll always go an extra mile if you keep seeing each other at work. I believe it was a mistake to put Luka in Infini, and I don't know why Marc Duval would even tempt it."

He's just as clueless as us about the reason then. And I can't even disagree. Me being in Infini—it changed everything.

"What else do I believe?" Geoffrey continues. "The only way to ensure you abide by the rules is for one of you to *quit* Aerial Ethereal."

"What?" we say together.

"I reread your contracts. There's a stipulation that says if you both leave the company, the no minors policy is enforced. But if only one of you quits, there's no harm done. You won't be able to ever talk to each other, you'll live your lives separately like you *agreed* to do years ago, and Infini won't be damaged."

I flinch back, numb to the bone.

Baylee's face is in her hands.

My thoughts speed up, and it hits me. "You don't want the no minors policy to happen, so you'll never rat us out to Marc. We don't have to comply." I'm grasping for a glimmer of control.

(It's always fleeting. I'm not holding my breath.)

"Wrong," Geoffrey snaps. "There's a timeline. Seven days to quit. If you don't by then, I'll say you physically attacked me today, in this vending area, and I'll *fire* you."

My stomach clenches, and I look to the ceiling for answers. We could break our contracts and leave our jobs together, but it'd also enforce the no minors policy.

I already know she won't do it.

Just like I won't. Not if there's another option, and he's giving us one, our second handout from someone I deplore. Only I despise him way more than I ever hated Marc Duval.

This seems worse than the first time.

Because I'm older.

I'm twenty, and what I feel for Bay isn't a dream or fantasy. I have my head somewhat on my shoulders, and the naysaying voices in our ears aren't even here. We don't need our stand-in parents to tell us where to go. What to do.

And I wonder what I would've decided if I had the two contracts at this time in my life. I wonder if I would've quit AE to be with Baylee right then and there.

Maybe.

But that's not what's on the table today. We can't walk away without hurting the dreams of potentially *thousands* of children. We're not going to do that.

One of us is quitting for Geoffrey's "offer" and it's about to be me. I open my mouth to volunteer so she can stay in the circus, but I see the way he's staring at me.

And a realization sinks in.

He directed his whole firing and quitting speech *to me.*

"We don't have a choice who quits, do we?" I ask, more calmly than he probably likes.

Geoffrey almost smiles like he won a game I didn't even realize we were playing.

Tears slip out of Bay's eyes, and she chokes, "No, let me—"

"I need you," Geoffrey cuts her off. "I don't need him." He steps off the vending machine, coming forward again. "They say you're irreplaceable because you're a Kotova? Because of chemistry with your siblings and cousins? You're just a number to me. I can easily rewrite the choreography of every act you're in. Like you weren't ever there. Invisible—"

"Wheel of Death," Baylee combats, voice cracking.

I whisper, "It's okay, Bay." She can't quit. Infini…it's her mother's memory.

She can't quit.

I can leave. I'll…do something. I don't know what. I blink a couple times, blocking out the names of my family members. Of never seeing Bay again. I crack my knuckles.

I don't want to confront all that I'm losing.

(I'll puke.)

Geoffrey says, "I can move Erik Kotova onto Wheel of—"

"You *don't* have that authority," Baylee interjects, and I frown. Does he?

"Shut up, and don't interrupt me again."

I instantly stand and step in front of Baylee.

Geoffrey laughs like it's too late.

I don't want to leave her in this dude's presence. I'll have to warn Brenden before I go. Who else? Dimitri? They'll make sure Geoffrey doesn't mess with her when I'm gone, right?

(What am I saying? It's like I'm preparing for my *death*.)

I can already feel the uncertainty tormenting me. Not knowing if she's happy or sad. Or just doing okay. All of it. All over again.

Looking directly at me, Geoffrey says, "I've been given the authority to swiftly axe Brenden and Zhen's aerial straps routine anytime I like, so *yes*, you better believe I have the authority to shift around artists and fire them."

Baylee caves into herself, and I turn to comfort her—

"Don't *touch*."

I freeze at his words.

"You're going to leave separately. Luka go first—"

"No fucking way," I actually say out loud. I think it stuns him, but I don't drink in his expression. I crouch down to Bay, careful not to touch her like he said. I don't toy with that risk. "Baylee. Hey, go outside. Call your brother to come get you? Can you do that?"

Brenden doesn't have a car, but he'll probably take a cab. I don't want her to be alone right now, and I'm not leaving first so she'll be alone with *Geoffrey*.

Baylee pinches her eyes, attempting to stop the waterworks. My gaze sears.

She curses, and she tries to stand. I know she must feel like a million pounds of sorrow, but she has to get up.

In a full minute, she rises on her own, her hand pressed to her collarbones.

"Call Brenden," I say.

She nods once.

"Please."

She nods again.

"Okay." I glance back at Geoffrey, who's watching too keenly. I hate this dude so *fucking* much. I try to follow her out of the vending area, but he clamps a hand on my shoulder.

He yanks me back, and I shove him off out of defense.

I lost sight of her, but I remind myself that I've been given a choice. To quit or to be fired. I have seven days until I decide, and that's seven days left with Baylee.

He's not taking that away from me.

ACT THIRTY-NINE
BAYLEE WRIGHT

Luka likes pretending that doom isn't waiting in the horizon. For six days, I've done a decent job at pretending too. We sneak off together when we can. As though Geoffrey never caught us. And we try not to talk about his impending departure.

Well, he's quitting *tomorrow*, and I couldn't stomach attending an Aerial Ethereal artists banquet in the Masquerade's ballroom tonight. Most go for the free food and booze.

But Luka gladly ditched with me.

With his suitemates at the banquet, we hang out in his kitchen. I sit on a bar stool and watch him burn my grilled cheese on a frying pan.

I'd cook, but he offered, knowing I typically smile when he *always* under-butters the bread and smoke billows in his face.

I haven't smiled at all today.

Reality is too close to stealing him from me, and my heavy mood won't rise. I slump forward, and I wonder if there's anything *more* I can do to keep him here.

To extend this moment for another day.

Another lifetime.

Anything.

Luka flips the charred grilled cheese onto a paper plate, and he tosses the smoking pan into the sink. Then he slides the paper plate to me with a growing smile. "I think I could be a good cook," he teases. "Maybe Steak 'n Shake will hire me."

My lips downturn. "That's not funny." I'd normally take a bite of the grilled cheese. He always burns the outside, but the inside is usually really good.

I can't even bring myself to pick it up. The act feels like running five hundred miles across the globe. I groan and wipe my leaking eyes with the hem of my cotton T-shirt. I've been involuntary crying *all* day. I'm sick of tears.

I'm sick of sadness. I just want it to leave me.

And I want him to stay.

Luka skirts around the counter and comes up to me while I sit. He cups my cheeks, his palms warm against my skin, and I wrap my arms around his waist.

"I could quit first," I say, surfacing our fate that we've avoided. "He said only one of us needs to, and if I quit before he can fire you, Geoffrey can't really do anything…" I trail off as Luka shakes his head.

"No, Bay." His brows rise. "*I'm* quitting tomorrow. Not you." He kisses me lightly on the lips, as though imprinting his declaration as a promise.

A tear slides down my cheek, onto his palm. "I'm sorry." My voice fissures.

Luka brushes his thumbs beneath my welling eyes. "I'm sorry too." He nods a few times, restraining emotion. He edges closer, his arms falling to my shoulders.

His body is pressed more up against my build. His warmth blankets me, and my legs instinctively curve around his waist, my ass on the end of the stool.

More in his possession.

I can't rid the lump in my throat. "You didn't do anything wrong," I say. "I'm the one who showed you the list."

I tried not to imagine being caught before finishing the list. It was always a possibility, but I just hoped we'd end things on our terms this time.

Luka almost laughs. "I'm *glad*."

I make a face at him like he can't be serious.

He actually smiles. "Everything we did wasn't a mistake to me, and it's definitely not all on you. The list was supposed to be about two exes *talking* through their past. Not redoing everything. I took it to another level, Bay."

"And I agreed to it," I remind him. "Because…" *I wanted you.* The list was supposed to be about me emotionally moving on, but we ended up using it as an excuse to stay together. "Shit." I'm really crying. I bury my face in my shirt, lifting the fabric and exposing my abdomen.

I feel him kiss the top of my head, and I sink against his chest. Luka draws me off the stool, but he keeps my legs secured around his waist. I pull my shirt down to see my surroundings. He carries me to the living area.

And he lies on the modern gray couch with me pressed up against his body.

Our limbs tangle together, his strong arms holding me like it's the first and last time. My ear rests over his heart, and I listen to the calming *thump…thump…thump.*

Silent tears cascade down my cheeks, and every now and then, he caresses them away with his thumb.

After a few minutes, I look up, and he smiles weakly at me. His gray eyes are glassed.

I turn on my side to face him more.

He turns with me, and his arm hooks over my waist, welding us together.

In the quietest voice, I whisper, "Will I see you tomorrow?" I ask what's been on my mind since he started cooking. He may leave in the early morning before practice starts, and there's a chance we won't find private time to meet.

A tear rolls out the corner of his eye. "I don't think so."

This is it then. I inhale a sharp breath, and he rubs my shoulder and arm before his hand travels to my cheek again.

I place my palm onto his hand.

His breath is uneven, staggered, and his lips touch mine so tenderly and lovingly. It fills me up.

We break slowly, and I wish my tears weren't all over his hand. My throat swells, but I find my voice to ask shakily, "Do you want to complete the list?"

His brows cinch. "Right now?"

I try to shrug, but I have no energy. "It's now or never." What we do here determines how we end our love story.

Luka rolls on top of me and hoists his weight off my frame, his hands on either side of my shoulders. I clutch his biceps, fine with him bringing his entire body down onto me, but he stays suspended above.

He combs pieces of my hair off my face. He smiles like I'm the most beautiful person he's ever seen, even tear-streaked. Even crying and sad. "I'd rather just lie here with you, Bay."

I think he knows that we're both not emotionally up for oral sex.

"What about the list?" I whisper. "It just stays unfinished forever?"

Luka thinks for a second, and then he says, "We've never had a close. Maybe we were never meant to." He lowers some, his forehead near mine. "One day, you'll find a man that you deserve, who'll make you *so* fucking happy." We're both crying. "I'm sorry that couldn't be me."

We tangle up again, hugging. Clinging.

And I whisper into his neck, "It was you. It was always you."

We stay like this until time ticks by, and footsteps patter along the hotel hallway. Voices growing louder, and we know the banquet has ended.

We gather the strength to stand, and we languidly head to the suite's door. He hangs onto my wrist, and I rub the wet tracks off my cheeks. He's still clasping onto me as I crack open the door.

And I look back, his chiseled yet angelic features only an inch away. I press two fingers to my lips, and I do what he had done.

I touch the imprinted kiss to his mouth. One beat passes, and he swiftly shifts my fingers before his lips urgently meet mine in a real, sweltering kiss. It pulls and curves my body into his. I grasp onto the back of his head, and his tongue parts my lips.

Driving the kiss deeper. More sensual than pained.

Tears slip down our faces, and I feel his pulse race against mine.

This is our goodbye.

At least it's better than the first time. I hope I can live with that.

ACT FORTY
LUKA KOTOVA

I start packing around 4:00 a.m., my bedroom dark. Dimitri sleeps on the bottom bunk, rolled onto his stomach, and his muscular legs hang off the edge.

I skulk to our dresser, trying not to wake him.

I don't need much, and it's not like I have furniture or many possessions. I empty my drawers into one duffel bag. That's it.

Home has never been the clothes in my closet or the bed beneath my body. Home is my family, and for the first time, I'm leaving.

Stress has been quietly crushing me.

I zip up my bag and pause for a second, breathing through my nose. I abandon my duffel and exit my bedroom for the suite's bathroom. I slip inside, kneel, and stick my middle finger down my throat.

I dry heave, nothing left to puke.

I hate that I can't puke.

I hate that I want to—that it's been controlling me this badly. I can't block out the guilt anymore. Regret assaults me, and I breathe heavily for a second.

(Come on, Luk. Fight this.)

My eyes tighten shut.

I stopped fighting this monster about a year ago. It's been with me since I was six, and I win sometimes. I lose just as often, but it's there, you know.

Lurking.

I always think, *I'll do better tomorrow.* When I'm this knee-deep in, I rarely do. But it eases me right now. The "I'll do better tomorrow" thought. It helps me stand up.

I close the bathroom door and return to my room—the lights are on. Cautiously, I slip inside, not surprised by what I find.

Dimitri is squatting beside my duffel and inspecting the contents, plus the empty drawers.

He catches my gaze. "Going somewhere?"

Look, I knew I couldn't tell my family I was quitting Aerial Ethereal. At least not until the last minute. They'd ask *why* a million times over, but I already emailed Marc Duval that I'm quitting, an informal written termination.

It's done.

"To hell," I say, pretty easygoing. My voice is never dry. "Want to come?" I pick up my duffel by the strap and zip it again. If I pretend like I'll be back, I can leave easily.

It won't hurt.

(Please.)

"Hell is too hot for your lily-white ass." Dimitri straightens to a stance, and his gaze narrows for answers.

I almost smile. "Thanks for the tip. I'll pick up some sunblock on my way." I nod to him. "See you on the other side, dude." As I turn, he guards the door with his six-foot-five frame. He's dropped some muscle mass this past week, per Geoffrey's request.

But he's still huge.

"If you won't talk to me, go talk to Nik," Dimitri says seriously.

"I'm about to."

He processes this, trying to trust me. I'm really telling the truth. I plan to tell Nik I quit AE, and then I'll hop in a cab. I already booked a plane ticket to New York.

I figured I'd find an apartment in Brooklyn. Tap into my *tiny* savings, and then I'll figure out where to go from there.

Simple as that.

(It's the hardest thing I've ever done.)

Dimitri cocks his head. "If you're in trouble, you know you can come to me."

"I'm fine." I try to pass, and he extends an arm across the door frame.

"Fine isn't waking up at two a.m. to go puke—"

"Don't."

"Don't what?" Dimitri points at my chest. "You made a promise to Nik when you were thirteen. Did you forget that?"

"No. I didn't forget." I promised that if I ever felt out of control, to the point where I couldn't function, I would tell him. I wouldn't lie. I wouldn't go at this alone. I'd ask Nik for help.

Dimitri stares at me like *so what the fuck are you doing.*

I rub my face once, wincing. Because I just want to leave, not confront these issues too. One is hard enough. Heaping them all on me at once—I can't.

I can't deal with it all right now. "Let me through, dude." I can't stay here.

Dimitri hesitates. "Tell me I'm not going to regret this."

My throat bobs, but I try to smile, duffel strap on my shoulder. "Stay beefy. Or everyone will start calling you *the Prius*." I pass him, patting his shoulder once, knowing he'll let me go.

He sidesteps, his features solidified in pained confusion.

(Bye, Dimitri.)

I HAVE A KEYCARD TO NIK'S SUITE.

I slip inside the darkened living area, curtains drawn closed over the windows. I glance left, and Nikolai is already exiting his bedroom, dressed in black boxer-briefs, hair disheveled and face set sternly.

He grips his cellphone, and I'm sure Dimitri called or texted him about me.

I don't drop my bag. I won't be here long. "Hey," I whisper in the quiet.

Nikolai stops a foot from me in the small space between the bar counter and the couch. Instead of asking questions, he assesses my features for answers, his concern palpable.

In one breath, I say, "I quit AE."

Nik frowns darkly. "No you didn't."

"Yeah. I did." I keep my voice low, my stomach and muscles coiling. "I'm leaving. My flight is at nine, so I'm heading out now—"

"Wait slow down." Nikolai raises his hands and then reaches out for my bag. "Take a seat."

I back up, only one step. "I have to go." It feels like someone is jumping on my ribcage. "I have to go," I repeat, cementing this agonizing fact.

Before I can spin to the door, Nikolai clutches my shoulders. "*Luka,*" he says my name with force and urgency. "*Luka,* you're not leaving. You have to talk to me."

I shake my head slowly. "All you need to know is that I quit."

Nikolai tries to steer me to the couch, but I put a hand on his chest. He instantly freezes, but his gaze drives into my core, trying to pry the answer out.

I wonder if he sees fear inside of me.

Anguish. Or heartbreak.

Maybe all three.

"I'll talk to the police," Nikolai says. "Whatever you stole, we'll make it right."

I laugh because I actually *wish* that my kleptomania was the problem right now. (And there you go, I gave one monster a name. It's so clinical that I usually avoid the term, but it's out there and real.)

"Look at me," Nik whispers. "*Luka.*"

I look up. "I'm fine. I'm leaving, and you'll have to accept it, Nik." I turn towards the door.

Nikolai sprints ahead of me, and I take only two steps before he pushes me back with his palm to my chest. His puts his phone to his ear.

He's calling someone?

"Nik, don't."

In Russian, he says, "*I need you over here right now. It's Luk.*" The call lasts point-two seconds, and then he hangs up.

I shake my head vigorously.

His jaw contracts, and he keeps one hand on me. Making sure I don't leave. "You weren't planning on telling them you quit AE." It's not a question. He just knows I couldn't stomach it.

"Don't make me do this," I say beneath my breath.

Nik wears dark confusion, his hand on my shoulder now. "You're *choosing* this. You chose to quit."

My bones lock.

Nikolai reads me well. "This isn't your choice. Luka—"

"I can't." My nose flares, and I raise my hands. "Just let me go, dude. You *have* to let me fucking go." The door whips open.

Our heads swerve, and I go motionless and cold as Timo walks into the suite, squinting. "Why are you in the dark?" he whispers and then flips on the kitchen light, a soft orange glow.

His face falls at the sight of us, squared off towards one another, and my bag—he hones in on my duffel. "What are you doing?"

"Wake Katya," Nikolai tells him.

"No," I say, but Timo quickly sprints to the other bedroom. He cracks open the door and whispers our sister's name.

My hands are on my head, and I start thinking that I have to tell them I quit. I have to rip off the Band-Aid, dodge their expressions, and then walk out of here.

I have to do this.

I have to do this.

I drop my hands to my thighs, slightly hunched over and already winded. Nikolai tries to bend down to my height. He used to do that a lot when we were younger. Try to be eye-level with us.

It should comfort me, but it just makes it harder to leave.

"We can fix this," Nikolai tries to assure me.

"No." My jaw tenses. "There is no *we*, Nik. There's just me. I take responsibility for my own actions."

Nikolai searches my features rapidly, hastily—*fearfully.*

"Luka?" Katya creeps out of her bedroom, shutting the door. I don't imagine Baylee on her bottom bunk in there. Overhearing this. I want the last image of us to be better than that.

I stand up straight, and I slowly make my way to the door. Nikolai follows, but I'm able to put my hand on the knob.

Katya and Timo are about five feet away in their pajamas. Facing me with panic and worry.

Timofei tries to smile. "That's just an overnight bag, right?"

"Sure."

"He's lying," Kat says, eyes already welling in hurt and anger. "You're a bad liar, Luka Kotova."

(You're a good sister, Katya Kotova.) I nod a couple times, fighting emotion. I look between the two people I chose five years ago. My little brother, life and youth personified.

My little sister, sweet and clever.

I already miss them.

I'm numb as I say, "I quit AE." I turn my back to them, twisting the knob, but their screams of "what?" and "why?" pierce my eardrums.

I tune out Timo who yells at me. Pleading with me to stop and stay and talk. He grabs my hand, and I shake him off. He curses at me.

He screams at me.

(I'm sorry.)

Katya is sobbing.

I exit the suite, my heart in my throat.

I shift my bag to my other shoulder, and I walk fast towards the elevator.

"Nik, you can't let him leave!" Katya cries. "Nik, *go faster!*"

Nikolai is chasing after me. I don't even look back before he runs up to my side, his lengthy stride pace-for-pace with mine.

My voice is hollow. "You can follow as far as you want, but I'm not stopping." I press the elevator button. As we wait, he stays silent, but his intense presence bears down on me.

I'm in a daze, remembering how Katya auditioned for Noctis, a touring show, during contract renewals last season. That hurt some, but I figured she needed to prove something to herself. She was accepted, and she declined, ultimately staying in Viva.

Timo never thought she'd leave.

It's even hard to believe I'm not just transferring shows. I'm quitting the company, and I'm a breath away from the elevator.

It dings, and in unison, we enter. The doors slide shut, and I watch the digital numbers tic down as we descend.

Nikolai hits the emergency *stop* button.

I should be mad. I should be angry.

But I'm relieved. And I don't know why. He's the one who'll harp on about *responsibilities* and hammer me over the head with what I've done wrong.

We face each other in the motionless, quiet elevator. Tensed. Uncertain of what'll happen here. Either I eventually walk out or he stops me.

There are only two outcomes.

"At least give me the facts," Nikolai says. "Let me understand what happened."

"Don't be too hard on Timo and Kat when I'm gone, okay?" I'm a brick wall that he's trying to crumble for my own good. I know it.

I just can't come undone that easily.

His features darken. "If you leave AE, they'll be *inconsolable*."

"So console them," I retort. "Don't wait for me to do it."

Nik must be clenching his teeth, his jaw muscle tensing. We stare at each other for a long, uncomfortable moment. He's the one who takes two steps forward, strong-minded.

And he asks, "What do you need from me? I will give you *anything*." The way he says that one word—it's as though he's offering his entire life to me.

But he already gave me his life, his time, his world years ago when he chose me over the touring show.

I speak as clearly and unemotionally as I can. "I need you to let me go."

He speaks firmly. Passionately. "Anything else but that."

I never detach from his brutally intense gaze. "It's all I need."

"Bullshit," he swears. "Something happened." He keeps searching my face for answers. "Did someone force you into this? Luka—"

"Just stop." I drop my bag, the weight killing me. "Just stop for a second." I stagger back and lean my body on the wall. I feel strangely ripped open but sewed up at the same time.

Nikolai's chest rises and falls, and he paces the width of the elevator, only one time, before halting. "You're right," he says, his eyes almost bloodshot.

"What?"

"I can't console them," he says flat-out. "I've always needed your help."

I shake my head on instinct.

"I text you *every single day*, Luka."

"Then you can text me from across the country—"

"It's *not* the same!" he yells from his core. I'm about to cite Sergei and Peter, who he didn't see for six years but he maintained contact with them through the phone—he beats me to this fact. "You mean *more* to me than them. I…"

He practically raised me.

Nikolai is only a foot away, his voice deep and low, cut with raw emotion that he doesn't hide. "I know you're in pain. You have to tell me what happened. Look at me."

I realize my eyes are on the floor. I can't lift them.

Nikolai places his hand on my shoulder, one on my jaw, guiding my face upward. His strict gaze is full of strength. It's not against me.

It's for me.

I imagine this is what a father is supposed to give a son. Support. A rock to stand on.

I want to tell him. I want to let it out, and I open my mouth—but I'm so used to suppressing the truth. How do I release it all now?

My eyes well. "Nik…" (I'm scared. I'm so fucking scared.)

His gaze bears into me. "I'm going to help you."

I shake my head again. "You won't." I rub my mouth, my breath stuck in my throat. "I already know what you'll say."

"It's about Baylee," he realizes, his hands slowly dropping off me.

My head is a million pounds at the hollowness of his voice. *It's about Baylee.* I stare at the frozen *34* number, and somehow, I tell him everything that happened in the numbest, most soulless voice imaginable.

It's easier if there's no hurt attached to the words. It's easier if I describe Geoffrey in plain detail. It's easier if it's all meaningless.

When I finish, I finally look to Nikolai. I can't comprehend his reaction fully, not as he stares stunned but harsh at the ground.

"Go ahead," I say, pain leeching my voice for the first time. "Say what you want to say. I'm the irresponsible fuck-up you can only count on Monday through Wednesday. I risked my career and my family for a girl. You'll say that she wasn't worth any of it. That she was just some fling."

Nikolai meets my gaze head-on, but saying all of this aloud—it snaps something inside of me.

I straighten up off the wall. "You'll never understand what I feel for Baylee. It's not fleeting. I can't wish it away. I *tried*. I fucking tried!" I scream through glassing eyes. I blink once, and tears fall. "And fuck you."

"Fuck me?" he repeats, his voice cold. "What did I do other than love you?" He takes a fierce step forward again. "My entire life, I've *protected* you."

I drop my head, silent tears streaming down my cheeks. "Then why do I feel like you're about to gut me?"

Nikolai looms close, but he stays still. "I would never hurt you. I'm on your side. Look at me—I'm on your side."

I meet his eyes, but skepticism lingers in mine.

He sees. "I'm human, too. I make mistakes. I wonder, all the time, about the choices I've made in life. Just like you. And I know what it's like to feel compelled to choose a woman over your career. To risk your job for someone else. You know, I cut out of Amour early for Thora."

I remember he thought she was in trouble, many months ago before she was part of AE.

"I would do more than that for her," he admits. "I can't picture my life without Thora, and I'm telling you, I understand what you're going through."

(Do you?)

Very deeply, Nikolai says, "Some love is infinite. And I'm going to help you fight for yours."

My knees almost buckle as he lifts an insurmountable weight off of me, my lungs ablaze. "Don't fuck with me, dude."

"I'm not, I promise." Nikolai rests his hand tenderly on the back of my head, and then he pulls me into a *hug*. A real hug.

(I'm not kidding.)

Hot tears run down my chin. I grip the back of his shirt and pinch my eyes with my other hand, crying. I can't tell you the last time a family member consoled *me* like this. And I never imagined it'd be from Nik.

He's a fortress. Something unbreakable, no matter how much I beat at him—and he's also something keeping me standing.

I feel it fully.

Trying to cut the waterworks, I mutter a couple profanities and rub my face with a rough hand.

Nikolai says lowly, "You spend too much time with Dimitri." Because of my language, probably.

I lean back some, both of our eyes reddened. "Jealous?"

He doesn't deny it, and severity hardens his features. "If anyone corners you and tries to manipulate or blackmail you, tell me the moment after. Not a second or day or week later." He pauses. "I'm *always* on your side, and I'm sorry I made you feel like I wasn't."

I let out a sound of relief and pain.

Nikolai clutches my face, and he says in Russian, "*I love you, brother. I need you whole.*"

I want that too.

ACT FORTY-ONE
BAYLEE WRIGHT

Curling up on Brenden's bottom bunk, I cry silently into his dinosaur Pillow Pet. I just listened to the most excruciating sobs from Katya and everything Timo said to Luka as he left.

I couldn't stay in my bedroom any longer.

Brenden sits up against the headboard, typing on his laptop. "Dr. Spiro is only available Monday at noon. Will you be okay until then?"

When I don't respond, he shakes my shoulder hard until I attempt to elbow him. It's feeble and weak.

"Weak," he actually tells me.

"You're weak," I say softly and turn my head, looking over at my brother. The computer screen illuminates his caring face in the shadowy bedroom. "I can't go at noon."

"Yes you can," he says.

"I have practice." I'm about to turn back into the pillow, but Brenden braces me up, his hand on my shoulder. I rub some of the involuntary tears, my cheeks wet.

"AE will give you an hour off to see your doctor. You should be going more anyway. I haven't seen you this depressed since..." Knowingness suddenly bathes his features, and his head tilts back. "Something happened with Luka? Didn't it?"

He seems more sympathetic and concerned than spiteful towards Luka. My lips part, wanting to be honest. Wanting to be free from every deceitful thing I've told my brother. I'm scared.

So, *so* scared.

I swallow and say, "I can just feel low for no reason."

"*Yeah*, but events can also push you into a deeper depression." He shuts his laptop and switches on a reading light attached to wooden slats above us. He likes dinosaurs, history museums, all languages, and literature—that's *my* brother. I'll claim him every day.

He's mine.

And he deserves the truth. He deserved it five years ago.

Brenden grabs a box and starts covering me in tissues. "Thanks for washing Rexy-Rex. He needed a bath."

I sniff his dinosaur pillow. "God, he smells bad."

"Like your sorrow."

I muster the strength to flip him off.

Brenden smiles.

I want to smile back. On another day, I would. I sit up partially and fold a few tissues, blowing my nose. Besides the occasional breathy snore, Zhen doesn't make much of a peep on the top bunk.

I can feel my brother thinking hard.

With a breath, I say, "I don't want you to stop prying." I want Brenden to dig the truth out of me and take the heaviness away.

"What happened?" he asks outright. "You know I won't judge or...I couldn't be mad at you. I *wouldn't*. I just want to know so I can help you."

I shrug tensely, and I sigh a pained breath before I let it *all* out. I mean every last thing that I'm contractually *not* supposed to say. From five years ago. From the past months. Past week.

I don't care about the no minors policy anymore. Everything seems pointless, and I just need someone to tell me what to do. What to feel.

Brenden only interjects to encourage. "Keep going," he says nicely. "You can tell me. I'm not mad." *I'm not mad*, he ensures me the entire time. Even when I confess about impersonating Luka in text.

I'm not mad.

It must be an hour when I finish, and I sob into his Pillow Pet again, hugging it tight. Brenden rubs my back in a circular motion, and he wipes a fallen tear quickly so I don't see.

I saw, obviously.

"I've been afraid to tell you," I reiterate for the millionth time.

"I would be too," he says. "I don't know if I would've ever…I don't think I could've crossed AE." Then again, he wouldn't have gotten in trouble in the first place.

Knees tucked to my chest, I rest my cheek on the pillow and look at Brenden, my waterworks slowing. He keeps his warm palm on my back.

"I'm sorry for lying," I whisper, "and for all the times I made your life harder."

Brenden shakes his head like I don't need to apologize for the twentieth time. "I love you, Bay. If I lost you with Mom and Dad…" He tries to sniff his tears away, and he wipes the corners of his eyes with this thumb. "You're my heart."

"Literally." I eye his tattoo.

His lips curve high.

"I love you too," I breathe, and the talk of love draws questions in his gaze.

"I didn't know how much Luka meant to you, you know?"

I nod once. I couldn't ever tell Brenden.

"You've never talked about him like you just did. *Never*. I mean, the way you just described the guy and all the time you've spent with him… it kind of reminded me of Dad's novel."

My eyes widen, surprised that he brought up Dad's books first. "Which one?"

"*Bones Against Bones*."

I know the quote before he says it aloud, and I shut my eyes and listen and feel the incoming words.

And Brenden recites, "I have lived partially. Halfly. Incompletely. To be whole, I did not know until my bones thundered and bellowed for more."

More, I mouth the word.

Brenden hugs me to his side, and I lean my head on his shoulder. He's the one who says, "Regardless of Luka, there's hope in the future, Bay. I know it might be hard to see or feel right now, but it exists. You have to believe in it. Not a lot. Just a glimmer. Hold onto it." He glances down at me. "You holding?"

I take a stronger breath. "Yeah. I am."

ACT FORTY-TWO
BAYLEE WRIGHT

In the performance gym, I stretch on the blue mats with Brenden and Zhen, yawning in my armpit. We stayed up most of the night and early morning talking, and then 7:30 a.m. hit and we needed to leave for work.

What's strange is that more than half of Infini's cast is *late*. All of the Kotovas are straggling, and other artists loiter around the locker room longer than normal.

I barely reach for my foot. I'm distracted by the constant mutterings from passersby. The side-glances and even some *pointing*. All directed at me.

I don't believe Brenden shared my secrets, but I grow antsy and turn to them. "You are seeing the same thing as me, right?"

Brenden and Zhen scan our surroundings.

"Maybe one of us has toilet paper stuck to our ass," Zhen quips and checks his butt. "Not me."

Brenden lifts his ass up to Zhen.

"Not you either."

"I thought for sure it was me." Brenden plops down with a grin.

I say, "I'm serious."

"We know," they both reply in unison.

I elbow Brenden and crane my neck for answers. *Dimitri.* I see him speaking to his brothers hastily by a water fountain, and they're all nodding in agreement.

They must all be distraught over Luka quitting.

I frown deeply at the tiny squared windows of the blue double doors, leading into the hallway. Offices on the other side.

I spy *bodies* darting down the hallway. I just see flashes of people through the windows. Moving quickly. Hurriedly. None of these bodies enter the gym yet, so I assume they're slipping into offices instead.

I have a nagging feeling something big is happening.

Zhen rises to his feet. "I think I should…ask around." He sees what I see.

"Good idea," Brenden says, zoned in on a group of girls gawking at me. "Try Reesha and Lanie. They look like they know something."

"Already there." Zhen waves us goodbye, even though he's going thirty feet or less.

I think Brenden would follow if I didn't soak his Pillow Pet with my snot. Meaning, he wants to keep me company while I'm blue.

Brenden scoots closer, and I half-heartedly stretch my arm over my chest. I could text Katya, but if it's just everyone upset about Luka's departure, I don't want to poke at her wounds.

Brenden takes out his phone. I kept mine near too, but I don't retrieve it.

"Can you text Luka?" I ask hesitantly. "See if he knows something—"

"I'm already on it," Brenden tells me.

I nod, but I'm still uneasy.

Zhen returns slowly, like he just saw a hoard of naked people, and he's unsure of how to relay the image.

I frown at him. "It can't be that embarrassing."

He opens his mouth but then tilts his head, quizzical? I don't know that look.

"I've heard all your boner stories," I say to prove a point. "Ninety-percent were boring, Zhen. Okay, so whatever's going on—it won't faze *me*. I'm cool." I feel like I'm trying to convince my older brother's best friend that I'm part of the "cool mature club"—which, really, is what's happening.

Zhen drops his gaze to gather his words. "I'm not embarrassed. I'm…shocked."

"Oh." I haven't seen him really surprised before? At least maybe not concerning me. "What is it…?" My eyes start welling again. I thought the tears had ended.

He pushes back his black hair. "In New York, you were caught having sex with Luka. Nothing with cocaine."

I'm stunned silent. Brenden is assuring me that he didn't tell, but I never doubted him. I think…Luka must've told someone.

Zhen lists off a few more things: the contracts we signed, the threat of the no minors policy, and Luka being forced into quitting by Geoffrey. Basically, *everything*.

It's all out in the open with the whole company. Blood drains out of my head, cold biting me.

I'd feel more at risk of being fired if this day didn't start out weird. But I just realize—there are young kids, no older than ten or twelve, crying by Viva's trapeze.

And I caused their grief. With the no minors policy. "Is it already enforced?" I stare off, a chill snaking down my spine. Brenden wraps his arm around my shoulders, but I'm as stiff as a board.

"It's all just talk right now," Zhen says. "I don't think anything official has happened."

Brenden's phone buzzes.

I lean over and read the text.

Brenden sent: is something going on? Baylee is freaked.

Things are up in the air — Luka

Another text comes in fast.

She's staying in Infini no matter what. It's boiling down to the policy & our old contracts — Luka

Brenden asks me, "What? You keep shaking your head."

"Who has that much sway in Aerial Ethereal to override a *contract* written by the company's creator?"

Not long after I say it, artists start collecting their bags. With quick glances at their cells, they leave the gym. Brenden checks his phone for any cancellations, but he shakes his head.

The hallway starts emptying, but no one rushes into the gym. Everyone seems to be headed for the elevators. Like they're going home to their suites.

Viva has an early-afternoon show soon. Most of the cast should be warming up. I look again at someone who may have answers.

Dimitri catches my questioning expression this time, and he nods heartily at me. Like *stay strong, Baybay. We're fixing this.*

We're helping you.

I blow back, my lips parting in recognition of what this all may mean. That they're not giving up on Luka. On *us.*

For the first time, we may actually have people on our side.

ACT FORTY-THREE
LUKA KOTOVA

One hour to 8:00 p.m. show-times and no decision has been made yet. I've been held in Antoine Perrot's office since this morning. He's the Director of Infini. In Corporate hierarchy, he's above Geoffrey Lesage. Beneath Marc Duval.

(Everyone is beneath Marc.)

The glass door is shaded with blinds. I can't even peer into the hallway. Trying not to stress, I kick back on a chair and I toy with a wooden puzzle from his desk. Also, I eavesdrop on his Corporate phone call.

"There's nothing more I can do on this end." Perrot (he goes by last name) perches his phone to his ear, anxious hand on his short silver hair. In his early fifties, he looks a lot like John Slattery, the actor from *Mad Men.* (Yeah, I looked him up on IMDB.)

I listen intently.

"Marc, I know. I've had the creative staff try to reason with the artists, but they aren't budging just like New York and Montreal."

My lips gradually lift. About three hours ago, Perrot shot out of his seat when he learned the cast of Nova Vega and Celeste were nowhere to be found. All taking the day off. It's now 10:00 p.m. in their respective cities, and the artists missed their openings.

To avoid local media coverage, Aerial Ethereal cancelled their shows five minutes before curtain-call, citing *illness within the cast.*

Like they all have the flu.

But the cast abandoned their shows to make a change. It's not all about me or Bay. Most refuse to perform until Marc agrees that the no minors policy will never be implemented.

Still, my huge family and the Wrights have been seeking a dissolution to the contracts we signed five years ago. Brenden is advocating for Bay. Her aunt has even hired a lawyer, her husband's colleague.

I eavesdropped on all the lawyer-talk. AE's representatives harp on one thing: the contracts we signed were an *opportunity.* A so-called gift that no other minors—at least the ones caught having underage sex—received. They were fired. We kept our jobs.

And we had a choice. We could've *not* signed the contracts, quit AE, and then we would've been a couple. Maybe we would've went to high school together.

Had a semi-normal teenage life. Been happy or sad. Who can really know what our lives would've been like?

All I know is what happened. Where we are now.

Our lawyers have been combating AE, calling the terms of the contracts "grossly extreme" and an "abuse" of power. I don't know if we really have a chance.

It could be wishful thinking, but to have her family, my family, fight for us this time—it's validation I didn't even realize I needed. Five years ago, we were just kids in their eyes, and nothing we said would've made a difference. We couldn't change their minds.

We couldn't make them *see* what we felt, and I really didn't think we could change them now. But somehow, someway, they see Bay and me as more than young love. Maybe they pity us—for all that we went through—or maybe they sympathize and finally understand our pain.

I don't know.

I don't need to know their motivations. It doesn't matter to me.

Just knowing their voices aren't rivaling ours, that they're shouting in certainty and solidarity—it's enough. Our families finally believe we're worth the fight.

Perrot has his hand to his forehead. "No. Marc, it's almost eight p.m. here. Viva already missed their show—I know. I also heard that Seraphine's cast is missing." He checks his watch. "It's almost one p.m. in Tokyo, so there's time…wait." He rolls forward on his chair, eyes widening at the computer screen. "Dammit. The artists for oceanic touring shows are leaving—*dammit*."

Perrot catches me smiling, and I can't suppress this one. Not even if I tried. Because I've *never* been on this side of power.

By banding together, individuals can be mightier than the hands that encase us. That control us. I've been witnessing artists across the globe tear at red tape and snip the strings that force us every which way.

It seems unbelievable. I smile more. *Unbelievable.* Just like the circus. Where the impossible becomes possible.

Perrot cups the speaker with his hand, anxiety wrinkling his forehead. "You'll know the outcome with everyone else," he says to me. "You're free to leave."

I immediately spring up. He doesn't have to tell me twice. I head to the glass door.

"Wait."

I stop.

"My puzzle."

It's in my pocket. I lick my dry lips and then casually return the unsolved, wooden puzzle to his desk. "Sorry." (I am sorry.)

He swivels in his chair, phone pressed to his ear again, and before I reach the doorknob, he exclaims, "Wait."

"I didn't take anything else."

Perrot raises a finger at me to *wait* and speaks to Marc in fluent French. I understand only a few words. *Billets* (tickets) is one of them. Then he gestures me to sit again.

My lungs are heavy, and I return to the chair and lean back on its wooden legs. Pretending I'm not stressed when so much weighs on me. I still hear Timo and Kat's screams…and I haven't seen or talked to them since.

Nik has texted me *they're okay* and sent me pictures of his suite. A lot of my cousins are drinking and playing cards. Eating takeout. Chilling.

Bay is there.

Nikolai said that Dimitri has been annoying her during their card game—his attempt at distracting her from everything.

I hope I made the right choice in letting Nikolai corral our family and confront Corporate. I hope I didn't fuck it all up for no reason.

Perrot pockets his cell and high-tails his ass to the door. "I'll be a few minutes. I need you to stay here. Do you understand?" His words almost slur together; he speaks that fast.

"Yeah, sure." I'm being honest. I won't leave.

Perrot is out the door in a snap-second.

Alone for the first time, I unearth my phone from my pocket and FaceTime Katya. I mutter beneath my breath, "Please don't ice me out. Please don't ice me out."

It rings and rings.

I stare fixatedly at the screen, not blinking. "Come on." I hunch forward, forearms on my thighs and phone cupped in my hand. "Come on, Kat."

The call rings out. She doesn't answer.

I inhale a sharp breath and run my hand through my hair. Okay, I'll try Timo. I click into my favorites and find his name near hers. I press *FaceTime* and the ringing begins. And my apprehension elevates.

My hand is on my mouth, waiting. Waiting.

Timo answers.

A ceiling pops up, and I hear Kat say, "Turn the camera around." She's with him? I'm unable to move, like if I do they'll disappear.

The camera spins. On screen, Timo and Katya sit side-by-side on her top bunk, an orange Noctis poster behind them. I don't pretend that they're emotionless beings who can accept what I did with a full-blown smile. I planned to leave without telling them, and they knew that.

They know everything now, and if I could do anything differently, it'd be saving them from the pain I caused.

Katya has dark circles beneath her eyes, and Timo wants to glare, a look he used to give Nik. Not me.

"Uh…" I start, lost for words for a second. I put my hand to my mouth, then my eyes. I break down, crying silently. "I'm sorry," I mutter. "I'm so sorry."

Katya sniffs. "How could you do that?"

I shake my head, and I drop my hand, my throat closed. I struggle to look at the screen.

Sounding wounded, Timo says, "We didn't even earn a goodbye from you? Nikolai was that high on your list, but you couldn't tell us or even leave a note. Would you've liked a note, Kat?"

"Yeah," she sniffs again. "I would've *loved* a note."

I stare off at the wall, dazed. Could I've written a note and changed this outcome? Probably not. We'd still be here, right now. Feeling each other's pain.

"And you *lied* over and over again," Katya cries. "I asked you about Baylee point-blank, and you told me…" She growls in frustration at her tears. "I really hate…what you did."

"I know." I shut my eyes closed. "I couldn't tell you though."

"Why?" Timo asks. "That's what I want to know. We trust each other with everything. So what if the company told you not to, we'd *never* let it slip, man."

My eyelids flit open, and I meet their hurt straight-on. "I couldn't put this on either of you. It seems easy, okay? One secret, but it's not like the time you two snuck out to a salsa club and I had to lie for you. It's not like when I broke curfew to eat pizza on the subway and you made a pillow dummy on my bed for Nik to find. It's *bigger* than that." I sit up more, chest on fire. "It's five years of holding your breath every time you see Bay in proximity to me. It's five years of checking over your shoulder to see if Corporate is breathing down your neck. It's five years of feeling like—*if I say the wrong thing, I screw everyone over.* And it's not just our lives at stake. You ruin children across oceans, across the *world*." I take the biggest breath of my life. "That's why I didn't put this on you."

That's why.

Slowly, they both begin to nod.

Understanding.

Timo combs longer strands of hair out of his eyes. "We should've been the first to know you were quitting."

"I love you two the most, that's why you were the last."

Katya huffs. "That makes *zero* sense. You know that?"

Timo's eyes soften and sweep me. "It makes some sense."

Katya frowns at our brother. "If he loved us the most, he'd tell us *first*."

"Not if it hurt him to say goodbye," Timo says. "It hurt that badly?"

My eyes burn, welling up again. "Dude, I don't want to do that again. Ever."

"You won't have to." Timo sits up straighter too, the bunk bed creaking, but my unknown fate strains the air.

This morning, I sent in a termination email. They could still fire me, even if I sent another that said: *Disregard the last email. I do not want to quit Aerial Ethereal.*

It's all up in the air.

"Will you promise something?" Katya asks, still sniffling. "That you'll tell us things in the future. I'd want to know if Geoffrey confronts you again."

"Aye aye." Timo nods. "Nik is the one who keeps us out of the loop in fear of hurting our childish sensibilities. We don't do that to each other."

Katya makes a circular motion, tying us all together.

"I won't block you out," I promise. "I'm not ditching you two for Nik or Serg or even Dimitri. It's us three."

"Until the end," Timo says theatrically, fist to his heart.

"Until the end," Kat smiles.

I smile back. "Until the—" The door whips open, and Perrot motions me forward, his face somber.

"Luka?" Katya says.

"Are you okay?" Timo asks.

"It's, uh, Perrot. I have to go." I stand up. "I'll see you." I end the call and pocket my phone. Perrot looks more uneasy than he did when Nova Vega's show tonight got cancelled.

The blinds smack the door as he shuts it behind him. Before he speaks to me, his cell rings. "Perrot," he greets, phone to his ear. "No, Marc just cancelled all three Vegas shows. It's madness." He sighs. "AE is telling the press it's for stage maintenance…I hope so. We'll see." His gaze flits to me. "He's here with me. I'm about to do it now." He pauses. "No. No. Marc is stuck in Seoul. His flight won't arrive until tomorrow."

After a few more words, he hangs up, and then his hand is on my shoulder. He steers me out the door.

I glance back as we walk, caught off guard. "We're leaving your office?" We're already *out* of his office. Into the hallway.

"Marc made a decision," Perrot says. "I'm about to tell everyone, and you're coming with me."

————— ◆ —————

ONE THING I'VE ALWAYS HAD IN COMMON WITH

Baylee Wright: neither of us prefers the spotlight. We will gladly pass the sweltering attention onto someone else.

I stand beside Perrot in a seated crowd of over a hundred, and I'd rather be on the blue mats next to Baylee and my family. Eating popcorn and smiling at the person who'd take my place.

Perrot canvasses the artists with a single glance. "I represent Marc today. He apologizes for not being here in person, but he's across the country at the moment. He's heard your concerns and your pleas, and he's taken this matter *very* seriously."

Eyes dart to me. Like I have the answers.

At this point, I have nothing but hope. And aren't most battles won with just that? *Hope.* I smile weakly to myself and look up at Baylee.

Her arms are loosely around her bent leg, and her uneasy gaze stays on Perrot. Until she feels me staring. Then she looks my way.

Our chests rise at the same time, and in a crowd full of people, with eyes all on me, I mouth, *I love you.*

Tears brim and she brushes them quickly. She nods repeatedly, expressing the same sentiment. She presses her forehead to her knee, trying to hide her sorrow.

Bay thinks it's over.

The worst has come.

My heart is in my throat, but I lift my gaze to the eighty-foot ceiling. I listen and wait for Marc's decision to either capsize the lives of hundreds or make it better.

Perrot clears his throat and reads a checklist off his phone. "I'll begin with the easiest point of contention." He places his hand on my shoulder. "Luka Kotova will still remain employed by Aerial Ethereal—"

Clapping from my cousins and siblings cuts into Perrot's speech.

It feels too bittersweet to smile. I stuff my hands in my sweatpants, my fingers skimming wrapped peppermints and keys to nowhere.

Perrot waits patiently for the noise to die before continuing. "The last two issues of concern are the no minors policy and the contracts signed by Baylee Wright and Luka Kotova." He pauses and points at a young girl and boy from Viva. "Please put away the phones. No recording."

Secrecy has always been important to Aerial Ethereal.

(Clearly.)

But I understand. This world is exclusive to those allowed to enter, and there's a whole section about "social media" conduct in everyone's contract. No one can make YouTube videos or live-stream any kind of footage from practices, rehearsals, and definitely not performances.

Marc would flip if any of this traveled to the press.

As soon as the phones disappear, Perrot speaks. "Marc wants to assure the entire troupe that he values and respects the opinion of every artist. He understands your fears and concerns, and with great consideration, he has made a decision." Perrot reads off his cell. "'To protect the integrity and morale of the Aerial Ethereal troupe across the globe, the no minors policy will not be instated or used as a future mode of...'" he trails off at the cheering. It explodes, especially from all the kids.

I end up smiling, but I also cage a breath.

It's good.

That's *really* good, and Bay's face says the same. It's good, but there's a part that still hurts. We have no idea where we stand in all of this.

"Quiet!" Dimitri yells, gesturing with his hands for everyone to sit.

Perrot talks over the fading cheers. "And lastly, Marc has decided to dissolve the contracts—" Baylee covers her face, bowing forward with emotion, and it hits me like a tidal wave.

We're allowed to be together.

Truly.

I barely hear Perrot say the reasoning: *to rectify any emotional and psychological distress inflicted upon the recipients.*

I beeline through the half-seated crowd. People spring to their feet. Hugging. Cheering louder. I aim for one person. One girl.

The sea of people starts parting for me, knowing where I'm headed. As soon as Baylee rises to her feet, I clasp her hand and draw her to my body.

"Come here," I breathe.

She clutches the back of my neck, and I hold her face gently, her cheeks slicked with tears. Our eyes dance over one another again. And again.

I tune out all the commotion. It's just me and her.

We sway like music plays, and her brown eyes smile before her lips do. My smile stretches wider and higher, and I dip my head down to whisper, "You know what I'm going to do, Bay?"

"What?"

"I'm going to kiss you *for the first time* in front of a crowd."

Isn't that fucking bizarre? That in all our lives, in all our time together, we've never kissed for other people to see. It's been private. It's been ours, but if we could've unrestrained it and let it free, we would've from the beginning.

Baylee's smile overpowers her features, and my lips touch her rising grin. Our kiss pulls us together like a magnet, and I clasp the back of her head, my tongue parting her lips. Deepening the kiss—and then loud, dry clapping breaks into our reverie.

We lean back only slightly to spot the source.

Geoffrey Lesage saunters through the troupe, still clapping, and his gaze is dead-set on us.

"Congratulations," he says loud enough for all to hear. "You got what you wanted. You won your dispute."

Why the hell is he bitter? The no minors policy isn't enforced, and the whole cast is intact. He got what he wanted too.

"It wasn't a game to me," I say easily. "It's my life—"

"It's my career."

Realization pummels me. I assume that Marc didn't appreciate his blackmail tactic or usurping his power. Geoffrey skipped rungs of the Corporate hierarchy, and I bet he was slapped on the wrist.

"You're not our choreographer anymore?" I ask.

"Would you like that?" he snaps. "For me to leave?"

I go rigid, my hands on Bay's shoulders, and Geoffrey stops about ten feet from me, his gaze flitting to Nikolai, who glares threateningly an arm's length away.

Geoffrey's focus returns to me. "Well?"

"I don't want you to leave." (Yes I do.)

He fixes his blazer. "Then you'll be happy to know I'm still your choreographer and *dedicated* to Infini's success."

Baylee nods, tensed. "We all want the same thing."

"Good." His voice is tight, and he scans the discomforted cast. "Dress rehearsal tomorrow for Infini. Don't be late." His scowl darkens at the two of us. "No exceptions."

We bruised his ego.

And I worry he's going to make us pay for it.

SPRING

ACT FORTY-FOUR
BAYLEE WRIGHT

Hurriedly, I exit stage left to raucous applause, my juggling torches snuffed out and sweat beading my forehead. My ribs jut out as I catch my breath, but I can't slow.

I have to do a quick costume change from the "nightmare" to the "dreamscape" aesthetic. And I *love* my current nightmare costume: a sheer skirt over a burgundy velvet leotard, turtleneck. Fiery ruby crystals are sewn in spirals across my breasts and waist.

I'm a beautiful, magical blaze of fire.

Sliding past artists backstage, the nervous-excited energy is high and it has nothing to do with boys or dating. All our hard work amounts to the moments we spend on stage together and the subsequent awed claps from the audience.

And the hope it won't end here. *It can't end.*

My mom's music echoes so triumphantly, the drum beats and trumpets that dive into your core and make you want to *move.* It instantly makes me smile.

And rouses my spirits beyond anything.

Backstage, Luka sprints fast, his cue coming soon since Wheel of Death is next. He's shirtless, his sculpted abs, arms and shoulders purposefully displayed to evoke sheer masculinity. It works too well.

My neck heats, and my gaze drops to his pants: skintight blood-red spandex. His costume leaves nothing to the imagination, not any carve of muscle or bulge. Luka is undeniably *hot.*

No pun intended. He's supposed to be a devil, and the costume department even attached sparkling horns in his dark brown hair. His bold black and red makeup is scary yet attractive.

I'm scarily attracted to him.

As he races past, he grins. "You were amazing!" He turns around, walking backwards and slowing his pace. Keeping our gazes locked for as long as possible.

I press my lips together, my smile out of control. I'm about to tell him to *kill it,* but he says, "Fuck it." And he *runs* back to me.

I shake my head, still smiling. Luka, always the risk-taker.

He carefully kisses my lips, just once. An out-of-this-world vigor floats me eighty-feet high in my brain.

It's the most bizarre feeling ever. His eyes drink me in, and our lungs inflate. I start groaning and laughing because my face hurts.

He dips his head to whisper, "Girlfriend." *We're together.*

Boyfriend.

I'm drowning in love. I push him before he misses his cue. "Go, *go.*"

Luka nods and raises his brows playfully. "See you, krasavitsa." He finally turns his back to me and bounds for stage left.

At a mirror, I ensure my hair is still secured into two high gelled buns, and while I remove my makeup and change into a sky-blue, turtleneck leo, I glance at my gold-stitched balls for the trampoline act.

I'll talk about juggling to anyone who'll listen, but it's not like the Mets or Jamaican food. My love for those two has never come into question. I'm not *living* inside of them.

But I live inside of juggling. It's my every day. No breaks. No time apart. Living with a passion isn't like sitting on top of the world twenty-four-seven. I drop down constantly and stare pointedly at my juggling props, and I question if they've revolted against me.

Every toss feels off. Every way I move feels *wrong*. Like I'm all out of whack, and in one moment, I *hate* juggling like it's my stubborn spouse. It's my foe.

Then one day, my clubs float in perfect symmetry. My heart soars as high as the props I toss, and my passion blisters bright inside of me. Juggling is my love.

I remember why I do this. Why I grind through the hard parts—I do it for these blissful, world-bending moments.

For the premiere, it's been happy. I pick up my gold-stitched balls, and I hope that I can keep it that way.

CURTAINS CLOSED ONLY A HALF HOUR AGO, but Geoffrey calls us over and tells us to take a seat on stage. A few Masquerade employees sweep up popcorn between rows, the auditorium nearly empty.

None of the artists have even washed off their makeup or changed out of costume yet. We were all excited and ready to celebrate the premiere. It went *really* well.

Full house. Sold out, and the Russian swing finale roused the audience to their feet. I'm pessimistic about my fortune and luck, but there's evidence *saying* that this was a good first show.

I know it.

My hand tightens in Luka's while we sit, and I rest my chin on my knee. Brenden whispers to Zhen close by, and they shake their heads, as confused as everyone else.

"Artists." Geoffrey surveys all of us, his face unreadable. "How did you think that went?"

A few people say, "Great."

"That's not what a critic from the L.V. Times said."

I frown, and Luka squeezes my hand like, *it's okay*.

But we performed for critics yesterday, a special pre-showing. We already read the one negative review that said "lacks the spark of its original" and "it sputters out like the juggler's torch"—that part was awful. I douse my torches at the end *on purpose*.

Other critics were positive.

"…you'll keep dreaming long after the curtains close…"

"…bold choices for an old staple show…"

"…the talent breathes life & fire into the classic Aerial Ethereal reverie…"

"…the music dominates once again…"

Geoffrey spreads his arms. "And I happen to agree with the L.V. Times. You know why? The proof is in the *numbers*."

We haven't heard about sales. No one in AE's financial has shared them with us.

I stiffen while he draws out the news.

Geoffrey skims his goatee with three fingers. "April and May have sold out, but summer sales are *shit*." He points a threatening finger. "If there are thousands of unfilled seats come June and July, you're all in boiling water. This is a sinking ship that *I'm* personally bailing out, and I will push you as hard and as far as humanly possible."

His gaze lands on me.

And Luka.

"How badly do you want this show to survive?"

So badly, but my belief in our choreographer's "talent" vanished around the time he tried to emotionally push Luka.

I don't trust him, and I'm afraid of playing into Geoffrey's hand.

But he's our boss, and as long as Antoine Perrot says to listen to Geoffrey, we can't disobey him.

ACT FORTY-FIVE
BAYLEE WRIGHT

In the crowded physical therapy room, I plop down in an ice bath, the metal tub uncomfortable and *cold*.

I feel like a monster truck ran over me. We perform for Infini twice a day, five times a week, and on our two days off, we're still in the gym for twelve hours, per Geoffrey's high-stress demands. With no guarantees that Infini will be renewed for another year.

Marc usually sends out congratulatory emails after a show's first month. We received none.

I could sink beneath the ice, but I try to remember we have time, still. I shiver from the cold bath.

My mom's music isn't lost yet.

I hold onto a glimmer of hope. Just a glimmer.

It helps.

Then I peer at Luka's tattooed leg. He stands close by, skillfully putting on Kinesio tape across his bicep.

When Luka notices me staring, he hikes his leg over the tub, foot on the edge. I have a complete view of his designs now, and he smiles while he bites off tape from the spool.

The way he's looking at me, I feel like he's remembering earlier this morning. We had *deep* sex on his bed. The kind that filled me to the brim and vibrated my limbs as I came.

Dimitri wasn't in the room, thank God.

But it's been hours, and the fullness stays between my legs. It's a good soreness. I feel like Luka is still completely and utterly inside of me.

I smooth my lips, the ice bath tempering my heat. "What's this one?" I skim a design on his shin with my finger.

Luka tilts his head. "A skyline…" He sounds unsure.

My teeth start to chatter. "You don't know." I try to give him a serious look, but he keeps smiling and my teeth keep clanking. "Stopiznotfunny." I slur, groan, and slump over the tub.

We have a date tonight watching the Mets vs. Cubs—I smile at the floor dizzily.

This is why I've blocked out the date. I feel like a love-struck fool.

Luka retracts his leg and crouches beside me, a full-on grin. "You always said it was 'cool' that I got random tattoos at the spur of the moment."

I whisper, "Because I was with you." I bite down to stop the teeth-chatter.

Luka's eyes twinkle. "Those are my favorite tattoos, by the way. The ones where you were with me. I remember all of them."

"Mmmhmm." I'm trying not to smile.

Luka pockets his tape and then snatches a cotton towel. I stand and step out of the tub, water dripping down my spandex shorts and sports bra. I walk straight into his embrace, and he wraps me up in the towel and his arms.

Hugs from Luka Kotova are the best of all time.

So tight and comforting, they deserve trophies and medals. This particular hug pulls me firm against his chest, even with my arms tucked to my A-cups.

"I'm getting you wet," I say.

He dips his head and whispers, "Not as wet as you're going to be tonight." He starts murmuring *all* the things he plans to do to me, and my cheeks start heating, my breath shallow.

I try not to smile when he mentions his cock filling me deep again. Then he presses his lips to my head. He's dirty and then so sweet.

"Kiss! Kiss!"

We flinch slightly at Robby's incoming presence. Luka's cousin snickers as he walks past and waves us to *go on, kiss.*

Other artists on med beds and in ice baths watch us curiously. I freeze, and Luka feels me tense up in his arms.

So it's not the first time all the attention has veered onto our relationship. This happens at least twice a day. I shouldn't be put-off; I'm a people-watcher, I understand the allure.

The problem is that people fought for us. I feel like we have to *show* we're the best couple in Aerial Ethereal. The pressure is already high at work. Now *this.*

It's a lot to live up to.

"Kiss! Kiss!" Robby claps to the word. "Kiss!"

Luka ignores him easily and digests my reaction. I'm not annoyed at Robby; I'm just thinking. I eye a couple young girls who whisper by a medicine cabinet.

Luka must see my mind reeling. "We don't have to prove anything to anyone, Bay."

I nod. It's really nice hearing that from the guy I'm with. So I inhale and try to relax more.

His right hand warms my cheek. Our eyes flit to each other's lips. Now I kind of want him to kiss me. And not because of Robby.

Luka whispers, "I can play into his joke just to shut him up."

I nod stronger.

He inches closer and kisses me full-force, my lips sting, and his hand dives to the small of my back. My skin heats like electricity zipping down my neck, breasts, hips, and lower…I pulse, beginning to throb.

Luka smiles, his tongue tangling with mine as we draw even nearer. His body thrums against my body, and he cups my ass.

I start laughing for no reason.

Robby cat-calls us with a whistle and drifts away.

Luka wraps his arms around my shoulders, laughing too. "You know I'm going to grab your ass more often now."

Luka Kotova likes hearing me laugh. "You're too much." I control my laugh and make a grave face.

He mimics my expression. "You always say that. Too much of what?"

"*Everything,*" I say seriously.

"Evidence?"

"I could spend hours detailing why, but not while I stare at you." *While he makes me smile.*

Luka playfully turns his back to me, and then checks me out over his shoulder. "What about now?"

I shake my head, almost about to burst into another laugh, and he's made me forget all about the sadness surrounding Infini. For a moment at least. My eyes suddenly well, and I can't describe the source of my emotion.

It just surges.

He spins back, noticing. "Come here, Bay." His voice is tender, and he brings me into another warm hug. I wrap my arms around his waist.

"Date night!" someone shouts.

I suddenly gape at Luka.

"Date night!" That's a Kotova, jeering at us about *our* date night later. I eye Luka. "You told who?"

He kisses my lips, my temple, my cheek, and he whispers, "Everyone."

I wear a more heartfelt smile, *swooning* at him. We sway now like we're slow-dancing. "Because you can," I realize.

He nods, a powerful, assured nod. "Because *we* can." We can tell the whole world we're in a serious relationship. I inhale a freeing breath, and that's when Sergei approaches, an envelope in hand.

Sergei opens his mouth, but an old female AE doc calls Luka over, "I need to do a short examination on you, Luka."

"I had a physical last month," Luka says while we separate. I tighten my towel around my chest, and Luka fits his baseball cap over his tousled hair, hiding his gaze from Sergei.

"It's a follow-up to that one. Just step over here." She ties her wispy gray locks back, and Sergei and I watch her lead Luka to the medicine cabinet.

I put my towel to my lips, nervous.

Early this morning, he stole a coffee canister from the grocery store. He helped me put away my veggie kits and protein bars—and I had to ask, "How bad is it?" We were both grabbing the refrigerator handle, frozen.

He knew I was referring to his kleptomania. "What kind of scale do you want?" he asked.

"*One* being you…"

"…have no desire to steal," he helped me out. "*Ten* I can't stop thinking about it?"

I nodded.

Luka contemplated for a second. "Maybe a six, six-point-five. It's like…about as bad as when I was…" He winces through his teeth, trying to find an age. "Eight-years-old?"

"I didn't know you then."

He smiles. "No kidding."

I tried not to smile back, but it was hard. "The other thing is worse right now though, isn't it?" I meant his bulimia, but he hates the clinical names, so I always avoid them in conversation.

"Yeah, it's not good." Luka sighed deeply and spun his Knicks hat backwards. "I'm trying to get ahold of it. I've just felt out of control lately." He chewed his bottom lip once in thought and nodded, coming to terms with that. "You sad?" he asked.

I made a so-so motion with my hand, and then we hugged, our hands dropping from the refrigerator, the door thudding shut.

My cheek to his chest, I asked, "Therapy?" I wondered if he was going.

"I never found a therapist in Vegas."

"You never tried?"

He shook his head, blinking a couple times. "No. I don't know, maybe I should." He used to go when he was little, and he returned in New York around when I first met him, on-and-off. AE used to pay a portion, but Luka mentioned that his health insurance didn't cover it anymore.

Sometimes it's easy to use money as a reason not to go, but therapy helps us both a lot.

I nudged him lightly and said, "You should try."

"…I'll think about it."

I replay our talk in my head as the female doctor nears Luka.

"Can you open your mouth, please?" she asks him.

He looks nonchalant as he lowers his jaw, mouth wide. She peers down his throat with a medical instrument and light.

"You're worried about him?" Sergei asks me.

I frown. "Yeah, he's my…" God, I'm smiling already. "Boyfriend." It's overwhelming being able to say that.

"No, I mean…" Sergei gestures from Luka to me and back again. "You know what he deals with. He's told you?"

I nod, and I look at the ceiling as I find the answer. "I think he told me when I was…thirteen? Yeah, thirteen." It was really hard for Luka to describe what had happened, which is why I don't ever repeat his past to anyone. Not even to someone who may already have the answers.

Like Sergei.

He scratches his short hair. "I should've known you two were together." His shoulders rise. "I just thought Luka would've told me that he had feelings for you. I never thought he legally *couldn't* say anything."

"I doubt Luka minds anymore," I say. "He's not really a grudge-holder."

"My apology is for you."

My brows jump.

Sergei laughs, more at himself than at me. "No one thinks I can apologize?"

I must not be the first stop on the Sergei Koto*v* apology tour. "It's just apologies usually begin with *I'm sorry.*"

"I'm sorry," he says honestly. "For more than one thing." He passes me an envelope.

My lips part. "Is this…?" I feel the outline of money without opening the flap. *The grand for my misplaced box.* I paid AE and depleted my bank account months ago.

"It's not all I owe you. I thought I could pay in installments. A hundred a month."

"I'm confused." I slowly shake my head to clear cobwebs. "Why now?"

Sergei rubs his throat. "It's not easy admitting that I'm in the wrong. Before I transferred to Infini and moved to Vegas—I honestly did *not* know this about myself. I guess confronting old choices puts your life into perspective…" He pauses. "And I've been mentally revisiting conversations and things I've done, and I realized I was stubborn and…an ass here. So." He motions to the money. "That's a start to an *I'm sorry.*"

"Okay," I say with a small smile. "I accept, thanks." Do we shake? Do we hug?

I guess I have to start with: what is Sergei to me exactly?

A co-worker?

My boyfriend's older brother?

Luka is on okay terms with him. They haven't built a close-knit relationship, but he's not cold-shouldering Sergei like Timo.

To my knowledge, Timo hasn't spoken to Sergei since The Red Death, and Sergei has respected his little brother's space.

Their disputes aren't mine though. I want to be friendly to someone who's been kind, so I extend a hand to shake.

Sergei smiles and shakes back.

"I have it under control," Luka says strongly to the doctor. Our eyes fix back on him.

She sighs. "You'll need to start writing down everything you eat and your feelings about the food before and after consumption. I'll give you a journal before you leave. I believe you did this before when you were…" She flips into his chart. "Six-years-old—"

"I am *not* that bad," he refutes, turning his back on us.

Sergei cracks his knuckles, on edge.

"I think it's best, Luka," she says. "Stay there, let me get you a journal."

"Baylee."

I *jump* so much at the sound of Geoffrey's voice, right by my ear. I end up bumping into Sergei, but he puts a hand on my shoulder, steadying me.

My lungs just shot out of my body, and Geoffrey wears *zero* humor.

Before I ask *what*, he says, "You'll need to stay late tonight."

Today is an "off" day—no performances. So Luka and I came in at 5:00 a.m. on the dot to workout and practice so we could have the night off. I reiterate this to Geoffrey, and he cuts me off mid-sentence with, "Shut up."

"That's not necessary, Geoffrey," Sergei tells him in a controlled voice.

Luka abandons the medicine cabinet to reach us. "What's going on?" His hand slips into mine.

My ribs hurt; I'm so stiff. "He's saying we need to stay late."

Luka shakes his head. "Why?"

"I need you both on trampoline *tonight*," Geoffrey explains. "We're changing your eight-ball, seven-up pirouette."

"I can't do *nine* balls," I emphasize, my pulse racing in fear. It's not possible. I've never done that before, not even on the ground. And any big changes we make now are risky. The show has already begun.

"Did I specify nine balls? No, I didn't," Geoffrey snaps. "You're not going to sit on Luka's shoulders anymore." He takes one beat. "You're going to *stand*."

Shit.

Shit.

I rub my eyes, already tired at the thought of nailing that trick down while standing on his shoulders. And the timing—God, the timing.

Perrot would tell us to deal with this change. So I nod. "Okay." All I can do is agree and work hard again and again.

Ignore the stress.

Luka asks, "Can we start working on it tomorrow?"

"No. You start tonight." He laughs once, his lips hiking, almost mockingly. "Why? Do you have a *date* or something?"

My face drops. He heard the Kotovas shouting *date night* at us. Didn't he?

Luka restrains emotion, not giving him more satisfaction, but Geoffrey spins around like he won a round in a battle and saunters out of the physical therapy room.

He ruined our baseball date night on purpose. "God, I hate him," I say.

Luka nods, his jaw muscle constricting. "Me too."

SUMMER

ACT FORTY-SIX
LUKA KOTOVA

"*Be responsible* today."

That declaration has rained down from Vince, Aerial Ethereal's marketing director and *no longer* a Corporate spy.

(Hallelujah.)

He's dreaming though. I may suck at math, but adding a hundred AE artists + the hottest July afternoon + free drinks + a *massive* Masquerade pool with hotel guests = a scenario with 0 responsibility.

In the same breath, Vince said, "Have fun." I'm sincerely trying to figure out how *responsibility* and *fun* intersect on the Venn diagram.

Three Amour artists understand the decree well enough. Taking running starts, my cousins do full-in full-outs, splashing into the water and garnering thunderous cheers from guests. The DJ increases the volume of a remix to a summer pop song, and people cheer and dance.

The Masquerade hosts very few promo parties a year, but when they do, they always ask AE artists to perform and to "blend in and drink and have fun"—that way we'll surprise the guests when we finally unleash a trick. Ticket sales normally skyrocket after these events.

Mandatory or not, stressed or relaxed—I don't bail on pool parties. The Nevada summer is too brutally hot.

This year, it's even better. I wade in the five-foot end and Baylee is standing on my shoulders, not a cousin.

I clasp her calves, completely secured, and she juggles eight mesh balls in a clean arc. She lets me catch one that falls, and I toss it back up to her.

In our section of the pool, the inebriated, sunburned guests stare open-mouthed and clap their hands to their margaritas and beers.

I meander around the pool, the water cool on my skin, and I ache to dip under. I know Bay must be scorching from the heat. No clouds in sight.

I chew a piece of gum and eye a dude who zigzags in the water towards us, his trucker hat says *beer me*.

"You have to stay back, dude!" I yell over the music, my voice nonchalant.

He floats *slowly* toward us now.

I almost laugh, and I look up.

In a red Adidas swimsuit, Baylee looks beautiful and in her element. She lowers, sitting on my shoulders, and she never breaks tempo. Balls sail in a new crisscrossing pattern, and I catch sight of her smile— which has been more fleeting this summer.

Infini isn't selling out. We fill more seats than Amour, but our auditorium holds more bodies. There's mutterings about music changes, too.

On top of that, Geoffrey has given us almost *no* time to recuperate and breathe. We're both losing precious sleep. I'm down to five hours a night, and she's not much better. But she works herself harder than me, deathly afraid of Infini's end.

I run my hand up her leg, and the trucker hat dude yells at her, "I wanna hold your balls!"

I lost count of how many times she's been heckled. I raise a hand at him in warning as he creeps closer, shaking my head.

(Drunk people, honestly. I have no other words than that.)

Baylee forces a smile. "Do you know how to juggle?!"

"Yeah!" he laughs and reaches out to grab Bay.

I splash him in the face. "That's not an invitation! Back up!"

He drifts back a little, and I end up walking backwards, putting space between him and Baylee. Look, the place is swarming with security and I've dealt with these kinds of personalities my entire life. My level of paranoia is low, confidence high, and I'm too used to this to be an overprotective, over-alarmed asshole.

"If you can juggle, then get your own balls!" Baylee shouts, her tone serious.

He puts his sunglasses on top of his trucker hat, laughing. "Baby, I can show you my balls. I have 'em right here!"

Baylee raises her brows, still juggling, and she watches the drunk Vegas guest out of curiosity. It's entertaining to see how far they're willing to take their wild vacation.

(What happens in Vegas, stays in Vegas. For them. Not me. This is my whole life.)

One second later, he actually commits.

Swim trunks down, dick out. Luckily, we are all saved by the image since five-feet of his body is submerged under water.

Girls squeal nearby and splash him for exposing himself. Others unhook their bikini tops.

"Skinny dipping!" a guy hollers, and more swimsuits fly off.

My hand slides up Bay's thigh. "You started that, you realize?"

"And Brenden said I fail at fun and relaxation," she says seriously. "Here, I just started a naked pool party." That must've been a recent conversation with her brother.

She does fail at relaxation. Around my neck, her muscles are tensed up again, even as I rub her thigh. Bay lets her balls drop in her palms.

I hoist her off my shoulders, and she instantly dunks beneath the water and then breaches the surface.

"You okay?" I ask, my hands on the curve of her hips. My back is to the trucker hat dude, shielding her from him, and we drift into the masses, their fists pumping at a popular song.

We bypass the in-pool bar. Bay switched her antidepressants, under advice from her therapist, and the new kind have bad side effects with alcohol, so I don't ask if she wants any liquor.

Baylee drapes her arms over my shoulders. "I want to be happy." She tries to release a heavy breath. "I just can't stop thinking about what happens if Marc says Infini is done. It's not just the music and my mom. It's so much more."

I frown. "Like what?"

She shrugs. "Where do I go? What do I do? It's the *only* show I've ever been in."

"Krasavitsa." I give her a look like it's obvious what would happen.

"Don't say what I think you're going to say. It's so farfetched."

I say it. "AE will hire you for another show, and it's only unbelievable to you because it hasn't happened before."

She seems uncertain.

"They *will* hire you again."

Baylee leans her head back like her head weighs a million pounds and groans. "You don't know that. I'm not a Kotova."

"They will," I say again, my lips rising.

She smiles off of my smile. "I'm being realistic here." Her smile leaves really fast. "All so when I'm without a job and a roof, I'm not crushed to pieces."

"Look." I cup her face in my hands, and her worried eyes meet my assured ones. "That's not going to happen. I'm not letting Corporate crush you. I'm *not*, okay?"

She nods, and I wonder if she really believes me.

Do I even believe I have that kind of control?

For now, I'm going to pretend to.

I THOUGHT I PICKED A SOMEWHAT QUIET CABANA

to disappear into with Baylee. Not to screw around, we're literally sleeping. I wake to familiar voices.

"My quota of drunk old men has been reached, surpassed, and pissed on profusely," John says.

I open my eyes and make sure they haven't woken up my girlfriend. My arms are around Baylee while she sleeps on my chest, head tucked in the crook of my arm to block out the sunlight. She's practically passed out, needing this.

"Old men must attract more old men," Timo says, his smile breathing inside his words.

They walk into view and nearly approach my cabana, but they're distracted by each other's presence.

(I'm not kidding.)

Timo is checking out John like he's not his boyfriend that he sees every day. And John is *fit*. I mean, a six-pack, toned, and he's bigger built than my little brother who has lean muscles. His dark trunks contrast my brother's neon-orange Speedo.

Most Kotovas are in Speedos. Mine is blue. Be warned: Dimitri will show off his muscular thighs to every woman he passes. He thinks they're god's gift to humanity.

(They kind of are.)

John sips his beer and then says, "What kind of schooling does AE give you? Twenty-six is nowhere near fifty—and I don't know why I'm asking. You believe you're twenty-one."

"Remind me, what am I, John?" Timo tilts his head, his cross earring swaying.

"You're nineteen, clearly delusional because you're dating me, and you hip-hop-around like a frog with ten legs."

Timo's smile bursts. "I must have weird taste when I go for the guy that calls me a frog over the one who calls me 'Adonis' incarnate."

"I'm honest to you. The other guy just wanted to fuck you."

"So you don't want to fuck me?" Timo questions.

"Please," John says dryly and then kisses my brother strongly. He urges Timo's mouth open with smooth force, his arm winding around my brother's waist. Subtly drawing him even closer.

Timo flushes while smiling, and he clutches the back of John's wind-swept hair. Lip-locked for a while, they only break when John pulls back.

"Hold still, babe," he tells Timo, his dark scowl trained on Timo's hair.

Timo stiffens, more uncertain than usual. He clutches his boyfriend's waist, stepping closer to him.

John wraps one arm around Timo's shoulders in comfort, and then he picks some sort of beetle bug out of my brother's hair.

It flies off immediately.

"Seriously!" John yells at the departing bug. "I was going to fucking stomp on you!"

Timo laughs and then he notices me out of the corner of his eye. He breaks apart from his boyfriend. "Hey, brother."

I wave with a smile.

He bounds over at first like a ball of lightning, but then he slows at the sight of Bay sleeping. "I'll be quiet," he whispers and stands on an ottoman with a bow.

He's taller than John now.

John eyes Baylee. "How is she sleeping? I can barely hear myself over the shrill music. I almost enjoy my own voice."

I give Timo a look like: *you tell him something. I'm too tired.*

Timo swings his head to John. "Magic."

John pauses for one beat. "I never thought I'd be with a dork for this long."

"I can expire our time," Timo banters. "Just tell me, John. I'll end it—"

John covers Timo's mouth with his hand. "Stop talking nonsense, babe. That's my job." With Timo taller on the ottoman, John draws him down some, just to kiss his forehead.

When Timo is at parties like this one, he gets hit on by young dudes and older men—really, all ages—about thirty times, at least. John is the one that has to constantly say, "He's mine."

But more than six-months into their relationship, they're at a good place together. I think both have trouble believing it, but for different reasons.

Noise explodes as a huge group of family bounds over, some crawling out of the pool and soaking the cabana bed. I sit up against the pillow with Baylee in my arms.

She stirs, squints at the incoming men, and just shrugs them off, sleeping again.

I'm glad she's used to my family, and she's not agitated or bothered by them. I can't excuse half the shit they do, I'd lose my voice.

I'm pretty sure Abram is pissing behind the cabana.

"Looking good, Thora James!" Timo calls, and everyone starts clapping as Thora approaches us with Nikolai. He claps too, nothing short of proud.

All the promo material for Amour has Thora's *face* front and center. A huge honor. Something they'd never think to do with me.

(I'm not aching to be on promo art.)

There's a reason they picked Thora. Daisy Calloway, one of the famous sisters, left a raving review about aerial silk in Amour, and Aerial Ethereal capitalized on that quote, the aerial silk act, and their new star Thora James.

After a hard start to the beginning of the year, she still worked her ass off. It goes without saying, she deserves this recognition.

Robby parades one of the *many* Amour posters, pumping it in the air like a boxing cue card.

Thora puts her hand to her mouth, a little embarrassed.

Nikolai whispers to her, infatuated with his girlfriend. That night at the hospital, months ago, didn't draw them apart. They're closer now than they've ever been.

And then Sergei slips into the cabana behind Erik, and there's an unmistakable shift in mood.

I try to stay relaxed, but the air pulls taut. Everyone glances between Timo, John, and Sergei.

Timo hops off the ottoman, and John looks to his boyfriend on whether he wants him to leave or stay. The cabana falls to silence.

It just got really awkward.

"I can go," Sergei says, about to turn around.

Timo hesitates. "Wait." He told me that Sergei texted him a five-hundred word apology for The Red Death, and he asked me, "What should I do, Luk?"

I said, "He seems sincere." It means something to me, but to Timo, I think what he's been searching for, all this time, *wasn't* sincerity or honesty.

It was just the smallest acknowledgement that Sergei still cares about him. About the little brother he used to put on his shoulders and find ponds to ice-skate on during wintertime. No matter which city we were in.

So as they meet each other's gaze, Sergei waiting on pins and needles for Timo's response, I'm almost positive I know what he'll say.

"You should *stay*," Timo tells him. "The party is here."

Sergei looks like a lot of emotion just slapped him at once. He says in Russian, "*I heard the party is wherever you are. I've missed it.*"

Timo lets this sink in, but his rising lips suddenly part in alarm. I follow his gaze that drifts across the pool.

I jolt up, stirring Baylee even more.

"What?" She rubs her eye, frowning until she meets the horror on my face.

Everyone is looking at what Timo and I see.

Frozen next to the DJ speakers and chaotic pool party, Katya stands tear-streaked. Black mascara runs down her cheeks, and she wipes at the makeup. Head swinging left and right like she's searching for something. Someone.

I know it's us.

Her family. Her brothers.

"I'm going to kill someone," Nikolai says lowly as he parts from the cabana, his stride urgent.

I slide Bay off, and she nods like *go, go*. I jump up and put a hand on his shoulder, just as Nikolai tears through the crowd. Other cousins follow. So do my brothers.

Thing is, Katya was on a *date* today.

I'm not sure anyone knows this fact besides me and Timo, and if I tell Nikolai, he really will want to kill some motherfucker.

More than I want to right now.

My lungs are lit on fire.

"Wait!" I shout at Nik over the commotion, servers flocking the area with trays of booze. Beach balls are launched rapidly into the air. "Wait, Nik!"

He stops, head dipping back at me.

"Let me talk to her first," I say. He'll turn whatever happened into a lecture, and she'll be more upset.

He contemplates for only a second before nodding. "Three minutes."

THE WORST DATE IN HISTORY OF DATES.

That's how Kat describes the event to me, each word like a fist to my heart. I'm not prepared for the worst date in the history of dates. I'm not ready to go *fuck this guy* to someone who's unhinged her life.

Nothing could ever make me ready for that.

My head is spinning, and I instantly ask, "Are you okay, like physically?"

Katya sits atop a counter in the empty boys' bathroom, tile floor wet from people dripping pool water, and our siblings stand guard outside. Timo waits for the three minutes like Nik. I think he's afraid of accidentally annoying her.

"Kat?" I pass her paper towels from a nearby dispenser.

She crumples them in a fist and stares faraway at the urinals.

"Hey." I touch her cheek gently. "What happened to living in sin city and being fazed by nothing, huh?" (Come on, Kat. Talk to me.) "Did he hurt you? Katya—"

"Not like you think." She sniffs and lifts her glassy gaze. "I…" Our heads turn as the door opens, all three of our brothers coming inside.

Nikolai stands uptight by a sink, and he crosses his arms, his authority masking every inch of his face. Body. And eyes.

Katya barely glances at him or Sergei, who leans against a stall, his jaw hardened in severe lines. Timo hops on the counter next to Katya, and he asks under his breath, "Did you use it?"

She sniffs harder. "No."

"Use what?" Nik asks.

"Yeah, *what*," I say, my brows furrowed.

Nik frowns darkly at me. "You don't know."

"No." I give Timo a look. "What happened to *the three of us*?" I gesture between us.

Timo brings up a foot to the counter. "John's cousin, Camila, you all know her—she kept calling you the *cool* brother." He picks his fingernail but gestures to me. "And I thought I'd officially become cooler. I gave Katya a condom. I wanted her to be safe."

I watch Katya stare off again, and I worry about that dazed look in her eye.

"Timo," Nikolai groans, his hand to his forehead.

"What?" Timo touches his chest. "Do we all not want our little sister to be safe? How am I being reprimanded for this?"

"So you didn't use a condom," I say to her, flying past Timo's words.

"Not because I didn't want to," Katya says, "and for the record, after Nik's sex talk I bought a *huge* box of condoms. I was *eleven*."

"Those are expired," Nikolai says. "Throw them out."

Katya bows forward, heels of the palms to her eyes. "I can't do anything right!"

We all tense. I edge forward to the counter and put a hand on Katya's back. "It's okay, Kat." We give her a minute of quiet, and then she lifts her head.

"I'll share details, but…" Her big orb-like eyes grow on Nik. "Don't be mad."

Nikolai looks like he's swallowing shrapnel. "I'll try not to be."

I don't know where this is going anymore than Nik.

Katya taps her knees with two fingers, nervous. "He complimented my flexibility, which was kind of nice. I thought it was suggestive. I mean, that's *suggestive*. Right?"

I don't want to be the one to answer these, so I look at Timo and then Nikolai.

"In what context?" Timo asks with a shrug. "I mean if he said I want to hike your leg—"

"Let's stay on course," Nikolai interjects.

"And we wonder why we can't solve crimes by dinner time," Timo quips.

Katya sniffs and says, "He saw Viva. He kind of knew about me, and he's from Vegas. I thought…the date was nice." She shrugs. "He paid for lunch, and since Teddy is a waiter at Imperial, he's never seen the top suites at the Masquerade. I knew…um, I knew you were all at the pool party. So I thought…"

Nik is rigid.

I'm a statue.

Timo is frozen.

And Sergei has his hand to his mouth in concern.

"You took him up to our suite," Nikolai says angrily. "How old is he?"

"Nineteen."

"You're only seventeen, Katya."

"That's old enough!"

Nik's already intense gaze darkens more. "You don't even know this guy."

"We chatted. He's *not* a stranger, okay? I wouldn't do that. I know the rules." She growls at the incoming tears and rubs her eyes with her arm.

(What the fuck happened.)

Sergei keeps shaking his head, and he mutters some words in Russian that sound like, "*...not safe.*"

My hand falls off her back, and I grip the sink counter.

"He *didn't* hurt me like you think, Luk," she repeats a sentiment she expressed earlier. "Just..." She makes a motion with her hands around her head like *I need space.*

Timo jumps off the counter, and I step back with him and Nik. Until we're all facing Kat, giving her room.

"Teddy just made me feel..." Her chin quivers, face twisting. "You're going to hate me more than him." Her voice cracks. "And I didn't do anything wrong. *I didn't.*"

"We're your brothers," Timo says, "no judgment. I've probably done worse."

"Me too," I say.

Nikolai doesn't add himself into the mix. He is pretty squeaky clean.

But in Russian, Sergei chimes in, "*Me, as well.*"

Katya rips the paper towel into pieces. "Teddy was impressed by the suite, and we were definitely flirting. I think." She frowns. "No, *I know* we were."

Timo whispers to me, "I'm scared." He's not joking.

"Same."

Kat blinks, silent tears falling, and she says, "I got on my knees, went for his zipper, and *he* freaked out."

What.

"He called me a slut…said he doesn't date girls like me. Then, other worse words." Her glassy eyes narrow at the floor. "And he ran out, and all I could hear is that one line: *girls like me.* For the…the *longest* time I wasn't sure what kind of girl I was, and then I do one thing that I've wanted to do, and he decides who I am like that." She snaps her fingers. "And I mean, don't most guys *like* blow jobs? What's wrong with me? Does he think I'm that ugly and unappealing that he'd rather run away?" Her voice hushes, and I have to strain my ears to hear. "I don't know. It just all hurts."

Silence leeches the bathroom, and I'm not sure who's ready to break it. I love my sister, and the only thought in my mind is that someone— some guy—hurt her.

She cringes the longer the room stays quiet. "Someone. Say *something.*"

"That guy is a real tool," Timo says. "You're beautiful, and any guy would love to have head from you."

I almost laugh at the look on Nikolai's face.

"This is not what we're going to take away from this situation," Nikolai says sternly. "*No.*"

"No?" Timo gapes at Nik. "So you're siding with the douchebag who rejected our little sister? How is that helpful? Where's the loyalty, brother?"

Nikolai looks quickly to Kat. "I'm on your side," he assures her, "but you don't need to be giving guys blow jobs." He's always been unabashed when mentioning sex to our sister. Like it's his duty to inform her—but also keep her safe.

We both haven't been ready for Katya to get older.

"I want to," she refutes. "You all do it. Why am I different? Because I'm the girl? It's just *sex.* I don't look at my virginity like a delicate flower any more than you all looked at yours like a petunia or daffodil."

I realize now that if I can view sex as just *physical*, no emotions required, she may be the same way. Timo was before John. We grew up around the same dudes. She wasn't ear-muffed because she was a girl either, but she is being treated differently because she's one.

"Kat has a point," I say.

She expels a relieved breath.

But Nikolai is stone.

Katya frowns at him. "I know you see me like…a little girl, but your job is done, Nik."

His eyes cloud, jaw tightens and he rubs his lips before saying in Russian, "*My job is never done.*"

She asks in a shaky voice, "Do you think…I'm a slut?" She's only looking for affirmation from Nikolai. His approval means more to us than we sometimes let on.

"No," Nik says.

"Even if I gave him a blow job?" she questions.

"Even if you slept with him," he says in a reassuring tone. "You're no more a slut than all of us in this room."

I'm smiling, the air less strained, and Timo grins back at Kat.

She takes a big breath.

"If you want to explore things, you need to buy new condoms and *be safe.*"

"I do, and I know," she says with a nod.

"And you're still young in a city with—"

"Nik," she says, holding his gaze. "I *know.* I plan to talk to Thora." Nikolai is about to raise another point, but Katya beats him to it. "I know she has few experiences, but I have Timo and Luk, too. You don't need to worry about me all the time."

Timo laughs. "He's physically incapable of such complex things."

We all break into a smile at the sound of Timo's laughter, and then Sergei asks, "Where does Teddy work again?"

"Imperial?" Katya says, confused. "Why are you…oh my God, *don't* talk to him."

Sergei sighs out frustration but looks to Nikolai.

Nikolai turns slightly, and they're whispering.

My eyes drift between them. I'm glad that Nikolai Kotova has an older brother to confide in now. I never thought he'd be able to look to his right and find Sergei there.

"What if Luka and I just talk to Teddy?" Timo asks Kat, and he mutters, "Maybe throw a cocktail in his face." He swings his head to me. "You want in?"

"Oh yeah."

"*No*," Katya says and spread her hands out. "N.O." She slides off the counter. "I do need you to do something though."

We all listen.

"Can you try to hold off on telling our cousins what happened? I know as soon as we exit, they're all going to ask, and I'd rather condense this *whole* thing into two sentences. And *I'd* rather tell them. Because I want to see their reactions and glare at them if they're rude."

"Damn, sister." Timo smiles bright.

"What?" Katya grows emotional at all of us smiling with Timo.

I'm the only one who says what we're thinking, feeling, and I nod to Katya, "We love you."

ACT FORTY-SEVEN
BAYLEE WRIGHT

y core flames with each sit-up. *One.*

Two.

Three.

Four.

I lift my body to meet Luka's intensely charismatic gray eyes. His pink lips curve, his hands securing my ankles, protective and tender. I feel so safe.

He disappears when I lower my back to the blue mats.

"*Five*," Luka counts aloud.

Rising up, he leans forward and places a gentle, warm kiss against my lips.

I smile, lowering back to the mat.

"*Six.*"

I use my core to bring my body up again, and my eyes widen, horrified. I try to scream, but no sound escapes.

Geoffrey replaced Luka; he kneels before me—gripping my ankles so tight, his fingers dig into my bones.

His ill-humored glare slashes at me, his goatee out-grown and hair curling in oily tendrils. Before I can lie back down, Geoffrey leans forward and *slams* his forehead forcefully against mine—

I gasp awake, breath stuck in my throat. My tank top and fleece pajama shorts suction to my sweaty skin.

"Baylee. *Baylee*," Luka repeats my name, his hands on my cheeks, hovering over me. I tighten my eyes shut. *I'm on Luka's top bunk.*

I'm not in the gym.

Geoffrey isn't here.

I repeat it all, tired tears slipping out of the corners of my eyes.

"Bay, can you look at me?"

I catch my breath, my pulse racing, and I open my eyes. Luka's concern blankets me, and I try to hang onto him. Metaphorically and physically. I clutch his wrists while he holds my face.

"Luka…" My face is frozen in a wince. I think I scared myself.

He quickly pulls my body onto his lap, sitting up, and his strong arms wrap around my back in a skintight hug. I press my forehead to his shoulder, my arms sliding underneath his, curving up his back.

God, Geoffrey is invading my nightmares, and I can't ever remember having one *that* vivid.

"You're okay," Luka whispers against my ear. "You're okay."

He's such a dreamer. Because I don't know if we are okay anymore. Luka has the darkest circles beneath his eyes, as sleep-deprived as me, and these past weeks, *months*, have been a giant struggle.

He searches my gaze. "What are you thinking?" His voice is a whisper since Dimitri is on the bottom bunk beneath us.

"That we're sinking in quicksand, and I'm afraid…" I shrug, unable to say the rest.

Luka combs back the sweaty pieces of my hair. "He won't be our choreographer forever. This will end at some point." His lips rise. "And we can watch the Mets lose to the Cubs in peace."

I start smiling. *How am I smiling?* "Hey, you have to admit, the Mets showed *spunk* and fought a good fight."

"Oh yeah," he says easily. "They never gave up."

Those four words hang over us for a moment, and our eyes dance over each other again. I don't want Geoffrey to hurt Luka, but our choreographer pushes him before and after performances in ways that he doesn't push anyone else. Not even me.

He has this gross fascination with Luka's emotional restraint, and he tries to trap him in different acting exercises. Just to break him down.

Each one ends the same way: Luka starts laughing and Geoffrey orders him to leave the gym. It plays out so often now, I'm scared that outcome will morph into something worse.

The bottom bunk creaks, a body rolling ungracefully out.

I rest against Luka. "We've woken the sleeping giant."

"Say that a little louder, I couldn't hear you over your dry-humping," Dimitri says, flitting on the lights by the dresser.

Luka and I squint.

"We weren't humping," I say flatly.

Dimitri rests an elbow on the dresser. "Sounded like dick against pussy to me."

Luka rubs the tired corners of his eyes. "Shut up, dude."

I yawn again. "You seriously make it impossible to forget human anatomy."

"I'm an educator," Dimitri agrees.

"No," Luka and I say in unison.

His eyes dart between us, waiting for one of us to explain the truth of the matter, but we both hesitate for a long moment.

Dimitri is concerned enough that he says, "I can always go find Brenden. I'm sure he'd love to hear about Luka's pecker in his sister—"

"Fuck you," Luka says with very little malice.

"Okay," I say, and as he spins to the door, I add, "No, *wait*. I meant *okay* I'll tell you." I rotate so I'm on Luka's lap, but I lean my back to his chest. He holds me comfortingly around the waist. "I had a nightmare."

Dimitri makes this grunting noise that sounds like a *hmm*.

"What?" I ask.

"Just wondering if it had anything to do with *Geoffrey*."

My stomach drops. "How'd you know?"

Luka frowns. "You had a nightmare about Geoffrey." It's not a question. His concern heats me up inside, and he rubs his face again like he wishes our torment would all end tonight.

Dimitri explains, "I've been having a reoccurring nightmare where Geoffrey starts screaming at all the girls in Infini. My brothers and cousins restrain me, but I eventually land a fist in his face. And I'm fired." He thinks for a second. "I thought maybe Geoffrey wasn't just penetrating my mind at night. Maybe yours too. That fuck-face."

Luka asks, "What happened to fart-face?"

"He became a fuck-face when he started penetrating brains at night," Dimitri nearly growls. He massages his knuckles and scans me in a once-over.

Luka extends his leg out, his muscle probably cramping. "Geoffrey needs to *relax*."

We wear weak, nostalgic smiles as we're subtly reminded about the sex toys and *relax* note someone slipped in Geoffrey's office.

"Did I ever tell you," Dimitri says, "I found out who gave him the blow-up doll and ball gag?"

My eyes grow, curious, but my phone buzzes. I search beneath the buried blankets while Luka asks, "Who?"

My ankle touches the hard phone cover, and I wrestle with the sheets for it.

"Sergei."

I freeze. "Sergei?"

"No," Luka rejects the idea. "Someone's fucking with you."

"If they were fucking with me, I'd know it," Dimitri says. "You forget that I grew up with Serg. Once upon a time, I knew him better than I knew you."

I find my phone. "Sergei is a rule-follower."

"To the core," Luka adds.

"Like me. Like Nikolai," Dimitri agrees, "but Sergei also can't turn down a dare. Erik dared him, and what do you know—it happened."

Luka looks dumbfounded.

Dimitri flips off the lights, returning to his bunk. "You're probably too young to remember all of Serg's dares. Nikolai once got him to streak buck-ass naked through a Waffle House in Atlanta."

The bed squeaks as he climbs on, the entire structure rumbling. I clutch Luka's thigh in case the bed collapses.

I've imagined the super shitty scenario a dozen times, and I always feel terrible for Dimitri Kotova. On the flip side, he told us that if he dies underneath our bunk bed, he'll haunt our asses for the rest of our lives.

It's a seriously terrifying threat.

Luka calls down, "How old were all of you, back then at the Waffle House?"

"Fifteen, seventeen," Dimitri says from below. Luka would've been nine-years-old at that time, and while he mentally sifts through his history, I click into the email notification.

Date: August 25th
Subject: New Changes
From: Geoffrey Lesage, Choreographer
Cc: Baylee Wright

Baylee Wright:

Starting tomorrow, you will practice with machetes for the opening number. Clubs are over. (You will still perform with fire for your juggling act and use balls for the trampoline act.)

I expect a completed, pristine performance with machetes on stage in **<u>one week.</u>**

Don't fail this show.

Geoffrey Lesage

Infini Choreographer

geoffreylesage@mailme.com

I have no reaction. None at all.

I spin my screen to Luka, the soft blue glow illuminating his angered eyes.

It's a rare sight, his anger. I keep soaking in his features. He's twenty-one now. He looks older, but more so from stress.

I pre-ordered the *Hamilton* soundtrack on vinyl for his birthday, August 21st. He's been obsessed with the musical, and the soundtrack is releasing soon, so he was happy and surprised I remembered.

But I wish I could've done more. *Hamilton* just moved from Off-Broadway to Broadway this month, and he would've loved to go.

It's not even the price that stops me. We don't have *time*. I mean, we celebrated his birthday in Verona, the club. Not the city. And even then, Luka and I had to leave early.

Geoffrey had the costume department make miniscule changes on our "nightmare" outfits. He scheduled us for fittings on that particular day, at *night*.

Luka shakes his head. "We'll get Perrot to change this."

"Perrot hasn't fought Geoffrey on anything. Even Nikolai called him *spineless*." I can't be surprised anymore that this is happening. I can't even be mad. I feel like I'm reserving all my energy for an apocalyptic scenario where Geoffrey attacks Luka.

Luka looks away, thinking.

"You know what's weird? Months ago," I whisper, "machetes seemed like the most dangerous, *worst* thing that could happen." I shrug. "Now they don't seem that bad."

Luka gapes at me. No one ever asks if I'm being serious because they always know I am. "Come on, Bay."

"What?" I frown.

"They're *bad.*"

"They're dulled, and I can put rubber on the edges while I practice."

His nose flares. "What happens when you drop the machete on your head and the blade hits your skull? You'll need twenty stitches, and you may form a stutter."

So that happened to one of my instructors when I was eleven. I shouldn't have told him that story. "Will you still love me if I form a stutter?"

"*Bay,*" he forces.

"You better," I say. I already know he would.

Luka hugs me again, and he presses a long, warm kiss to the top of my head. As though healing a wound that hasn't arisen yet.

FALL

ACT FORTY-EIGHT
BAYLEE WRIGHT

A moan tickles my throat, my lips parted in an O-shape, and I accidentally thwack the handle of the shower for something to hold onto. Hot water cuts off, steam vanishing from the glass inside Luka's bathroom.

My mind is on an earth-shattering ascent while my bare body is in Luka's possession, my right leg hoisted over his shoulder. He kneels on the tiles, his fingers pressing in the soft flesh of my thigh.

I tingle all over, and my hand finds his thick hair, gripping as he kisses me right between my spread legs. As his tongue flicks and laps my sensitive clit, I tremble against him. *Oh God.*

Oh God.

I cry out, and I pinch my eyes closed, losing sense of place and time. I force my eyes open for one reason. To see him.

Breath tight in my chest, I look down.

His mouth encloses my pussy, kissing deeper, harder. His tongue is a force that I know intimately now. And his gaze, locked on mine, almost sends me over, soulful grays devouring me whole.

My muscles tighten, and I clench and clench. My pulse dives straight down. Throbbing. God, I'm throbbing so badly. In the *best, best* way.

He hits another sensitive spot, and my back arches. I feel myself slipping, my legs shuddering, and I'm unable to hold myself upright. Reaching out, I knock over a shampoo bottle and soap. I clutch onto the tiny ledge with one hand, the other, I fist his wet hair.

"Luka," I moan. *Luka.*

Luka.

I can *feel* his smile against my heat. And then his fingers slowly fill me, pulsing in and out. Slow and firm. I inhale a sharp breath.

Holy shit. My world rotates, and I tighten around his fingers. My moans turn inwards, caught deep in my throat. I shudder and shudder, my body bowed towards Luk.

And then the door flies open.

My face drops as Dimitri and I look straight-on at one another. The glass shower isn't fogged anymore. There's no more running water, and he can *easily* distinguish me from waist-to-face. Nipples, boobs— all exposed. And Luka's head is between my legs.

Great. Just great. I have the shittiest luck. Thankfully, Dimitri growls a curse and spins his back to the shower.

Luka casts a quick glance over his shoulder before rising. Both of my feet are now on the tiles, and Luka snags a towel off a shelf in arm's distance and wraps it around my body.

"I saw nothing," Dimitri says, solidified in the doorway. "That's a lie. I *wish* I saw nothing. I saw Baybay's tits."

I cringe. Is this karma for that one time I saw his dick in my peripheral?

"Dude, you can leave now," Luka says.

Dimitri adds, "This would've never happened if I heard the mother-fucking shower."

So now it's our fault. I refute, "You need to fix the bathroom lock."
It broke yesterday when Dimitri said the wood couldn't handle his
brute strength.

"*My* bathroom lock. Not *the*. You're the one crashing in my suite.
You're my guest—"

"She's my guest, my girlfriend," Luka interjects, "and seriously, *leave*."

"I can't." He rotates towards the mirror, but he trains his gaze on
the sink.

I secure my towel and squeeze out my wet hair. Luka opens the
glass door, completely naked. His tattoos just barely stop at his ass, and
he doesn't even bother cupping a hand around his dick.

"Why not?" Luka asks.

"Tell me what I just saw aren't bruises from work." He's worried.

Luka and I exchange a look, and our eyes travel down each other's
body. Yellowish and blackish bruises mar Luka's back, waist, legs, his
pale skin dotted with them, and I'm not any better.

Big purple and blue welts bloom across my brown skin, saucer-like
patches around my hips, knees, and my shoulder.

I shrug at Luka. Neither of us wants to lie to family and friends.
We were forced to, and now that we have the choice, we're choosing
honesty.

Luka explains, "We were having trouble with her standing on my
shoulders—the timing, and this past week Geoffrey has been running
us in drills off the mats. Look, I combatted him, got Perrot on the
phone, but he said, *it didn't sound bad.*"

I tighten my towel, a chill in the air. It's known that Perrot mostly
sits behind a desk, not very knowledgeable about the ins-and-outs of
disciplines and athletics. If asked what a burpee is, I question whether
he'd know the answer.

Dimitri looks out of the corner of his eye, noticing me covered,
and he faces us. Luka still stands unabashed and naked in the shower
doorway.

Taking in the welts all over his younger cousin's body, Dimitri cocks his head. "I never saw you two off the mats. When was this?"

"At night."

"How much sleep—"

"Don't," Luka starts. "There's nothing we can do but deal with it, and we're dealing." We feel trapped, but in a different way than when the contracts loomed over us. Luka already went to medical on my behalf.

And coincidentally, I went to medical on *his* behalf.

We were both called in. They examined our bruises and said it's normal in our profession. They don't feel the harshness or cruelty in each one. So I've become more and more resigned.

Dimitri glowers. "This shit isn't work. That's abuse. And it's ending." He storms out of the bathroom, but he calls back, "Get dressed! We have plans to make!"

ACT FORTY-NINE
LUKA KOTOVA

At a 1:00 a.m. stage rehearsal, I slump a bit on a midnight-blue velveteen seat, just to kick up my feet on the chair in front of me. The cast fills the middle rows, watching Infini's acts until our turn arrives to perform.

On stage, Zhen and Brenden clutch ivory straps rigged to the ceiling, and they slice through air, circling each other. In sync as the music crescendos to a heart-stomping beat. The breathy, celestial lights sweep their bodies, and they gracefully collide like two archangels born together.

I'm drawn in for a full minute, and I've seen their act before.

The only reason it may be axed: Corporate thinks there are too many "aerial" acts in Infini, and aerial straps could be replaced by Cyr wheels. (Which is ridiculous—it's called *Aerial* Ethereal.)

Bay is worried, but I don't think it'll happen. We're in October, and contract renewals are coming in January. If anything, Infini has a greater chance of being cancelled. Sales are only up 4% from last year, and I think the Masquerade and AE were expecting a 20% increase.

(That's the monthly gossip, provided by Luka Kotova.)

Quietly, I shake Junior Mints into my mouth, my left arm around Bay's chair. She conked out about an hour ago, and I'm not waking her since she's done with rehearsal. We've all just been ordered to *stay put* until everyone finishes.

Brenden stretches in a split midair, and Zhen balances on his head with one hand, their limbs extended in clean angles. Even without costume and makeup, they've hooked in the attention of the cast.

My cousin Abram draws forward, his eyes lit up, and his chest lifts as trumpets infiltrate the score. Zhen and Brenden increase their momentum, soaring.

This is why I love art. The circus moves people.

Art *moves* people.

To me, there's very few other things more amazing than that. After their act ends, Geoffrey nears the stage to speak to them.

He's been testy since trampoline performed. The four oldest guys— Sergei, Dimitri, Erik, and Matvei—have been purposefully fucking up their routines at rehearsals only. Just to distract Geoffrey.

It works sometimes. His attention veers on them more than us, but I really didn't want my cousins and brother to risk their reputations. Professionalism matters to them.

I'm the one who doesn't give a shit.

But once Dimitri gets an idea in his head, there's no stopping him.

"Take a seat on stage," Geoffrey tells Brenden and Zhen, and then our choreographer slips into the row in front of mine.

He struts forward, and I dump the rest of the candy in my mouth. For some reason, this attracts him to me. I'm not even loud.

I'm quiet.

No one else was looking at me, but his gaze daggers my face. I chew casually, and I crane my neck over my shoulder.

All of my older cousins and Sergei are rigid one row behind me, their grays and Dimitri's ocean-blues pinpointed on Geoffrey.

The choreographer saunters closer, and his overbearing presence wakes Bay. She tensely lifts her body up and rubs her eyes. Watching as he halts directly across from me, but I prefer his focus to fix on me, never her.

Geoffrey rests his ass on the back of a chair. He has a great view of my Adidas soles.

I spin my baseball hat backwards, nonchalant. Waiting. (Come on, Geoffrey, what do you have for me?)

Like he's mentioning the weather, he says, "Tell me an excruciating moment that involves your sister."

This again. "No," I say simply like I've done before.

Sergei interjects, "We're not doing acting exercises, Geoffrey."

His gaze is still latched on me. "Luka has room to be more emotive. I'm helping him." (Yeah, he's not.) To me, he says, "Tell me an excruciating moment that involves your brother."

I shake my empty Junior Mint box. "Which one?"

"Timofei."

I almost laugh, finding this whole thing ridiculous. "With Timofei, there are none."

"You're lying," Geoffrey shoots back like he had the gun cocked and loaded, ready for my response.

My muscles constrict, but my facial features don't change shape.

Geoffrey stands straighter, nearing my row, his waist an inch from my soles. I bet he wants me to drop my feet to the floor. (I'm not going to.)

"Nothing excruciating has ever happened to you?" Geoffrey asks like he already knows the answer. I blink a few times, processing. He doesn't know.

He can't know.

Artists are aware that I have an impulse to steal worthless shit. Some think it's funny. (It's not to me.) There are rumors that I purge after I eat; some people know it's fact. And Geoffrey has this information from medical—what he can't have, what he doesn't have, is how it all started.

Only my extended and immediate family know, plus Baylee, Thora, and John. That's it.

"Your sister…" he trails off, a smile appearing. "You're glaring."

Baylee's hand slips into mine.

"We're getting warmer," Geoffrey says. "Let's try this again. Tell me an excruciating story involving your sister and little brother or I'll describe a scenario that *will* bring something out of you."

My chest elevates in a breath like I'm running in place. Not sitting. I drop my feet and let go of Baylee's hand.

She glares at Geoffrey. "You *can't* do this to him."

Before he hones in on Bay like he's tried before, I immediately stand up and sidestep, blocking her completely. I feel all of my cousins and my brother rise with me

"Luka," Baylee protests, springing to her feet. I'm taller, so she's hidden from Geoffrey.

Now I stand face-to-face with the motherfucker I loathe, a row of chairs separating us. Our eyes latched again, I cup my hands in front of me.

And he says, "I'll describe a scenario then."

"Go ahead," I reply.

"You were six."

My nose flares; I shake my head dazedly. "No."

"No, what? You weren't six?" (I was.)

The air is thin. Silent, a pin drop could be heard.

"Your sister was three."

I snap, eyes ablaze—and I *charge.* Someone fists my shirt before I reach Geoffrey's face. Yanking me backwards.

He's smiling. "Your brother was five."

I tear out of a cousin's hold, or maybe it's Sergei restraining me, my pulse beats and bleeds. "You *motherfucker,*" I sneer.

Geoffrey thinks he has a piece of me. A part of me that I don't give anyone else. He's cradling my anger and pain.

Just to use against me.

"You were in the Midwest for a few months."

I rip out of another hand, and I storm forward, my pulse on searing ascent. I'm being dragged back again. My cousins yell in Russian for me to *take a breath* and *stop, Luka*. I'll be fired if I hit him, but he should be fired and sucker-punched for *all of this*.

I can't sit quietly by and let him run over me.

I can't.

I can't.

"Your parents became friends with a few locals while you all lived there."

I somehow bolt out of my cousin's grip, and I launch a right hook at Geoffrey—a strong hand clasps my wrist, stopping me.

"*Fuck you!*" I yell through my teeth, veins rising in my neck. My face reddened in ire, I can hardly see straight.

Geoffrey soaks in my raw, unfettering emotion, but he just keeps going. "They were invited to a neighborhood summer barbecue."

"Is this what you want?!" I scream so loudly my lungs scald inside-out—someone wraps their arms around my collar. "You want to hear me yell?!" I thrash against a muscular build. "Well, fuck you, you *motherfucker.*"

"The party was unrelated to the circus or AE. Only your parents, four brothers, sister, and you went."

I spew threats, screaming *fuck yous*, my chest bursting open. Hot tears scratch my eyes, and knives stake my insides. I want Geoffrey to stop speaking, but he's not going to stop. My anger does nothing to hurt him. It just pummels me, and I'm growing cold.

And numb. A voice whispers in my ear, "Shhh."

Raging tears drip off my chin, and I breathe. And breathe, my chest rising and falling heavily. Two arms swoop underneath mine, putting me in a body-lock, and then…their large palms cover my ears.

Protecting me.

I blink and blink, my widened, bloodshot eyes flitting to the forearm that holds me. I see a tattoo of a lightning bolt striking a tree, and I know.

It's Sergei.

My brother is the one shielding me from Geoffrey's words.

And I shut my eyes.

Geoffrey is gone. I can't hear him. I can't see him.

Quiet tranquility pours through me. At ease. Calm.

Peace.

My past is still mine to give. Mine to share. I breathe and breathe, *in control.* I feel more in control, and that's what it is: a state of mind.

In this moment, I can reach my past. I can touch it myself.

Geoffrey isn't prying into me. He didn't rip it out. I can cradle it within my own assured hands.

I can remember. I remember being a kid. Being led upstairs with Timo and Kat to a game room. The kind with a pool table, foosball. The person who led us—it was the teenage son of the host. Barbecue neighborhood party, normal people. In a normal place.

What happened wasn't normal. He took off his clothes—it's blurry. I don't know.

I remember being naked. We were all naked. Confused. So fucking confused.

I was just a kid.

Later, we had to be told by adults that he touched himself, forced us to undress and to watch. But these memories sit repressed in my head. Trauma that I can't fully reach, but it affects me—and Timo. Katya remembers nothing. Timo and I, we obsessively fixate on things but in different ways, craving control, and I can't shut if off.

I'll never be able to, but some days, many more days than most people can imagine, I feel empowered. I break free, and I hold onto those. I'm holding onto this moment.

Where I can think about it. Breathe deeply. Touch the past and not drop to my knees.

I'm okay.

I promise this time.

WINTER

ACT FIFTY
LUKA KOTOVA

Aerial Ethereal's end of the year holiday party is my absolute favorite of all Corporate events. It surpasses the promo pool parties by a million leagues.

The Masquerade's grand ballroom is decked out in garland, snow-flakes, twinkling lights, about ten different fir trees, and a row of country flags, representing the homelands of AE artists. And everyone brings a dish, either cooked or store-bought, the buffet table overflowing with homemade recipes, passed down from generation to generation.

And the music.

It's holiday music; and look, I like anything with a good beat.

I dance with Bay, our heads nodding, silly shoulder-pumping while we hold holiday-patterned disposable plates. We're off in a corner, doing our own thing by a popcorn-garland tree, and I catch her free hand and twirl her in a circle.

Her smile instantly grows, and mine stretches higher. Last year, I didn't have Baylee. I was just dancing by myself for a while.

This is a thousand times less boring, but this particular year is also laced with gravity. Her smile fades quickly, probably remembering what I do.

The whole cast of Infini has been on edge ever since we received an email. It said Perrot would announce the show's fate at *this* holiday party. He'll tell us if our contracts will be renewed for another year or if this is the end.

If the worst happens, I know it's the close to one chapter of our lives, but I worry Bay will feel like it's the end of the entire book.

Our dance slows with a song switch and Bay's approaching aunt. She flew in from New York for the weekend, and Baylee finally met her baby cousin last night. I haven't had a chance to talk to her aunt. Not since she's been in town, and definitely not before that.

Even though she supported my relationship with Baylee the second time around, I want to make a better impression.

Baylee wears a funny look.

"What?"

"You're nervous, aren't you?"

I nod and wipe my lips with a flimsy napkin, my plate half-filled.

"She'll be nice to you," Bay has to whisper as Lucy nears.

Her aunt slows to a stop, sipping a cup of eggnog. "I love the dress." She appraises Bay's simple red sweater-dress. "You didn't find anything CC?"

"Calloway Couture looks best on Posh Spices," Baylee says.

Lucy wears a white-knit dress, the collar high. "CC looks great on every woman, every girl." She steals a Polish sweet off Bay's plate. "As the niece of the brand & marketing exec, you should write this down."

"I'll remember this," Baylee says seriously. "No more journaling for me."

Her list is completed and done, but we're not over. We're still going strong. I slide my arm around her shoulders, and Bay rests her weight against my side.

Lucy dusts crumbs off her lips. "How have you been, Luka?" It should be a light phrase, but she wears deeper concern than a stranger would. Lucy knows everything that happened a couple months ago.

I start nodding. "Better. *A lot* better."

Geoffrey Lesage was fired.

That day inside the auditorium—while he began unearthing my past about me and Kat and Timo for the *whole* Infini cast to hear—Dimitri called Nikolai to come help me.

Nik was halfway across the hotel, too far from the auditorium to reach me in enough time, so he told Dimitri, "Film him."

Without Geoffrey knowing, Dimitri slyly took out his cellphone and recorded the choreographer harassing me. Nik sent the footage to Corporate. Geoffrey was fired within two hours.

A significant weight has lifted off the cast, off Bay and me since then. Bay said it was like the Mets won the World Series, and I said, "Or the Knicks winning the NBA Finals."

"Or Infini surviving," she added more solemnly, and I hugged her, kissed her, hoped that it'd turn into reality.

(We'll see.)

"That's good to hear," Lucy says. "Anything new?"

I smile. "I'm pretty boring."

"That's *so* false," Bay tells me.

I can't help but laugh at how she says this like it's written in the stars. "You're the most exciting part of my life, Bay."

"Aw," Lucy says.

"That's not true," Baylee says pointedly and looks to Lucy. "He did a backflip off a casino machine with Timo and was chased by security for a full hour."

(Yeah, that happened this morning.) I also called Baylee in my hiding spot. That was one of my favorite parts, but the thought drifts off.

Lucy holds my gaze, and I wonder if she thinks I'm too rebellious for her niece. And then she says, "I just had a realization."

"What?" I ask.

Her eyes ping between us. "Baylee smiles the most when she's around you."

Baylee doesn't restrain her next smile, lips pulled high.

I grin down at her, and she shrugs like it's fact.

I shrug back the same way.

Lucy gets a phone call, and I hear the words *explosive poop* and *diapers* before she leaves to help her husband.

"You're lucky she didn't ask you about babies," Bay says seriously.

"Why'd that be bad?" I bite into a pizzelle, a flat waffle-shaped Italian cookie.

"I don't know. We never discuss that far into the future." She shrugs slowly. "I guess we never thought there'd be *a future*…but I'm not suggesting or assuming anything."

She's nervous.

Bay.

"Come here," I whisper to my beautiful girlfriend, drawing her close again. And again. Her arm is around my waist while mine hooks around her shoulders.

I nod to her. "Later in life. Like thirties, I can picture us in the circus, and we'll wake up each morning and dance with our kids in our kitchen."

Tears well in her brown eyes.

I mention Trivial Pursuit after dinner, and she puts a palm to my chest. My eyes burn, but this is one of the best paternal memories I have. And it's not even my dad.

"I'll lose on purpose, every time," I tell her. "Though, knowing your genes, our kids will be really intelligent. The Kotova part…" I wince through my teeth. "Sorry about that."

She smiles a shaky, tearful smile. "You're smart, Luka." Then she wipes at the corners of her eyes; no tears have fallen, but I feel her swelling emotion. She stares off for a second, thinking.

"What is it?"

"It's weird talking about years into the future when in ten minutes, Infini could be cancelled and I might be *out* of the circus."

"Baylee the Realist is on the rise," I tease.

(Don't doubt my love for the realism inside of her.) I love every part of Bay.

She gives me a look. "It's true."

"Sort of, partially. Maybe not at all." I smile.

"Luka the Dreamer is on the rise," she says pointedly, starting to smile off of my smile—but we're both distracted as Nikolai's lengthy stride aims for us.

He looks antsy.

"Yeah?" I ask him.

"Erik said you know Katya's porter."

I easily spot Kat from across the ballroom. She reads a paranormal paperback with Thora, both on velveteen stools.

I look back at Nik. "The porter that dropped her?"

"That one." His gaze darkens. (Yeah, he's not my favorite dude either.)

"I talked to him once in passing."

I remember I said *try to stay focused.*

Katya asked for a show transfer about a month ago because she doesn't trust that porter. Since she's already in AE's artist database, HR will direct her to a show that has an open slot. Then she would have to audition for the director, etc.

Problem is, she's a minor and Nik is her guardian, leaving her with only two real possibilities.

1.) our parents could agree to look after her, and she'd go on tour with Noctis. (I'm praying that's not happening.)

2.) she'd be transferred to Infini, which is…unstable at the moment.

She can't join Amour; it's too risqué, no minors allowed. It's more plausible she'll stay in Viva.

Nikolai clutches his phone in a tight fist. "Auditions are open for Somnio. I thought you could try to convince him to attend."

I nod, understanding. If he leaves on his own accord, then Kat will have a new partner. "I'll see what I can do." I barely hear him say thank you, my attention on Bay who stares at the carpet, deep in thought. A cookie is frozen between her fingers.

If Infini is cancelled, it's possible I could be shifted back to Viva and return to my old job as Kat's porter. And I don't know where that'd leave Bay.

I'M OUTSIDE THE MASQUERADE'S BALLROOM.

Sitting in the semi-quiet lounge area, I hunch forward on the edge of a leather chair. Before I forget, I take a moment to jot everything I ate in a tiny spiral notebook.

"Hey, man."

I look up at Brenden and nod in greeting, but it's not like we've talked without Bay present. We haven't since that long, awkward time ago we made sandwiches.

Brenden motions to the adjacent leather chair. "Can I sit?"

"Yeah." A pianist must be playing somewhere on this hotel level, music echoing towards us.

His eyes ping from my notebook to a paper plate in his own hands. "I don't know if you're allowed, but Bay said to give this to you. She's in a long conversation with our aunt about PoPhilly." He stretches forward and hands me the plate. "She said to tell you it's not an 'air patty'—and the meat quality is a solid A."

My lips stretch. "It's from a restaurant in New York?" Bay had been trying to convince Lucy to freeze a box of beef patties and bring them on the plane.

"Yep."

My lips fall as I remember the first part of what he said. "Why wouldn't I be allowed to eat it?"

"Sorry," he immediately apologizes, being considerate of my feelings.

And I think of Bay. How important Brenden is in her life, and while I don't like getting deep with a lot of people, I think I should make a better effort with him.

"You can ask, dude," I say. "It's okay."

He slides forward to the edge of his seat like me. We're closer, and he lowers his voice so no one can overhear. "Do you have to change your diet? If you're working on controlling it, do you need to eat healthier?"

That's why he's unsure if I should eat the beef patty. "No, everyone is different, but for me, my issue is more about moderation and timing… like if I overeat or if I eat too close to practices."

I stare at my notebook, not able to talk in detail, but I know my issue well.

I convince myself that I'm in control by doing something Corporate would disallow—eating before practice—but then I *have* to purge at that point. And I become a prisoner to a different monster.

I love candy, hamburgers, all junk food, and I always randomly order off of menus, and in my healthiest months, I still eat the same kind of food—just at healthier times and portions.

When I'm really stressed, I will start believing that puking will make me feel better and more in control. That's what happened this year.

Brenden slowly nods. "And the notebook helps?"

"Yeah, sometimes. I'm not always at a place where I need it."

I haven't thrown up in three weeks, which is good. *Really* good, and I'd say that my compulsion to steal is down to a 4.5 rating. (Decent for me.)

A long moment passes. It's an awkward beat, and the more we stare at one another, I think he's looking at me differently.

The answer hits my head—why he's being so cool with me. I give him a look, setting down my beef patty.

"What?" he asks.

"Don't pity me," I tell him. "I'm the same guy you disliked. I haven't changed. I've been the same person."

He shakes his head. "I thought you were an adrenaline junkie who stole crap for the hell of it." He heard about my childhood trauma from Geoffrey in that auditorium. He's had a couple months to reevaluate who I am.

I'm still Luka Kotova.

A kleptomaniac.

A bulimic.

And I'm more than that. I'm a brother to five siblings. A fourth generation circus performer and a high-risk acrobat. I'm Russian-American, a proud Kotova. A dreamer and a rebel.

"Look," I try to explain, "it doesn't change the fact that I *steal*. It's still wrong."

"It changes something."

No. I don't want it to. Here's why. "When I was a kid," I say slowly, these words edging to the forefront of my brain, "my therapist used to tell me that I need to be accountable for my actions. If I get caught stealing, I can't just blame it on my issues. I have to take responsibility. I could've turned around, set the item back—I could've paused one moment longer, and I have to try to be better." I capture his methodical gaze. "I don't want it to be okay with you that I steal, is what I'm saying. Because it never was before."

He understands, clarity flooding his eyes.

I wonder if Bay told him that I found a therapist in Vegas.

I'm going once a week. It's more expensive than I really like, but I forgot how much it helps. I can't really put a price value on my health. So Baylee tells me.

Brenden sits back. "Where does this leave you and me?"

We hear commotion in the hallway, our heads turning slightly. Dimitri is inbound. He must've taken a piss break.

Brenden and I acknowledge each other again. The awkwardness is literally still there. I don't think it'll ever leave. Maybe that's just how the two of us are meant to be together. Awkward.

I almost laugh. "I like how we were before. In New York, before I got caught with Bay." We weren't friends, but we were cool enough to play board games together. For him to share his family moments with me—I was a part of his world.

That's all I'd want.

His smile gradually appears. "I did too."

I think we'll be able to return to that.

"Princess!" Dimitri calls across the lounge area. Our heads swing to the right. Camila is with her boyfriend, Craig.

He's a redhead. That's all I can hone in on. Dimitri looks like a kid in a candy store, grinning from ear-to-ear as Camila's eyes grow like a deer caught in headlights.

Brenden says, "He has no chill."

I nod in agreement as we stand. I grab my beef patty and pocket my notebook. By the entrance to the ballroom, Dimitri extends his palm to Craig.

"Dimitri," he says, "Camila's friend."

Craig reluctantly shakes. "She's never mentioned you before."

"Probably because she nicknamed me." Dimitri doesn't say that the nickname is *tiniest dick*—and it's not for the obvious reason. He's not embarrassed. He just doesn't want Camila to be in hot water with her boyfriend by mentioning his dick.

It's why Dimitri isn't peacocking. He's assessing Craig like he's learning more about Camila by meeting him. Nothing more than that.

Camila sees me nearing. "Hey, cool brother."

I nod to her in reply, eating the last of my patty that's stuffed full of beef. I can definitely imagine Bay melting in heaven when she took a bite of hers.

Craig looks irritated. "Let's go, Camila. I don't want to be here all night."

Camila sighs lightly, and she smiles at Dimtiri. "See you Saturday."

"See you, princess."

They are really friends. Been that way since the summer.

Brenden looks to me as we walk. "I meant to ask you. Did you ever figure out why you were put in Infini with Bay?"

"No clue."

"Little Kotova," Dimitri says as we reach the door. Craig and Camila already disappeared inside the ballroom.

"What?"

He cocks his head, and I figure out that he just heard Brenden.

"Do *you* know why I was put in Infini?" I sway back, surprised. Has he known this whole fucking time?

"Have you ever asked Sergei about himself? Not if he's a titty or ass guy or likes to rub it out in bed or the shower." Only Dimitri has to clarify that he's not talking about body parts or sex. "His hobbies. His interests."

"I…" (No, I haven't.)

Dimitri pats my shoulder. "Start there."

ACT FIFTY-ONE
LUKA KOTOVA

I beeline for Sergei in the ballroom, skirting past clustered groups of people and ten-foot fir trees. My brain churns through weeks, months, nearly a *year* with Sergei—and I still can't comprehend why he'd have this answer that's always eluded me and Bay.

I round a mammoth tree, and by a dove ice sculpture, I find Timo, Sergei, and Nikolai in mid-conversation.

"…mountain vaca, beach vaca." Timo uses his palms as mock scales, and the beach vacation is higher.

"I miss the Swiss Alps," Sergei says, eggnog in hand. I skim him. He wears all black. Black slacks, black belt, black button-down, black leather bracelets—I feel like I'm missing the smallest, tiniest detail.

"If it's not in driving distance, it'll cost a fortune," Nik states.

Timo catches sight of me. "Luka, beach or mountains for the Great Kotova Road Trip?"

I rake a hand through my hair. "I don't mi…" Timo is mouthing *beach, beach, beach* repeatedly. So I say, "Beach." I open my mouth to cut in and ask Sergei, but Timo is like lightning. Speeding ahead and whiplashing my train of thought.

"I second the beach." Timo raises a palm like he's taking an oath. "Kat will third, and now it's three to one. Beach wins." Timo makes a cha-ching motion.

"What about Nik's vote?" Sergei asks.

"Nik's not invited." Timo beams as he says it.

Nikolai rolls his eyes, but his lips curve upward.

"It won't stop him from tagging along," Timo says. "You may not know this now, Serg. But you'll come to find that Nikolai has an obsession with following me around." *Serg.*

As soon as Timo says his nickname, Sergei's face lights up. It's taken almost the whole year, but they're finally on good terms.

Sometimes all it takes is time. Sometimes it takes more than that.

Nikolai interjects, "If you told us where you were going, no one would need to follow you."

"Don't let him fool you," Timo tells our oldest brother. "His favorite game is *Where In The World Is Carmen Sandiego? – Timofei Kotova Edition.*"

Nikolai shakes his head, his charismatic eyes smiling, and Sergei laughs.

I butt in, "Sergei, can I talk to you?" I motion towards the window. In the corner. Away from family, from most of the artists.

"Yeah." Sergei looks to Nik, who's suddenly stone-faced, letting no emotion pass.

Nik shakes his head once in reply. He wouldn't know what this is about. I haven't even told Baylee yet.

Timo tries to capture my gaze, but I avoid. I'd rather not spin this into a huge family discussion.

Half a minute later, Sergei and I reach the semi-private corner, and he sets his eggnog on the windowsill.

"Will you be honest with me, please?" I start off.

"From the start, *I'm* the one who said honesty is important," he says. "I've been honest with you."

I blink quickly, thinking. How did he get Geoffrey to return the tempo of our act's music to the original? That has always bugged me. And what Dimitri just said…

"Luka," Sergei says. "Just ask me outright. I'll answer."

Is it me? I haven't asked him anything personal. Not one thing. I've empathized with him, but I never reached out and reconnected with my brother. Not beyond work.

Sergei twists his bracelets, anxious. "You realize I'm not Nikolai? I'm not going to assume what you're thinking by reading your body language." Yeah, Nik is really good at that.

I stuff my hands in my slack's pockets, and my fingers touch a pack of Skittles. "Do you know why Marc Duval would risk putting me in Infini with Baylee?"

Sergei's expression morphs from somewhat worried to *amused*.

I raise my shoulders. "I'm missing the joke here, dude."

He rests his elbow on the windowsill. "I tried texting, emailing— *talking* with you at the start of the show. You could've had this answer back then. It's funny." He tilts his head from side to side, reconsidering that word. "In a sad way."

(That's my life. Funny but sad.)

"Yeah, well…" I run my fingers through my hair and gesture to him. "I'm asking now, and it's not like we were ever close when our family was together."

Sergei nods, knowing that age separated us. Growing up, he was like the untouchable brother to me. The oldest, the strongest, the fittest—I made him into this humongous, godly figure. Intimidating, more so than Nik, who's already hard to confront at times.

Timo could reach *anyone*, anything, but not me—I just hung back. It's why I can't recall that many memories with just Sergei and me. I don't know if any exist before Infini.

"I was told," Sergei explains, "that Wheel of Death *needed* to return to Infini. Marc believed that removing that act was the reason Infini's sales were down."

I don't ask why the act was removed in the first place. When Timo joined the cast of Amour, they had to erase *Wheel of Death* off Infini's program. It was his discipline before it ever became mine.

"There are only a few Kotovas who've mastered the discipline." Sergei is one of them. "I didn't ask to join Infini. I was told to." He pauses. "But I did ask who my partner would be."

"Who was it?" I just know—it couldn't have been me.

"A cousin I'd never met." His gaze drifts to the window, Vegas lit up in an array of neon colors tonight and every night.

"Why me then?"

Why am I standing in front of Sergei and not a no-named cousin?

"I wanted to be paired with a brother." His softened gaze meets mine. "And not just any brother. I wanted to be paired with you."

I let out a laugh. "You're joking." When I see that he's not, I say, "Peter would've been better. Nik, *Timo*. If they were available—"

"I would've still chosen *you*," he emphasizes. "For some reason or another, we were never in a single act together growing up. I was never able to perform side-by-side on a stage with you, Luka. I've worked closely with Timo, with Nik, with Peter—but not you. And my best memories are coaching my brothers."

Coaching. Because he's the oldest. The know-it-all.

He has been coaching me.

Bettering me, enhancing my skills at this discipline from the jumpstart.

My carriage elevates in a big breath, but I can't wrap my head around another loose thread. "How could you ever ask for me and get me? Corporate listens to *money* and these strict contracts, not us. Not what we want."

"I told Marc over coffee that if Wheel of Death seemed that important for Infini, I needed to be in it, and that I wouldn't go if you weren't my partner."

I rock back. "You gave Marc Duval an ultimatum?"

"It wasn't that harsh." He laughs. "We were talking about everything. Music, movies, family, and when the topic of Infini and contract renewals came up, it was casual…" He laughs harder, probably at my befuddled expression.

My brows must be knit together.

"Luka." Sergei smiles wide. "I'm friends with Marc Duval. Every time we cross paths, we grab coffees, lunch, always dinner. We don't usually talk business, but when we do, it's laidback. He respects my opinion, and I respect his. In some ways, he's always seen me as a voice for the artists, and my relationship with Marc occasionally gives me sway with the staff."

"What…" The. Hell. It's hard for me to believe.

Which is why he steps nearer and says, "I'm best friends with Christian Duval, his *son*. We were in a band together. Wherever the circus went, the band followed."

A band.

None of this should be shocking. Dimitri told me to ask Sergei about his hobbies. *A fucking band.* And I've always known nepotism exists. Playing favorites, preferential treatment—it's all real. It's why Baylee and I were even given a chance to stay in the circus after we were caught. And apparently it's why I went to Infini.

It hits me now that *he's* the reason I got the chance to look at Baylee Wright again.

To say her name out loud.

To hold her hand.

If I didn't return to Infini, Bay and I would've never taken the risks. I'd still be in Viva. Trying not to think about a girl that I was helplessly, wholeheartedly, *infinitely* in love with.

His decisions changed my life.

Again.

But this time, he actually led me to the wish-upon-a-star, blow-out-all-your-birthday-candles kind of happiness.

"Thank you," I say, my emotion encapsulating the two words.

Sergei nods like he feels them.

I replay his answers, my lips rising, and I ask, "So what kind of band was it?"

Sergei picks up his eggnog. "Metal. A cross between Disturbed and Celtic Frost." He gestures to his chest. "Stryke Manner."

My lips pull high. "Your band name was *Stryke Manner.*"

"It's cool," he says as though it can't be rivaled.

I laugh. "You played guitar?"

"Drums." Sergei drinks a swig of eggnog. "I could teach you. You'd be good. Your rhythm is…" He falls quiet as the holiday music dies down.

Antoine Perrot stands on an apple box, microphone to his lips. "Is this working?" His voice booms. "There we go."

He's going to make an announcement about Infini, and the only thought I have in my head is: *find Baylee.*

I tell Sergei why I'm leaving, and then I weave through frozen bodies that face and listen to Perrot. Everyone may as well be a marble statue, and I'm the only one moving.

Perrot thanks everyone for attending and then starts recalling his memories being the Director of Infini while in Vegas. He's being too sentimental, and Baylee will draw a conclusion from that. No doubt.

Find Baylee.

I pick up my pace, dodging a group of my cousins. I dip beneath a low-hanging string of garland.

"The press release will reach the entire Aerial Ethereal troupe tomorrow, but I wanted to tell the cast before and in person. For your hard work and the difficult year, you all deserve that."

I find her.

She stands tensed by the dessert bar and three-foot chocolate fountain. I come up behind Bay, and she instantly sinks her back against my chest.

I snake one of my arms around her collarbones, my other across her abdomen. I hold her tight, and her ribs expand in a breath.

We sway back-and-forth some, and I watch her wide-eyed, concentrated gaze on Perrot.

Perrot sighs heavily. "There's just no other way to say this. Creative and financial teams have come to the conclusion that no matter how much effort our artists give, there is no saving Infini."

Baylee goes completely still in my arms. Like an arrow struck her heart, and as I stand behind her, against her—it impales me too. I can practically feel her grief and pain fist her lungs.

And there's nothing I can do but hold Bay.

"To garner more tickets, we need a completely new show narrative, a new name—and at that point, it's no longer Infini. It's something else."

No one whispers. No one moves.

We just listen.

Perrot adjusts his clammy grip on the microphone. "To the cast of Infini, you gave your all. I speak on behalf of the company when I say, you made us proud."

People are starting to cry.

Baylee wipes beneath her eyes with a trembling hand, and I fight emotion.

Perrot's gaze glasses. "This is the end of the line for me." There must not be a role for him in the company. Show director positions are scarce. "I wish that I could promise the entire cast a job. I'd hire you all." He laughs weakly, but the humor doesn't catch on with his audience.

I feel Bay's heart pounding hard.

"But there are no job guarantees," Perrot says. "Come January, you'll learn if Aerial Ethereal has a place for you. Something else may be in the works, but my advice is to audition for open-slots in Somnio. It's on a European tour, and you should take advantage of every opportunity while you still can." He pauses. "So it's with great sadness and honor that I announce New Year's Eve as Infini's last show."

That soon.

We figured, but hearing the news gives it permanence. Validity. And pain.

"Bay?" I whisper in her ear.

She nods once as though to say *I'm dealing*. And she clutches my bicep around her collarbones like she doesn't want me to let go anytime soon.

I'm not.

I'm holding on forever.

"Raise your glasses."

Baylee and I don't separate to reach for a cup. Champagne flutes and eggnog glasses are hoisted all around us, watery gazes set on Perrot.

And he says, "To Infini."

"To Infini," everyone repeats.

And so softly, Bay breathes, "To Infini."

ACT FIFTY-TWO
BAYLEE WRIGHT

Our very last performance in Infini, the globe auditorium is packed to the brim. Every chance I can, I stand in the wings of the stage with other Infini artists, all of us watching our friends, our *family* lay their hearts bare for this show.

One final time.

There's not a dry eye, and we dab the corners with tissues, careful not to rub off our makeup. For as much loss I thought I'd feel, my heart is so full right now. This show has meant the world to me, but to witness the soul-deep passion these artists have for Infini as their feet touch the stage—the grief inside this ending has given way to love.

I *feel* such strong love today.

Before I change into my sky-blue leo, I linger by the left wing, other artists congregated around me, watching.

I watch Luka perform Wheel of Death to hypnotic percussion and roaring horns. Sergei and Luk run on the *outside* of their opposite wheels, the danger escalating with the music's pulse-stomping pace.

As the wheel rotates vertically, Sergei hangs on the lower wheel, and Luka, on the top, *jumps*.

He flips and twists, his feet seemingly about to land nowhere. But the wheel swishes ahead, catching Luka in perfect timing, and he reaches out devilishly to the little girl Milla on stage. She draws forward, her nightgown billowing.

Sergei lands a trick that causes the audience to gasp, and Luka whips his head to his brother, acting like he's never noticed him before. He suddenly *darts* through the metal apparatus. Entering the middle space frame beam.

Then he jumps down on the same wheel as his brother.

Sergei slips into the wheel and he makes a face at Luka like *you can't catch me.*

Their cat-and-mouse routine causes Milla to take a few steps backwards, but I'm entranced. I'm stuck here watching how *beautiful* Luka is, how much he loves the circus.

As the routine nears the end, Luka smiles at his brother, and Sergei smiles back, their hands clasp—and I have to turn away before tears cascade.

I rub my nose, and I quickly dress.

Intermission hits, and everyone tries to change fast. High-risk trampoline is next, and Luka enters, his chest and ribs jutting in and out as he catches his breath.

He wipes off his red nightmare makeup, grinning at me.

I don't restrain my smile as I pass him brushes and a pallet of his sapphire and gold makeup. His dreamscape spandex still makes him look like a celestial god.

Time passes fast, and we hurry in our new costumes, new makeups, and it seems like before I even blink, we're taking our cue stage left.

I rise and fall on my toes, my gold-stitched balls in my hand.

"Bay," Luka says, dipping his head to mine. He pecks me four quick times on the lips. It's routine after he kissed me playfully like that months ago, and that night's performance was considered one of the best.

I may not always believe in random good fortune, but Luka keeps the superstition alive. I do it for the kisses, and for him.

"Ready, krasavitsa?" His gray twinkling eyes drink me in.

I inhale a humongous breath, and I realize that each act has been armoring me for the end, protecting me for a final goodbye. And I wholeheartedly believe this act with Luka will wrap me in indestructible metals and steels that no pain could infiltrate.

"I'm ready," I say strongly.

And we go.

I'm dancing to my mom's music. I am breathing in every lively cord that thrums through my veins. We are heaven and peace on this stage, and balls take flight in symmetry. Kotovas scale poles around me, their vivacious energy and chemistry at a peak.

I twirl and juggle, nearing the apparatus, and I'm lifted onto the trampoline by an angel named Luka—and we bounce.

We fly.

There are no words to describe the feeling of being alive.

After all our work, I can stand on his shoulders. He rotates me, eight gold balls taking flight. I catch them to applause, and Luka squeezes my ankles, proud of me.

I'm so proud of *us*.

At the end of the act, he wraps his arm around my shoulders, kissing the top of my head, and we watch the show together.

We're quiet. Holding onto one another. Listening. *Feeling.*

He's out of my arms for Russian swing, the final act, and the joyous chorus of the finale's score alleviates all tension. All discord. Kotovas move in celebration of what they do and who they are, and I feel the same.

Proud to be a part of this heart-rendering world.

Proud to be a Wright.

Proud to be my mom's daughter.

Tears wet my cheeks, and I don't worry about the makeup. I'm smiling, and just as the curtains fall to the close, someone shouts, "Last curtain call for Infini."

Last curtain call for Infini.

This is the final goodbye.

I walk on the bright stage with the rest of the cast, and I engrain everything in my mind: the velvet curtains, all the spotlights, the floor beneath my feet, the chatter and the quick side-hugs before the curtain slowly rises to a standing ovation.

A warm arm is around my shoulders. "Luka," I breathe.

He smiles and wipes some of my tears. "This is only the start, Bay."

I nod over and over. Life continues after tonight, and I'm clinging to more than Luka. I have hope.

The contortionists rush forward first, with a bow and a wave. They step back, and I push Luka, his turn is up. He's already grinning, jumping far ahead, and his arms hook around cousins. Who hook their arms around him. Together, in unison.

The audience roars, clapping harder and louder. I can't stop smiling.

The Kotovas stand statuesque, teeming with charisma and pride, and I clap and clap. I cheer for Brenden and Zhen as they take the spotlight.

It's my turn.

Artists let me through, and I come forward, passing the Russian swing apparatus. I juggle three balls and twirl before I bow.

I hear Luka's loud whistle, and I grin inside-out.

Just when I think it's the end, most of the cast shuffles back—but they push *four* of us to the front. To the spotlight.

Luka lightly pushes my arm, his lips stretched wide. "Go, Bay."

I'm about to shake my head, but Brenden clasps my hand, and Dimitri suddenly takes my other. Zhen grabs Brenden's—and I realize why we're being honored.

We're the only ones who stayed with Infini from *beginning* to *end*. The original four.

So we walk forward together. Hand-in-hand. And before the curtain falls, I see the admiration and respect from my peers as they clap all around me, and I see the audience overflowing with emotion that we built.

I can't think of a happier goodbye than this one.

"I HAVE SOMETHING BIZARRE TO TELL YOU,"

I say to Luka, after we sneak into the Masquerade's biggest globe auditorium. We finished performing Infini about four or five hours ago, showered and changed in comfier clothes.

We sit on the midnight-blue velveteen seats. In the very middle row of the middle section. It's empty and peaceful, and the stage curtains are still drawn open. The last set piece, a painted soft blue sky floating into star-speckled space, still hangs as the background, omnipotent and breathtaking.

Luka dumps three types of candy into a bag of popcorn, already smiling.

"You're not nervous?" I give him a serious look.

"No," he says with a laugh. "I like bizarre things as much as you do."

I bring my right foot to the seat, angling my body slightly towards him. "What's bizarre," I say, "is that when I sit *here*, in an empty auditorium with no one around but you"—I make a grand sweeping motion at our scenery—"it's not quiet to me, and it's not because I'm talking."

Luka listens and watches intently, his smile not mocking at all.

I lean forward, my hand on his armrest. "It's like…" I put a hand on my chest like the words are in me but I can't articulate. "I hear music. It's hushed, but there's this *sound* that can't be contained—and God, I am in…"

"Love," he finishes, his gray eyes encapsulating what I feel.

I nod, tears welling. I laugh into a smile. "Love is bizarre."

His arm slides on top of mine. "You want to hear something bizarre?" He tosses a piece of popcorn in his mouth.

"What?"

"I figured that out way before you."

My smile matches his. "Not bizarre at all," I say as his fingers lace mine. "I can believe that easily."

Luka reaches down and finds my Infini souvenir tote bag. After the final performance, there was a wrap party, and we were all given mementos to remember the show. We have time to kill before we learn where our futures are headed.

Sergei said he'd text us by 3:00 a.m. with details. He's calling his friend, Marc Duval's son, and seeing if he's heard any rumors about where we'll all end up.

I sit up straighter and stare at the glittering gold *Infini* logo on the sapphire-blue bag.

"Spectacular!" Luka reads off the back of the tote. "Splendid!" He pops a green Skittle in his mouth. "Only two words. They could've used your thesaurus, Bay."

"No one's taking my thesaurus," I say, digging through the contents of the bag. "The doodles are invaluable to me."

He grins, his arm stretching over my shoulders. He watches me pull out a blue T-shirt, stationary, a hardbound program, and I pause when I reach the DVD.

I know it's footage of Infini from New York. They filmed during the first year, and the dreamy and whimsical cover is the other artist who used to play The Girl. Before Milla.

My eyes drift to Luka, and I sweep his angelic yet chiseled face, dangerous like a nightmare but enthralling like a dream. "You should've been the poster," I say what I'm thinking.

Luka laughs.

"I'm serious." I start smiling *again*, my face hurting. "Stop. It's true. You *evoke* Infini."

He's staring straight into me. I think my overly passionate emphasis hooks him. "I already believe you," he says, "and I don't even know what that means exactly." He offers me the popcorn, and I grab a handful. He nods to the DVD case. "You weren't in any extras, were you?"

"No. You weren't either, right?" I remember they were trying to limit the number of children shown on the DVD. I flip the case over, the extras listed out like *a day in the life of an artist* and *before the show.*

"No, but Nik had a five-minute extra about his workout regime."

"I remember that. Dimitri had a fit when they chose Nikoali instead of him." We smile at the memory.

Luka adds, "Then Dimitri stood in the back of the shot while they were filming Nik." We burst into laughter because Dimitri took that time to *flex* in each camera frame like he was posing for *Sports Illustrated.*

And it's all caught on tape.

Our laughter slowly fades when my finger skims the credits on the DVD case.

Next to *Composer* is *Joyce Wright.*

I won't dance to her music on stage anymore. Audiences won't hear all the melodies she strung together, and it hurts. It will hurt for a while, but Marc was wrong.

I was wrong.

My mom's memory doesn't end here. She lives on inside of so many people. She has touched thousands on and off this stage, and not even this bag of mementos or this DVD can encapsulate all of my mom.

Quietly, I say, "I thought she'd disappear or vanish if Infini ended, but I still feel her presence. As long as I remember her, I don't think she'll ever leave me." A hot tear rolls down my cheek, and I wipe it away.

Luka draws me to his chest where it's safe and warm, and just as we hug, our phones buzz, a text from Sergei.

This is it.

We wait to look, our eyes dancing over each other, and he whispers,

"You're not scared."

"No," I say, thinking about how we're together. We've been together, and wherever we go from here I'm certain that won't change. "I'm hopeful. You?"

He nods strongly. "The exact same."

We inhale together, and then on the count of three, we check our phones. "One. Two," we say in unison. "Three."

The text thread includes all of the Kotovas, my brother, Zhen, and several Infini cast members.

I'm only sharing the rumors I'm 100% sure are fact. If you don't see your name, there's still some indecision. First what I know: Aerial Ethereal has been developing a new show for the past six months. The name is a little straightforward, but they're trying new things, and the concept is really fresh. Most of you will like it: celebration of 4 seasons. In the summer, the sets and costumes reflect the summer. The fall, it reflects the fall, etc.

"Did you see the show concept?" Luka asks right as I digest the details.

"Yeah, it sounds like it'll get people to return to the show all year."

"That's what I was thinking." He's excited.

I hope they need a juggler. Luka clasps my hand and kisses my palm while we read the rest.

Also, the new show has late-night viewings. The name they gave the show is meant to reflect this.
It's called Midnight.

Midnight.
Here's the cast of Midnight that I'm 100% sure of:

Erik Kotova
Robby Kotova
Anton Kotova
Abram Kotova
Sergei Kotova

Sergei typed his last name out with an *a*. It's so subtle, but he must identify as Kotova more now than when he first arrived in Vegas.

The list of Kotovas goes on and on and on, but four names jump out at me.

Luka Kotova
Dimitri Kotova
Timofei Kotova (pay raise + major lead)
Katya Kotova

"Luka." My head whips to him, and he looks overwhelmed, hand to his mouth. He hasn't been in a show with both Timo and Katya since New York.

"Keep reading, Bay," he urges.

So I do, and my heart stops.

Zhen Li
Brenden Wright
Baylee Wright

I'm in the circus. I'm with my family. His family. No one is splitting up. Not this time, and the fact breathes something powerful inside of me.

As I look up, Luka stands and hurdles over a row of chairs. He walks backwards, his gaze nothing but inviting. "Follow me, *krasavitsa*."

I'm already on my feet. I'm already hurdling the same rows at a blood-pumping speed. We're smiling, and he reaches the stage before me, hoisting himself swiftly and effortlessly. He slides on the surface but he leans down.

And Luka outstretches his hand to me.

I grab hold.

He lifts me in one movement, and I'm against his chest, my palms on his face as he spins round and round in a dizzying circle with me in his arms. His smile magnetizing my smile—and I hear music.

And I think, *I have lived partially. Halfly. Incompletely.*

To be whole, I did not know until my bones thundered and bellowed for more.

I am whole and happy.

And this is more.

EPILOGUE
ONE MONTH LATER

LUKA KOTOVA

"Jump!"

I jump straight up with over a hundred other artists. All of us in a huge casual circle, the middle empty. We wear workout clothes for a troupe warm-up. Morning light crests the windows of the performance gym, and the air is loose and free as we all bounce in unison.

"Hands up!" someone else calls out.

Arms raise as we jump, and Nik slips into the open center, claiming the attention. He may be my uptight older brother, but performing, he's as smooth and graceful as water.

He dances, his feet and body in harmony, and his eyes glimmer at Thora who jumps on the outskirts with the rest of us.

She's scowling, but her RBF begins receding at the sight of her boyfriend. She signed a two-year contract for Amour, but Nik and Thora will most likely be in aerial silk for much longer than that. The Masquerade signed paperwork to keep Amour in the hotel for twelve years.

"Pat!"

We drop to our feet and pat our thighs. The soft drumming noise reverberates off the eighty-foot ceilings.

Nik extends his arms and points at two people. Not wavering, Sergei and Dimitri slide on either side of him, and they mimic Nik's dance to the tee. Watching the three of them together, I can almost picture them as teenagers. Not as many responsibilities, daring Sergei to streak, ribbing on Dimitri for everything, and fighting over Nikolai.

Then again, they still do all of that shit, and they're in their late twenties.

"Timofei," Serg calls.

Timo bounces in front of all three men, and his aura literally outshines them. He backflips, slides his feet out and then together, twirls and finishes with an aerial. Everyone is smiling.

"Clap!"

We all clap to a new beat.

Older guys slipping back to the outskirts, they leave Timo alone in the center. My little brother is now the highest paid Aerial Ethereal artist. He's carrying the weight of Midnight, his time spent on stage tripling some of us, but if anyone thrives best inside a spotlight, it's Timofei Kotova.

"Stomp and clap!"

Someone sets the rhythm: *stomp stomp, clap clap*. We all fall into the beat.

Timo juggles *invisible* balls, his face pulling theatrically, pretending to be surprised at his own talent. I grin wide, and he calls out, "Sister!"

Katya steps into the center, and Timo tosses an invisible ball to her. She pretends it's on fire and hot-potatoes it, her hair billowing down her back.

I love being in a show with my little sister, but more than that—I'm happy she's not working with anyone she can't trust.

And that she's safe.

"Brother!" Timo calls cheerfully, and he chucks an invisible ball at me.

I catch the ball with two hands, and I eye my girlfriend next to me. "Bay."

She wears her cool-as-steel New York attitude, but as we join the center circle with Kat and Timo, I dribble my invisible basketball around her frame.

My eyes are teasing, saying: *what? Can't catch it?*

Wearing a tank top, Baylee mimes rolling up her imaginary sleeves and she tries hard not to smile.

I act like I dribble between her legs, and then I stand an inch from her face and spin the invisible ball on my finger.

Baylee steals the ball and pretends to kick it away, and my smile stretches and I nod my head to the beat the artists make around us.

Bay mimes a baseball bat dropping from the air into her hands.

Then she gears up for a pitch.

Timo, Kat, and I angle our bodies like we're eyeing the pitcher.

"Bases are loaded," I call out. "She's the indomitable, *undefeatable* Baylee Wright. Never missed a ball in her life."

Bay's gaze flits to me, smile peeking, but she tries to act concentrated on batting. Then she swings, and in unison, Kat, Timo, and I whip our heads to the right and shield our eyes from mock sunlight. Gawking at a homerun.

Timo whistles a fading whistle like it's the baseball, flying off into the distance.

Baylee mic-drops her invisible bat.

I rush up to her, our lips a breath away, and in a split-second, I pretend the invisible ball just landed on my finger.

Baylee shakes her head, trying to keep her lips pressed together. Trying to look serious.

"Whisper!" someone shouts. Everyone *shhhhs*.

I spin the ball faster, and she's close enough to murmur, "You're unbelievable."

I grin more, and she can't suppress her own smile any longer. I dip my head, forehead nearly touching hers, and I murmur, "You're just now realizing this moment never ends?"

It can't disappear.

It's already invisible, unseen. Something we *feel*.

We'll never lose this. It burrows into us like an endless light.

SPECIAL THANKS

Our deepest thanks is given to Nori Amada.

We are believers in fate, and we wholeheartedly believe that the universe brought us together. Had we not met, this book wouldn't carry a portion of the joy and heart that exists inside of it. Thank you for sharing your love of music with us. For answering our countless questions on soca and the Caribbean. And for being the singer/songwriter to lift Baylee up during dark times. Hearing you talk about your music, and your passion for it, breathed fire into our own art.

Readers:
We highly recommend that you discover more of Nori Amada's music. It never fails to lift our spirits.

You can find Nori Amada on iTunes, Spotify, and Soundcloud.
www.noriamada.com

ACKNOWLEDGMENTS

We are dreamers. Huge, boundless, ridiculous and bizarre dreamers—and we once dreamed up being able to write this magical acrobatic world that seems beautiful and impossible. Then we dreamed up the possibility of someone reading our story and *feeling* something from these pages and characters.

That someone, maybe, is you.

So thank you. Whether knowing or not, you are our dream, and we're forever grateful for you.

It's always hard for us to list out names—because it truly tears us apart leaving out anyone who's helped us—so when we say a big thank you to the Fizzle Force, it encompasses *everyone* who knows us or who has simply read our books. Those we've chatted with and those who've stayed quiet. We love you all, and we're so very thankful for the support you've given us, especially throughout this novel.

To our mom, you are the rock behind this book. Thank you so much for always being there when we need you. Especially on such short deadlines. Not many may know, but you are always our first reader. Our first supporter and cheerleader. We love you so very much.

To Nori, we're honored to have met you, and we thank you so much for sharing your passion for music with us. You're possibly one of the sweetest people in the world, and we're wishing you only immense success.

To our sensitivity readers Maya and Ebony, thank you for the feedback and for the insights you shared on Baylee's culture and identity. It was invaluable to us, and of course, any mistakes or misrepresentations are our own.

To Kimberly, our agent, thanks for always being in our corner. We can say, without a shadow of a doubt, you've brought magic to our lives.

To Lanie, you are such a powerhouse, a sweetheart, our superhero—we adore you to the very ends of the Earth. Thank you for the endless support for *The Secret Ex-Boyfriend* and all the hard work you've put into spreading the word about the Circus Is Family Series. It has meant more to us than words can express.

To Jenn, thank you for all you've done with the Fizzle Force Group—but mostly, thank you for being such a great friend throughout the years. And sticking by us. And being here. We're so very appreciative.

To Jae, your graphics, your kindness and bright spirit are literal sunshine. Thank you so much for making the Fizzle Force Group so welcoming. For all the celebrations you've thrown in spirit of *The Secret Ex-Boyfriend* and the cast of Aerial Ethereal.

To Siiri, we want to thank you for the constant support from beginning to the not-yet-end (hopefully we'll be here for a while!) You've been a great friend to us and a big advocate of our work. Thank you, always.

To bloggers, thank you for taking the time out to read and review our books. We're so very grateful for all your love and enthusiasm.

And thank you to Sue, Amy, and Bella for all the Aerial Ethereal happiness you've stirred up on Tumblr and Goodreads. You're magical in our eyes.

Lastly, we'll return to the Fizzle Force, our readers. To you. With one final goodbye, just as the curtains to Infini—this very novel—draw close…

We thank you.